THE
PENGUIN BOOK
of

BENGALI SHORT STORIES

Translated and edited by
ARUNAVA SINHA

PENGUIN BOOKS

PENGUIN CLASSICS

UK | USA | Canada | Ireland | Australia
India | New Zealand | South Africa

Penguin Books is part of the Penguin Random House group of companies whose
addresses can be found at global.penguinrandomhouse.com.

Penguin
Random House
UK

This selection first published in Penguin Classics 2024
001

Translation, selection and editorial matter © Arunava Sinha, 2024

pp. 481–4 constitute an extension to this copyright page

Set in 11.25/14.75pt Adobe Caslon Pro
Typeset by Jouve (UK), Milton Keynes
Printed and bound in Great Britain by Clays Ltd, Elcograf S.p.A.

The authorized representative in the EEA is Penguin Random House Ireland,
Morrison Chambers, 32 Nassau Street, Dublin D02 YH68

ISBN: 978–0–241–56263–5

www.greenpenguin.co.uk

MIX
Paper | Supporting
responsible forestry
FSC® C018179

Penguin Random House is committed to a
sustainable future for our business, our readers
and our planet. This book is made from Forest
Stewardship Council® certified paper.

Contents

Contents

Contents

Introduction

I will go out on a limb and claim that the short story is the brightest jewel of Bengali literature. Nurtured by a profusion of magazines, Sunday newspaper supplements and innumerable literary journals throughout the twentieth century, and read avidly by millions with virtually no other form of quick entertainment available, the short story tells the many stories of Bengali literature like no other literary form can.

And yet the irony is that it is Bengali novels that people remember. Perhaps this is true of all languages – many classic novels are etched permanently in the collective memory of readers, but there is no such collective memory for short fiction, except for a handful of stories. I will now go back out on that same limb and state that Bengali short stories are living testimony to the injustice of this act of remembering and forgetting, remembering and misremembering.

The Bengali language is spoken and read by some 250 million people, largely in two countries – the Indian state of West Bengal and the country of Bangladesh. Both these regions were part of the original province of Bengal, albeit with fluid boundaries, even before the advent of British colonization in India. The spoken and the written language had evolved over the centuries from one of the offshoots of the ancient tongue of Sanskrit. By the time the East India Company and then the British Crown took over the administration of Bengal – and, gradually, other parts of India – the Bengali language was much closer to its current versions. With the coming of the printing press in Bengal in the second half of the eighteenth century, the language gradually acquired a standard version – with, of course, a fair amount of regional diversity in the vocabulary – that became the one in which literature began to be produced. This, with some evolution, is the version that has persisted.

As with most of the literatures of India, Bengali literature also began in oral form, which in turn meant that verse was the primary medium.

When writers finally discovered the possibilities of prose in the nineteenth century there was, inevitably, an explosion of writing of all kinds. It was from this sudden expansion of possibilities that Bengali fiction emerged, both in the form of the novel and, a little later, the short story. These forms were taken from the West, due to the spread of English literature in Bengal, channelled by the British rulers who had made Calcutta, the present-day capital of West Bengal, the capital city of their Indian colony.

Starting in the late nineteenth century, the short story in particular found millions of readers over the next decades. There was a large literate readership in Bengal, thanks to the growth of education during and after the period referred to as the Bengal Renaissance. Given this demand, Bengali fiction writers wrote short stories with a ferocious energy, creating in the process a steady stream of make-believe, and yet starkly real, experiences that their readers willingly became a part of.

Bengali fiction has always been written in a time of turmoil. It is hard to identify even a single period of relative calm in the social and political history of Bengali-speaking people in India and, subsequently, erstwhile East Pakistan and Bangladesh. By the time the first short stories appeared, India in general, and Bengal in particular, were already in the throes of the freedom movement demanding the withdrawal of British colonizers and the right to self-rule. In Bengal this took a particularly violent form, as hot-blooded young crusaders decided that bombs and guns were the way to frighten the British into leaving. Gandhi's non-violent movement was still in the future, and there was both a romantic and a heroic appeal in the possibility of wreaking havoc within the orderly administration of the British. The 'Swadeshi' movement also tried to wage economic warfare by demanding the boycott of British goods in favour of home-grown ones – which were, ironically, a luxury, for the latter were far more expensive than the former, making the cause accessible only to the relatively rich. These themes were reflected in the Bengali fiction of the time, most notably in some of the works of Rabindranath Tagore 1861–1941 who was to win the Nobel Prize in Literature in 1913, and, before him, in the writings of Bankim Chandra Chattopadhyay (1838–94), whose historical novel *Durgeshnandini* (1865) is considered to be the first Bengali novel.

However, there were other manifestations of turmoil that society was being forced to confront. There was the continued exploitation of the landless by feudal landowners, with the former having to suffer terribly in both physical and mental terms. A political movement for their rights lay several decades in the future. Added to this was the ruthless demonstration of hierarchy in India's complex caste system, with the so-called upper-caste people grinding down the members of the so-called lower caste with claims of quasi-divinity, power and entitlement. All of these themes featured prominently in the stories written in the hope of seeing social change.

Patriarchy continued to rule in vicious forms. Even though the relentless efforts of nineteenth-century social reformers like Rammohun Roy (1774–1833) had led to the outlawing of the practice of sati – where a woman joined her husband on his funeral pyre – and the introduction of the facility of remarriage for widows, education for women, and a raising of the minimum age of marriage – championed by another reformer, Ishwar Chandra Vidyasagar (1820–91) – these changes evoked, quite literally, howls of protest from the orthodox. Before the second half of the nineteenth century, it was common practice for parents to get their daughters married soon after they turned eight – women still enjoyed very few rights and almost no freedom. The only exceptions were those whose fathers or husbands were enlightened, but there again it was the decision of men. Thus the genuine plight of women became the subject of much of fiction, with a number of stories bringing out the hidden desires, aspirations and frustrations of women in domestic spaces, both urban and rural, enabling half their readers to see the concealed elements of their lives reflected in these stories. Not surprisingly, they gained a huge following, especially among women readers who, confined to their homes for all intents and purposes, could only live through the lives of fictional characters.

It would be no exaggeration to state that all these forms of social injustice and inequity became the staple of much of Bengali fiction at the time. Short-story writers in particular wove their tales with the threads of real life around them. The trajectory of the characters in these stories, whether they led to hope or despair, was representative of a brutal reality. These characters are almost always victims of one or more forms of oppression, with the oppressors also getting considerable play. Some writers fused these narratives with the psychology of individuals, but up until the 1920s or so Bengali fiction was clearly intent on depicting social reality. There was really no way to avoid or escape this, nor would it have been moral to do so, since the grimness of daily existence was a palpable presence in most people's lives.

In 1905, the British decided that the political resistance was getting too hot to handle in Bengal and the protesters had to be divided. The British government of India announced that the province was going to be partitioned along religious lines, with a separate region being created for those areas where Muslims were the dominant population, leaving the rest for the Hindu majority. This rehearsal of the Partition of India, which took place when it eventually gained independence in 1947, was not met with approval. There was vigorous and violent opposition and the writing was on the wall quite early on, but the colonizers held out till 1912 before giving in and announcing the reunification of Bengal. While this temporary separation asserted the unity of the Bengali identity in some ways, much of it thanks to powerful cultural statements made by writers and artists, it also underscored the nascent fault lines between the two major religions of Bengal, Hinduism and Islam. Caste was already a strong divider, and religion now joined it, with a single Bengali word, *jaat*, being used to combine both religion and caste and partition people into separate groups – based on caste among Hindus, and on religion between Hindus and Muslims – where each considered the rest 'the other'. Alert to this development, many writers began to explore its impact on individual lives through their fiction.

A year before the reunification, the British government of India shifted the capital from Calcutta, on the eastern side of the country, to Delhi, which is located more centrally in terms of longitude if not latitude. With the rulers of the country no longer as invested in the development of Calcutta and its surroundings, economic changes started to take place in the region, as the engines of business and commerce – and the resultant prosperity for many, though by no means all, in Bengal – began to move to other parts of the country, closer to the seat of government. In any case, Bombay and the western part of India were also becoming mercantile powers in their own right. This inequality would lead to economic despair and the resultant pushback in disruptive forms soon after the country gained independence in 1947.

The intellectual domains of the sciences, the arts and culture flourished in Bengal in the early decades of the twentieth century, thanks in no small measure to the Western education that the British had brought to the region. The latest ideas in philosophy, art, physics, biology, medicine and, above all, literature all made their way to Calcutta. By virtue of being the capital for many decades, Calcutta had consolidated its importance in Bengal in a manner that has lasted ever since, even after the Partition, when Dhaka became the most important city in East Pakistan and, later, the capital of Bangladesh. As a result, writers from all over Bengal gravitated towards Calcutta sooner or later. Even if they didn't necessarily spend their entire lives there – some of them preferred to write in rural or semi-rural surroundings – their works were almost entirely published in Calcutta in magazines and books.

Soaking in ideas from elsewhere, many thinking women and men adopted the ideals of socialism and, subsequently, Marxism. Viewing the world around them through these lenses, a number of writers interpreted the misery of the masses in Marxist terms in their fiction. Like their predecessors, they too wrote about the oppressed, but their stories offered narratives not so much of human oppression as of the tyranny of a system whose effects on humans were to be seen in uncompromisingly raw storytelling that pulled no punches.

In the 1940s, even as Independence, the Partition and the riots associated with them began to loom, Bengal faced one of the worst-ever crises in its history when a famine in the state, artificially engineered by the British, led to millions starving to death, even though there was no overall shortfall of grain. The famine led people to beg, steal and even kill for food. Ever since then, food, hunger and, of course, social injustice have been the leitmotifs of many works of Bengali fiction, with the theme taking on increasingly symbolic overtones.

The 1940s were a truly turbulent decade for Bengal. There was widespread fear of a Japanese invasion as the Second World War spread to the east. Japanese planes bombed Calcutta in December 1942 and in December 1943. There was panic, mass evacuation and a shortage of all essential commodities, leading to chaos in daily life. In between these two attacks came the famine. And barely had these subsided when violent riots broke out across Bengal between Hindus and Muslims, Calcutta being badly affected.

The riots drove a spiteful wedge between the two communities and sealed the decision to partition India on the eastern as well as the western front. Most of the districts of Bengal where Muslims were in the majority were allotted to the newly formed country of Pakistan – more specifically, to East Pakistan, for independent Pakistan comprised two segments, to the west of independent India and within the eastern part of independent India respectively.

Independence and Partition saw one of the largest movements ever of people across international borders. These borders were drawn by the British government of India before leaving India. Many of the Muslims whose homes were in the regions allotted to India decided to move to West or East Pakistan, whichever was nearer. And many of the Hindus whose homes were in areas given to Pakistan chose to settle in independent India. In Bengal, along with the Indian state of Punjab, as well as in Pakistan, this naturally led to a huge influx of people who came to be known as refugees. Bengali was now the language spoken by almost everyone in East Pakistan as well as the newly formed Indian state of West Bengal – the part of the original Bengal that had been allocated to India. The trauma of having to leave one's home and settle in what was now a new country – even if the cultural affinities were strong – naturally became the subject of a great deal of Bengali fiction, art and cinema. The stories didn't so much capture the process of the migration as they did its after-effects on the everyday lives of their characters on both sides of the new international border.

A new upheaval began in East Pakistan soon after its formation. The people here complained about the attempts of the Pakistani government in West Pakistan to impose Urdu as the official language of Bengali-speaking people in East Pakistan. The Bhasha Andolon – the movement for Bengali – erupted in Dhaka soon after the formation of Pakistan in 1947. On 21 February 1952 there was a crackdown by the Pakistan military on planned protests in Dhaka, which were led by college students, in which several young men were killed. The date of the killings has been memorialized among Bengali-speaking people since then, and it was later adopted by the United Nations as International Mother Tongue Day. This movement gathered pace through the 1960s, eventually culminating in a liberation movement and, finally, the liberation war that saw the emergence of the independent country of Bangladesh – the name comes from the language, which is known as Bangla among those who speak it – in 1971. The war for freedom against Pakistan was in fact won with the help of the Indian Army; India and Pakistan had by then become bitter enemies, having fought their own war in 1965. Much of Bengali literature in East Pakistan and, subsequently, Bangladesh adopted as its principal themes the liberation war, independence from Pakistan and violent post-independence politics during the 1970s. In this wave of violence even Sheikh Mujibur Rahman (1920–75), considered the architect of the independence of Bangladesh, and its first president, was assassinated along with his family by a group of Bangladesh army officers in 1975. The trauma of this event has been a recurring subject of writings from Bangladesh.

At the same time, in West Bengal fiction writers were evolving new literary styles for themselves – moving away from traditional storytelling to explore language and its possibilities more freely, much as was being done in the West – and confronting the new realities of the rise of a violent ultra-left movement known as Naxalism. This also led to the most openly political work seen in the annals of Bengali fiction, as a number of writers examined the violence and the doomed ideology behind it through a critical and creative lens. Many of them expressed their support for the movement and used their stories to depict, dramatize and despair of the human tragedies of this time in explosive and unconventional language.

Perhaps this long-lasting overdose of social and political turmoil delayed the examination of modern-day relationships between people in Bengali fiction. It began in some of the short stories and novels written in the late 1960s and continued into the 1970s, but it wasn't until the 1980s that the complexities of personal lives and relationships took centrestage; they have continued to inform the fiction written in Bengali on both sides of the border between India and Bangladesh.

If you were to conclude that a collection of Bengali short stories picked from various decades is effectively also a telling of the history of the times, people and places from which these stories come, you wouldn't be wrong. And yet, of course, the stories here are far more than history – either of the land and the people or of Bengali literature. As with any literature, they are individual, unique dialogues between the writers and the world they perceived, the world they dreamt of and even the world they abhorred. The 'Bengaliness' of these stories is not in-your-face. They are not works of ethnography masquerading as fiction, nor clever guides to those who want to know more about Bengali-speaking people and their universes.

After all, these stories were written in Bengali for family, friends, neighbours and fellow inhabitants of the worlds they depict. They were meant to be not doors through which to enter an unfamiliar world, but windows through which to gaze into a familiar world brought afresh to readers. They don't represent Bengal, they represent only these particular writers' work at the time that they were written. And yet you may find, dear reader, a thread – or a dozen – that seems to bind them together. It might be something as simple as longing for what is not, or a suppressed anger about the world being the way it is, or a confession that human existence is too peculiar to be understood and can only be acknowledged and recorded – it might be all of these, and other things as well.

There is no science to the choice here, no cast-iron logical framework, no effort to be representative, no literary justification. Call this collection, if you will, the personal choice of someone who found these stories worthy of full-bodied reading – with mind, heart, muscles, organs, imagination, ecstasy, melancholy, love . . . everything that a human being is capable of bringing to reading a short story and adoring it. I thank you for holding this book in your hands. *Dhonnobaad.*

RABINDRANATH TAGORE

Dead or Alive

I

The widowed daughter-in-law of Sharadashankar, the zamindar of Ranihat, had no family of her own on her father's side; one by one, all of them had died. She had no one to speak of on her husband's side either – neither husband nor son. Her elder brother-in-law's youngest son was the apple of her eye. His mother had been severely ill for a long time after giving birth to him, which was why his widowed aunt Kadambini – whom he addressed as Kakima – had brought him up. Rearing someone else's child seems to strengthen the bond, for one has no right over the child; there are no social demands, only the demands of love – but unalloyed love cannot cite any documentary evidence to establish its right, nor does it wish to. It only adores the uncertain object of its affection twice as fervently.

After she had showered all the suppressed love of the widow on the little boy, Kadambini died unexpectedly one monsoon night. For some unknown reason her heart stopped beating suddenly; everything else in the world continued to function as before, but only the spring in her tiny, tender heart – ever thirsty for love – stopped working forever.

To avoid the unwelcome intrusion of the police, four Brahmin employees of the zamindar proceeded to cremate the body without any delay.

The crematorium in Ranihat was a long way from any habitation. The enormous burning ground was completely bare, except for a hut next to the lake and, close by, a huge banyan tree. A river used to flow here in the past, but it had completely dried up now. A section of the dried riverbed had been dug up to create the lake. People hereabouts considered the lake a legitimate representative of the river in full flow.

I

Placing the corpse inside the hut, the four of them awaited the arrival of the wood for the pyre. It was taking so long that Nitai and Gurucharan went off to enquire about the delay, while Bidhu and Banamali stayed back to guard the corpse.

It was a dark monsoon night. The sky was overcast, not a star was visible; the pair waited in silence in the darkness of the hut. One of them had a box of matches and a lamp. But despite all their efforts the dampness prevented the matches from being lit and the lantern they had brought had died long ago.

After a long silence, one of them said, 'I'm dying for a smoke. We came away in such a hurry that I forgot to bring any along.'

'I can get some at once,' offered his companion.

Sensing Banamali's desire to flee, Bidhu exclaimed, 'Really! And I suppose I'm expected to wait here alone, am I?'

The conversation ended. Every minute seemed like an hour. The pair that had stayed back cursed the pair who had supposedly gone off in search of wood – every passing moment deepened their suspicion that the other two were having a cosy smoke and chat somewhere.

There were no sounds to be heard besides the constant chirping of crickets and the croaking of frogs from the lake. Suddenly the bed appeared to shake, as though the corpse was turning over on its side.

Bidhu and Banamali began to tremble and muttered prayers. A sigh was heard inside the hut. Bidhu and Banamali leapt out of the room in an instant and raced off towards their village.

Nearly three miles away, they ran into the rest of their party, who were returning with lanterns. They had in fact stopped for a smoke, and had not done anything about the wood. Still, they informed the other two that the wood was being chopped and would be despatched shortly. Whereupon Bidhu and Banamali proceeded to describe all that had taken place in the hut. Dismissing their account in disbelief, Nitai and Gurucharan reproached them angrily.

Without further ado, all four of them returned to the hut at the burning ground. Entering, they discovered the bed empty and the corpse missing.

They exchanged glances. What if a jackal had dragged the corpse away? But even the sheet covering her was missing. Investigating, they spotted a woman's small footprints, fresh in the mud gathered outside the door.

Sharadashankar was not an easy man to deal with, and telling him this ghost story was unlikely to yield dividends. After prolonged discussions, the quartet concluded that it would be best to inform the zamindar that the cremation had been completed.

Those who finally brought the wood for the pyre at dawn were told that because of the delay the body had been burnt already, using some wood kept in the hut. No one was likely to be suspicious about this – a corpse was not a valuable object for anyone to steal.

2

As everyone knows, even when there are no signs of life in a person, sometimes life still persists, and the body resumes its normal functioning at the appropriate time. Kadambini had not died either; only her vital signs had stopped for some reason.

When she regained her senses, she found herself enveloped in darkness. It seemed this was not the place where she normally slept. 'Didi,' she called out, but no one answered in the dark room. Sitting up in fear, she recollected her experience of dying. The sudden pain in her chest, the inability to breathe. Her sister-in-law had been warming the milk for Khoka – her son – on a fire; unable to stay on her feet any more, Kadambini had tumbled on to the bed and in a choked voice said, 'Didi, ask Khoka to come to me, I am dying.' Then everything grew dark, like a bottle of ink overturned on a sheet of paper covered in writing, and Kadambini's entire memory and consciousness, every letter in the book of the world, dissipated in an instant. The widow could not remember whether Khoka had addressed her as Kakima one last time in his endearing voice, could not recollect whether she had succeeded in collecting a final allowance of love for her everlasting, alien journey of death from this ever-familiar world.

At first she thought that hell was eternally desolate and eternally dark, just like this – that there was nothing to see there, nothing to hear, nothing to do, that she would only have to stay awake like this till eternity.

But when a cold gust of moisture-laden wind blew in through the door and she heard the croaking of the frogs, all the memories of the rains that

3

she had amassed since childhood in her brief life condensed in her mind in a single moment, enabling her to feel the touch of the real world. There was a flash of lightning; the lake, the banyan tree, the huge burning ground and a distant row of trees became visible for a moment. She recalled bathing in this lake on auspicious dates, and how horrifying death had seemed at the sight of corpses here.

Her first thought was to go back home. But, she reflected the very next moment, why will they take me back since I am not alive any more? It will be bad luck for them. I have been exiled from the kingdom of the living, after all. I am my own dead spirit.

If that were not so, how could she have arrived here at this desolate crematorium from Sharadashankar's well-protected ladies' chambers? If she had not been cremated yet, where were the people who had come to cremate her body? Her last memory was of the final moments of her death in Sharadashankar's well-lit residence. Discovering herself alone the very next moment on this distant, barren, dark burning ground, she realized: I am no longer a member of the human tribe on this planet; I am dangerous, a harbinger of ill fortune, I am my dead spirit.

As soon as she was struck by this thought, the rules that bound her to the world seemed to melt away. She felt possessed by extraordinary power, infinite freedom – as though she could go where she liked, do as she pleased. Driven into a frenzy by this unprecedented new ability, she swept out of the hut like a sudden gust of wind and walked across the burning ground without a trace of diffidence, fear or concern in her heart.

As she marched on, her footsteps faltered, her body weakened. The fields and meadows just wouldn't end – they were interspersed with paddy fields, some of them knee-deep in water. When the first light of dawn became visible, a bird or two could be heard from a bamboo grove located near a cluster of houses not too far away.

Now she felt a kind of trepidation. She did not know where her relationship with the world and the people who inhabited it stood. As long as she had been at the crematorium, in the fields, in the darkness of the monsoon night, she had been unafraid, as though in her own world. In daylight, the settlement seemed a treacherous place. Humans fear ghosts, ghosts fear humans too, they occupy opposite banks of the river of death.

3

Her mud-spattered clothes, the strange state of her mind and the unhinged demeanour brought on by a sleepless night had transformed Kadambini's appearance to one that would have made people afraid and young boys pelt stones at her from a distance. Fortunately, the first person to see her in this state was a gentleman travelling on that road.

'You seem to be from a genteel family,' he said to her. 'Where are you going in this condition all by yourself?'

At first Kadambini looked at him without responding. She could not summon an answer quickly. That she was still in this world, that she looked like a gentlewoman, that a passer-by on the village road was asking her a question, seemed unbelievable.

'Let me take you home,' the passer-by said to her again. 'Tell me where you live.'

Kadambini considered what her reply should be. She could not entertain thoughts of returning to her in-laws' home, and she had no home of her own – suddenly she remembered a childhood friend of hers.

Although they had been separated as children, her friend Jogomaya and she still wrote to each other now and then. At times this escalated into a fully fledged war of love. Kadambini attempted to convey that hers was the stronger emotion, while Jogomaya insinuated that Kadambini did not reciprocate her sentiments adequately. Neither of them harboured the slightest doubt that, if only some miracle were to bring them together, they would be unable to let each other out of their sight even for an instant.

'I want to go to Sripaticharan-babu's house in Nishchindapur,' Kadambini told the gentleman.

The traveller was on his way to Calcutta; although it was not near, Nishchindapur was on the way. He personally escorted Kadambini to Sripaticharan-babu's house.

The friends were reunited. It took a few moments for them to recognize each other, but the resemblance to their respective childhood selves soon became obvious to both.

'How fortunate I am!' exclaimed Jogomaya. 'I had never expected to set eyes on you in my lifetime. But how did you happen to visit me, my dear? How did your in-laws let you go?'

After a pause, Kadambini said, 'Do not ask me about my in-laws, my dear. Let me live like a maid in one corner of your house, I will perform all your household tasks.'

'What do you mean?' responded Jogomaya. 'Why should you live like a maid? You are my friend, you are my . . .' et cetera.

Sripati entered. After a brief gaze at him, Kadambini left slowly – neither covering her head with the end of her sari in a show of respect, nor displaying any sign of diffidence or uncertainty.

Jogomaya quickly began to explain to Sripati, lest he think badly of her friend. But so few explanations were required, and Sripati approved of every one of her proposals so easily, that Jogomaya was not particularly satisfied.

Kadambini had come to her friend's house, but she could not feel close to her friend – death was a gulf between them. Constant self-awareness and doubts about oneself made socializing impossible. Kadambini would gaze at Jogomaya, her thoughts drifting; she felt as though her friend occupied a distant planet with her husband and household. With all her love and tenderness and responsibilities, she is an inhabitant of the world, while I am nothing but an empty shadow. She is in the realm of existence and I am in the universe of the infinite.

Jogomaya, too, found all this strange, but she could fathom none of it. Womankind cannot tolerate mystery – for you can make poetry with uncertainty, you can be valorous with it, but you cannot live in a household with it. That is why women either eliminate the very existence of what they cannot understand, maintaining no relationship with it, or else they convert it with their own hands into a new form where they can put it to some use. If they can do neither, they become exceedingly angry with it.

The more obscure Kadambini's behaviour seemed to become, the angrier Jogomaya got with her. What kind of menace is this that has descended on me, she reflected.

There was another problem. Kadambini was afraid of herself. She simply could not run away from herself. Those who are afraid of ghosts fear their own backs – they are terrified of whatever they cannot keep an eye on. But Kadambini's biggest fear lay within herself, she was not afraid of the external world.

That was why she would scream sometimes alone in her room in the middle of the afternoon. In the evening, she would tremble on spotting her own shadow in the lamplight.

Her fear made everyone in the house afraid too. The maids, the servants and even Jogomaya herself began to see ghosts everywhere, at all hours.

One night, Kadambini ran sobbing from her own room all the way to Jogomaya's, saying, 'I beg of you, didi, don't let me be alone.'

Jogomaya was as angry as she was scared. She felt an impulse to throw Kadambini out of her home at once. A compassionate Sripati calmed her down with a great deal of effort and let Kadambini occupy the room next to theirs.

The next day, Sripati was summoned to the ladies' chambers at an unusual hour. Turning on him unexpectedly, Jogomaya said, 'What kind of man are you! A woman leaves her own in-laws' home and ensconces herself in yours, a month goes by and she shows no sign of budging, and I don't hear a word of protest from you! Please explain what you have in mind. All you men are the same.'

Men indeed have a natural bias in favour of women, and women hold them responsible for this. Even if Sripati had been willing to swear on Jogomaya's head that his compassion for the helpless yet beautiful Kadambini was not inappropriately great, his behaviour would have proved otherwise.

'Her in-laws must have tortured the childless widow,' he mused, 'and, unable to stand it any more, Kadambini must have arrived here to seek shelter from me. Since she has no parents, how can I abandon her?' With this thought he had desisted from making any kind of enquiry; nor did he have the inclination to cause Kadambini any pain by asking her questions on this unpleasant subject.

Thereupon his wife proceeded to assault his numbed sense of responsibility. He realized that sending word to Kadambini's in-laws had become absolutely crucial to the maintenance of domestic harmony. Finally he decided that the outcome of sending an unexpected letter might not be ideal, and that he would make enquiries personally at Ranihat before deciding on a course of action.

While Sripati went off, Jogomaya went to Kadambini to tell her, 'It isn't proper for you to stay here any more, my dear. What will people say?'

Looking gravely at Jogomaya, Kadambini said, 'What do I have to do with people?'

Jogomaya was astonished at this response. 'You may not, but we do,' she said in a fit of rage. 'How can we hold on to the daughter-in-law of another family?'

'What family am I the daughter-in-law of?' Kadambini responded.

Oh my god, thought Jogomaya to herself. What does the woman think she's saying?

'Do you think I really am one of you?' Kadambini continued slowly. 'Do you think I belong to this world? You people laugh, you love, you cry, you live with your own families, I can only watch. You are people, and I am a shadow. I cannot fathom why god has chosen to keep me among you all. You are afraid too, lest I bring misery to your happy lives, and I cannot understand either what relationship I have with all of you. But since the Almighty has not earmarked a place for me, although the ties have been snapped I continue to haunt your lives.'

Because of the way she kept speaking, Jogomaya made some sense of it without grasping the real meaning, but she could neither respond to nor repeat her question. Weighed down with concern, she left.

4

It was almost ten at night when Sripati returned from Ranihat. The world was flooding under torrential rain. The continuous sound suggested that neither the downpour nor the night would end.

'What did you learn?' Jogomaya asked.

'A great deal,' answered Sripati. 'We'll talk about it later.' He changed his clothes, ate his dinner, had his late-night smoke and went to bed. He looked rather disturbed.

Having suppressed her curiosity for a long time, Jogomaya asked as soon as she got into bed, 'What did you hear?'

'You must have made a mistake,' Sripati responded.

Jogomaya was enraged at this. Women never make mistakes, and even if they did, the duty of wise men was not to refer to them but to accept them as their own. 'Such as?' retorted Jogomaya a little hotly.

'The woman you have given shelter to in your household is not Kadambini,' declared Sripati.

Such a statement could easily provoke anger, especially when it comes from one's own husband. 'So I don't know my own friend: I have to consult *you* to identify her – what a thing to say!'

Sripati explained that they could not argue over the nature of his statement, for they had to consider the evidence. There was no doubt that Jogomaya's childhood friend Kadambini was dead.

'Listen to you,' countered Jogomaya. 'You must have made some mistake. There's no telling where you've really been, what you've really heard. Who asked you to go yourself anyway? A letter would have clarified everything.'

Extremely disappointed with his wife's lack of faith in his efficiency, Sripati proceeded to present detailed evidence – with no effect. Their arguments ran on into the middle of the night.

Although there was no difference of opinion between husband and wife over throwing Kadambini out of their home this instant – for Sripati was convinced that their guest had deceived his wife all this time under a false identity, while Jogomaya believed that she had abandoned her family – neither of them was willing to concede the current argument.

As their voices became progressively louder, they forgot that Kadambini was in the very next room.

'What a predicament,' said the one. 'I heard it with my own ears.'

'Why should I believe you?' said the other with conviction. 'I can see her with my own eyes.'

Finally Jogomaya said, 'Very well, tell me when Kadambini is supposed to have died.'

She assumed that she would be able to find an inconsistency between his date and one of Kadambini's letters, thus proving her point.

The date that Sripati mentioned turned out, when they had both calculated backwards, to be that of the day before the one on which Kadambini had arrived at their house in the evening. Jogomaya's heart trembled at this and Sripati began to get an eerie feeling too.

Their door opened suddenly, a gust of rain-laden wind snuffing out the lamp. The darkness rushed in instantly, filling every inch of space. Kadambini appeared in the middle of the room. It was past two-thirty in the morning, and it was raining incessantly outside.

'I am the same Kadambini, my dear,' said Kadambini, 'but I am not alive any more. I am dead now.'

Jogomaya screamed in terror; Sripati couldn't utter a word.

'But what crime have I committed other than dying? If there is no room for me in this world or in the next, where should I go then, tell me?' Her plaintive cry seemed to awaken the creator, asleep at this hour on this monsoon night, as she asked, 'Where should I go then, tell me?'

With these words, Kadambini left the couple sleeping in their room to seek her place in the world.

5

It is difficult to explain how Kadambini returned to Ranihat. But she did not show herself to anyone at first, spending the day without food in a ruined temple.

When the monsoon evening descended early, and villagers anxiously took shelter in their own homes in anticipation of the imminent deluge, Kadambini went out on the road. At the threshold of her in-laws' house she felt a moment of panic, but when she entered, her face covered by the end of her sari, the doormen mistook her for a maid and did not block her way. The rain intensified at this moment, and the wind picked up.

The lady of the house, Sharadashankar's wife, was playing cards with her husband's widowed sister. The maid was in the kitchen and an ill Khoka, who had a fever, was sleeping in the bedroom. Evading everyone's eyes, Kadambini arrived in the bedroom. She did not know herself what impulse had brought her to her in-laws' house, but she did know that she wanted to set her eyes on the little boy one more time. She had not thought of where she would go, or what would happen thereafter.

In the light of the lamp she saw the sickly little boy sleeping with his hands clenched tightly. The sight made her agitated heart yearn – how could she live without clasping the child with all his sickness to her bosom once? She pondered, Now that I am gone, who will look after him here?

His mother enjoys company, enjoys chatting with people, a game of cards, she was happy all this while entrusting the responsibility for the child to me, she has never had to bear the burden of bringing him up. Who will take care of this boy now?

The little boy turned on his side, saying in his sleep, 'Water, Kakima.' Oh my! You haven't forgotten your Kakima, my darling! Quickly pouring out a glass of water from the pitcher kept in the corner, Kadambini took the child in her arms and gave him his water.

As long as he was under the influence of sleep, the boy was not the least surprised to have his aunt giving him his glass of water. When she had fulfilled her long-cherished desire and tucked him back into bed after kissing him, he woke up. Putting his arms around her, he said, 'Did you die, Kakima?'

'Yes, Khoka,' she replied.

'You've come back to Khoka now? You won't die again?' Before she could answer there was a commotion. About to enter the room with a bowl of food for the boy, the maid dropped it with a clatter and collapsed on the floor, exclaiming 'Oh!'

The lady of the house came running at the sound, her cards forgotten, turning into a block of wood the moment she entered, unable to speak or to make her escape.

All this scared the little boy, who sobbed loudly, saying, 'Go away, Kakima.'

After a long time, Kadambini was now feeling as though she had not died – the familiar house, the boy, her love for him, all of it was as alive as they had ever been, she could sense no gap, no gulf. At her friend's house she had felt that her childhood friend had died but in the boy's room she realized that nothing of his aunt had died.

'Why are you afraid of me, didi?' she pleaded. 'Look at me, I'm just as I always was.'

The lady of the house could stay on her feet no longer; she fainted in a heap on the floor.

Informed by his sister, Sharadashankar-babu appeared personally in the ladies' chambers. His palms joined in supplication, he said, 'Is this fair, Chhotobouma? Satish is my only male heir, why must you cast your eye on him? Are we not your family? Ever since you went he has been wasting away, his illness won't leave him, he calls for you all the time. Since you have left the world, you must cut the strings now. We will perform your last rites suitably.'

Kadambini could take it no longer; she cried out frantically, 'But I am not dead, I am not dead. How do I convince all of you I am not dead? Look, I am alive.'

Seizing the metal bowl from the floor, she struck herself on the forehead with it and her forehead began to bleed immediately.

'Look, I am alive,' she declared.

Sharadashankar was transfixed, like a statue. The little boy called out to him in fear. The two women who had fainted remained on the floor.

Shouting, 'I am not dead, I am not dead, not dead,' Kadambini left the room, climbed down the stairs and plunged into the pond behind the ladies' chambers. Sharadashankar heard a splash from the room upstairs.

It rained incessantly all night and the next morning; the rain did not let up in the afternoon either. Kadambari died to prove that she had not died.

SARAT CHANDRA CHATTOPADHYAY

Paradise of the Wretched

I

Thakurdas Mukherjee's aged wife died after a seven-day fever. Old Mukherjee's rice business had made him a man of means. He had four sons and three daughters, the children had children of their own, and with the sons- and daughters-in-law, neighbours and servants all present, it was as though a festival had erupted. The entire village turned out for a glimpse of the grand final journey of the corpse. The dead woman's daughters wept as they lined the soles of her feet with the traditional red *altaa* and put a thick layer of vermilion on her hairline to signal that she had died a married woman. Her daughters-in-law adorned her forehead with drops of sandalwood paste, dressed her in an expensive sari and touched her feet in reverence for the last time. The profusion of flowers, fragrances and garlands did not make it look like an occasion of grief – it was as though, after fifty years, the lady of the house was on her way once more to her husband's home. Old Mukherjee bade farewell for the last time to his lifelong companion with a tranquil expression, wiped away a few tears out of sight of everyone, and consoled his daughters and daughters-in-law. Rending the morning skies with the invocations to the gods that normally accompany a dead person's final journey, the entire village walked alongside the funeral procession.

One more living being joined the group, though from a distance. This was young Kangali's mother. She was on her way to the market to sell a handful of eggplants she had picked from the yard in front of her hut, but the sight she saw made her stop abruptly. The market was forgotten, and so were the eggplants – wiping her eyes, she followed the crowd to the crematorium. It stood in a corner of the village, by the river. All that was needed for the funeral pyre had been collected there already. Belonging as she did to a lower caste, Kangali's mother did not dare go closer. Standing at a slight distance behind a high mound of earth, she watched the last rites with great interest and attention. When the body was placed on the wide and generous pyre, she found the view of the red *altaa*-lined soles beautiful, and had the urge to run up and smear a little bit of the *altaa* on her own forehead. Her eyes streamed with tears when the son lit the pyre, accompanied by invocations to the divine in a chorus of voices. In her head she repeated: you are fortunate, you are going to heaven – bless me so that I too may have Kangali as the one who lights my pyre.

Having one's son light one's pyre. No small achievement. This leaving of one's sons, daughters, grandsons, granddaughters, servants, maids, family – a shining family – behind and ascending to heaven made Kangali's mother's breast swell with pride; she seemed unable to measure the extent of this good fortune. A profusion of smoke from the freshly lit pyre curled upwards, casting a blue shadow – Kangali's mother clearly saw a small chariot in its coils. Someone was sitting in it, not quite identifiable, but there was vermilion in the parting of her hair, and the soles of her feet were lined in red. Kangali's mother gazed skywards tearfully. A boy of fourteen or fifteen tugged on the end of her sari.

'What are you doing here, ma, aren't you going to cook?'

Startled, she looked at Kangali. 'I will.' Pointing upwards, she said, 'Look, there she is, going to heaven.'

The boy stared at the sky in surprise. 'What?' After a brief inspection, he said, 'Are you mad? It's nothing but smoke.' Angrily he said, 'It's past noon, aren't I supposed to be hungry?' Then, spotting the tears in his mother's eyes, he said, 'Some upper-caste Brahmin woman has died, what are *you* crying so much for?'

Kangali's mother finally came to her senses. She was embarrassed at weeping for someone else in the crematorium. In fact, fearing this might bring bad luck upon her son, she even tried to wipe her eyes and smile.

'Why should I be crying, the smoke got in my eyes, that's all.'

'Hah – the smoke got in my eyes, that's all. You *were* crying.'

She didn't protest. Taking her son by the hand, she went down to the waterline to give him a bath, and took one herself too. She was not fortunate enough to witness the completion of the rites.

2

When parents name their children, god does not content himself only with laughing in the sky, but also protests vehemently. Which is why their names taunt them all their lives. However, Kangali's mother had only a short life story, and it had escaped the creator's joke. Her own mother had died in childbirth, leading her angry father to name her Awbhagi, to remind her that she had brought misfortune upon them. With her mother dead, and her father spending his days fishing in rivers to earn a living, no one took care of her. It was a matter of great astonishment that little Awbhagi still succeeded in growing up and becoming Kangali's mother. The man she was married to was named Roshik Bagh, who, true to his surname denoting tiger, had another tigress. With her he shifted to another village, leaving behind Awbhagi with her misfortune and her young son Kangali, whose name signified destitution.

Today the same Kangali had turned fourteen. He had begun to learn cane-weaving, and Awbhagi was now hoping that after another year of battling misfortune their suffering would cease. Only the one who had allotted this suffering to them knew the extent of it.

Returning from the pond after washing his hands, Kangali found his mother covering the leftovers on his plate with an earthen bowl.

'Aren't you going to eat, ma?' he asked in surprise.

'It's too late to eat, I have no appetite.'

'No appetite? I don't believe it. Show me the pot.'

Kangali's mother had used this ruse many times to fool her son. He insisted on inspecting the pot, which did in fact have only enough rice for one person. Now he sat down contentedly in his mother's lap. Boys of his age did not often do such things, but because he had been ill for a long time he had not had the opportunity to wander away from his mother's arms and make friends with boys and girls of his age. Her lap had been his playground. Putting his arm round her, he touched her face with his, only to jump up in alarm. 'You have a fever, ma, why did you have to stand under the sun to watch the dead body being burnt? And then why did you have to bathe? Is a dead body being burnt something that . . .'

His mother clamped her hand on his mouth at once. 'You must never say dead body, it's a sin. A chaste and pure woman has gone to heaven in a chariot.'

'The things you say, ma,' Kangali said sceptically. 'As if anyone goes to heaven in a chariot.'

'I saw for myself, Kangali,' said his mother, 'she was seated in a chariot. Everyone saw her red-lined feet.'

'Everyone?'

'Every single person.'

Leaning back against her, Kangali began to ponder over this. He was accustomed to believing everything his mother told him – from childhood he had learnt to believe her – and if she was saying everyone had seen it for themselves, there was nothing more to doubt. A little later he said, speaking slowly, 'Then you'll go to heaven too? The other day Bindi's mother was telling Rakhal's aunt, there's no one here as chaste and pure as Kangali's mother.'

Kangali's mother was silent. Kangali continued as slowly as before, 'So many people begged you to marry them when baba left you. But you said no, all my trials will be over once Kangali grows up, why should I marry again? Where would I have been today if you'd married again, ma? I might have starved to death.'

His mother folded him to her bosom. A great many people had in fact advised her to get married, and when she didn't agree in any circumstances, they had given her a good deal of trouble too. The recollection brought tears to Awbhagi's eyes again. Her son wiped them away, saying, 'Do you want to lie down?'

His mother was silent. Kangali laid out the mat, put a thin quilt on it, fetched a small pillow and drew his mother towards the bed he had made. 'No need to go to work today, Kangali,' she said.

Kangali found the proposition most attractive, but said, 'Then they won't pay me the day's wages, ma.'

'Doesn't matter, let me tell you a story.'

Kangali needed no further inducement. He nestled close to his mother at once, and said, 'Go on, then.' Awbhagi began the story about the prince, the general's son and the flying horse.

She had heard and told this story many times. But within moments there was neither a prince nor a general's son – she told a story that she had not heard from anyone else, it was her own creation. The more her fever rose, the faster did the heated blood swirl in her head, and the more she wove newer and ever newer tales. There was no ceasing, no pause even – Kangali's frail body thrilled with every episode and in fear, wonder and delight he put his arms round his mother's neck and tried to nestle into her breast.

Daylight waned outside, the sun set, the dark shadows of evening grew deeper and spread across the earth, but no lamp was lit inside, no one rose to perform the last task of the day, only the mother's humming poured music into the silent son's ears in the intense darkness. It was the story of the funeral procession and the crematorium. Of the chariot, the red-lined feet and the journey to heaven. Of how the grieving husband said goodbye in tears after touching his dead wife's forehead with his feet, and then the son lighting the funeral pyre.

'Those were not flames, Kangali, those were god himself. And the smoke spreading across the sky was not smoke but the chariot to heaven. Kangali!'

'What, ma?'

'I too will go to heaven if you are the one who lights my pyre.'

'Don't say these things,' said Kangali, his voice barely audible.

His mother probably did not hear him. Through her fevered breathing she said, 'No one can hate me then for being low-caste, no one can talk about my misfortune. When my son lights my pyre the chariot to heaven will have no choice but to take me.'

Pressing his face to hers, Kangali said, 'Don't say these things, ma, you're frightening me.'

His mother said, 'And Kangali, can you fetch your father so he can touch my head with his feet the same way to say farewell. The same *altaa* on my soles, vermilion in my hair – but who will do all this? You will, won't you, Kangali, you're my son and my daughter, you're my everything.' She held her son close.

3

The final act in the drama of Awbhagi's life was about to end. Its extent was brief. Not even thirty years may have passed, and the end was ordinary too. There was no doctor in this village, he lived in another one. Kangali went to him with entreaties, wept at his feet and finally pawned a vessel to give him a fee of one rupee. He did not visit the patient to examine her, only prescribing three or four pills, which required an array of accompaniments to be taken alongside. Kangali's mother was unhappy with her son. 'Why did you have to pawn the vessel without asking me?' Accepting the pills, she touched her forehead with them reverently before throwing them into the burning oven. 'If I have to get well I will, no one in our clan has ever taken pills.'

Two or three days passed this way. The neighbours paid visits, everyone recommended their own version of guaranteed cures and went away. When young Kangali grew increasingly flustered, his mother drew him close and said, 'The doctor's pills didn't work, and you think these treatments will? I'll recover on my own.'

'You didn't take the pills, ma, you threw them into the oven,' Kangali said through his tears. 'How can anyone get better this way?'

'I'll get well on my own. Can you boil some rice for yourself? I want to watch you eat.'

Kangali busied himself trying to make rice for the first time with great ineptitude. He could neither drain the starch nor get the rice out of the pot properly. The oven refused to be lit correctly – water fell into it, sending up plumes of smoke. Rice grains spilt on the floor, and his mother's eyes filled with tears. She tried to get to her feet but fell back in bed. After her son had eaten she asked him to come closer and began giving him instructions, but her voice, already faint, faded altogether, and all she could do was weep continuously.

Ishwar the barber knew how to check the pulse. The next morning he placed his fingertips on the patient's wrist and then looked grave, sighed, shook his head and left. Kangali's mother deciphered the message, but she felt no fear. When everyone had left she told her son, 'Can you fetch him?'

'Fetch whom, ma?'

'You know, the one who's gone to the other village.'

Kangali understood. 'Father, you mean?'

Awbhagi was silent.

'Why will he come, ma?' Kangali asked.

Awbhagi was doubtful herself, but she said softly, 'Tell him ma only wants to pay her respects to him one last time.' As Kangali made to go at once, she gripped his arm and said, 'Tell him ma's going, let him see you cry.' After a pause she said, 'Get a little *altaa* from the barber's wife on your way back. She's very fond of me, she won't say no.'

Many of the villagers were fond of her. Ever since his mother's fever had set in, Kangali had heard her talk about these things many times. He set off, weeping.

4

Awbhagi was in a stupor by the time her husband Roshik did in fact turn up the next day. The shadow of death had fallen on her face, and her vision had completed its task on this earth and left for an unknown destination. 'Baba is here, ma,' Kangali said, sobbing, 'didn't you want to touch his feet?'

Perhaps his mother understood, or perhaps she didn't, or maybe her deep-rooted desire knocked on the doors of her consciousness like an ancient tradition. Bound for death, she held out her hand.

Roshik stood there, bewildered. That someone could actually seek to touch his feet in reverence was beyond his imagination. Bindi's aunt, who was present, said, 'Go on, let her.'

Roshik took a step forward. He had given no love to his wife in her lifetime, no attention or care, but now he burst into tears as he let her touch his feet.

'Why did such a chaste and pure woman have to be born into a low caste like ours?' said Rakhal's mother. 'Send her on her way now, it's as though she gave up her life with the expectation that Kangali will light the pyre.'

I cannot tell what the god presiding over Awbhagi's misfortunes out of sight of everyone made of this, but to young Kangali it was like an arrow to the heart.

The day passed and the night too, but Kangali's mother did not wait for the morning to arrive. Who knows whether there are arrangements for someone from such a low caste to be taken to heaven in a chariot, or whether they have to set off on foot before dawn, but it was clear that she had left this world before the sun had risen.

There was a wood apple tree in the yard. Roshik had barely plunged a borrowed axe into its trunk when the feudal landlord's guard ran up and slapped him resoundingly. Snatching the axe away, he said, 'Is this your father's tree, you bastard?'

Roshik caressed his cheek, and Kangali said tearfully, 'My mother planted this tree, why did you slap my father?'

Uttering an expletive, the guard tried to slap him too, but decided not to as it would mean becoming unclean, since Kangali had been touching his dead mother all this while. A crowd gathered because of the uproar, but no one denied that Roshik had not been wise in attempting to chop the tree without seeking permission. They also pleaded with the guard to allow him to do it. For Kangali had earnestly expressed Awbhagi's last wish to everyone who had been to see her.

The guard was not one to melt. Gesturing with his hands and face, he informed the gathering that he was not going to be taken in by their cleverness.

The feudal landlord was not a local. He did have an office in the village, however, presided over by the bill-collector Adhar Roy. While everyone pleaded in vain with the guard, Kangali raced off to the office. He had heard it said that guards took bribes, and was convinced that if only he could convey news of such unwarranted injustice to the powers that be, steps would be taken. How green behind the ears he was! He had no familiarity with feudal landlords and their employees. Confused and dazed by grief and desperation after losing his mother, he went directly up to where Adhar Roy had just emerged for a frugal meal on completing his prayers.

'Who are you?' Adhar Roy asked in astonishment and anger.

'I am Kangali. Your guard slapped my father.'

'Serves him right. Did the swine not pay his tax?'

'No sir,' said Kangali, 'he was chopping a tree, my mother has died . . .' He could not hold back his tears.

Adhar was irked at all this crying so early in the morning. The fellow had just touched a dead body, what if he touched something here? 'Go downstairs if your mother's died,' he rebuked Kangali. 'Someone purify this place with some cow dung and water. What caste are you?'

Going downstairs, Kangali revealed his caste fearfully.

'That's a low caste,' said Adhar. 'What do you need wood to burn the body for?'

Kangali said, 'Ma told me to light her pyre. Ask anyone if you don't believe me, everyone heard.' He was about to burst into tears on recalling his mother's plea.

'Bring five rupees for the tree if you want a pyre for your mother,' said Adhar. 'Can you afford it?'

Kangali knew this was impossible. He had seen for himself that Bindi's aunt had taken his brass plate to pawn it for a rupee so that a shawl could be bought for the last rites. 'No,' he said, shaking his head.

Contorting his face, Adhar said, 'If you can't pay, go bury your mother by the river. How dare your father take an axe to someone else's tree, the swine?'

'We planted the tree in our own yard,' said Kangali. 'My mother did it herself.'

'Planted it yourself! Someone throw him out.'

Someone appeared and threw him out, uttering words that only the employees of feudal landlords could summon to their tongues.

Kangali rose to his feet, slapping the dust off his body, and left slowly. He could not for the life of him understand why he had been beaten up and for what crime. The bill-collector's dispassionate expression showed no change. He would not have got this job if it had. 'Check whether the scoundrel's taxes are overdue, Paresh,' he said. 'If they are, one of his fishing nets should be confiscated, the bastard might run away.'

There was just a day to go to the ritual post-death ceremony at the Mukherjees'. The arrangements were worthy of the departed housewife. Aged Thakurdas Mukherjee was on his way back after supervising everything personally when Kangali confronted him, saying, 'My mother has died.'

'Who are you? What do you want?'

'I'm Kangali. Ma said to light her pyre.'

'Then do it.'

Word had spread already – someone said, 'He probably wants a tree', and explained everything.

Surprised and annoyed, Mukherjee said, 'What demands! I need all the wood I can get for the ceremonies. Get out of here, you won't get anything from me.' He left.

The Brahmin priest sitting nearby and making a list of the items needed for the rituals said, 'Who burns bodies in your caste? Just do the formalities and bury her by the river.'

Thakurdas Mukherjee's son was passing, looking extremely busy. Listening to the exchange, he said, 'Have you noticed how they all want to be high-caste these days.' He dashed off in pursuit of some important work.

Kangali begged and pleaded no more. His experiences during the past two hours seemed to have aged him several years. He went back in silence to where his dead mother was lying.

A hole was dug by the river and Awbhagi was laid down in it. Rakhal's mother lit a few hay stalks, put them in Kangali's hand, and guided his hand to touch his mother's face with the flame before throwing the stalks away. Then the people present filled the hole to erase all remaining signs of Kangali's mother's existence.

Everyone went back to whatever they were doing. Kangali alone sat there, gazing unblinkingly at the wisps of smoke from the burning stalks of hay spiralling up into the sky.

PARASHURAM

The Philosopher's Stone

Paresh-babu had found a philosopher's stone. When and where, how it got there, or whether there are more is none of your business. Be quiet and listen.

A middle-aged, middle-class man, Paresh-babu occupied ancestral property, and was a lawyer by profession. His earnings were nothing to write home about; they barely covered his household expenses. He picked up a pebble from the road on his way back home one day. Not that he had recognized it for what it was, but because it looked unusual he put it in his pocket. When he was home he took the key to his ground-floor office out of his pocket and discovered it was yellow. Paresh-babu wondered how the iron key had turned to brass. Maybe the original was lost, and his wife had had a duplicate made with brass, which he hadn't noticed all these days.

Entering, Paresh-babu emptied his pockets on the desk, keeping only his wallet, and climbed upstairs. The key was forgotten. After some food and an hour of rest, he went back downstairs to go over some work documents, and switched on the light. The first thing that caught his eye was the stone. A nice, rounded, shiny pebble. He would give it to his youngest son the next morning to play marbles with. Paresh-babu deposited it in a drawer that held his scissors, knife, notepaper, envelopes and other stationery. How strange, the scissors and knife turned yellow at once. Paresh-babu touched his inkpot with the stone, but there was no change in the glass. Then he held the stone against a lead paperweight, which turned yellow and twice as heavy. With a trembling voice Paresh-babu called for the manservant and said, 'Haria, fetch my watch from upstairs.' Haria brought his cheap nickel watch with a leather strap. As soon as

Paresh-babu touched them with the stone, the watch and the buckles all turned to gold. The watch stopped working, for the spring had turned to gold and was not strong enough any more.

Paresh-babu was in a state of bewilderment for some time. Gradually he realized that he had found that extremely rare object, a philosopher's stone, which turned all metal to gold on contact. Joining his palms together in prayer and raising them to this forehead repeatedly, he muttered, 'Long live Ma Kali, why such kindness? You are the only true god, Hari, are you playing with me? I'm not dreaming, am I?' Paresh-babu delivered an almighty pinch to his left arm, but still he didn't wake up. Not a dream, then. His head began to reel, his heart began thumping loudly. Putting his head on his breast, he declaimed like the classical heroine Shakuntala, 'Be quiet my beating heart. If you give up on me now, who is going to enjoy this enormous wealth granted by the gods?' He had heard of a man who had leapt so high in the air with elation after winning four lakh rupees in a lottery that his head had struck the rafters and been split open. Paresh-babu clutched his own head with both his hands, just in case he leapt as well.

Like extreme grief, one also grows accustomed to extreme joy. Paresh-babu returned to his senses and began to reflect on what he should do now. It was best for the news not to get out suddenly; you never know which of your enemies might put a spanner in the works. For now only his wife Giribala would be told, although women could never keep a secret. Paresh-babu went upstairs and broke the news to his wife slowly instead of springing it as a surprise, and, making her swear on the 3 million gods and goddesses, warned her not to let it out.

But although Paresh-babu had cautioned his wife, he lost control personally. Touching an iron beam beneath the bedroom roof with the philosopher's stone softened it because it was turned into gold, making the ceiling cave in. He converted all the pots and pans in the house to gold. Anyone who saw them wondered why they had been gilded. Paresh-babu told them off unceremoniously, 'Don't bother me, what business is it of yours?' Fed up with being interrogated, he more or less stopped socializing, and his clients decided he had gone mad.

After this Paresh-babu moved slowly, for haste could spell danger. He sold some of the gold, deposited part of the takings in the bank, and bought shares with the rest. He built a colossal house and a factory on twelve acres of land in Ballygunge. There was no shortage of bricks, cement or iron, since it was child's play for him to win over the authorities. Coming across a pile of rusted car parts in disuse, he asked, 'How much?' The owner was devoid of greed and said, 'Take it all, sir, it's garbage, I can't pay for transport though.' Paresh-babu proceeded to gather fifteen or twenty kilos of the scrap every day. All he had to do in his private chamber was to touch it all with his philosopher's stone to create gold instantly. Ten Gurkha security men and five bulldogs guarded the factory premises, where no one was allowed in without Paresh-babu's orders.

Making and selling gold was the easiest of businesses, but producing it on a large scale was not possible alone. Paresh-babu put an advertisement in the papers, and, rejecting a mass of applications, appointed Priyotosh Henry Biswas, who had just acquired an MSc degree, at 150 rupees a month. Priyotosh had no family to speak of, and moved into Paresh-babu's factory. He did not take more than an hour to clear his bowels, bathe, and eat his meals. He slept for seven hours, worked at the factory for eight, and spent the remaining eight hours writing long poems and love letters addressed to Hindola Majumdar, his classmate from college, besides smoking and drinking tea at frequent intervals. He was a fine young man who did not spend time in the company of others, did not go to church on Sundays, displayed no curiosity about anything, and never asked where all this gold was coming from. Paresh-babu considered himself in possession of a second gem in addition to the philosopher's stone in the form of his new recruit. Priyotosh melted the gold down in large moulds using electric bellows and made thick bars which Paresh-babu sold to a syndicate of Marwari businessmen, fattening his bank balance. There was no limit now to his wife's wealth, she was in fact in physical pain from all the jewellery she used to wear, and was quite sick of gold. Giribala had discarded all of it and had switched to saffron robes.

Still, Paresh-babu's activities didn't stay under wraps very long. The police began to investigate him on the Bengal government's orders. But they succumbed easily, for they had not yet mastered the policies of the ideal state; all they needed to be mollified were a few grams of gold. Scientists gave up food and drink and began to speculate. Had they been born two centuries ago, they would have realized that Paresh-babu had found a philosopher's stone. But there was no room for such objects in modern science, which was why they concluded that he had put together a machine that could split the atom, and was making gold by reassembling the fragments, just like making a quilt from pieces of cloth. The trouble was that Paresh-babu never answered letters, and Priyotosh was nothing but an idiot who only said when pressed, 'I merely melt the gold, I have no idea where it comes from.' Scientists abroad had at first dismissed the whole thing as a rumour, but eventually they became active too.

Flustered by the advice of specialists, the government of India decided that Paresh-babu was a dangerous person, but there was nothing they could do about it, since he had not done anything illegal. There was a proposal to arrest him and seize his factory, but various powerful people from India and abroad came in the way. The ambassadors of Britain, France, America, Russia and other nations kept a vigilant but benevolent eye on him, inviting him repeatedly to dinner. Paresh-babu went, ate quietly, and said yes and no sometimes, but no one could worm his secret out of him, not even after plying him with champagne. 'For the good of the nation let a few of us know your secret,' some Congress leaders in Bengal suggested. 'Don't even think of listening to anyone,' the Communists told him, 'just go on with what you're doing, the world will benefit.'

The ranks of friends, relatives and flatterers kept swelling, with Paresh-babu even handing out suitable rewards, but still no one was happy. As for his enemies, they were stunned into silence. Despite his expanded wealth, he did not lead an ostentatious life, and his wife was too old-fashioned to know how to squander money. Still, Paresh-babu was now known all over the world. He was reputed to be capable of supporting half a dozen kings of the princely states financially. What he said and ate and wore was published in the newspapers of Europe and America in bold type. Love letters had begun to pour in from home and abroad. Beautiful women sent photographs and catalogues of virtues, writing, 'Dearest sir, you may retain your old wife, we have no objection. You are a liberal Hindu, purify me and enrol me in your harem, or else I shall consume poison.' Letters like these arrived in large numbers every day, and Giribala snatched them out of his hand. She engaged a foreigner as her secretary to read out translations of the letters and send replies according to her orders. Giribala said many harsh things out of anger, but the foreigner was under-educated, and wrote the same thing in every letter: damn you. In other words, you wretched woman, can't you find a rope to hang yourself with? Ten renowned scientists wrote to Paresh-babu to tell him that if he revealed the secret behind the gold they would try to ensure that he received the Nobel Prizes in Physics, Chemistry and Peace all at the same time. Assuming this too was a love letter, Paresh-babu's wife sent the same reply through her secretary: damn you.

Paresh-babu kept pushing the price of gold down: from 100 rupees per ten grams it had dropped to seven. The British government had bought gold cheap and used it to repay its dollar loans to America. The American government was furious, but it could not find grounds to object. Britain had wanted to repay its pound sterling loan to India down to the last penny in the same way, but the prime minister of the country said, 'We lent you neither gold nor dollars, we supplied material during the war, you have to repay us with the same material.'

Unable to find a solution, the mavens of economics and politics were frantic with worry. If it had been one of the three older cosmological periods of the Hindu calendar, they could have taken the ascetic's route to secure the help of one of the top gods and teach Paresh-babu a lesson. But there was no scope for this in the modern age. Some experts were advocating the use of platinum or silver standards, but others argued, no, those might be manufactured cheaply too, radium or uranium would be best, or go back to the barter system of yore.

Churchill could not be restrained any more. Flying into a rage, he said, 'We will not allow the Commonwealth to be destroyed, we won't waste time griping to the United Nations either. Let British rule be re-established in India, let our soldiers capture this Paresh, let him be kept under confinement on the Isle of Wight. Let him produce as much gold there as he likes, but all of it will belong to the British Empire, we will decide how to distribute it.'

George Bernard Shaw said, 'Gold is a useless metal, it cannot be used to make ploughs or sickles or axes or boilers. Paresh has done well to destroy its undeserved reputation. He should now try to make gold as strong as steel. As soon as I am given a gold razor I will start shaving.'

A Russian spokesperson wrote to Paresh-babu, 'We extend a warm invitation to you to reside in our country, sir, we are sure you will enjoy it. There is no discrimination between whites and blacks here, we will make you the apple of our eye. You have received a miraculous gift, but, forgive me for saying so, you are not particularly intelligent. You know how to make gold, but not how to capitalize on it. We will teach you. Should you harbour political ambitions, you will be made the president of the Soviet Union. We will allot a magnificent mansion to you on a hundred acres of land in Moscow. And if it is privacy you seek, you can live in Siberia; we will give you an entire city. A wonderful land, which your ancient texts have named North Kuru.' Giribala treated this missive as a love letter too and gave the same reply. Damn you.

Paresh-babu lowered the price of gold to where it now cost forty-five paise per ten grams. The amount of gold mined around the world every year was about 750,000 kilograms. Right now Paresh-babu was single-handedly releasing five times that quantity every year. The gold standard had gone to hell. There was great inflation in every country, currency notes and coins had become useless trifles. Even with their wages and salaries increased greatly, everyone was in a sorry plight. Prices were sky-high and no one could afford anything.

Ten people each from different groups had laid themselves down outside Paresh-babu's front gate with a vow to fast unto death. From time to time he received anonymous letters – you're an enemy of the world, we will murder you. On his part, Paresh-babu had lost his taste for wealth. Giribala wept all the time, saying, 'What's the use of all these riches if we cannot be at peace? Get rid of that horrible stone, discard the gold in the river, let's give up everything here and go live in Kashi.'

Paresh-babu made up his mind, and informed Priyotosh of the secret behind the gold the next morning.

Priyotosh was unmoved. Handing him the philosopher's stone, Paresh-babu told him, 'Destroy this at once. Burn it, melt it with acid, or use any other method.'

'Righto,' said Priyotosh.

In the afternoon one of the security guards ran up to Paresh-babu and said, 'Come quick, sir, Biswas sahib has gone mad, he's asking for you.' Paresh-babu rushed off to find Priyotosh lying on his bed, weeping. 'What's the matter?' Paresh-babu asked. 'Read this letter, sir,' Priyotosh answered.

Paresh-babu read:

My Priyo, my dearest, goodbye. My father is not willing, he has several objections. You have no prospects, you live in someone else's house, you make only 150 a month, and to top it all you are a Christian and a year younger than me. This marriage is impossible, he said. Let me give you some more news. Have you heard of Gunjan Ghosh? A fine singer, handsome, curly hair. Makes 600 a month at the civil supply office, the only son of a father who has apparently made millions from his contractor's business. My wedding has been arranged with this Gunjan. Don't be upset, my darling. You know Bokul Mallik, don't you? Three years junior to me, we were in Diocesan School at the same time. She can't hold a candle to me, and yet she's one in a thousand. Bag Bokul, you will be happy. This is my final love letter to you, dearest darling. From tomorrow you will be my brother, and I your affectionate elder sister. Yours, but only till today, Hindola.

Paresh-babu said, 'What a fool you are. Hindola has left you voluntarily, this is exceedingly good news, why are you unhappy? You cannot pray in thanksgiving at the temple of course, you'd better light a couple of candles at the church. Now get out of bed, wash your face, come and have a cup of tea and breakfast. By the way, have you managed to dispose of the stone?'

In anguish Priyotosh said, 'I have swallowed it, sir. This life is not worth preserving, the stone will go to the grave with me. Can you imagine so many years of love culminating in Gunjan Ghosh?'

'What did you swallow it for?' Paresh-babu asked in surprise. 'Is it poisonous?'

'I am not aware of its composition, sir,' said Priyotosh, 'but I think it is. Even if it is not, and I am not dead by tonight, I am determined to consume ten grams of potassium cyanide tomorrow morning, I have measured it out. Don't worry, sir, your stone will be buried with me and remain there till the day of judgement.'

'What a madman!' Paresh-babu said. 'Abandon these horrifying notions, I shall try to get you married to Hindola. Her father Jogai Majumdar is a childhood friend of mine, a canny fellow if there ever was one. I will provide a handsome dowry, he may be ready to give his daughter's hand to you once he knows this. But you're a Christian . . .'

'I'll convert to Hinduism, sir.'

'Now this is true love. Now come on, we have to see Dr Chatterjee.'

Paresh-babu informed the doctor that Priyotosh had absent-mindedly swallowed a pebble. An X-ray was taken the next day on the doctor's advice. Scanning the plate, Dr Chatterjee said, 'You don't usually see such cases, I'm sending a report to *The Lancet* at once. Next to his ascending colon the young man has developed a small semicolon, which is where the stone is trapped. It might descend on its own. Let it stay as it is now, it won't do any harm. If there are adverse symptoms I'll operate on him and take it out.'

Jogai Majumdar hurried to meet Paresh-babu on receiving his letter. After their conversation he rushed back home and told his daughter, 'Priyotosh has agreed to convert to Hinduism, Dola, you must marry him. No need to delay things, let his purification ceremony be conducted today, and the marriage tomorrow.'

Hindola was astonished. 'What do you think you're saying, baba? Yesterday it was Gunjan Ghosh, and today it's Priyotosh? Look, Gunjan has given me a diamond ring, how do you suppose he'll feel? You've given him your word, I've given him mine, how can we go back on it? How can Priyotosh match Gunjan? There's simply no comparison.'

'You think you know everything,' said Jogai-babu. 'Priyotosh has a goldmine in his stomach now. It will come out one day or another, and when it does the philosopher's stone will be yours. Paresh-babu won't take it back, he has given it for Priyotosh's dowry. Give that diamond ring back, Priyotosh can get thousands like that. Can your Ghosh and his contractor father be compared to a groom like this? No more arguments, it's Priyotosh you must marry.'

Her voice soaked in tears, Hindola sobbed, 'It was him I loved. But he's such a fool.'

'Why would he want to marry you if he's not a fool?' said Jogai-babu. 'With a philosopher's stone in his stomach he can marry the most beautiful woman in the world.'

Priyotosh Henry Biswas harboured no regrets. His purification ceremony was conducted, a ritual fire was lit with a kilogram of vegetable clarified butter, five upper-caste Brahmins were served a sumptuous meal. And then Hindola and Priyotosh were wedded at an auspicious moment. But Jogai-babu's and his daughter's wishes were not fulfilled, for the stone did not drop. Sometime later, there was a strange phenomenon – all the gold Paresh-babu had created began to lose its sheen, and within a month all of it turned back to iron.

There was a simple explanation. As everyone knows, just as unrequited love leads to failing health, being lucky in love revives it. All the organs function efficiently, improving metabolism. It had taken Priyotosh only a month to grind down the pebble; not even a fragment was to be seen in an X-ray. And with the dissolution of the stone, all of Paresh-babu's gold had reverted to its original form.

Hindola and her father were furious. 'Priyotosh is a liar and cheat,' they said. They had trusted this fraud, they complained, and wasted their time with this Christian garbage out of sheer hope. But Priyotosh was fortified mentally after digesting the philosopher's stone. He had become more intelligent, and ignored his wife's and father-in-law's verbal assaults. He would not consume cyanide even if Hindola threatened to divorce him. He had realized that St Francis and Ramakrishna Paramhansa had got it right – women and wealth were both worthless, nothing compared to iron. He now ran Paresh-babu's iron factory, casting fifty tons of various products every day, and was enjoying life to the full.

BIBHUTIBHUSHAN BANDYOPADHYAY

Drobomoyee's Sojourn in Kashi

For two days they packed. Only three families lived here – usually none of them spoke to the other two. The area was surrounded by clumps of false white teaks, tamarind trees, bamboo groves and very old orchards of mango and jackfruit. There was a dense growth of trees around Drobomoyee's house, which meant the sunlight never entered it. There was a pond in front, overflowing in the rainy season, with the monotonous croaking of frogs in the daytime and the buzzing of mosquitoes at night.

Drobomoyee's grandson said, 'Is there anything at home you can eat, or should I get something?'

Her reply was faint, for she had been suffering from malaria for two months; an intermittent fever had returned on alternate days by the clock in the afternoon. Drobomoyee slipped under her ancient quilts, groaned piteously and became delirious every time.

A woman from one of the neighbouring houses, universally addressed as Naw-thakrun, went up to her window and asked, 'What's the matter, do you have a fever?'

'I want to die. This fever, all the time. Oh god how my arms and legs ache. It won't even let me get to my feet, what is this illness?' Then she would add an entreaty. 'Even with these quilts I feel so cold, will you get that old mattress there and put it on me, Naw-bou?'

'Should I press it down on you, didi?'

'Do, do, press hard ... I think ... this ... is the end ...'

'Don't say that, don't be afraid. Tebu will be here as soon as the letter reaches him, Kanu will come, Bindey will come – may your grandsons live long, didi, wonderful boys all of them, what do you have to worry about?'

'No ... one ... looks after ... me ...'

'Of course they will, didi, of course they will. Don't speak, rest quietly.'

'My ... cow ... in the ... northern ... field ...'

'Where did you leave her?'

'Next to ... milkman Jotey's ... field ...'

'Never mind, I'll bring her home. My cow's there too. Rest.'

Naw-thakrun returned to the window half an hour later to ask, 'Has the shivering stopped, didi?'

A faint voice came from beneath the pile of torn quilts and sheets, 'But my cow ...'

'Don't worry, I've brought her back. Has the shivering stopped?'

'Hmm.'

Every year Drobomoyee suffered from malaria through the rainy season. Her eldest grandson, Srishchandra aka Tebu, worked at the Gun and Shell factory in Ichhapur. The middle one was an employee of Eastern Bengal Railway in Pakshi. The youngest one lived somewhere there too. Only the eldest grandson was married, with a son of his own. He had visited Drobomoyee with his family for the past five or six years, each time staying a week. His wife Manorama was from the urbanized district of Hooghly, she sniffed at everything. 'House nothing, it's just a ramshackle room with bamboo slips for walls. It's such a jungle here you can see wild pigs in the daytime. And those mosquitoes! God, the mud. Is this place fit for humans?' Manorama's scimitar-like nose grew sharper and higher. Seven days later Drobomoyee had to allow her heart to be broken as her great-grandson left. She could not contain her tears. To Naw-thakrun she said, 'I cannot tell you how sweet he is ...'

Unable to understand the desperate anticipation of many years now drowned in Drobomoyee's uncontrollable weeping, the barren widow from next door was nonplussed. Perhaps Naw-thakrun told herself, 'How she exaggerates everything!'

Naw-thakrun was not a relative of Drobomoyee's, merely a neighbour. The two old women stopped talking to each other for an average of four months every year, refusing even to set eyes on one another. And yet, once they had made up, it was Naw-thakrun who did the most to look after Drobomoyee. When Drobomoyee couldn't get out of bed because of fever, Naw-thakrun took care of her cow along with her own. She even brought the ailing Drobomoyee some food sometimes, or at least peeped in on her through the window and comforted the sick woman.

But this time Drobomoyee was suffering more than usual. The fever began in mid-June and attacked her frequently. She grew progressively weaker, and everything tasted foul. For a month now she had been afflicted by an intermittent fever.

In the evening Drobomoyee kicked away her quilts and rose to her feet. The trembling had stopped, though the fever hadn't receded yet – there was a bitter coating on her tongue, her head felt heavy and her body numb.

'Did you bring my cow back, Naw-bou?' she called out to her neighbour.

Naw-thakrun answered after two or three attempts. 'Who's that, is that didi? You're up?'

'Did you bring my cow back from the fields?'

'I did. Can't you think of anything but the cow? Is the fever gone at last?'

'It has. Where did you put the cow?'

'In the cowshed. Mad to go on about the cow all the time . . .'

There was a spot of kerosene oil in one of the earthen lamps. Drobomoyee lit it. Two birds were conversing on a hog plum tree. To Drobomoyee's fevered brain the conversation seemed to go like this –

First bird: 'Kutli kutli . . .'

Second bird: 'Kya kya kya . . .'

First bird: 'Kutli kutli . . .'

Second bird: 'Kya kya kya . . .'

First bird: 'Kutli kutli . . .'

Drobomoyee was irked. So monotonous. On and on they were going, it had been half an hour at least. Who wanted this on top of a headache? Stop, for heaven's sake. How could she cope with man and beast harassing her together . . .

Drobomoyee went to the cowshed for a glimpse of Mungli, her cow, to calm herself down. She never ate till Mungli had eaten. Here she was in this desolate home of her husband's in the wilderness, everyone had deserted her, some for distant lands and some for heaven. She had two sons, two daughters, several grandchildren – a large family, if only they had all lived together.

But no one had remained here. She was alone with Mungli in this house in Gopinathpur. No wonder Drobomoyee loved her cow so much, going back several times after tethering Mungli in the field to make sure she was all right and taking her to the river for water.

When she woke up in the morning Drobomoyee felt she couldn't stand upright for hunger. She picked some figs from the tree behind the house, and some leaves from the horseradish tree in the yard. On her way to the river she met Mrs Mukherjee, none of whose sons were educated and simply smoked ganja all day. Drobomoyee's grandsons were all gainfully employed, because of which Mrs Mukherjee's envy knew no bounds.

'They said you were ill,' she told Drobomoyee.

'Yes. Going to make some rice today. That's why I'm off to the river early in the morning ...'

'How sad it is, you have everything and yet nothing. All these grandchildren but look at you ... it's all fate.' In other words, no need to boast about your grandsons having jobs, your condition is as miserable as ever.

The path to the river was flanked by wildly growing trees and plants and gardens. None of the gardens was fenced, and some of the cleanliness-obsessed widows had broken the branches of the orangeberry and dog teak trees because they brushed against them when they went to bathe in the river. Drobomoyee had just wandered into the undergrowth to peep at something when one of the Mukherjee daughters-in-law said from the back, 'What are you looking for, Khurima?'

'Whether any of the jackfruits are left on that tree there. The tree's usually full of fruits but the rogues will never leave any for you ... I'm ill most of the time ...'

'Who took the jackfruits?'

'Do you expect me to keep guard? The neighbourhood is full of thieves, do you think there's any honesty left in this day and age?'

'Let's go to the river, Khurima ...'

Drobomoyee proceeded to the river, still muttering to herself. Going back home after her bath, she had just cooked some rice with the figs and horseradish leaves and sat down to eat when she heard a rustling sound beneath the fragrant lime tree behind the house.

'Who's that?' she called out.

'It's me, Kanak,' came the faint response in a girl's voice.

'What are you doing there? Come on out.'

The figure of a ten- or eleven-year-old girl, withered by malaria, appeared in the yard confidently to face Drobomoyee's merciless gaze.

'My mother finds all food tasteless, she told me, go get a lime ...'

Flying into a rage, Drobomoyee said, 'Of course, it's your father who planted the tree after all, pick all the limes you want. Thieves, the whole lot of you. Why can't you buy your limes in the market? Why are you here? Is this your father's tree?'

The girl stood in silence.

Drobomoyee continued seething to herself. After a while the girl said, 'Thakuma ...'

'What? What is it?'

'Should I go?'

'Have I tied you up? Go.'

'You won't let me take the lime?'

Drobomoyee absently ate some rice, picked up her pot of water with her left hand and swallowed its contents. Then she said in a relatively softer voice, 'Are your clothes freshly washed? Pour me some water from the pitcher there ...'

The girl complied. Drobomoyee said, 'Why tasteless? Is your mother having a baby?'

'I don't know.'

'Take a lime, but no more than one, all right?'

Drobomoyee had just laid out her mat for a nap after lunch when Atul, the eldest son of the Mukherjees, appeared and asked, 'Are you sleeping, Thakuma?'

'What? Oh, it's Atul.'

'Do you have a false white teak tree? Someone from a matchbox factory in Calcutta is here to buy false white teaks and silk cotton trees. Good price, in case you have any ...'

'No, I don't.'

'But there are so many of them behind your house thanks to Hari Roy ...'

'No, I'm not selling.'

Drobomoyee was far too attached to the trees behind her house. Whatever little land her husband had left behind was now overgrown and covered with large, useless trees. Selling them as kindling could have fetched her some money in these times when coal was short, but she refused to entertain the possibility. It was said that someone had come to pluck fig leaves for his silkworms, but Drobomoyee hadn't allowed him. The story may have been an exaggerated one, but it revealed her attitude.

Drobomoyee began to feel quite well in the afternoon. Not too many people came to this part of the village, and no one besides Naw-thakrun dropped in. But Drobomoyee quite liked socializing. She was rather keen on having visitors, but no one came besides the girl who had already been here in the morning, though it was only for her own selfish reason.

'May I have a lime, Thakuma?'

'But why? You already . . .'

'We've used up the one I took in the morning, we need another one now, ma said . . .'

'All right, come sit with me for a bit.'

Unwillingly the girl obeyed, or she wouldn't get the lime. She had no wish to give the old woman company. Her friends of her own age were playing by the pond in another part of the village, she had left her heart there. But the lonely Drobomoyee was ready to cling to anyone she could find on this desolate afternoon – she would at least be able to talk to someone.

Drobomoyee ranted on unmindfully, about her grandson's badly behaved wife, about her great-grandson's miraculous virtues, about how much her youngest grandson Paresh loved her. Her young listener began to yawn. In a pleading voice she said, 'Ma told me to get the lime quickly, it's getting late . . .'

'All in good time . . . now listen . . .'

'Ma will scold me, she can't eat without the lime . . .'

'Yes, now listen . . . So Khokon is insistent on having the guava, and his mother won't let him have it either, she's so obstinate. I tell her, let him have a slice, then she tells me, be quiet, what do you know about bringing up children? Mothers these days are not like in our times, those days are gone. Imagine me not knowing how to bring up children, where did your husband come from, you're nothing but an immigrant's daughter.'

'I have to go now, Thakuma . . . a lime . . .'

'Oh all right, take one ... You heard the whole story, didn't you ... She hates me ...'

Suddenly a bullock cart was heard outside. Her eyes widening with surprise, the little girl said, 'Someone's come, Thakuma ... stopped beneath the tamarind tree ...'

Drobomoyee's second grandson, Niradchandra, entered with two heavy bundles in his hands. 'Thakuma ...' he cried.

Drobomoyee jumped to her feet, a big smile spreading across her face. 'Is that Kanu? Come to me, you've made me so happy.'

Kanu put his bundles down and bent to touch his grandmother's feet in deference. Looking at the girl, he said, 'Isn't this Hari-kaka's daughter Kanak? How you've grown ... Wait, here's a sweet for you.'

Unwrapping one of the bundles, he handed her a sweet, but Kanak remained standing with her hand held out, smiling and waiting to see what else was in the bundles. No one in her low-income family worked outside the village – she had no idea of the wonderful things that those who were employed elsewhere brought back home.

'Well?' said Drobomoyee. 'What's behind this sudden visit? So you finally remembered your old grandmother. How I've suffered all month, I'm not cured yet. No one here to even give me water to drink ... Naw-bou saved my life ... I wrote so many letters, no one came, not Tebu, not Bindey, not you ...'

Naw-thakrun came over in the evening when she heard. Kanu had been born in the village, she was delighted to see him. Having asked after him, she said, 'Tell me Kanu, do you want your grandmother to die without treatment? She's got kala-azar, fine today, shivering with fever tomorrow. Who's going to look after her? And then there's her cow to take care of ... you'd better do something about it ... Otherwise ...'

'That's what I'm here for,' said Kanu. 'Her letter came long ago, but I simply couldn't get leave earlier ...'

'Take a couple of sweets home, Naw-bou,' Drobomoyee said. 'Kanu brought them for me ... But have you seen my teeth ... take them Naw-bou.'

'All right, give me a couple. We get no delicacies here. May your dutiful grandsons live long, didi, you have nothing to worry about. Kanu especially ... nobody in the village like him ... I don't mind telling the truth ...'

And so Naw-thakrun went back home happily after a while with four sweets instead of two.

The grandmother and grandson had a discussion at night. Kanu had made a plan – he wanted to take his grandmother to Kashi and have her live with other Bengali widows there. The mother of one of his friends lived there, he would deposit his grandmother in the same place. Naw-thakrun was delighted to hear of this plan the next morning, Drobomoyee's grandsons would never leave her in the lurch. And this was the right age to go and live in a holy city. If only her own son had been alive. He had died nearly forty-five years ago, at the age of just seven months. Her first child and her last.

On the day she was leaving Drobomoyee entrusted her dearest Mungli to Naw-thakrun's care, making her neighbour swear to look after the cow. 'The cow is yours now Naw-bou,' she said, 'bless me so that I may lay my bones to rest in Kashi. May the load be lifted off my grandsons' shoulders. The eldest of them is affluent, they eat good food, I'm an old woman now, people like me have no room in households such as theirs ...'

Drobomoyee had gathered a pile of dried coconut leaves and twigs for use as kindling for the oven during the rainy season. She was off to Kashi now, and living in a holy city would be impossible if she remained attached to things back home. She gave away most of the kindling to Naw-thakrun, and the rest to others.

Kanak had arrived with a ripe cucumber. 'Want some, Thakuma?' she said.

'Take some of those twigs, Kanki, you won't forget old Thakuma will you?'

'Never,' said Kanak, shaking her head vehemently.

Naw-thakrun wept as Drobomoyee left.

Drobomoyee arrived in Kashi, having somehow managed to keep herself untouched by anything she considered impure during the train journey. Kanu's friend Satya's mother lived on the ground floor of a house in a lane. A room next to hers had been rented for Drobomoyee. The old woman had the key and unlocked the room, whereupon Drobomoyee established herself in it with her belongings.

Within an hour she discovered with some trepidation that her neighbour was from the district of Nadia in Bengal. The woman's manner of speaking was polished. Being a native of the largely rural Jessore district, it was natural for Drobomoyee to be fearful. Entering Drobomoyee's room, the other woman said, 'You can make arrangements to cook tomorrow, I've got some milk and sweets for you to eat today.'

'All right,' said Drobomoyee apprehensively.

Bringing the food, the neighbour said, 'Get your sacred shawl.'

Drobomoyee had no idea what this was, but she said, 'I don't have one.'

'You don't? What do you wear when you say your prayers?'

'My usual white sari, I don't have anything else to wear.'

Even though it stood in a lane, the house looked out on the main road. The sound of traffic did not die down till late into the night. Used as she was to living in a remote, rural place, Drobomoyee began to feel most uncomfortable. When did the people of Kashi sleep?

Submitting his grandmother from the village to his friend's mother's care, Kanu left the next day. His leave was exhausted. His friend's mother's name was Neerajabashini, she was three or four years younger than Drobomoyee, and her hair hadn't greyed yet – but that could also be on account of her robust health.

Drobomoyee went with her to Kashi's famous Dasaswamedh Ghat in the evening. There was a huge crowd, songs, speeches, storytelling. Many of the people had gathered around a monk dressed in saffron; Neeraja went up to them. The monk was spouting wisdom on karma and servitude, most of which Drobomoyee didn't understand. On the way back she asked, 'Who was that?'

'He's an important, umm, from the Ramakrishna Mission, Swami Sevananda.'

'From where?'

'Haven't you heard of the Ramakrishna Mission? They're the sage Ramakrishna's ... it's a very large organization.'

'Are Rama and Krishna two sages?'

Neeraja stared at Drobomoyee in astonishment. 'Haven't you heard of the most holy Ramakrishna Paramhansa?'

'No. Who is he ... Is he here?'

Neeraja didn't prolong the conversation. Her companion was a savage who had not even heard of Ramakrishna. But Drobomoyee was not to blame, she had not kept up with the times, and besides, she had never left her neck of the woods. No one had mentioned Ramakrishna in the wilderness of Gopinathpur. She was conversant with the usual members of the pantheon, but not of a god with such a long name.

Drobomoyee lived in fear. What if her companion considered her an ignorant, uninformed, godless woman?

It took her only a few days to realize that Neeraja was obsessed with religion. She was a diehard devotee of hermits. No monk newly arrived in Kashi was safe from her; she would visit him at once and chatter constantly, asking all sorts of questions about her karma and so on. Every time they went out Neeraja spent hours on the streets, showing no signs of returning home. This irked Drobomoyee no end, but what was she to do? Not yet familiar with the roads of Kashi, she could not go back without her companion.

One evening they went to the Kashi Vishwanath temple for a glimpse of the evening prayers.

A female monk was seated inside, dressed in saffron, a tangle of matted hair on her head. A number of women had gathered around her. Always eager for the company of hermits, Neeraja joined the crowd at once.

Drobomoyee could hear the questions of the devotees.

'Can we see god, maiji?'

'Will my daughter get her amulet today, maiji?'

'Will you read my palm, maiji?'

'Why do I not feel devotion within me, maiji?'

Drobomoyee couldn't stop laughing in her head. You've surrounded yourself with monks and ascetics, prayers here, incantations there, you pinch your nose two hours a day – if all of this doesn't give birth to devotion within you, drown yourself in the Ganges. I'm sick of your posing.

Everyone left eventually – but not Neeraja. She had closed her eyes and settled herself into some kind of meditation and refused to budge. Drobomoyee didn't dare say anything either. Meanwhile she suddenly recollected there was no wheat flour at home, she had forgotten until now. Where would they get some at this hour? The usual fare of sweetened semolina would have to be forsaken tonight thanks to the pressure of religiosity.

Drobomoyee grew irritated as she waited. Most of the women from Bengal had left the temple; only those who spoke the local language of

Hindi were still present. She could neither speak their tongue nor understand what they said.

It had been three months since she had arrived from the village. It was quite cold in Kashi now. She couldn't help thinking of her cow Mungli, for whom she would light a fire in the cowshed on winter nights. The fig tree must be full of fruit – she wondered who was eating them. Was Nawbou taking care of Mungli the way Drobomoyee did? She treated Mungli like her own daughter . . . Her eyes filled with tears.

Naw-bou's letter had arrived today, which was why memories of home kept flooding her mind. The letter said Mungli was well and would soon be giving birth to a calf. The posts holding up the roof of Drobomoyee's house simply had to be changed, Kanu or Bindey should be informed.

Sighing, Neeraja came out of her trance and said, 'Let's go, didi. How sacred this place is, isn't it? I have no desire to go back home and cook and eat.'

Drobomoyee said to herself, 'Why don't you just stay here and waste away till you die, who's begging you to go home and cook?'

'I'm practising the hand position during prayers,' said Neeraja, 'I've almost perfected it.'

Drobomoyee was silent. Was the hag mad? It was impossible to understand the things she said. It's almost midnight, can we go home, please?

But there was no respite at home either.

'Shall we read the *Gita*, didi?' Neeraja would say from her room.

Drobomoyee joined her with great reluctance. She had no interest in intellectual holy texts like the *Gita*. She was used to down-to-earth religious instructions in verse, she could make sense of those. But she didn't understand a word of these difficult sentences. And the less said the better of the way the whore read, rolling her eyes and sounding tearful. Drobomoyee could neither laugh nor suppress her laughter. Really, the kind of trouble that people could get into!

'Oh, magnificent,' Neeraja would marvel as she read.

'If only she'd stop,' Drobomoyee told herself as she nodded off.

In the morning Neeraja said, 'My guru will be here today, make something special for him in my room, didi.'

A monk arrived at two in the afternoon. Corpulent, with a big paunch and a flowing beard. Neeraja lay down flat on the floor to hammer her head twice on his feet in a show of deference. The day passed in getting the ingredients and preparing his food. In the evening Neeraja sat down with her guru to learn some obscure technique of spirituality, some nonsense. They matched each other with their gibberish. Drobomoyee was deafened.

The guru was from Bengal. He sent for Drobomoyee after nine at night.

'Where did you live earlier?'

'Gopinathpur in Jessore district ...'

'Family?'

'Grandsons, one of them is married with a child.'

'You want to live in Kashi?'

'Yes.'

'What is your name?'

'Drobomoyee Debi ...'

'Have you been initiated formally to spiritual life?'

'No.'

Neeraja's eyebrows shot up. 'This is a disaster. You haven't had your initiation yet? I had no idea.'

'You will have to be initiated,' the guru said.

'I have no money, it's too expensive. My grandsons send me eleven rupees a month – I have to use it for rent and food. Where will I get the money?'

'What is the use of being in Kashi without living the spiritual life?'

'I didn't come for a spiritual life, I came to improve my health.'

'Which comes first, health or the afterlife?' asked Neeraja angrily.

Drobomoyee was silent.

'Answer her,' said the guru, 'you cannot remain silent.'

Oh for heaven's sake, the hag was talking nonsense again.

What Drobomoyee said was, 'As you say. I don't understand these things. But not now. My grandson sent me seven rupees, it's been used up for rent. Without any money ...'

But both of them were adamant. She would have to be initiated.

'You are living in Kashi,' said the guru, 'and you are quite old too. It will all go to waste unless you are initiated by a guru. You are here today, you will be gone tomorrow. This world means nothing, this life means nothing ...'

'There are only Brahma, Vishnu, Maheshwar. In this life and in the afterlife . . .' droned Neeraja.

The whore just won't stop, Drobomoyee said to herself. If it's only the gods who rule their lives, where are women supposed to keep their husbands? Still, Drobomoyee wasn't to be persuaded.

Neeraja felt she had honestly tried to do something good for a seventy-year-old on her way to death, but what could she do in the face of such resistance? Her own devotion was something to behold. She would not eat a.morsel till she had taken a sip of the water in which her guru had dipped his feet. His instructions were more valuable than the scriptures. She sold an old necklace of hers, giving her guru the money.

When she heard this, Drobomoyee said, 'You gave so much money to your guru!'

'For a good cause, didi.'

'Your own necklace?'

'Came from my in-laws when I got married . . . My husband gave it to me himself . . .'

'And you sold it.'

'Family is temporary, didi, everything is temporary. It's all an illusion woven by the creator. An illusion that makes us forget everything . . . But the guru alone is constant . . .'

'Of course, of course.'

This bitch always talks big. By all means hand over everything you have to your guru – what did Drobomoyee care? How can anyone give away a necklace her husband had given her himself? This was the thought that haunted Drobomoyee late into the night. Those days had faded, her mind was now covered by the clouds of forgetfulness. The house in Gopinathpur was not dilapidated on their wedding night.

Suddenly she recalled that last June she had spotted a cucumber plant sprouting in a crack in the northern wall. Gathering some dry strips of bamboo, she had built a frame to support the plant. It must have grown bigger now, who was eating all the cucumbers? Maybe Kanak went there every day for limes – Drobomoyee had left an entire tree behind, after all. Kanak might be the one who plucked the cucumbers.

Drobomoyee was startled by a horrible sound. It was coming from Neeraja's room.

What was the hag up to at this hour? Why was she exhaling so loudly? Was she choking in her sleep?

'What is it, what's the matter?' Drobomoyee cried out.

'What are you saying, didi?' Neeraja said.

'What's that sound?'

'I'm practising yogic breathing . . . it can only be done late at night . . . my guru has given instructions.'

What on earth! The whore wouldn't even let her sleep at night.

'All right then. I thought you were choking in your sleep.'

'No didi, I'm not asleep yet. Yoga is impossible in sleep. If I spend my life sleeping when will I prepare for the afterlife?'

'True, true.'

'Are you going to sleep now, didi?'

'No, why?'

'I cannot rest until I can immerse my ego, I will not be able to, either. What is the body meant for, didi? Not for sleep, not for comfort – but only to do one's work. Buy your days, all you can do is buy your days . . .'

Drobomoyee felt her blood boiling. Go buy them, you bitch, if you have the money, but let me sleep at night at least.

Winter was here. Kanu went to Kashi during his Christmas holidays to meet his grandmother.

'Can't you find me somewhere else to stay, Kanu?' Drobomoyee asked him.

'Why, what's wrong with this place?' Kanu asked in surprise. 'Satya's mother is here too, isn't this the best arrangement?'

'The bitch is mad.'

'Mad! What do you mean?'

'She's far too religious-minded. I can't be like her. Take me away from here.'

Kanu laughed her off. His grandmother said the strangest things.

'You've come to Kashi late in life, Thakuma,' he said. 'Why don't you be a little religious-minded too? Yes, that's what she's like. Satya was saying she refuses to stay at home. Satya's younger brother got married in May – her youngest son. They sent so many letters, requested her so many times, but she refused. Said she couldn't get tied down again in bonds that she had broken free of. Her youngest son even sent her a telegram, but to no avail.'

'Really, Kanu?' Drobomoyee asked in astonishment.

'Would I lie to you, Thakuma?'

'Take me away from here, please.'

'How can you ask for such a thing? Why are you so godless, Thakuma? Can't you learn to be spiritual from her? You've spent your entire life with material things.'

'I feel so short of breath here I'll die.'

'There you are again, talking like a godless person. What is this, Thakuma?'

Winter passed, summer arrived, and made way for the rains. It was the middle of June. There had been no news from home in a long time. Naw-thakrun used to write, but the past three or four months had seen no letters from her. One day Neeraja brought it up in the course of conversation.

'I've heard there's no one back home, didi, is that true?'

'I have the house, the trees . . .'

'Are you still attached to these things, didi? Submit yourself to god, all ties will dissolve. No one is real – god alone is,' said Neeraja and raised her eyes to the sky.

'Oh no, I think the cat is drinking the milk in the pan,' Drobomoyee butted in swiftly. 'These cats, honestly, and there are as many monkeys. My towel . . .'

'Come with me to Kedar Ghat today, didi. Upeen the storyteller is going to read and explain the Kashi episode of the *Skandapuran*. Truly worth hearing. When in Kashi you must listen to the Kashikhanda being read . . .'

'I don't feel well, why don't you . . .'

Neeraja was adamant, and Drobomoyee had to go with her. She had been to Kedar Ghat once or twice before with Satya's mother. A slim, fair-skinned storyteller had begun his narration on a flat terrace adjoining the river – he was surrounded by Bengali-speaking women and men. There were more women than men.

'Didi, have you brought some money to give him?' Neeraja asked.

'Oh, you didn't tell me . . . I didn't bring any . . .'

'Less than eight annas won't do. All right, I'll pay for you too for now . . .'

'Pay four annas for me. My grandsons don't send me much money.'

'Whatever you pay now is a deposit on your afterlife, didi . . .'

The river was brimming over after the rains. An enormous barge was moving downstream, and well-dressed men and women were out on the water in two or three small sailboats. The sun was setting over Ramnagar, the vermilion-tinged sunlight glittered like liquid gold on the parapets of tall buildings. The storyteller was singing melodiously. Kashi was the finest of all sacred places, the god Vishwanath personally whispered holy words in the ears of those who died at Manikarnika Ghat, leading humans directly into the divine circle – this was the burden of his song.

Drobomoyee's mind flew into the distance. It was June, which meant her jackfruit tree was laden with fruit, they went all the way down to the roots. The three mango trees must have had a lot of fruit too – it was unlikely that her grandsons had gone home to eat them. They couldn't care less. The villagers must have plundered the mangoes from her trees.

Night fell. 'Let's go back, didi,' said Neeraja.

Drobomoyee had noticed the bitch weeping loudly and saying, 'How beautiful!'

If only she could shake off the whore. But no such luck, Kanu wouldn't allow it.

Back home Neeraja found her companion looking pensive and distracted, and not saying much. She must have been immersed in the storytelling. Perhaps the tide had turned.

'What are you thinking of, didi?' Neeraja asked.

'I have a jackfruit tree back home. You've never eaten its fruit, or you'd have known how delicious they are.'

'You are still not able to break the ties, didi? You have one or two trees, I have three large orchards, so many varieties of mangoes. I never even gave them a second glance. My sons shed tears, you're too young to live in Kashi, they say. I tell them, no, no more of being tied down to the material life. You know what they sing – Who is your own, who is distant . . .'

(Oh hell, the bitch has started again!)

'So I tell them,' Neeraja continued, 'I have spent a long time living the householder's life, dreaming of hope, it's time to think of the afterlife now. My guru, he is a free spirit in a human body . . . by his grace . . .'

'Of course, of course,' said Drobomoyee.

'Come to the Vishwanath temple with me this evening, didi, let me take you to maiji. You're older than me, you should be initiated into the spiritual life, free yourself of all ties, and take up residence in Kashi. How much time on earth do we have, didi? The summons is waiting at the door – I have seen and heard so much.'

'To hell with you,' Drobomoyee said to herself, 'just listen to the hag talk. Considers herself a spout of spiritual wisdom.' Out loud she said, 'I used to have a cow named Mungli, she was so attached to me, followed me everywhere, wouldn't eat unless I fed her myself. I'd give her tender leaves to eat, and . . .'

'How can you still be talking of these things? You know the story of Bharat, don't you? Such a wise man, but attachment to a fawn deprived him of freedom from rebirth. Meditate on god, on god. Everything else is a lie, a lie.'

Drobomoyee did not respond. She hated the things Neeraja said. The bitch was most peculiar. And so hard-hearted, didn't even go to her own son's wedding. Shame on her, no one should have to even set eyes on her.

Drobomoyee dreamt all night of Mungli in her home in Gopinathpur, gazing at her mournfully with tears in her eyes. Naw-thakrun wasn't taking care of her, she was old now, couldn't give as much milk as before. Drobomoyee had pulled Mungli out of her mother's womb and treated the cow like her own daughter all these years – who was going to look after her now? How plentiful the jackfruit was this year, the best in the past three or four years. She was on her way to the river for her bath, Mrs Mukherjee was saying, 'So much fruit on your tree this year, give me one, I'll let your grandsons eat it.' The straw was falling off the thatched roof. Neither Kanu nor Bindey had been home. How would the roof survive the monsoon unless the posts were strengthened? Kanak was saying, 'May I take a lime, Thakuma? My mother finds her food tasteless . . .'

In the morning Neeraja had been to the Ganges for her bath and had begun cooking her frugal meal of boiled food. Having completed her sacred incantations, she was now engaged in rituals to the god Shiva, which included percussion with the use of her cheeks. Drobomoyee had slept in, and had woken with a heavy heart. Her nearest and dearest – Mungli, the jackfruit tree, the fig tree – were far away. And thanks to the whore . . .

Neeraja's rituals ended. To Drobomoyee she said, 'I have received some excellent news today, didi . . . I met my friend from Guptipara when I went for my bath . . . She lives in Kashi too . . . She said my guru is coming here on Monday. He will meet us on his way back from Haridwar. My friend has been initiated by him. What a glorious day. My survival is at his feet, this time you must receive your initiation too, didi, I won't take no for an answer. The body isn't purified without it, when we sail across the sea of mortal life it is his feet that will be our boat . . . or we will drown.'

'Of course, of course,' said Drobomoyee.

Kanu arrived by the morning train on Saturday, before Neeraja's guru could reach Kashi. Drobomoyee burst into tears. 'Take me back to Gopinathpur, I don't want to have anything to do with this sacred city – let the gods stay where they are. Two months more with this whore will drive me mad.'

And so on the auspicious day of Neeraja's guru's arrival in Kashi, Drobomoyee, accompanied by her grandson, stepped off the train with her bundles and trunk in the station that served her village.

Naw-thakrun rushed to meet her. 'Didi . . . didi . . .'

'Yes, Naw-bou, is my Mungli well?'

'She isn't well, didi, she doesn't get up, doesn't eat, she's only been lying in her shed since you left.'

'My heart said as much, I wasn't waiting for you to tell me. I couldn't stay there any more after dreaming of her. Take me back, I told Kanu, let the gods remain in their place. Where's Mungli? I dreamt I was feeding her tender bamboo leaves.'

Naw-thakrun led Mungli by her rope to Drobomoyee a little later. The cow did not look her old self. Drobomoyee ran to her, caressing her face and shoulders. Mungli wept, so did she.

'She was your daughter in a previous birth, didi,' Naw-thakrun said, 'a mother's bond from an earlier life cannot be . . .'

'For heaven's sake, Naw-bou, are you also going to start talking like the bitch? Mungli is my daughter in this life, never mind earlier lives.'

'What bitch? Who are you talking about, didi?'

'I'll tell you everything, I'm so relieved to be back home . . .'

Kanu smiled. 'Thakuma is impossible, such a godless woman! Passing the rest of her life in Kashi is not in her destiny.'

'Tell them, Naw-bou ... May I leave from my own home when I go, taking leave of all of you. I have no need to die in Kashi ... this home of mine is as good as any sacred place. My husband died in this yard there beneath the tree, when it's my turn you must ...'

Drobomoyee wiped her eyes on the end of her sari.

Daylight had dwindled. After a long day the sun was about to set behind the dense bamboo grove in the west. Arum flowers had bloomed somewhere in the wild, their strong, pungent smell filling the air. Drobomoyee's heart filled with enthusiasm, with peace and joy. She had stepped into this house as a nine-year-old bride, she was seventy now.

Kanak came up to her with a smile. 'How are you, Thakuma? I came running when I heard you're back. You didn't forget us, did you?'

BANAPHOOL

What Could Happen?

'Mrs Mitra, you're late today as well. It's past eleven-thirty . . .' Mrs Mitra looked abashed. Then she smiled her lovely smile, saying, 'I'm really very sorry about this, Mr Lahiri. But my mother-in-law has been ill for some time. The doctor is inevitably late. So . . .'

Mr Lahiri was a stern civil servant. Pursing his lips, he said, 'Really? I'm sorry to hear that. But I still have to inform you that you cannot be so late. How will anything be accomplished if you're not here on time? So many files awaiting your attention . . .'

'I'll finish all the pending work today, I will.'

'Very well. By the way, why do *you* have to wait for the doctor? Isn't there anyone else at home?'

'No. My husband's been transferred to Siliguri, you see. There's just a maid, besides myself. The doctor says my mother-in-law's got typhoid.'

'You really should engage a nurse.'

'We can't afford to, sir. It costs twenty-five rupees a day. The doctor's fees and medicines already add up to fifteen rupees a day.'

'Get her admitted to a hospital then.'

'It isn't easy to get a hospital bed. Besides, she doesn't want to be hospitalized.'

'I see. Well, do get on with those pending files now.'

As soon as Mrs Mitra sat down at her desk, Manoranjan appeared. He used to be her classmate. They had taken their MA exams together. There was another, far from irrelevant, fact. Manoranjan was also in love with Mrs Mitra. He'd been suffering from this romantic fever from the time they'd been students together. He hadn't been cured yet. A handsome and strongly built man, Manoranjan didn't need to work for a living. He was the only son of a wealthy father. But as soon as he heard that Mrs Mitra had got a job here, he pulled strings to secure employment in the same place. He worked as a petty clerk on a paltry salary. The authorities had not expected to be able to hire someone with a first-class MA degree in English Literature on a salary of just 100 rupees. They had appointed him instantly.

Manoranjan had proposed marriage when they were still at university. He met every criterion except one – his caste did not match hers.

Mrs Sushila Mitra belonged to an orthodox family. She didn't want to oppose her parents. It was on their instructions that Miss Ghosh had become Mrs Mitra. Not too long ago – it had been just six months. She had started working even before her marriage, continuing afterwards. Her husband Baldeb Mitra had asked her to give up her job. But Sushila Mitra had refused. She had sensed that her husband's income would not be enough for them. Running a household on 250 rupees would be impossible at a time when prices rose every day. So she hadn't resigned. But Baldeb was unhappy. And then he was suddenly transferred. He was even more annoyed at not being able to take Sushila along. His mother said, 'I'll stay with my daughter-in-law. I don't want to leave my home.' But she had been ill for the past few days. Sushila did feel it would be better not to go to work and stay with her mother-in-law instead. But she couldn't get leave of absence. Her superior officer berated her even for being late.

However, Sushila's biggest problem was Manoranjan. If he'd been the nasty type, she could have told him off. But she knew he was a rare sort of man. Although she hadn't been able to accept his proposal, he hadn't walked away. 'Whatever happens,' he kept saying, 'I'll always be with you.' Not in as many words, but that's what his behaviour suggested.

That day he said, 'Let's share those pending files – they'll get done today. That's not a concern. What I'm saying is, go ahead and get a nurse for your mother-in-law. Don't worry about the expense.'

'I have to. That's why I haven't been able to afford a nurse.'

'I'll pay . . .'

'Why should I take your money?'

'You would have if we'd been married. Just because we're not, do I have to be a stranger? Don't you believe I care for you?'

Sushila lowered her head in an attempt to hide her embarrassment.

Then she said, 'There's more. What will my husband think if I take your money?'

'Why should he take it badly? Don't friends help one another when in trouble?'

Smiling her lovely smile, Sushila said, 'If the friend in question is a handsome young man like you, people are bound to read more into it.'

There was an extremely stubborn, unrelenting personality lurking within Manoranjan. It had made him perform many incredible feats in the past – swimming across a river in full flood, or eating a huge dessert after an enormous meal. This personality suddenly asserted itself.

'I *shall* help you,' he said.

'You can't. I simply won't take your money.'

'You have to.'

She was even later getting back home that day. But the sight that confronted her made her extremely anxious.

In the throes of a fever, her mother-in-law had fallen off her bed. She had been unconscious since then. 'Concussion,' said the doctor.

She died the next day.

After the last rites, Baldeb told Sushila, 'You were busy with your pen-pushing office job while my mother lay dying. All that is over and done with. Now I'm telling you clearly – leave the job, or leave me. You can't keep sailing on two boats . . .'

What happened after this?

Here's what could have happened:

1. Sushila said, 'I cannot leave my job, I'd rather leave you . . .'

2. Sushila left her job. They barely survived on a single salary.

Then something extraordinary took place. A letter arrived by registered post. Sushila opened it to find a will. Manoranjan had died by suicide, leaving her his estate of two-and-a-half lakh rupees. But Sushila didn't accept the money for herself. She used it to set up Manoranjan High School.

3. Sushila didn't give up her job. A few days later, her husband Baldeb was grateful that she hadn't. For both his hands were injured in a bus accident and had to be amputated.

Actually, none of this happened.

Things went on just as before. Baldeb and Sushila had frequent rows over her decision to continue working. But Sushila didn't resign. She didn't leave her husband either. And Manoranjan didn't leave Sushila. The living embodiment of Platonic love, he kept hovering around her. This out-of-tune triangular song kept playing. Nothing dramatic happened.

JIBANANANDA DAS

Women

A summer afternoon.

Chapola had barely napped for half an hour when she woke up. The poincianas were visible through the window, shedding flowers.

She could smell a strong cigar in the next room – so her husband was back from work?

Chapola stood up. Hemendra entered with his cigar and said with a glance at her, 'I've asked for the car to be brought round.'

Stretching, Chapola said, 'Don't feel like going today.'

'But it was you who said it's Saturday . . .'

'I did, but where can one go? To the cinema? What's on today?'

'Let me get the paper.'

As soon as Hemen returned with the newspaper Chapola said, 'Never mind, I don't feel like the movies.'

A trifle disappointed, Hemen said, 'But the races won't start before the monsoon . . .'

'No need to go to the races . . . all that money down the drain . . . let me see the paper.'

Exhausted by the effort of tossing the newspaper towards his wife, Hemen sat down on a cushion and began to pant with the cigar in his hand. He looked like a bullfrog in a tie with a coat hanging from his shoulders.

Chapola was over forty – and Hemen forty-nine. Both of them had put on weight steadily, while their hair thinned . . .

Hemen's belt no longer seemed capable of keeping his belly in check; and his face was a replica of his paunch. Chapola's face was no different from Hemen's – dreams or imaginativeness never seemed to have encroached on their visages.

Hemen was a businessman, with a fleet of medium-sized trucks laden with building material criss-crossing Calcutta for the past ten years. He had several related enterprises too. Having started as a mere contractor in the districts, he had now consolidated his businesses in his head office in Calcutta, with some 300,000 rupees invested in them.

Chapola was leafing through the newspaper.

The Marwari businessman Dhondhonia had hosted a lavish dinner, with more than a hundred invitees. Chapola was scanning each of the names with great concentration – it took her half an hour, in which time Hemen consumed his entire cigar. With a sigh Chapola put the newspaper down. No, they weren't rich enough yet for their names to appear in these columns – but her husband had in fact been a guest at Dhondhonia's dinner – why, so had she. No, they were nowhere near as important as they considered themselves to be, they trailed far behind. Their names were not to be among the chosen hundred, not even today, when they were about to turn fifty.

Chapola grew restless. Sitting idly led to a feeling of disgust – with people – with the world – with one's own unsuccessful life.

Stirring herself, she said, 'Shall we go to Leela's place?'

'Very well, get dressed then.'

Completing her toilette in half an hour, Chapola came out fully dressed and said, 'Have you had your cup of tea?'

'No,' Hemen shook his head.

'Let me tell Yasin, he'll make you some.'

'Never mind, I'd rather have another cigar. Where do you want to go?'

'Let's go to Leela's . . .'

'Leela's? I heard Dwijen's taking her away.'

'Taking her away where?'

'To Shillong.'

'It's so hot in Calcutta, we could have gone away too for a few days, everyone's going . . .'

'Hold tight for a while, I've got some large orders – just hold tight like a good girl for a few days, my dear.'

'But Dwijen's really taking Leela?'

Hemen smiled.

'You do know they don't get along at all, don't you?' said Chapola.

She expressed her sympathy for Dwijen. Hemen felt the same way – about Dwijen.

The car seemed to be out of order. Hemen gazed at it hopelessly. 'Something's happened to the motor car.'

'Oh dear,' said Chapola. 'In that case . . . let's just go upstairs . . .'

Hemen fiddled with the parts, then stared in bewilderment at the car. He continued with his efforts for another five minutes, but the vehicle didn't budge.

Depositing it in the chauffeur's hands, he said, 'Let's take a bus.' Which was what they did.

Hemen had built a house in posh Ballygunge Avenue – Dwijen still lived in one of the older neighbourhoods, Shyambazar. Not all of Hemen's entreaties could get him to move. 'Yes, I will,' he kept saying, but ten years had gone by and he hadn't succeeded. Dwijen didn't lack for money, and he was by no means a miser – nor was Leela, for that matter. But the fact was that they didn't get along, though why this was the case between husband and wife was something Hemen didn't understand. Why did they do nothing but hurt each other?

The bus was full, no one gave up their seat to Chapola. A passenger rose to his feet at the next bus stop, and Hemen propelled Chapola in that direction. But when he realized a couple of minutes later that a labourer or some such man was sitting next to Chapola, Hemen dragged his wife away by the hand and got off the bus.

Then they took a taxi.

They had barely reached the second floor when they heard Leela's voice . . .

Maybe she was scolding the servants. Definitely a disobedient and impudent servant – and Leela's voice was shrill too. Hemen felt it was a truly bellicose tone, which his wife did not possess. Without a voice such as this the household servants took everything for granted and could not be bullied. But then he didn't speak this way either, and his business problems had still been resolved easily at every step. With these thoughts running through his head, Hemen scraped his boots on the first-floor doormat with great satisfaction. Chapola did the same with her heels.

'Don't lock horns with Leela in any circumstances,' Hemen told Chapola. 'You must maintain your dignity.'

Unsure of whether to light his cigar, he took it out of his pocket, only to return it by the time they had got to the second floor.

Leela could be heard shouting in the dining room – must have been something to do with the servants. Chapola and Hemen didn't go in that direction. Maybe Dwijen was in the drawing room – Hemen entered with Chapola. But there was no one there.

'Dwijen . . .'

No response.

It was a quarter to three on the clock.

No one in the bedroom either.

There was no choice now but to go into the dining room. There they found Leela perched on the dining table – a veritable virago flashing a bread knife in each hand. Dwijen was seated quietly on a chair on one side with a slice of bread in his hand.

'Dwijen . . .'

'Dwijen-babu . . .'

'Enough, no need to indulge him,' Leela interrupted them.

Tossing one of the knives on a plate and holding on to the other, she said, 'We just had a cup of tea.'

Chapola said, 'Excellent.'

Hemen had drawn up a chair to Dwijen and was whispering to him with his arm round his shoulders. Leela said, 'Don't indulge him more, please.'

Chapola said, 'Poor man has just come home after a hard day's work . . .'

'What do you mean poor man?' Leela asked, her eyes flashing.

'I was saying Dwijen-babu is . . .'

'Dwijen-babu is a poor man, and what about me?'

'The poor thing works hard all day and . . .' Chapola was silent after this.

Leela said, 'And what must I do with him because he comes home after working hard all day?'

'We heard you're going on a holiday,' said Chapola.

'Who told you that? Going where?' said Leela, filing her fingernails with the knife.

'Don't use the knife to file your nails,' said Dwijen.

Leela turned to Dwijen, gripping the handle of the knife firmly in her hand. Hemen's heart quaked. Withdrawing his arm from Dwijen's shoulders, he glanced at Leela with great kindness.

'Isn't that a bread knife?' said Dwijen. 'Why do you forget?'

Clapping Dwijen lightly across the shoulder, Hemen said, 'Never mind, let it be.'

'Let it be? I'll show you how to let it be.' Leela suddenly threw the knife in the direction of Dwijen's head. It missed and struck the wall.

Everyone sat in silent stupefaction for a few minutes.

There was another knife on the table, but Leela didn't pick it up. Slipping his glasses off, Dwijen began to polish them as he said, 'What harm would a blunt bread knife have done even if it had hit my head?'

'If it had hit you in the eye though . . .' Leela said.

'What if it had?'

'The eyeball would have come out, that's all.'

'That's not nice,' Hemen said.

'Would you like such a thing to happen to your husband, Leela?' said Chapola.

'My husband!' Leela said. 'Some husband I have!'

'What does she think she's saying?' said Hemen in astonishment.

Chapola signalled him with her eyes to be quiet.

Dwijen kept smiling, his eyes on the floor. Leela sat sullenly for a few minutes and then said, 'Completely spoilt by all the attention he gets from everyone . . .'

'Who's spoilt?' said Hemen. 'Dwijen?'

'Who do you suppose?'

'Who's spoilt him?'

'Why, you, of course – and your wife . . .'

The blood rushed to Hemen's face as he glanced at Leela. Would he create a scene now? Chapola stared at him, holding her breath.

Dwijen nudged Hemen. 'Want some tea?'

'Didn't Dwijen-babu enjoy his tea then?' said Chapola. 'All right, I'll make some.'

A livid Leela said, 'So he will enjoy his tea if you make it but not if I do.'

Chapola made to light the stove without replying.

Leela gripped her wrist.

'I dare you to light the stove. Go on, I dare you.'

Her wrist was twisted so terribly that Chapola just about saved herself from falling. She sat down on a chair – her entire body seemed to be throbbing.

Turning the fan on, Dwijen deposited Chapola under it along with the chair, and stroked her head.

'You think I don't know this is what you're up to all the time,' Leela said. 'It's not for nothing that I get furious with you – the moment I look away . . .' Leela jumped to her feet.

Dwijen retreated slowly to his original position.

'Aren't you ashamed of yourself?' said Leela. 'Chapola isn't a blood relation, how could you pick her up in your arms? How could you even touch her?'

Hemen stirred; Chapola signalled to him again with her eyes not to interfere.

'And even if she were a relation,' Leela continued, 'she's neither your wife nor your sister, how could you touch her? And in front of my eyes, at that. You think I don't know what you're up to all day and night under the pretext of your High Court?'

'What's he up to?' said Hemen.

Leela said, 'And then he's started a business too . . .'

Hemen said, 'It's because of the business . . .'

'What business?' said Chapola. 'What does Dwijen-babu . . .'

'Why, T B Armstrong & Company, of course – you didn't know?'

Hemen felt a modicum of relief at this turn in the conversation towards matters of business. Finally he took his cigar out, lit it, drew on it luxuriously and said, 'Armstrong & Company is . . .'

Glancing at Leela, Chapola said, 'Never mind . . .'

'. . . A Bengali firm,' said Hemen. 'Not one Britisher or European or American, in fact no one who is not a Bengali.'

Hemen was under the impression he had astonished everyone by disclosing the secrets of Dwijen's company, but in truth no one was astonished, because no one was listening to him.

'No Marwaris, no Punjabis, no one from any other region, only Bengalis,' continued Hemen. 'It was started during the war. In Rangoon to begin with, where there was in fact a lot of fraud, but Dwijen had nothing to do with that. There's no fraud now.'

Drawing on his cigar for a minute or two with great satisfaction, Hemen said, 'Dwijen purchased all its goodwill three years ago', and glanced at Leela pleasantly. 'He's giving up his practice soon.'

'Why?' said Chapola.

Looking fondly at his lit cigar, Hemen said, 'What's a legal practice compared to a business like this?'

'What's the use of making so much money?' said Leela.

Hemen looked at her in great surprise.

'I saw with my own eyes what he was doing with Chapola,' Leela said. 'She's not a relation, still he strokes her head and rubs her back and whispers in her ear, what kind of lewd behaviour is this? If he can do this in my presence, who knows what goes on behind my back? He spends eleven to twelve hours outside, I've kept track.'

Hemen was glowering already, but no sooner had Leela finished speaking than Fate chuckled.

'Well, my husband is outside eighteen hours a day . . .' said Chapola.

'Oh him,' said Leela. 'Show me a woman who will have anything to do with him after she's seen his hairless head and witless expression.' Turning to Hemen, she laughed and said, 'My goodness, your nose sticks out like a swollen thumb!' Rolling with laughter, she continued, 'Stupid face, idiotic nose, moronic eyes, who's going to find you attractive?'

Hemen leapt to his feet. 'Oh really? You think you're very clever, don't you? Even now all it needs is a wink to have two dozen women throwing themselves at me.'

Leela was in splits. 'A wink! You'll wink at a woman! Oh please!'

'Shame on you,' said Chapola, 'what's all this about winking? Why are you boasting about something you never do?'

To Leela she said, 'Never, you know, I've been with him for twenty-five years, not once have I seen him so much as glance at another woman – all his business associates know there isn't a stain on his character – everyone in Calcutta knows . . .'

Hemen was deeply insulted – he didn't register a single word that Chapola said. He was burning with rage now that Leela had ruthlessly attacked his masculinity. Shaking with anger, he slammed his fist down repeatedly on the dining table and said, 'To hell with morality! I don't need a character certificate from anyone, I will let the cat out of the bag myself.'

'Have you gone mad?' said Chapola.

'I can have all the women from Calcutta's top families lined up on the streets,' Hemen roared. 'Have you any idea, Leela?'

'Dwijen-babu . . .' Chapola said.

'Let me walk you to your car,' said Dwijen.

Shoving him aside, Hemen said, 'Do you think I hold my character up like a flag? Are you under the impression Hemen is morally unblemished, that women consider him an also-ran? I can turn Calcutta into a city of willing women in three days.' Trembling, he continued, 'Never mind Calcutta, which is filled with all these hideous hags like Leela and Chapola, when I went to Jaipur to see the palace, I was on my way back when . . .'

But Hemen did not finish his story about his romances with the royal tigresses Debala Debi and Chanchala Kumari. With no one responding, and concluding he had whipped Leela enough, his heart was telling him to desist.

Having pulled out a fresh cigar, Hemen was now at peace. As he lit it and drew on it, his temper cooled, and his entire being was flooded with pity for Chapola, for Dwijen, even for Leela.

'Come, Leela, let's go to the cinema,' he said.

But it was past four o'clock now, too late for the first show. Hemen asked everyone to get ready for the second show at six, and then went up to the stove himself.

'Why?' said Leela.

'To heat the water.'

'For what?'

'Can't you see? Since you women won't do it, we men will have to grind the spices and make the tea. Wait and see how well I make it.'

But there was no sympathy or reassurance forthcoming from Leela.

'Who's going to have tea now?' said Chapola. 'No need.'

'Of course they will,' said Hemen.

'No one will,' said Chapola, 'put out the stove.'

With a wink and a smile Hemen said, 'The grandmas will have tea . . .'

'Who?' said Chapola.

Looking at her husband, she discovered he was indeed not looking remotely handsome – stupid face, idiotic nose, moronic eyes.

'Leela and you,' said Hemen.

'We're grandmas?' said Leela.

'You know, Dwijen,' said Hemen, 'they make fun of us about our looks, who's going to say they're middle-aged women? Get closer to them and you'll be asking yourself, my goodness, what are the grandmothers doing here, isn't that so, Dwijen?'

But before Dwijen could answer, Leela overturned the pan along with the stove. There was a spray of boiling water, and Hemen escaped narrowly from being scalded. The stove was on fire, the servant rushed in from the pantry and put out the flames with Dwijen's help.

The plan to watch a film didn't materialize.

Three days had passed.

Hemen was driving slowly past the office of T. B. Armstrong & Company; he wondered whether to pay Dwijen a visit. Stopping on the main road near a lane, he gazed at the Armstrong office. The sight of a fledgling business always turned him soft and tender – transporting him into the magical world of commercial transactions on the wings of all the imagination he could muster.

It seemed to Hemen that the Armstrong office was not particularly large – about the size of a room in Stephen Court or No. 100 Clive Street.

Hemen sighed. How large was his own office, for that matter? But he had at least had it whitewashed – a company owned by Bengalis had done it – whereas Armstrong's walls were as faded as ever, with the plaster peeling off in places. Hemen got out of his car.

All businesses were sinking these days, he reflected – he himself had been making continuous losses in the past year and a half. If things continued this way he would simply close down his company. The interest on his savings in the bank would suffice for both of them comfortably. They had no children. Hemen lit his cigar with a feeling of infinite peace.

Dwijen was thinking of leaving.

'Hello, Hemen!' He looked at the visitor with great eagerness.

Today they spoke only of business, with neither of them referring to the trouble and humiliation and agony and hopelessness they had experienced three days ago. It was their business crises that had made both of them feel gloomy and unsuccessful.

Dwijen collected Hemen from his office four or five days later and drove his car in the direction of a grill or some such place in the part of the city where the Britishers lived.

'Might as well go in.'

They did. Various pork, lamb and chicken dishes, coffee, pudding, fruit and ice cream arrived in succession at their table. Hemen said, 'The thing is, Dwijen, there's still a hundred and fifty thousand in the bank . . .'

'A hundred and fifty thousand!' said Dwijen.

'The trucks are still running all over Calcutta to fulfil orders. But Chapola and I can easily live in luxury off the interest on this hundred and fifty thousand – we already have the house in Ballygunge.'

After a pause, he continued, 'That's what we'll do. What's the use of running a business? I don't enjoy any of it, honestly.'

Dwijen didn't try to ask why Hemen didn't enjoy any of it. He had 100,000 in the bank himself. And a house too, in Shyambazar if not in Ballygunge, quite a nice house. But still he had been overcome by a feeling of despair and uselessness for quite some time now, in fact. It was quite different from Hemen's freshly minted dissatisfaction.

Hemen said, 'Can you tell me why I don't enjoy any of it, Dwiju?'

'Why do you think you don't, Hemen?'

'Can't tell, my mind has slipped off the rails . . .'

'Why?'

'Truly, Dwiju, is money everything?' Without waiting for an answer, Hemen continued, 'It's true, what Leela said was right, she's made me doubt everything . . .'

Dwijen was eating with his head lowered.

'This paunch, this baldness, this stupid face, this idiotic nose, these moronic eyes, really, what *have* I turned into?'

'Why not lose some weight?' said Dwijen.

'What's the use, my whole appearance is unattractive. I was chasing a woman the other day . . .'

'What!'

'It's not as though I don't go after women. Chapola doesn't know. But all this while I used to think going to the cinema with one of those Anglo-Indian girls was enough to fulfil my desire. But that's not enough – I need something more . . .'

'But you have Chapola for that . . .'

'It's not what you think . . .' Hemen threw a glance at the knife with which he was eating his roast. 'No, it's true, Chapola is certainly there, she's a wonderful wife, I couldn't have done without her, you cannot possibly complain about such women . . .' he said. After a pause, he continued, 'But you know what I want?'

Lifting his eyes, Dwijen chose a fresh knife.

Hemen said, 'I want women to forget everything when they see me, to throw themselves at me. Which man doesn't desire such things, Dwijen?' After this there was a silence of two or three minutes, during which Hemen operated his knife and fork rapidly. Then he said, 'But what Leela said is right, I'm not the kind of man whom women will flock around. Why should they? Around me? What's so special about me?'

'What's so special about me either?' said Dwijen.

'Oh come on, you have your good looks. I'd give up my goodwill any day for your looks . . . You've always bagged women, you think I don't know? In England and in India. You're a rich man's son, you have your own income, and then these looks, I know very well you've bagged women . . .' Hemen simply couldn't get over this suffering, the agony had overwhelmed him.

'Is bagging women all there is to life?' said Dwijen.

'But you *have* bagged them – many women.'

'What does bagging women achieve, Hemen?'

'Plenty. You've had so much fun, you can die happy now, can't you? Can't you?' Without waiting for a reply, Hemen continued, 'You should be able to. If I were you I'd certainly have been able to die peacefully . . .' Picking up his cup of coffee with deep resentment, he said, 'Even in middle age you fool around with half a dozen barristers' wives, I've seen it for myself.'

'Just fooling around and nothing more, Hemen?' Dwijen said.

'But that fooling around is so delightful, I've watched you at it many times. You think anyone wants me to fool around with them?'

'What about Chapola?'

'Don't joke, Dwijen.'

'Laughing and joking with one's own wife is the most delightful of all.'

Lighting a cigar, Hemen said, 'You've lost out there though.' He drew on his cigar with satisfaction for some time because Dwijen had lost out somewhere. But then Dwijen's handsomeness and perfect tie and thoughts of his flirting with the beautiful wives of barristers turned Hemen grim again. He continued smoking, nursing a grievance in his heart all the while. Then he said, 'It won't even matter to you if your business goes under, Dwijen. You have found the real thing in life, women love you. You can fulfil your romantic needs with so many people . . .'

Dwijen took out his cigarette case.

Hemen said, 'You're a happy man. Leela has made you bitter about her, which is why you can get along like a house on fire with other women. If Leela had been a worthy wife you wouldn't have had the urge to flirt with others. You might not have enjoyed it then, don't you think?'

He continued a little later, 'Flirting of course is always enjoyable, especially the way you have women milling around you. But if Leela had been different would you have had the chance to turn your back on her and wander about like a spurned lover to have dalliances everywhere?'

Hemen was overcome by a resentful greed. If only just one day in Dwijen's life could be his! Even if Dwijen's wife was a harridan, no one else had his skills when it came to warming up to other people's wives.

'And is it just harmless romance?' Hemen said. 'Who actually knows what it is you do with them, or how many homes you have broken in the course of your life?' After a pause he continued, 'I wouldn't get the genuine love of a single woman even if I spent my entire life seeking it, and here you have so many women lining up to offer you their love . . .' A little later he said, 'Why does it have to turn out this way, Dwiju?' Then he answered himself. 'But then consider my looks. It's not possible to attract women with this appearance.'

Sinking into a bottomless pit of misery, Hemen smoked in silence. There was no love in his life, no romance, not even flirtation. Even being caught up in a court case for abducting someone else's wife would have relieved some of his bitterness. And now his flesh and blood and reason and intelligence and conscience were all gnawing away at him hungrily. Why had things turned out this way? Why had he spent his life, his entire life, really, as an also-ran? There was an age at which you could think of bagging women, you couldn't talk about such things after thirty . . .

Perspiration began to drip from Hemen's face and bald pate. Clamping his teeth by mistake on the glowing end of his cigar, he felt a painful,

66

burning sensation in his mouth. All his agonies seemed to be converging.

Dwijen said, 'It's best to admit we've grown old, what will we do with these things any more . . .'

'Who's grown old? Not you, not me either.'

'Everyone's old after twenty-five – when it comes to playing around with women, seventeen or eighteen to twenty-one or twenty-two, that's the right age.'

Hemen stared at Dwijen in consternation.

'Whatever I did was also at that age,' said Dwijen.

'But why? You're still . . .'

'Nothing, nothing at all, I swear. All I want is a little peace and quiet – not from chasing women, Hemen, but in my own home, with my own wife, you have no idea, no one really loves me.'

'No one?'

'No one.'

Hemen gaped at Dwijen.

'Why should women of twenty love me,' Dwijen said, 'I'm pushing fifty. Doesn't matter whether they're Bengalis or Anglo-Indians. We have lost all claims over the hearts of women who are nineteen or twenty or twenty-one, they probably think of us as their uncles – or even grandfathers.'

A vastly amused Hemen began to giggle. Dwijen's plain speaking had lifted a load off his mind. What Dwijen had said had to be right, he was a barrister, after all, he was good at skilfully extracting the sweet core of the fruit.

A little later Dwijen said with great concentration, 'Maybe not twenty or even twenty-five, but at least women of thirty.'

'Not even them. For them there are young men of thirty-five. There's no lack of beautiful people in the world either. I've often seen them romancing with even twenty-five-year-old men – in desperation. I've seen it – often.'

'A housewife of forty or forty-five or fifty might develop a soft spot for you briefly, you too might feel a stirring when you see her – but it isn't love . . . it's nothing . . . it's rubbish,' said Dwijen. Raising his head to look at Hemen, he continued, 'Picture this, I'm in a car with two young men, one of eighteen and the other of thirty. In the next car I see three women, of eighteen, forty and fifty, let's say all of them are pretty. But still, I will be drawn to the eighteen-year-old.'

'Indeed you will,' said Hemen.

'But will she be attracted to the fifty-year-old man – even if she were to get the entire world in exchange?'

Hemen gaped at Dwijen again.

Dwijen began to chortle.

'It's my nephew whom she'll like, or my son, but not me.' After a pause, he continued, 'Don't talk to me of love or romance or even desire, Hemen. Even thinking about these things is painful.'

Taking a matchbox out of his pocket, Dwijen said, 'In our declining years the thought of beauty and love makes life seem worthless.' His cigar had gone out. Lighting it again, Dwijen said, 'We will get nothing more ever again, nobody but the wife at home, no one is left for us.'

The thought that the wife in question was Leela for Dwijen and Chapola for him gave Hemen great satisfaction. He paid the entire bill.

'You're a little boy,' said Dwijen. 'You don't have a mother or a sister, my heart bleeds for you.'

It was evening by then. 'Come on, Dwiju,' said Hemen. 'Let's drive around Tollygunge and Alipur and Chetla and Behala.'

'You really want to go to all these places now?'

'Of course!' Hemen nodded vehemently.

'Why?'

'No particular reason.'

'Something to do with your business?'

'No.'

'For no reason at all?'

'All these bad habits of mine . . .'

'It'll be terribly late by the time we get back.'

'Doesn't matter.'

'You go,' said Dwijen, 'I have some other work to attend to.'

A business matter! Hemen could release Dwijen then. His entire being had withdrawn from love, desire and women by now and had ensconced itself with great devotion and comfort in his seat of business. His life no longer seemed a failure, there were no pinpricks in being alive, the world was filled with infinite wealth.

Hemen looked up at the sky – a darkness like the seeds of a custard apple had descended on Calcutta. It was overcast, and a gentle drizzle had begun. Hemen felt happy, and his thoughts turned to Chapola. His heart was flooded with the sensations of his wife's love and caring. There wasn't another man on Calcutta's streets tonight as deeply content as Hemen. He would love Chapola all night tonight – he would feel an infinite sense of peace on this rain-filled night.

But he wouldn't go to Chapola just yet.

Business was business, and he was a man of business. He had resolved, he told Dwijen, that he would now drive around Tollygunge and Alipur and Chetla and Behala. It was a whim – there was no business objective behind it, so be it. He wouldn't be back before eleven, it didn't matter. But he had told Dwijen he was going to drive around Tollygunge and Alipur and Chetla and Behala, and he wasn't going to go back on his word, for that was a weakness which could raise obstacles in a businessman's path.

Hemen twisted his steering wheel and set off.

Dwijen followed him in a taxi.

By the time Dwijen's taxi turned into Ballygunge Avenue, Hemen was well on his way to Tollygunge. Dwijen knew the obstinate Hemen only too well, he wouldn't be back before midnight.

Climbing to the second floor, Dwijen found Chapola lolling on a divan.

At first the sight of her corpulent body made his heart recoil, but beneath the fat lay a heart so wonderful – so soft and pliable. Dwijen spent half an hour, then an hour, and then two, with this woman. But then – it was past ten-thirty – his heart began to thump. Hemen might arrive at any moment, clip-clopping upstairs like an arthritic pony.

He began to feel somewhat irked.

But still he would have to get out. It was true that he was a visitor to many drawing rooms in the city, he had to leave eventually. Eventually the wives wanted their husbands to come home – and their guests to leave. So leave Dwijen did.

SARADINDU BANDYOPADHYAY

The Rhythm of Riddles

I

Byomkesh had been to Cuttack on official work, and I had accompanied him too. It became evident after a few days that the task would not be accomplished quickly, that it would take time to rummage through a mountain of deeds and documents in the government office to unearth the truth. Accordingly, Byomkesh stayed on in Cuttack, while I returned to Calcutta. How could a Bengali household be expected to run without the presence of a man at home?

On my return to Calcutta, however, I had no work. I was feeling a little helpless in Byomkesh's absence. Winter was setting in, the days were getting shorter; yet the hours refused to pass. Occasionally I would visit the bookshop to supervise Prabhat, who ran it, and read new manuscripts if any. But still there was nothing to do for most of the day.

Then an opportunity to pass the evenings presented itself unexpectedly.

We lived in a three-storey building, occupying five rooms on the top floor, while a dozen or so office-goers shared quarters on the first floor. On the ground floor were the manager's room, the pantry, the kitchen and the dining room, with just one corner room being occupied by a solitary boarder. We were familiar with all of them, but not particularly intimate with any.

That evening, I had just switched on the light after darkness had fallen and opened a magazine when there was a knock on the door. Opening it, I discovered a middle-aged gentleman standing outside, smiling deferentially. I had seen him once or twice on the first floor, where he had taken up residence recently. He occupied the best corner room on the floor all by himself, and appeared to be a man of refined tastes, being dressed as he was in a warm Nehru jacket and silk churidars, his hair more black than white. He was well turned out.

Greeting me, he said, 'Excuse me, my name is Bhupesh Chatterjee. I live on the first floor.'

'I've seen you now and then,' I replied, 'though I was not familiar with your name. Do come in.'

I gave him a seat. 'I came to Calcutta a month and a half ago. I work for an insurance company; there's no telling where I'll be next. Tomorrow they might transfer me somewhere else altogether for all you know.'

'You work for an insurance company,' I said with some unease. 'But I have never taken out a policy, nor am I planning to.'

'That's not what I came for,' he smiled. 'It's true that I work at the insurance office, but I'm not an agent. I came because ...' After an awkward pause he said, 'I'm addicted to bridge. I haven't had a game ever since I came here, I'm dying for one. After much effort I've managed to find two more players. They live in Room No. Three on the first floor. But we haven't been able to find a fourth. We tried cut-throat bridge for a few days, but it isn't the real thing. I thought I'd find out today whether Ajit-babu is interested.'

I was indeed interested in bridge once upon a time. Not merely interested, obsessed. But the obsession had died from abstinence. Still, I felt that playing bridge was preferable to passing companionless evenings reading dull magazines.

'Very well, very well,' I said. 'I am long out of practice, of course, but still – why not?'

'Then come with me,' said Bhupesh-babu, springing to his feet. 'I have made all the arrangements in my room. Why waste time?'

'Please lead the way, I'll follow as soon as I've had my cup of tea,' I said.

'Oh but you can just as well have your tea in my room,' he replied. 'Come along.'

I was amused by his eagerness. I used to be just as enthusiastic once upon a time; the evenings seemed wasted without a game of bridge.

I got off my chair. Informing Byomkesh's wife Satyabati of my plan for the evening, I accompanied Bhupesh-babu downstairs.

The first room when you went down the stairs to the first floor was

Bhupesh-babu's. Pausing near his door, he called out loudly, 'Come along, Ram-babu, Banamali-babu. I've got hold of Ajit-babu.'

Two heads popped out of Room No. 3, which was situated halfway down the corridor, and then disappeared with the word, 'Coming.' Bhupesh-babu took me into his room and switched on the light.

It was a commodious room. There were two barred windows on the wall looking out on to the road. On one side was the bed, covered with a bedspread, and on the other was a cupboard, on top of which reposed a shining portable stove and everything you needed to make a cup of tea. Four chairs were arranged around a low table in the middle of the room; it was clearly a card table. The other small items of furniture, including a dressing table and a chest of drawers, all indicated good taste. Bhupesh-babu had slightly Westernized tastes.

Settling me in a chair, he said, 'Let me put the kettle on, the tea will be ready in a few minutes.'

Lighting the stove, he put the kettle on. Meanwhile, Ram-babu and Banamali-babu had arrived.

Despite our prior acquaintance, Bhupesh-babu introduced all of us once more. 'This is Ramchandra Roy, and this is Banamali Chanda. They live in the same room and work at the same bank.'

I observed other similarities too; I had not noticed them earlier, possibly because I had not seen them together. Both were aged between forty-five and fifty, both were plump and of medium height, their features cut in the same mould – thick nose, invisible eyebrows, square chin. The resemblance was obviously genetic. I was tempted to surprise them. After all, I was a friend of Byomkesh's.

'Are you related?' I asked.

They looked at me in surprise. 'No,' answered Ram-babu a little brusquely, 'we're from different castes.'

I was taken aback. Just as I was trying to stammer out an explanation, Bhupesh-babu brought a plate of snacks to rescue me. Then the tea arrived. Finishing our cups of tea quickly, we got down to the game. The subject of their being cousins was abandoned.

As we played I discovered I had not forgotten the art of bridge even after all these years; my playing and bidding expertise were both intact. The stakes were low; the most one could win or lose at the end of the rubber was a quarter of a rupee. But playing was no fun without stakes.

Ram-babu and I were partners in the first rubber. He lit a thick cigar, Bhupesh-babu and I lit our cigarettes; Banamali-babu was content with slices of clove and betel nut.

The cards were shuffled and the pairs changed after every rubber. All three of them were good players; there wasn't much conversation as everyone was immersed in the game. Only the ends of the cigar and the cigarettes glowed constantly. Bhupesh-babu rose at one point to open the window and resumed his seat in silence.

It was past nine by the time we finished our game; the servant had already reminded everyone twice of dinner. When we totted up, I turned out to have won an eighth of a rupee. Pocketing my winnings, I rose to my feet joyfully. 'We'll play again tomorrow, won't we?' asked Bhupesh-babu with a smile.

'We will,' I said.

When I went back upstairs, Satyabati remonstrated with me. Nine-fifteen on a winter night was quite late. But, happy with my game of bridge after such a long time, I laughed away her scolding.

After this the bridge became a daily affair, the session beginning as soon as the evening lamp was lit and continuing until nine at night. I had formed a distinct impression of each of them after four or five days. Bhupesh-babu was kind-hearted, soft-spoken and hospitable, extremely fond of bridge. Ram-babu was grave, taciturn, not given to protesting against others' mistakes while playing. Banamali-babu held Ram-babu in the greatest of regard, trying without success to emulate his gravity. Both were reticent, deeply addicted to bridge. Both had faint Eastern Bengali accents.

We had been happily playing bridge for six days, our sessions on the verge of becoming a permanent institution, when a ghastly incident on the floor below upset our regular gathering. Natabar Nashkar, the only inhabitant of the ground floor, was suddenly murdered. While it is true that we had no direct relationship with him, even when a ship sails along the middle of the river the waves end up reaching the banks.

At six-thirty that evening, I was on my way to our evening game, wrapped in a shawl. Because I was a little late I ran down the stairs, my sandals flapping loudly. Just as I had reached the last step, a bang made me stop in my tracks. I could not identify the source of the sound. It could have been a car backfiring out on the street, but the sound was rather loud. Surely it couldn't be deafening if it was from the street.

After a brief pause I continued on to Bhupesh-babu's room. The lights were on. Bhupesh-babu was looking out of the window, gripping the bars, while behind him Ram-babu and Banamali-babu were trying to peep out as well. Bhupesh-babu was saying excitedly when I entered, 'There ... there ... he ran out of the lane just this minute, did you see him? He had a brown shawl on ...'

'What's the matter?' I said from the back.

Everyone turned towards me. 'Did you hear the sound?' asked Bhupesh-babu. 'It came from the lane beneath this window here. I'd just opened the window when there was a bang down there. I looked out and saw a man racing out of the lane.'

Our building was situated on the main road. A narrow, winding, paved blind lane connected the road to our back door; the servants took this route in and out of the house. I felt a misgiving. 'The room beneath this one is occupied. Could that be where the sound came from?'

'No idea,' said Bhupesh-babu. 'Someone does live in the room below, but I don't know his name.'

Ram-babu and Banamali-babu exchanged glances, after which Ram-babu cleared his throat and said, 'The room downstairs is occupied by Natabar Nashkar.'

'Let's go and see,' I said. 'If he's in he can tell us what the sound was.'

None of the three seemed keen, but I was Byomkesh the truth-seeker's friend. How could I not investigate the source of the sound? 'Let's take a quick look before we start our game,' I said. 'I wouldn't have bothered if it had been an everyday sort of sound, but even if someone came through the lane to throw a cracker into Natabar-babu's room we should find out, shouldn't we?'

They accompanied me reluctantly.

There was a lock on the manager Shibkali-babu's door, and the door to the pantry was shut too. The dining room was unlocked, for it held nothing but a few low stools. Only the door to Natabar-babu's room was closed without being locked. It would not be incorrect to presume that he was in, therefore. 'Natabar-babu!' I called out.

There was no reply. When a relatively louder call did not elicit a response either, I pushed on the door gently. The doors parted slightly.

The room was dark, nothing was visible; but there was a faint smell. The smell of gunpowder. We exchanged startled looks.

'There must be a switch by the door,' said Bhupesh-babu. 'Wait, let me turn on the light.'

Pushing me aside, he peeped into the room, then reached in to grope for the switch. There was a click, and the light came on.

The first thing we saw in the unforgiving overhead light was Natabar-babu's corpse. Dressed in a white sweater and a dhoti, he lay on his back in the middle of the room, his limbs splayed out. A thick stream of blood had flowed out of his chest. Natabar Nashkar had not been particularly handsome even when alive; he was of medium build with a protruding stomach, his bloated face deeply pockmarked. But death had made his appearance even more grotesque. I shall not describe that horror. You could tell from his expression how hideous an emotion the fear of death is.

Frozen briefly into a statue by the sight, Ram-babu emitted a sound like a hiccup. He stared at the corpse with unbelieving eyes, as if in a trance. Suddenly sinking his nails into Ram-babu's arm, Banamali-babu said, 'He's dead, dada!' It wasn't clear to me whether his expression was one of sorrow or wonder or joy.

'There's no doubt he's dead,' Bhupesh-babu said, his face pale. 'He died of a gunshot. There. Can you see it on the window sill?'

The window, which had no bars, was open – on the sill lay a pistol. The picture became clear: the assailant had shot Natabar Nashkar from outside the window, and then left after depositing the pistol on the window sill.

I turned on hearing rapidly approaching footsteps behind me. Shibkali Chakraborty, the manager of the boarding house, was approaching. An emaciated man, he was walking with undue haste, and his eyes were unnecessarily distraught; when he spoke, he wasn't satisfied unless he had repeated himself several times. 'All of you here? Here? What's the matter? What's the matter?' he said when he was near us.

'See for yourself.' We moved away from the door to give him a clear view. Shibkali-babu jumped out of his skin when he saw the blood-soaked corpse. 'Oh my god, oh my god! Natabar Nashkar is dead. Blood, blood. How did he die?'

'You can find out for yourself over there,' I said, pointing at the window.

'Oh god, a pistol, a pistol,' Shibkali-babu babbled again in terror as soon as he saw the gun. 'Natabar-babu has been murdered with a pistol. Who murdered him? When was he murdered?'

'I have no idea who murdered him,' I replied, 'but I do know when he was murdered. About five minutes ago.'

I explained everything to him briefly. He stared at the corpse in distress.

I had not noticed earlier, but suddenly I realized that Shibkali-babu was dressed in a brown shawl. My heart leapt into my mouth. Controlling my palpitations, I said, 'Weren't you home? Did you go out?'

'What? Yes, I . . . was out on work,' he replied in agitation. 'But . . . but . . . what is the way out? What is to be done . . . what is to be done?'

'The first thing to be done is to inform the police,' I said.

'True, true,' responded Shibkali-babu. 'That's right, that's right. But I do not have a telephone. You have a telephone, Ajit-babu, if you could . . .'

'I shall telephone the police immediately,' I said. 'But none of you must enter the room; wait here till the police arrive.'

I dashed upstairs. As I was about to enter my room I saw my own reflection in the mirror. I was dressed in a brown shawl too.

We were acquainted with Pranab Guha, the police inspector in our locality at that time. A competent, middle-aged man, he was not, however, favourably inclined towards Byomkesh. While he did not express a lack of amiability in any manner of harshness of speech or rudeness, he spoke to Byomkesh with excessive obsequiousness, chuckling softly at the end of every sentence. Possibly their natures were mutually abhorrent; besides, Pranab-babu did not care for the coarse touch of an unofficial hand in official matters.

After listening to my account on the telephone, he said sarcastically, 'Really! A crime in the detective's den! But when you have Byomkesh-babu there, why do you need me? Let him conduct the investigation.'

'Byomkesh is not in Calcutta,' I said testily. 'He would definitely have taken up the case had he been here.'

'Oh all right, I'll come round then,' said Inspector Guha. He put the phone down with a chuckle. I went back downstairs.

Pranab-babu arrived with his entourage half an hour later. He chuckled when he caught sight of me, then inspected the corpse gravely. Lifting the pistol gingerly from the window sill, he wrapped it in his handkerchief and put it in his pocket. Eventually, having despatched the corpse, he occupied the only chair in the room and proceeded to interrogate all the inmates of the house.

I told him whatever I knew. I am summarizing the statements of the others –

Shibkali-babu, the manager, was sworn to a vow of celibacy – a bachelor, in other words. He had been running the boarding house for the past twenty-five years; it was his wife, his child, his family . . . Natabar Nashkar had taken up residence in this ground-floor room three years earlier, and had occupied it ever since. He was approximately fifty years of age, and not given to consorting with the others. Ram-babu and Banamali-babu used to visit him in his room once in a while. Shibkali-babu bore no ill-will towards Natabar Nashkar, for Natabar paid his dues promptly on the first of every month . . . Shibkali-babu had learnt that afternoon of potatoes being sold cheap at a particular warehouse, so he had gone there to buy some. But the potatoes had been sold out already, so he had returned empty-handed.

Bhupesh-babu worked at an insurance office; he had been transferred to Calcutta a month and a half earlier. He was about forty-five, a widower with no children. He had no home to speak of; he had travelled all over the country in the course of work. Bhupesh-babu gave an accurate account of how he had gathered a group of people to play bridge, and of that evening's incidents; he mentioned the man in the brown shawl too. He had not seen the man's face clearly; from the back you cannot see the face of someone who is running away; so he was unlikely to recognize the individual were he to see him again.

The statements given by Ramchandra Roy and Banamali Chanda were similar. I observed that although Ram-babu remained composed throughout the questioning, Banamali-babu appeared somewhat perturbed. Both of them used to live in Dhaka earlier, working in the same British firm. Their wives, children and family had all been killed in the riots at the time of the Partition, and they had somehow managed to escape with their lives. Ram-babu was forty-eight years old; Banamali-babu forty-five. They had lived in this boarding house after crossing over to Calcutta, and worked in a bank. Three years had passed this way.

They were fond of playing bridge, but had not had an opportunity to play since moving to Calcutta. Bhupesh-babu had made arrangements for a game of bridge in his room a few days earlier, and the evenings had been passing pleasantly since then. Within five minutes of their entering Bhupesh-babu's room this evening, there was the sound of an explosion in the lane outside . . . They had been acquainted with Natabar-babu in Dhaka; it had been a slight acquaintance, without any particular closeness. Natabar-babu had worked as an agent for various enterprises in Dhaka. They used to meet occasionally by virtue of living in the same boarding house; Ram-babu and Banamali-babu would drop in sometimes for a chat. They did not know whether Natabar-babu had any other friends . . . They had seen the man in the brown shawl for a split second in the dim light of dusk at the head of the lane; they would not be able to recognize him again.

The remaining inmates were unable to reveal anything. A game of dice had been in progress in a room at the other end of the first floor. Four players and four other spectators had been present there; they had not heard the gunshot. No one else in the boarding house had anything more than a nodding acquaintance with Natabar-babu.

Only the servant Haripada said something that could be either irrelevant or significant. At six in the evening, Suren-babu from the first floor had sent him to the restaurant on the main road to buy some snacks. On his way back through the back lane, Haripada had heard someone murmuring in Natabar-babu's room. He had been unable to see who was inside because the door was shut; nor had he recognized the voice. Haripada had noticed this specifically because Natabar-babu did not usually have many visitors. He could not specify the time, but Suren-babu stated clearly that he had asked Haripada to get the snacks at six in the evening.

In other words, Natabar-babu had had a visitor in his room half an hour before he died. It wasn't anyone in the boarding house, for no one admitted visiting him. Therefore it had been an outsider. Perhaps it had been the man in the brown shawl. Or some other person altogether; Haripada's statement proved nothing.

After he had taken everyone's testimony, Inspector Guha said, 'All of you may leave now, we will search the room. And yes, this is for Ajit-babu and Shibkali-babu – do not attempt to leave Calcutta without my permission until this murder mystery is solved.'

'What do you mean?' I asked in surprise.

'I mean that both you and Shibkali-babu are dressed in brown shawls,' answered Inspector Guha. 'Heh heh. You may leave now.'

He slammed the door in our faces. We returned to our respective burrows. The game of cards was forgotten.

The following day passed in inactive tedium. The police made no noise. Inspector Guha had left the previous evening with some documents after searching Natabar-babu's room and locking the door. The man was hostile towards us, but he expressed his hostility so courteously that you could say nothing. He knew I had a watertight alibi, but had still used a flimsy pretext to issue instructions forbidding me to leave Calcutta. Since I was a friend of Byomkesh's, harassing me was his only motive.

In the morning, all the gentlemen at the boarding house left for their respective offices. No one seemed the slightest bit perturbed. There was no regret among any of them for the death by gunshot of a person named Natabar Nashkar, who had lived in the same boarding house for three years. 'If thou beest born, die thou must' – everyone appeared to harbour a philosophical attitude.

In the evening I went to Bhupesh-babu's room. Ram-babu and Banamali-babu had turned up as well. All of us seemed to be lacking in spirit. No one suggested a rubber. Our session broke up after miserably discussing Natabar Nashkar's death and criticizing the incompetence of the police over a cup of tea.

As I climbed the stairs, a thought occurred to me. No matter how efficient Inspector Guha was, he would not be able to solve the mystery of Natabar-babu's death. Byomkesh wasn't here; the evening sessions were flagging. It would not be a bad idea to write an account of the entire affair instead of sitting by idly. I would have something to do, and maybe Byomkesh would be able to get to the bottom of the matter if he could read my account when he returned.

I began writing that very night. Starting at the beginning, I wrote down every last detail from my perspective in a way that would not allow Byomkesh to pick holes in the narrative. I finished writing the next afternoon.

I may have finished writing, but the story was not finished. Who knew when and where the story of Natabar-babu's murder would end? Maybe the murderer's identity would never be known. Feeling somewhat dissatisfied, I had barely lit a cigarette when Byomkesh strolled in holding his suitcase.

'Byomkesh! You're back!' I jumped to my feet. 'So your work's done?'

'The work's not even begun,' Byomkesh said. 'Two government departments are at loggerheads with each other. Each wants to be the first to lay down its life for the cause. I decided to leave, I'll go back when they've finished battling each other.'

Satyabati came running on hearing Byomkesh's voice, wiping her hand on the end of her sari. They were not newly-weds any more, but even now a joyful light appeared in Satyabati's eyes when Byomkesh appeared unexpectedly.

When the couple's reunion had ended I brought up the subject of Natabar's murder and gave Byomkesh what I had written for him to read. Byomkesh started reading my notes over a cup of tea.

He returned them to me at six in the evening, saying, 'So Inspector Pranab Guha has confined you to the city. What the fellow must think of us! We shall meet him tomorrow. Let us go and meet Bhupesh-babu now.'

I realized the case had intrigued Byomkesh. 'By all means,' I said, pleased. 'We may run into Ram-babu and Banamali-babu too.'

I took Byomkesh to Bhupesh-babu's room on the first floor. My assumption had not been incorrect; Ram-babu and Banamali-babu were indeed there. Byomkesh did not have to be introduced to anyone, for everyone knew who he was. Bhupesh-babu welcomed him warmly, and put the kettle on for tea. Ram-babu's gravity remained intact, but a nervous wariness was occasionally evident in Banamali's eyes.

Taking a seat, Byomkesh said, 'I was once addicted to bridge. Then Ajit taught me chess. But now I no longer enjoy playing.'

Turning to look at him as he was putting the tea leaves into the boiling water in the kettle, Bhupesh-babu said, 'Now for only the sport unto death with my life.'

I was startled to hear Bhupesh-babu quote Rabindranath Tagore. He not only worked at the insurance office but also read poetry!

'Right you are,' responded Byomkesh quietly. 'Playing against death all my life has ensured that I can no longer train my mind on light-hearted games.'

'It's different for you,' answered Bhupesh-babu. 'I deal in death too; what else is insurance but the business of death. But still I enjoy bridge.'

Byomkesh may have been talking to Bhupesh-babu, but his eyes kept drifting towards Ram-babu and Banamali-babu. They sat in silence, unfamiliar with such light but refined conversation.

Bhupesh-babu brought the cups of tea and a plate of cream crackers. 'Yours is a different kind of personality too. Bridge is a game for the intelligent; those who are intelligent are naturally attracted to this game. Some people play bridge as a means of respite from the agony of living. Many years ago I knew someone who used to play bridge to forget the agony of his son's death.'

Three pairs of eyes turned mechanically towards Byomkesh. No one spoke, all of them could only stare in surprise. A heavy silence descended on the room.

We finished our cups of tea without a word. Then Byomkesh broke the silence and said matter-of-factly, 'I was in Cuttack, I have only just got back. Ajit informed me of Natabar Nashkar's death as soon as I arrived. I was not acquainted with Natabar-babu, but the news of his death made me curious. You do not often have a murder on your own doorstep. So I thought of making your acquaintance.'

'How fortunate then that the murder took place,' said Bhupesh-babu, 'or else you'd never have graced my room. But I know nothing about Natabar Nashkar. I had never even set eyes on him when he was alive. Ram-babu and Banamali-babu knew him slightly.'

Byomkesh looked at Ram-babu. A shadow of fear seemed to fall over his gravity. He fidgeted, cleared his throat as though about to say something, then shut his mouth. Thereupon Byomkesh turned his gaze towards Banamali-babu, saying, 'I'm sure you know what kind of a man Natabar-babu was.'

Startled, Banamali-babu stammered, 'Uh ... ar ... he wasn't a bad sort ... quite a decent sort, in fact ... but ...'

Ram-babu finally regained his power of speech, cutting in on Banamali-babu's incomplete utterance. 'Look, we were by no means friends of Natabar-babu's. But when we lived in Dhaka, he lived next door to us, so we were acquainted. We know nothing about his character.'

'How long ago did you live in Dhaka?' asked Byomkesh.

'Five or six years ago,' answered Ram-babu, gulping. 'Then the Partition riots began, and we came away to West Bengal.'

'So you worked in the same firm in Dhaka?' Byomkesh asked Banamali-babu.

'Yes, we did,' he answered. 'You must have heard of Godfrey-Brown; it's a large British firm. That was where . . .'

Before he could finish, Ram-babu suddenly rose from his chair. 'You haven't forgotten we have to call on Narayan-babu at seven, have you, Banamali? . . . We shall take our leave now.'

Ram-babu made a quick exit, with Banamali-babu in tow. Byomkesh turned to watch them retreat.

Bhupesh-babu smiled. 'Your questions sound innocuous, Byomkesh-babu,' he said, 'but Ram-babu's offended.'

'I don't understand why,' answered Byomkesh innocently. 'Do you have any idea?'

'I have no idea,' Bhupesh-babu shook his head. 'I was in fact in Dhaka during the riots, but I didn't know any of them at the time. I know nothing about their past either.'

'You were in Dhaka too during the riots?'

'Yes, I'd been transferred to Dhaka about a year earlier. I returned after the Partition.'

Silence reigned for some time. Byomkesh lit a cigarette. Looking at him for a few minutes, Bhupesh-babu asked, 'Is your story about the man who used to play bridge to forget the pain of losing his son true, Byomkesh-babu?'

'Yes, it's a true story,' Byomkesh told him. 'It happened a long time ago, when I was in college. Why do you ask?'

Bhupesh-babu did not answer. Instead, he rose and fetched a photograph from his drawer, handing it to Byomkesh. It was a photo of a boy of nine or ten, his face glowing with the brightness of a child. 'My son,' Bhupesh-babu mumbled.

'Your son . . .' Byomkesh said, raising his eyes from the photograph to look at Bhupesh-babu anxiously.

'He's dead,' Bhupesh-babu shook his head. 'He had gone to school the day the riots began in Dhaka; he never returned.'

Breaking the unbearable silence, Byomkesh asked half a question. 'Your wife . . .'

'She's dead too,' answered Bhupesh-babu. 'Her heart was weak, she couldn't bear her son's death. I neither died nor succeeded in forgetting. It's been five or six years, I should have forgotten by now. I go to work, I play cards, I laugh and joke, but I cannot forget. Is there a medicine to wipe out memories of grief, Byomkesh-babu?'

'Eternity is the only medicine,' Byomkesh sighed.

2

'Let us call on Swami Pranabananda,' said Byomkesh over our morning tea the next day.

I was already under a pall of gloom after hearing of the tragedy of Bhupesh-babu's life the previous night; the thought of an encounter with Inspector Guha depressed me further. 'Is a meeting with Pranabananda absolutely imperative?' I enquired.

'Not if you do not wish to be free of police suspicion,' answered Byomkesh.

'Very well then.'

Taking the stairs to the first floor at nine-thirty, we observed a lock on Bhupesh-babu's door. He must have gone to the office. Ram-babu and Banamali-babu were emerging from their room in full finery – they retreated on seeing us. Throwing me a sidelong glance, Byomkesh smiled.

Shibkali-babu was going over the account books in his office downstairs. When he saw Byomkesh he leapt to the door, asking with anguish in his eyes, 'Byomkesh-babu! When did you return from Cuttack – what time? Have you heard about Natabar Nashkar? And now look, the police have involved me in the case – they've involved me.'

'Not just you, they have involved Ajit too,' said Byomkesh.

'Yes, of course, of course. Brown shawl. Ridiculous ... ridiculous. You must save us.'

'I shall try.'

Stopping abruptly on the road, Byomkesh said, 'Come, let us take a look at the lane.'

He was referring to the lane that ran past our home, the one down which the man in the brown shawl had escaped after shooting Natabar-babu. It was so narrow that two people couldn't walk abreast in it.

We entered the lane in single file. Byomkesh advanced slowly, his eyes fixed on the paved surface. I didn't know what he had in mind, but it was rather far-fetched to find clues to the murder three days afterwards.

The window to Natabar-babu's room was shut. Pausing outside it, Byomkesh trained his probing eyes on the paved surface of the lane. The window was at a height of four feet from the ground; it would be easy to fire into the room if the shutters were open.

'What's that stain?'

Following the direction of Byomkesh's finger, I observed a discoloured mark on the ground; star-shaped, with a diameter of about three inches. The lane was swept from time to time, but despite the urgency of all the cleaning, the stain had not been obliterated. It appeared to be two or three days old.

'What *is* that stain?' I asked.

Without answering, Byomkesh suddenly lowered himself to the ground like someone doing push-up exercises and planted his nose on the stain. 'What on earth are you doing?' I asked in surprise. 'Why are you rubbing your nose on the ground?'

'I was not rubbing my nose,' said Byomkesh, back on his feet. 'I was sniffing it.'

'Sniffing it! How does it smell?'

'You can sniff it too if you'd like to know.'

'No need.'

'Then let us go to the police station.'

Leaving the lane behind us, we went off towards the police station. I glanced at Byomkesh once or twice out of the corner of my eye, but it wasn't clear whether he had discovered anything after sniffing the lane.

Inspector Guha was lording it over the police station. He was on the whole of pleasing appearance, medium build and not too dark a complexion; the only flaw was that he was barely five feet three inches tall.

At the sight of Byomkesh walking in, his eyes first expressed surprise, followed by feigned humility. 'Byomkesh-babu!' he exclaimed. 'How fortunate I am to be in your august company first thing in the morning. Hehe.'

'I am no less fortunate,' countered Byomkesh. 'The scriptures clearly state the outcome of seeing a dwarf in the morning – you are freed from the cycle of rebirth.'

Inspector Guha was taken aback. Byomkesh had always ignored his jibes, but today he was in a different frame of mind. Unprepared for a riposte, Pranab-babu said glumly, 'I admit my appearance does not resemble a lamp post's.'

'You have no choice but to admit it,' Byomkesh smiled. 'Lamp posts have lights on their heads; that is where they differ from you.'

Pranab-babu's face fell. Forcing out a laugh, he said, 'I can't help it; not everyone is so bright inside their heads, after all. Was there anything you needed?'

'Of course there is,' said Byomkesh. 'First, I have marched Ajit to the police station to prove to you that he is not absconding. You may rest assured that he is under my surveillance; he will not be able to escape under my nose.'

Pranab-babu attempted a disarming laugh. 'I do not know what the commissioner will say if he learns that you have restrained Ajit from leaving the city,' Byomkesh continued without mercy, 'but I would certainly like to know. We have courts of law in this country; even police officers can be punished for unnecessarily interfering with individual freedom. But still, all that can come later. My second question is whether you have been able to gather any information concerning Natabar Nashkar's death.'

Pranab-babu debated whether to answer this question rudely. But, realizing that it would not be wise to antagonize Byomkesh in his current frame of mind, he answered calmly, 'Do you have any idea of the population of Calcutta, Byomkesh-babu?'

'I have never counted,' answered Byomkesh contemptuously. 'Probably five million or so.'

'Let's say it is five million,' said Pranab-babu. 'Is it a simple task to apprehend an individual in a brown shawl from these teeming millions? Can you do it?'

'I might be able to if I have all the information.'

'Although it is against our rules to share information with outsiders, I can tell you all I know.'

'Very well, do so. Has Natabar Nashkar's family been located?'

'No. We had advertised in the papers, but no one has come forward.'

'What did the post-mortem reveal?'

'The bullet penetrated the ribs to enter the heart. The bullet was matched with the gun; it was the same pistol.'

'Anything else?'

'He was quite healthy, but on the verge of developing cataracts in his eyes.'

'Who's the owner of the pistol?'

'It's an American Army pistol, available on the black market. There's no way in which to identify the owner.'

'Did you discover anything significant when you searched the room?'

'All the relevant items are there on that table. A diary, about five rupees in cash, a bank passbook and a true copy of a court judgement. You may take a look if you like.'

There was a table in the corner of the room. Byomkesh went up to it, but I did not. Inspector Guha was not a decent sort; an unpleasant situation would arise if he objected. From my chair, I saw Byomkesh examine the bank passbook, leaf through the diary and read the court document with the judicial stamp carefully. 'I have seen all I had to,' he said on his return.

By then, the devil in Inspector Guha had awoken again. Peering at Byomkesh, he said, 'You saw exactly what I did. Have you found out the name and address of the culprit?'

'Yes, I have,' Byomkesh told him.

'Really!' exclaimed Pranab-babu, his eyebrows shooting skywards. 'So quickly! You are extraordinarily sagacious! Would you be so good as to reveal the culprit's name, so that I may arrest him?'

'I shall not reveal the culprit's name to you, Pranab-babu,' Byomkesh said, tightening his jaw. 'That is my own discovery. You are paid a salary for your work; you will have to find out on your own. But I can offer you some help. Search the lane running beside the building.'

'Has the culprit left his footprint in there? Hehe.'

'No, he has left a mark even more incriminating . . . One more thing. I shall be taking Ajit to Cuttack with me in a few days. Stop him if you dare . . . Come, Ajit.'

'Have you really identified the culprit?' I asked in excitement when we left the police station.

'I had identified him even before we came to the police station,' Byomkesh nodded, 'but Inspector Guha is a good-for-nothing. He is not unintelligent, but his intelligence is destructive. He will never be able to get to the bottom of Natabar's murder mystery.'

'Who murdered Natabar Nashkar? Was it someone we know?' I asked.

'I shall tell you later. For now, let me tell you that Natabar Nashkar was a blackmailer by profession. You had better go back home, I am going to the city. Godfrey-Brown has a large office here in Calcutta too. I might get some information there. It may be some time before I am back.' He left with a wave.

I returned home alone. It was one-thirty by the time Byomkesh came back.

'You have to do something for me,' he said after his bath and lunch. 'You have to invite Ram-babu, Banamali-babu and Bhupesh-babu to tea. We shall gather here in this room this evening.'

'Very well. But what's going on? Why did you go to the Godfrey-Brown office?'

'There was a court judgement among Natabar Nashkar's belongings at the police station. When I read it I discovered that two brothers named Rashbehari Biswas and Banabehari Biswas were the treasurer and assistant treasurer, respectively, at the Dhaka office of Godfrey-Brown. They were caught embezzling funds seven years ago. They were taken to court. Banabehari was sentenced to two years' imprisonment and Rashbehari to three. Natabar Nashkar had got hold of this judgement. Then his diary revealed that he used to get eighty rupees every month from Rashbehari and Banabehari Biswas. I went to Godfrey-Brown to verify the misappropriation of funds. It is true. I had no more doubts that Natabar was blackmailing them.'

'But . . . Rashbehari, Banabehari . . . who are they? Where will you find them?'

'They aren't far away; you only have to go as far as Room No. Three.'

'What! Ram-babu and Banamali-babu!'

'Yes. You were very close to the truth. They are not just related, they are brothers. To honour the idiom, you could say they are not just brothers-in-arms but also thick as thieves.'

'But . . . but . . . they could not have murdered Natabar. When Natabar was killed they were . . .'

'Patience,' said Byomkesh, raising his hand. 'You shall hear the whole story at tea.'

A variety of snacks and tea had been prepared to entertain the guests. Bhupesh-babu was the first to arrive. Dressed in a dhoti and kurta, he had a folded grey shawl over his shoulder and an eager smile on his face. 'Have you made arrangements for bridge too?' he asked.

'We can make arrangements if everyone wants to play,' Byomkesh replied.

Ram-babu and Banamali-babu arrived a little later, their coats buttoned up to their necks, their eyes wary. 'Welcome, welcome,' said Byomkesh.

Byomkesh led a witty conversation over the tea and snacks. I observed after some time that Ram-babu and Banamali-babu had shed their stiffness. Feeling quite at ease, they were participating in the exchanges.

After twenty minutes or so, when the snacks were exhausted, Ram-babu lit a cigar; offering Bhupesh-babu a cigarette, Byomkesh then held the tin out to Banamali-babu. 'One for you, Banabehari-babu?' he said.

'I don't smoke ...' said Banamali-babu, and turned pale. 'Er ... my name ...'

'The two of you are brothers, and I know your real names – Rashbehari and Banabehari Biswas.' Byomkesh sat down in his chair. 'Natabar Nashkar was blackmailing you. You were paying him eighty rupees a month ...'

Rashbehari and Banabehari had turned to blocks of wood. Lighting his own cigarette, Byomkesh spoke as he blew the smoke out. 'Natabar Nashkar was a criminal. When he was in Dhaka, he was to all appearances an agent, but behind that façade he blackmailed people whenever he had the opportunity. When the two of you went to jail, he procured a copy of the court judgement, keeping future possibilities in mind. His plan was to wait till you had got jobs again after your release and then start sucking your blood.

'Then the Partition took place. Natabar could no longer continue his business in Dhaka, he escaped to Calcutta. But he did not know too many people here; there was no opportunity to pursue either his legal or his illegal profession as there was no one suitable for blackmailing. His business reached a low ebb. He took a room in this boarding house, surviving on whatever little money he had managed to bring over.

'Then he suddenly saw the two of you one day and recognized you. You lived in the same boarding house. On making enquiries, he discovered that you were working at a bank under false identities. Natabar Nashkar found a channel for earning. God seemed to have delivered the two of you to him. Pay up, or else I will reveal your real identities to the bank, Natabar told you. Helpless, you began paying him every month. Not a large sum, admittedly, only eighty rupees. But not bad for Natabar – at least it paid for his accommodation and food.

'So it went on. The two of you had no peace, nor could you escape Natabar's clutches. Your only hope lay in his death.'

Byomkesh paused. Breaking the breathless silence, Banabehari burst out, 'I assure you Byomkesh-babu, we didn't kill Natabar Nashkar. We were in Bhupesh-babu's room when he was killed.'

'That is true.' Leaning back in his chair, Byomkesh said carelessly, 'I do not care who killed Natabar. Only the police do. But the two of you work at a bank. If there is ever a discrepancy in the accounts I shall be forced to reveal your true identities.'

'There will be no discrepancy in the bank's accounts,' Ram-babu aka Rashbehari-babu finally spoke. 'We will not repeat our mistake.'

'Excellent. Ajit and I shall remain silent in that case.' Byomkesh looked at Bhupesh-babu. 'What about you?'

A strange smile flitted across Bhupesh-babu's face. 'I shall remain silent too,' he said softly. 'Not a word will escape my lips.'

The room was silent for some time after this. Then Ram-babu rose, speaking with his palms joined together, 'We shall never forget your generosity. May we leave now? I am not feeling very well.'

'You may.' Byomkesh saw them to the door, then came back after shutting it.

I saw Bhupesh-babu smiling at Byomkesh. Byomkesh returned his smile. 'I did not know there was an illicit connection between Natabar Nashkar and Ram-babu and Banamali-babu. That is a coincidence. You have probably unravelled everything, have you not?'

'Not everything, but the sum of it,' Byomkesh sighed deeply.

'Why don't you tell the story? If I have anything to add I shall do so afterwards.'

Giving Bhupesh-babu a cigarette and lighting one for himself, Byomkesh turned to me and began to speak, slowly. 'You wrote an account of Natabar's death. When I read it, I was struck by a doubt. The sound of a pistol being fired is never so loud. This seemed to be the sound of a shotgun, or a bomb bursting. Yet Natabar had been killed by a pistol shot.

'You had noticed the similarity in appearance between Ram-babu and

89

Banamali-babu. When I spoke to them, they appeared to be concealing something. Since they used to frequent Natabar's room, I became curious about them.

'But they were in Bhupesh-babu's room on the first floor when the gun-shot was heard. The atmosphere in Bhupesh-babu's room was peaceful, normal. He was in his own room; at six twenty-five p.m. Rashbehari and Banabehari came for the game of bridge. But the game could not begin till Ajit had arrived. A couple of minutes later Ajit's sandals were heard flapping on the stairs. Bhupesh-babu rose and opened the window looking out on the lane. At once there was an explosion. Rashbehari and Banabehari went up to the window. "There . . . there . . . he ran out of the lane just this minute, did you see him? He had a brown shawl on . . ." Bhupesh-babu exclaimed.

'There were several people walking past the lane on the main road. Rashbehari and Banabehari assumed one of them had just run out of the lane. They were left in no doubt that Bhupesh-babu was right. It is possible to induce such mistakes if you want to.

'Later the pistol was found on the window sill of Natabar's room. Naturally the question arises, why had the assailant left the pistol behind? There was no justifiable reason. I suspected that there was serious deception at work behind this apparently simple occurrence.

'Haripada, the servant, had heard someone in Natabar's room at six in the evening. What if that person had killed Natabar? And had then pushed back the supposed time of the killing in order to create an alibi for himself? A difference of fifteen minutes in the time of death cannot be detected by a post-mortem.

'I was convinced that the murderer was not an outsider, but someone who lived in the boarding house. But who was it? Was it Shibkali-babu? Rashbehari and Banabehari? Or someone else? I did not know who had a motive, but only Shibkali-babu had the opportunity. Everyone else had a watertight alibi.

'My mind was fogged; I could not see anything clearly. I had noticed that Natabar's room was directly beneath Bhupesh-babu's, and Natabar-babu's window was directly beneath Bhupesh-babu's. But the thought of a cracker hadn't even occurred to me then. Yes, a cracker. The kind that explodes when hurled, or when it is dropped from a height on a hard surface.

'I was on my way to the police station this morning in the hope of some fresh information. As I was leaving, I thought of checking for clues in the lane near Natabar's window.

'I did find a clue. The discoloured stain left behind by a cracker which burst on the paved surface of the lane directly beneath Natabar's window. When I sniffed it I discovered a faint tang of gunpowder. All my doubts were now dispelled. An excellent alibi had been created. Who had created the alibi? It could not have been anyone except Bhupesh-babu. Because he was the one who had opened the window. Rashbehari and Banabehari had gone up to the window after hearing the bang.

'Bhupesh-babu went downstairs quietly at six that evening under cover of darkness. The pistol had already been procured; he entered Natabar's room, introduced himself and shot him. Opening the window looking out on the lane, he placed the pistol on the window sill and returned to his room. Fortunately no one saw him on his journey to and from Natabar's room. But just in case they had, he needed an alibi. Returning to his room, he waited. Rashbehari and Banabehari arrived in ten minutes for their game of bridge. But Ajit had not arrived yet, so the three of them waited for him.

'Then Bhupesh-babu heard Ajit's sandals flapping on the staircase. He was prepared, holding a marble-sized cracker in his clenched hand. On the pretext of stuffiness in the room, he opened the window looking out on the lane and dropped the cracker. There was a bang downstairs. Rashbehari and Banabehari rushed to the window; Bhupesh-babu showed them the imaginary murderer in the brown shawl.

'Bhupesh-babu did not have to do anything more; the corpse was discovered in due course. The police came and took the corpse away. Curtain.'

Byomkesh stopped. Bhupesh-babu had been listening without a word, without stirring. He remained the same way. 'Any errors?' Byomkesh asked him, arching his eyebrows.

Bhupesh-babu stirred now, shaking his head with a smile. 'None whatsoever. I was the one who made the error. I didn't imagine you'd be back so soon, Byomkesh-babu. I had expected Natabar's case to have died down by the time you returned.'

'Two questions remain unanswered,' Byomkesh smiled. 'First, what was your motive? Second, how did you muffle the sound of the pistol being fired? Even if you fire a pistol in a closed room, the sound is likely to be heard outside. Did you take no care to prevent this?'

'I shall answer the second question first.' Removing the shawl folded over his shoulder, he unfolded it and held it out before us with both his hands; we saw a small hole in the new shawl. 'I was dressed in this shawl when I went to Natabar's room, hiding the pistol under it. I shot Natabar without taking the pistol out of my shawl; the sound was muffled by it, no one heard.'

Byomkesh nodded slowly. 'And the answer to my first question?' he said. 'I can guess some of it; you had shown us your son's photograph yesterday. Still, I want to hear it from you.'

A pulse began to beat in Bhupesh-babu's forehead, but he spoke calmly. 'I had shown you my son's photograph because I realized you would discover the truth. So I was justifying myself in advance. Natabar tricked my son into accompanying him from school on the day the riots broke out in Dhaka. That evening he came to my house to tell me he would return my son for a ransom of ten thousand rupees. I did not have ten thousand in cash, I gave him whatever I had; my wife took off all her jewellery and handed it to him. Natabar left with all of it, but we did not get our son back. We did not see Natabar either. Several years had passed since then. When I came to Calcutta after losing my wife and son, one day I suddenly spotted Natabar on the road. And then . . .'

'I see,' said Byomkesh. 'There is no need to say anything more, Bhupesh-babu.'

Bhupesh-babu remained immobile for a few moments. Then he said, 'What do you wish to do with me?'

Byomkesh looked at the ceiling for a while. Then he said, 'No one hangs for killing a crow, the writer Sarat Chandra Chattopadhyay has said. I believe no one should hang for killing a vulture either. You need not worry.'

PREMENDRA MITRA

The Tale of a Coward

Karuna brought me my morning cup of tea herself.

I couldn't help laughing at the accompaniments to the tea. 'The climate here in your part of the world may be excellent,' I told her, 'but my digestive system is still a hundred per cent Indian – a couple of days here have not changed it much.'

When Karuna only smiled in response and made as if to leave after arranging the cup and saucer and other dishes on the table, I called her back. 'Are you getting formal with me? I'd have understood Bimal-babu's standing on ceremony, but . . .'

Interrupting me, Karuna said, 'Let's say if I were to do it on Bimal-babu's behalf, would that be a crime?' With a smile, she left.

The tea got cold while I thoughts things over for a long time.

No, there was no harm admitting even to myself that Karuna's behaviour was causing me some unease.

Not that I'd expected her to do anything dramatic. Far from making me expectant, it would have given me cause for anxiety. That's why her initial lack of stiffness had actually reassured me. But gradually, an injured pride lurking somewhere within me seemed to be rearing its head. She needn't have gone to such extremes, I felt. Maybe the sun had set, but couldn't its rays have been delayed a bit to tinge the clouds to the west?

I think I'd have been happiest had Karuna appeared excessively forbidding and remote. A constant wariness on her part would probably have satisfied my ego the most.

But Karuna resorted neither to theatrical exuberance nor to rigid indifference.

I could easily have decided that it didn't matter to me even remotely.

And so I should have. After all, I had harboured neither the hope nor the wish to meet Karuna. It hadn't been on the cards either. Having disappeared without a trace among the countless millions on this earth, the possibility of rediscovering each other one day was completely unforeseen.

But when the unforeseen did materialize, I realized I had not been able to shed a lurking smugness at Karuna's inability to forget me, even though I had forgotten her quite effortlessly.

This conceit probably wasn't entirely unnatural.

After all, you couldn't forget the past entirely. Especially that particular evening years ago.

It had been raining incessantly all day, making it impossible to go out even if one wanted to. The servant informed me that a woman had come to see me.

A woman to see me here at this hotel! I was mystified at first. When Karuna followed the servant into my room, astonishment must have been written large on my face.

'You must be very surprised to see me,' said Karuna, coming up to me after the servant had left.

'I am a bit, yes, but you're sopping wet.' I was genuinely concerned.

Taking a chair, Karuna said, 'Don't worry, going out in the rain inevitably means getting wet.'

Then she laughed. 'What can you do anyway? How will you find women's clothes in this completely male world of yours? Surely you don't have an amateur drama troupe here either!'

'There's a married couple in No. Ten upstairs,' I said after a little thought.

'Are you proposing to borrow a sari and a blouse from her?' Karuna laughed again. 'How will you explain it?' Quickly turning serious, she said, 'I'll be fine in my wet clothes. Don't worry, I won't fall ill.'

I had no choice but to sit down by her side. And even before I could ask a question she said, 'You must be wondering why I've suddenly come here to see you.'

I didn't answer this time either. Karuna seemed distracted for the next few minutes. Then there was a sudden transformation. I realized she had been holding a torrent of emotion in check all this while.

Falling into my arms, she said frantically, 'They're taking me away to Patna tomorrow. My uncle wrote yesterday.'

It wasn't as though I didn't understand. But, still refusing to acknowledge the painful truth as long as possible, I said, 'Your college is closed, isn't it?'

Karuna said even more desperately, 'No, it's not that. You don't understand. They won't let me stay here any more, this will be my final departure!'

Holding her icy hand in mine, I sat in silence. Yes, there was pain in my heart too that evening, but it was nothing in comparison to Karuna's anguish. My love lacked the passion that could have made it rebel against the obstacles posed by fate.

Raising her tearful face a little later, Karuna said with determination, 'I won't go, never. Why should I?'

I didn't know what to say. Even that evening, somewhere in the recesses of my mind, I probably did not support her mutiny. I knew already that it would be in vain.

Trying to change the subject, I said, 'It may not be what you think, maybe your fears are unfounded.'

Karuna became distressed again. 'No, I'm sure, they want to keep me there by force. They think it's an infallible cure for my childishness.' She smiled bitterly. 'I'm supposed to be going to college,' she continued. 'I didn't mean to put you in a spot by turning up here. But I had no choice; you hardly visit my aunt's house any more. I wouldn't even have been able to inform you.'

After a pause, Karuna was distraught all over again. 'Will they really take me away by force and get me married to someone else? Is there nothing we can do?'

There's no need to describe in detail here the assurances and consolation with which I deposited Karuna at her aunt's house that evening years ago, but although it hurt terribly, it was indisputable that I hadn't been able to do anything about it.

Whether by coercion or not, Karuna's uncle did indeed take her away to Patna; we didn't even get a chance to meet again before she left.

Although I wasn't invited, I got to hear of Karuna's wedding. I cannot claim to have received the news either impassively or dispassionately, but when I look back and analyse it today, it's obvious that the next few days turned grey with despair because I was looking at things from Karuna's perspective – I did not have the ability to make out whether there was some self-satisfaction mingled with the pain of my realization.

Even after my memory of her had faded, I probably had the conviction somewhere at the back of my mind that, even if I could forget her, she would never forget me.

I embarrassed myself a little with the unexpected reaction I experienced to this cruel blow to my conviction, but still I couldn't restrain myself.

When Karuna returned to my room a little later, she would have been able, had she wanted, to detect a subtle change in my behaviour and in the way I spoke to her.

'What's this! You haven't eaten anything at all,' she said, looking at my plate.

I glanced at her as I buttoned my shirt; with a smile, I said, 'Formality begets formality; what would you have thought had I cleaned the plate like a starving man in a famine?'

'. . . You're still harping on the same theme!' Karuna sounded a little disappointed.

'Harping on the same theme is a weakness of mine, Karuna, I haven't been cured yet.' My voice was deep with emotion.

Karuna was putting away the plate of food, her face averted. I couldn't see her expression. But her response revealed nothing but light-hearted banter.

'So you've overcome all the other weaknesses.' Turning towards me again, she said, 'What's this, are you going out already?'

'Yes, I'd better check what progress they've made with the car.'

'Checking won't make the repairs go any faster. My husband said he'd enquire. He'll be home soon, he's asked for you to wait.'

'Therefore you and I should talk until then?' I tried to say, smiling.

'We could,' said Karuna with an amused expression.

'How easy it is for you to say something like this, Karuna!' My tone had become intense.

'What's so difficult about saying something like this?' Karuna's face held both a smile and traces of astonishment.

'Not all that difficult then, Karuna? Really? Aren't you afraid to be with me all by ourselves? I fear myself still, you know.'

'You really have gone quite mad.' Karuna left with a laugh, leaving me feeling rather foolish. Turning back from the door, she said, 'Don't you go away, I'll be back soon.'

But Karuna didn't return for the longest time. As I paced up and down in the room, I felt a resentment burning within me – whether against Karuna or against myself, I couldn't tell. Perhaps it was against destiny.

Why did I have to meet her again this way? What could this meeting be but an act of fate?

Having got some unexpected leave from the office, I was on a motoring holiday. When the engine collapsed suddenly last night in the middle of this town, I was grateful to fate for ensuring it had happened in a civilized place rather than in the middle of the forest. If I'd known what the future had in store I may well have preferred the forest.

Not only was it night, but the place was also unfamiliar. Unable to secure a bed for the night either at the waiting room at the station or at the cheapest of hotels, I hopelessly directed my horse-drawn cart back to the workshop where I had deposited my car for repair. That was where I met Bimal-babu. Employed at a nearby coal mine, he was visiting the workshop on business. Volunteering to come to the aid of another Bengali in a foreign land, he offered a room for the night in his house. I may have demurred mildly, but he brushed aside my objections.

He lived in a remote corner of the town. When we reached the house it had already fallen silent. As he rattled the knocker on the door, Bimal-babu said, 'I wasn't supposed to be back today, you see. The damned servants are all blissfully asleep.'

A little later a woman with a lantern opened the door, saying drowsily, 'I'm so sorry, I was fast asleep. But didn't you say you weren't coming back today?'

'Fate was probably going to give me a chance to be a Good Samaritan, so it led me back home. If I hadn't, this gentleman would have found himself in a bit of a spot in an unfamiliar town.'

Finally Karuna saw me. About to retreat, covering her head with the

97

cowl of her sari at the sight of a stranger, she suddenly stopped in her tracks.

Bimal-babu was still talking. 'Can you call the servants, they can unlock the drawing room and make up a bed for him in there. The gentleman may not find it very comfortable . . .'

He was forced to stop when he heard what Karuna was saying.

'So what if the gentleman does find it a little uncomfortable so far away from home,' smiled Karuna.

Bimal-babu looked at both of us in surprise. 'What do you mean? Do you know him?'

'Of course I do, just a little,' Karuna laughed.

'How strange!'

'Why should it be strange? Am I not allowed to know anyone you don't? I've only been married to you these past three years, do you suppose I was in solitary confinement the previous twenty?'

'But perhaps you could choose not to display this sample of our married life to the gentleman while he's still waiting outside in the cold,' Bimal-babu laughed too.

Karuna pretended to turn serious. 'Oh, so you want him to conclude that I'm perpetually quarrelling with you.'

Since it really was time that I said something too, I tried to laugh as well. 'Selling is my profession, Bimal-babu, you cannot fool me with samples.'

The manner of Karuna's first exchange of conversation with me after all these years struck a false note in me somewhere.

After a long wait, just as I was wondering whether to go looking for her, Karuna arrived. She answered the question I was about to ask her on seeing how she was dressed. 'I have to go out for a bit. Will you come with me?'

Taking my shawl from the clothes rack, I said, 'Your wish is my command. But where are you going?'

'To buy groceries,' Karuna smiled.

'Groceries?' I asked in surprise.

'I do the shopping myself quite often,' she smiled again. 'It's true that local women here don't usually go shopping themselves, unless they belong to families visiting on holiday, but I don't care for such restrictions; when my husband isn't here I go myself with the servant.'

'But Bimal-babu is here today, isn't he?'

'Oh, I forgot to tell you! He's sent word he's been held up on important work, he won't be back today.'

Karuna said all this quite casually. But I stopped in the middle of the road. 'What do we do then?'

'You seem concerned. Do you think you won't be looked after in his absence!' An amused, mischievous smile played on Karuna's face.

'It's not that, Karuna, I was thinking . . .' I said without a smile.

'If you start thinking here in the middle of the street I'll have to go on alone.'

So I had to walk along with her, in silence. The roads in this part of town were quite deserted. The houses were few and far between – many of them unoccupied. There was hardly anyone on the road to speak of.

We continued walking in silence. After a few glances at me, Karuna smiled again. 'Why so serious? What are you thinking about?'

'I'm thinking about leaving today.'

'But your car won't be ready so soon.'

'They can send the car on afterwards. I'll take the train.'

'Why so impatient to leave? What are you afraid of?'

I stopped again in the middle of the road. 'I told you, didn't I – I'm frightened of myself; it's me I don't trust.'

This time Karuna laughed loudly. 'What if you don't, it won't hurt anyone.'

No, I couldn't take this any more. Suddenly losing all self-control, I took her hand. 'What if you're the one that's hurt . . .'

Karuna didn't withdraw her hand. But, cruelly making light of my passion with a mocking smile, she said, 'But how? I trust myself, after all.'

'Couldn't that trust be shattered in an instant, Karuna?' I said, letting go of her hand. 'Couldn't a wave come along to dislodge you from your moorings?'

Karuna's eyes still held that indecipherable, amused smile. 'No idea, but then I haven't been tested either.'

I don't know what I might have said after that, but the roads were filling with people. I was forced into silence.

The Karuna who had gone shopping in the morning was completely different from the Karuna who sat opposite me at an elaborate lunch. Dressed in a sari with a broad red border over a white chemise, she came up to sit near me, her wet, loose hair draped over her back. She had never looked so extraordinary.

'What are you staring at? Haven't you seen me before?' she smiled, fanning me as I ate.

'It really feels as though I haven't.'

'Maybe you really haven't,' she said with an odd smile, and then asked, 'Tell me something, what did you think when you saw me shopping?'

'I was thinking that you're a new discovery for me.'

'Really! But I beg of you, don't deny Columbus's claims.'

'What if my claims predate Columbus's?'

'Even if they do, there's no deed of proof.' Karuna laughed uproariously at her own sense of humour.

I ate in silence for a long time. Then I said, 'Not everyone values a deed. Deeds are the easiest thing to burn.'

Karuna didn't smile this time. Looking at me strangely for a while, she suddenly rose, saying, 'I forgot your dessert.'

It was the cook and not Karuna who brought the dessert.

But she brought me some paan herself a few minutes later in my room and blurted out, 'So you're leaving by the evening train?'

I looked at her in astonishment. Was I imagining things, or was there a trace of anxiety on her face?

'Very well, I will,' I replied.

'What do you mean, very well, I will? As if I'm forcing you to go. I asked you to stay, it was you who insisted on leaving.' The acid in her tone was unmistakable now.

'Do you think I'm blaming you?' I smiled. 'I simply have to go.'

Karuna smiled too, perhaps a little embarrassed. 'I know, what can possibly hold you back in a place like this? But listen, you do know there's only that one train. Exactly at six-thirty, don't forget.'

I didn't have to take the trouble of not forgetting. Well before evening Karuna had made all the arrangements for my luggage to be packed, the motor workshop to be informed, and a carriage to be fetched to take me to the station. Just in case there were any disruptions during the fifteen-minute journey to the station, she saw me into the carriage an hour earlier and only then relaxed.

I didn't even get an opportunity to say anything through all of this.

As I was about to leave, she came up to the carriage to say, 'Heaven knows what you must be thinking about me. Probably that I'm dying to get rid of you, isn't that so?'

'That's the only source of consolation.'

'If consolation is so easy to obtain how will you ever get the real thing?' Karuna laughed.

The echo of her laughter was drowned in the clatter of the carriage drawing away.

It would have been best for this story to have ended there – but it didn't.

When I reached the station there was a long time to wait for the train. Unable to make the clock run faster after depositing my luggage in the waiting room and strolling aimlessly all over the platform, I was standing at the bookstall, wondering which of the books to buy. Suddenly I jumped out of my skin.

'Karuna! What are you doing here?'

'Nothing in particular,' she said with a wan smile.

Whether because of the faint light on the platform, or because she really felt that way, Karuna looked defenceless.

Moving away from the stall, I said, 'I can't quite understand why you're here, Karuna.'

Karuna smiled again. Then, suddenly looking serious, she said, 'I've burnt the deed.'

Genuinely perplexed, I stared at her idiotically for a while. Then I said frantically, 'Do you know what you're saying, Karuna?'

'Is it impossible, what I'm saying? Can't a wave ever come along to dislodge you from your moorings?' Karuna's voice acquired an intimacy of tone.

Stepping up very close to me, she raised her eyes to mine to say, 'Can't you take me away? Won't you?'

I was overcome. 'Take you away . . . I . . .'

'Are you wondering where to take me? Wherever you like.'

I couldn't say a word. I only felt an upheaval within me.

'I know what awaits you – difficulties, humiliation. But then I'm prepared for all that too, I'm risking all the shame and condemnation in the world to come to you.'

Karuna gazed at me in distress. What would I tell her? What could I say now? Thoughtlessly I had opened up the floodgates; how could I reject her now?

'But have you thought it through, Karuna? Will you be able to withstand the storm that will ensue? We might get so fatigued fighting it that one day we'll end up hating each other.'

Karuna was still looking at me intently, but gradually – very gradually – a contemptuous smile appeared on her face. 'Thank you for your valuable advice. The moorings would have been loosened in another moment.' Karuna laughed loudly this time.

I looked at her in surprise. Had she staged the whole thing just to mock me?

'There, the bell's gone for your train,' Karuna spoke quite casually. 'Mine's almost here too.'

'Your train!'

'My aunt and her family are coming from Calcutta. They don't know the way to our house. My husband isn't here either, so I came myself. Very disappointed?'

Without another word I set off for the bridge that would take me to the other platform. My last view of Karuna was of her bent over the books in the bookstall.

Was she really at the station to meet her aunt?

I'd never know.

BUDDHADEVA BOSE

A Life

Gurudas Bhattacharya, Vachaspati, the most senior teacher of Sanskrit at Khulna's Jagattarini School, had an accident during Bengali literature for Class Nine.

'Amaar projagawn amaar cheye tahare bawro kori mane . . .' The pundit stumbled on the sentence. 'Cheye'? Did that refer to the Bengali word for glance? Or for desire? After some thought, he explained the sentence as 'The king says his subjects want him, they desire his sanctuary, but they respect the king of Kaushal more. Grammar has been distorted a little here.'

The boys on the first bench exchanged glances. Then one of them stood up to say, 'The usage is correct, sir. The word "cheye" in this case is used for comparison, in the sense of "than". My subjects consider him more noble than me. See, it says a little later, "Are you so bold as to imagine you can be more pious than me?"'

'If only I were an Arab bedouin rather than who I am,' the boy next to him recited.

Gurudas did not respond. Accepting the correction made by his students, he continued teaching the poem. The bell rang.

It was the last period. Collecting their umbrellas and books, the other teachers left for their homes, while Gurudas made his way to the school library. The library was nothing but three cupboards full of books in one corner of the staffroom, most of them textbooks obtained as free samples. Among the more valuable volumes were several hardbound sets of the Bengali literary magazine *Probashi*, a Philip's atlas of twenty years' vintage, a Chambers Dictionary and three Bengali and English-to-Bengali dictionaries used by students. Clearing his throat, Gurudas said, 'Can you unlock this cupboard, Nabokeshto?'

Not even the servants at school paid much attention to the Sanskrit teacher. And Nabokeshto wore the mantle of bearer, doorman and gardener single-handedly. 'The library is closed, sir,' he answered with a touch of insolence.

'Never mind, just unlock it. I need some books.'

'But I have to leave for Rasoolpur right away – my daughter's in-laws have invited us . . .'

'That's all right, you can go. Leave the keys with me.'

'All right then. Don't forget to give them back to me before eleven tomorrow. You know how strict the new headmaster is. And lock the door of the room before you go . . . here's the padlock, see?'

Unlocking the cupboard, Gurudas planted himself in front of it; with a glance at his back, Nabokeshto gathered his bundle, wrapped in a homespun towel, from its place beneath the table – he was taking a bunch of grapefruits from the tree in the school yard as gifts for his son-in-law.

No one was allowed to take the dictionaries home; Gurudas spent a good deal of time leafing through the two Bengali dictionaries. The light grew dim, the silence of a provincial evening thickening inside the room. He forgot to sit down, forgot his hunger. His internal senses seemed to soak up the rows of letters. Today's incident had wounded him – he had not been able to capture the meaning of a word which millions of adults and children used every single day without a thought. How could he – he was a teacher of Sanskrit? He had learnt Sanskrit, but not Bengali. But he was a Bengali – that was the language he spoke. He seemed to realize for the first time that the Bengali language was not Sanskrit, not even a corrupt form of it – it was a complete, living, changing, evolving, independent language, the spoken language of 70 million people, their mother tongue. 'A living language, the mother tongue' – he repeated the words in his head several times. But prowess in one's mother tongue was not automatic, it needed nurture.

Gurudas noticed that none of the dictionaries included the word he had tripped over that morning. He was reminded of other words used in similar fashion – 'thekey', the Bengali word used for 'from' or 'since', or 'dyakha', used for 'seeing' or 'meeting' or 'looking after'. This was how the Bengali language performed the task of the Sanskrit verb ending. None of this was in the dictionary. There were mistakes in these dictionaries – wrong explanations, even inaccurate spellings. How were the students to learn? And I – how am I to learn?

It was late evening by the time Gurudas returned home. His wife Hori-mohini asked, 'So late?' Gurudas did not answer. He ate his dinner in silence. 'Are you ill? You aren't eating.'

'I am not ill.' He went to bed early that night.

Jagattarini School began at eleven in the morning, and the district school at ten-thirty. Gurudas went to the district school around a quarter past eleven the next morning, spending half an hour in the library before breathlessly entering his own class in the nick of time. The next day was Saturday – from the school he went to the only college in Khulna. He had a nodding acquaintance with the Sanskrit teacher there (here, too, it was he who taught Bengali). They conversed for some time, and he flipped through three or four books in the library – but his restlessness did not spare him.

No, he had not found it – he had not found what he was looking for anywhere. Could there not be a complete Bengali dictionary, which had room for every single word, both Sanskrit and vernacular, in the language, which included every combination, every application, every colloquial usage, which would enable the Bengali language to be learnt, its nature to be understood, its unique creative spirit to be appreciated? The college professor had said there was no such book. There were a few good ones among those he examined, but they were workmanlike – where was the dictionary that one could use for real scholarship?

The biggest bookshop in town was Victoria Library. In the evening Gurudas asked for a look at a major Bengali dictionary and the *Concise Oxford Dictionary*. Having leafed through them for a few minutes, he said softly, 'There's something I want to discuss, Reboti-babu.'

In a small town, everyone knew everyone else. The owner looked at Gurudas over the rims of his glasses.

'It's Saturday – may I take these two books home? I'll return them to you first thing Monday morning.'

'Take them home?'

'I'll handle them very carefully – won't soil them, won't crease them – I'll look after them. I need them urgently, you see.'

'Someone's already ordered those books, Ponditmashai.'

'I see.' Gurudas's fair, lean face reddened. A little later he said, 'Then I'd better buy them.' He had to wage a terrible war against himself, but ... he had spoken, he couldn't take his words back now.

'Pack these books for Ponditmashai ...' Reboti-babu made no further reference to the books having been ordered.

'But I can only pay next month.'

'Hmm ...' Gurudas sent up a silent prayer, 'Let him not agree, O lord.' But Reboti-babu's mouth softened.

'Very well. But on the first of the month, don't forget. We run a very small business, you know ... sign here, please.'

He had got them at a discount by virtue of being a teacher. Thirteen rupees and fourteen annas – nearly a third of his monthly salary.

Gurudas browsed through the two books late into that night by the glow of a lantern. His grasp of English was poor, but he had no difficulty in realizing the difference in the presentation of the two books. And yet this was just a condensed version; he had heard that Oxford had a giant dictionary too.

Before going to sleep he mused over Panini, considered the sheer extent of the Sanskrit dictionary *Shabdakalpadruma*, and recollected Vidyasagar. An extraordinary talent for grammar, an unmatched enthusiasm for analysis, a vocabulary that knew no limits. He used to possess them all. What had happened to them?

Horimohini had planted flowers in a fenced-off corner of the small yard. She was watering them with her daughter on Sunday morning when Gurudas came up to them, smiling.

'Shibani, go check if Nidhu-r ma has brought the milk,' Horimohini said.

'Later,' said Gurudas. 'Listen to me first.'

Horimohini paused and looked at him.

'I'm about to start on something new.'

A ray of hope flashed across Horimohini's face. Had the match for Shibani been finalized with the Chatterjees of Nimtala then? Their elder daughter Bhabani had been married into a high-born family – this was the other daughter. She had turned fifteen, if she didn't get married now, then when?

'Have they sent word?'

'Who?'

'The Nimtala Chatterjees.'

'No, that's not it. I am going to write a dictionary of the Bengali language. I made up my mind last night.'

There was no flicker of expression on Horimohini's face.

'You know what a dictionary is, don't you? A collection of words. The meaning of words in the Bengali language, similar words, usage of words, and so on. There isn't a book like this at the moment.'

'Not a single one? You're going to write it?' Horimohini felt a burst of pride. 'Will it say anything about gods and goddesses?'

'Everything.'

Yes, everything. Unknown to Gurudas, a smile spread across his face. He had fallen asleep last night as soon as he had come to this decision – a deep sleep. And when he awoke this morning, he discovered his mind was calm, his heart cheerful, and his body healed and rested. Support for his endeavour radiated from the branching rays of the sun in the sky, as though Nature had been waiting these last few days only for his resolve to do this. As soon as he accepted the task, satisfaction spread across the heavens, and the movements in his body acquired an easy rhythm. Gods and goddesses – of course he would have to include them. But all the gods? All their names? He would have to determine which of them belonged to an encyclopaedia and which to a dictionary. Which of the Sanskrit words could be considered Bengali? What to do with Brajabuli? What were the indications that a word was part of the Bengali language? Would he have to add words which were not in circulation but might be required? There was so much to think about. So much to ponder – but even Horimohini's flowering plants were urging him to start at once.

Gurudas had been to Puri once as a student; he was reminded now of his visit. He could see a similar ocean stretching ahead of him – a succession of waves, depressions, whirlpools, effort . . . the horizon in the distance. On this ocean his raft would have to float, this was the sea he would have to cross. For a moment Gurudas felt his skin prickle.

After lunch he brought the subject up again with his wife.

'I was thinking of the dictionary.'

'Yes, what about it?'

'The thing is, I need some material. Books and things.'

'Very well.'

'Very expensive books. I was thinking, Chakraborty-moshai had made an offer for that acre of land back home . . .'

'You'll sell it?' A shadow fell across Horimohini's face. 'We have nothing else, and the girl's growing up too.'

'We can survive on what we have.' Gurudas could not inject too much confidence into this assertion, so he tried to compensate with a soft smile. 'That is to say, I will survive, and once your son's grown up you'll have nothing to worry about.'

'The things you say! I think only about myself all the time, don't I? But I shan't let Nobu be a teacher like you. You know Netai, my nephew? He's passed his matriculation examination and joined the railways. Sixty rupees a month already – and extra earnings on top of that.'

Gurudas did not approve of the final statement, but, swallowing his criticism, he returned to the original subject.

'Why stop at the railways? Nobu might even become a deputy magistrate like my brother,' said Gurudas, throwing a sidelong look at his wife. It was a calculated ploy – he was fully aware of Horimohini's reverence for his stepbrother's status as deputy magistrate.

'Do you suppose I could ever be so lucky? But then, everything is possible if the gods smile on us, isn't that right? That reminds me, I'd sent you sweets after Lakshmi Puja the other day, but Shibani said you didn't have any.'

'I touched my forehead with them – that's better than eating them. Listen, I'm giving the land to Chakraborty-moshai then, all right?'

'Giving it? We hardly own anything anyway – and there's not only the girl who has to be married off but also the boy whom we must leave something for.'

'Everything will be done. But I cannot turn back now.'

'Cannot turn back – what do you mean?'

'Wealth is by nature temporary, but . . .' The scholar groped for the right word, and then turned helplessly to emotional appeal. 'I have made up my mind – are you going to stop me now?'

The land they owned was in Nandigram, about an hour away by steamer. Gurudas paid a visit during the Janmashtami holidays. A house, fruit-bearing trees, a small pond, some farmland. It used to be nearly seventy acres in his grandfather's time. After the division, about eight acres had come to Gurudas. He had had to sell nearly two acres for his elder daughter's wedding, and now another acre. Never mind, at least he was getting 150 rupees. Rummaging through the books at home, he even found the old Sanskrit dictionary printed in Bombay – it had belonged to his father – and, how fortunate, the Sanskrit grammar textbook that he had borrowed from a schoolmate and forgotten to return. The first thing he did on returning to Khulna was to buy two reams of the cheapest paper, which Shibani laced into a notebook.

On the first day of the Durga Puja holidays at school, Gurudas travelled to Calcutta, where he had to put up for three days at a boarding house in Sealdah. He bought two more Bengali dictionaries, Suniti Chatterjee's book on linguistics, an ancient (but excellent) Sanskrit-to-Bengali dictionary found after scouring the pavements of College Street and Chitpur, a Bengali grammar book written by an Englishman, *Alaaler Ghawrer Dulal* and *Hutom Pyachar Naksha* published by Basumati, and Kaliprasanna Sinha's *Mahabharata*, published by Hitabadi. He didn't dare ignore Rabindranath Tagore's *The Theory of Words* when it caught his eye – poets were the creators of language, might as well find out what he had to say. All this accounted for nearly fifty rupees. Then there were new clothes for everyone for Durga Puja, for Horimohini and Bhabani a pair each of the bangles that married women wore, a dhoti for his son-in-law, rubber slippers for Nobu costing a rupee and thirteen annas. He had to spend eight annas on his way back on a porter to carry all the books – that really pinched.

They had a wonderful time back home that year during the Durga Puja. Horimohini stayed back with the children while Gurudas returned to Khulna the day after Lakshmi Puja. He cooked his own meals and read all day. He found the English difficult, but managed to make sense of it, and the more he read the easier it grew. Drawing one of the notebooks made by Shibani to himself on the day before Kali Puja, he wrote the first letter of the Bengali alphabet, 'Aw', in a large hand. Fifty words were done that day. The school opened three days later, the family returned, and his leisure hours shrank.

Gurudas set himself a routine. He woke up at five in the morning to write for two hours, and then drank his share of milk, went out to tutor students, bought the day's provisions and returned home. This gave him a little time before his bath. He had to take private classes in the evening too – the exams were approaching – but he didn't go to bed until he had put in a couple of hours of writing. Gurudas was making smooth progress.

Winter came. There was no light before six in the morning, and this was when the pressure of checking annual exam papers intensified. But the Christmas holidays were approaching.

He had to visit Calcutta again during the Christmas vacation. The subject was like Draupadi's sari – unfolding constantly, an unending mystery, one whose depths you kept sinking into. How would he prove equal to this task – he, merely Gurudas Bhattacharya, a minor Sanskrit scholar? He did not know his way on this road, had no clear idea of where he would find the bricks and mortar needed to build this structure. In Calcutta he laid siege to the Imperial Library; the days passed navigating his way through the dense jungle of comparative linguistics. Many of the books were written in German, with an abundance of Greek letters and a thick growth of Latin, Gothic and Persian references, as though the immense vegetation of the Aryan languages had stretched up to the sky, spreading its branches far and wide. Sanskrit alone had never given him this feeling of kinship with the West, with the entire world. For the first time he set eyes on the Monier, Williams Sanskrit dictionary, he discovered Skeat's etymological dictionary too. Ten days passed cramming his notebooks with jottings.

When he was about to set off for Calcutta again during the summer holidays, Horimohini could not keep herself from objecting mildly.

'Why must you go to Calcutta again?'

'Do you need me here?'

'I was thinking of the expense. The boarding house costs money too.'

Gurudas had thought about this as well. The examination season was in the past, and not many studied Sanskrit these days. He had no one to tutor. Thanks to a supply of food from the land back home they managed to survive on forty-five rupees – but barely. They could afford coarse rice and daal and their clothes – anything more was virtually impossible. But . . . he simply had to go.

'Doesn't your mother's brother live in Calcutta?' said Horimohini. 'You could always . . .'

'Of course not, how can I stay a month at someone else's house? And he's only my mother's cousin – I haven't met him in years . . . it's impossible. But I'll manage – don't worry.'

'It's all very well for you to say that, but I spend sleepless nights.'

'But why?'

'Have you decided that Shibani will remain a spinster?'

A valid question. He had to accept that his daughter was showing signs of womanhood. It was time for her to be married. But . . . how?

'Why are you so anxious? She's only just turned fifteen. Many people don't even think of marriage till eighteen these days.'

'You of all people are saying this? Your very own family, the Brahmins of Nandigram, didn't allow their daughters to remain unmarried after ten.'

'Why shouldn't I? Didn't Rammohun Roy speak up against idol worship? Didn't Vidyasagar introduce widow-remarriage? They were Brahmins too.'

'Those who get their daughters married at eighteen also give them the chance to go to school and college, all right? They don't let them rot at home and turn into liabilities. Do you have it in you?'

Gurudas's lean, fair face grew pale. She was right. He had no response. He must try to arrange a match.

From the matchmaker he learnt that Rameshwar Banerjee of Hatkhola in Calcutta was looking for a bride for his third son. Rameshwar had been a professor at Sanskrit College during the solitary year that Gurudas had studied there. He decided to plead with Rameshwar in Calcutta to provide a safe passage for his daughter.

In Calcutta, Gurudas rented a 'seat' in the cheapest room in a boarding house he was familiar with. His meals were at a 'pice hotel' (which he had discovered on his previous visit; for four paise you could eat so much that you didn't need a second meal). His days were spent at the Imperial Library, at the university library, wandering among second-hand book-shops and seeking audiences with renowned professors. He had sensed a new requirement: instructions, advice, discussions – he had brought along all the pages in his notebook, in case anyone had any constructive comments to offer. It wasn't easy to meet professors – some had gone to Darjeeling, others were busy. Only two deigned to meet him. Leafing through the notebooks apprehensively, both of them said, 'Excellent, it's coming along very well, you must complete it.' When he enquired whether a detailed discussion was possible, he learnt that both were engaged as chief examiner for the BA exams, and did not have the leisure even to die at present.

One day he overheard a young man at a bookshop on College Street. The buyer was looking for a book on the history of Bengali literature; turning over the pages of two or three, the words he uttered were clearly weighed down with nausea. 'Dead! All dead! Rotting and ingested with worms which this swarm of professors picks out to eat. They collapse when they see living literature. Rabindranath was born in vain.' The young man disappeared, his sandals flapping.

Chuckling, the shopkeeper said, 'Subrata Sen speaks as forcefully as he writes.'

'Who was that?' Gurudas stepped forward. 'What did you say his name is?'

'Subrata Sen. You haven't read him? Powerful writer.'

At the boarding house he normally drank a tall glass of water by way of dinner and went to bed – his exhaustion taking him beyond the hot weather, the stench and his hunger in an instant. But sleep eluded him that night, the young man's statement ringing in his ears constantly. And you, Gurudas Bhattacharya, engaged in composing a dictionary of the Bengali language – what do *you* know of Bengali literature? Ishwarchandra Gupta, Bankimchandra Chattopadhyay, Michael Madhusudan Dutt – and that was it. The young man had named Rabindranath Tagore – some people said he had injected new life into the Bengali language, but you know nothing about him, you haven't read him at all. And these new writers – take Subrata Sen, for example – language lived through transformation in every era. It would die if it were to lose this power. And if a dictionary could not provide a portrait of this evolution, what use was it?

He had to think of the whole thing afresh. A dictionary was not a compendium of explanations for students, not a list or collection, not an immovable, static, ponderous object. Its essence lay in the flow, in movement, in showing the path to the future – to move ahead it had to gather sustenance from the creative work that writers were engaged in constantly. It would have to be replete with hints, allusions, advice, even imagination – just like a flowing waterfall glinting under the light. He would have to read literature – living works, current, changing literature – all that was being written, read, said, heard in the Bengali language. These were his ingredients.

He came back home bathed in a new glow. Within five minutes of his return Horimohini asked, 'Did you meet Rameshwar Banerjee?'

'I did.'

'What did he say?'

'In a minute.' Gurudas sat down on a mat, leaning back against a post. 'They have many demands. They're well off, you see.'

'Who'll marry your daughter on the strength of her appearance alone?'

'A thousand rupees in cash. Nearly three hundred grams of gold. All expenses. Provided they like the girl. But ... can we afford all this? I'd better make some more enquiries ...'

Sighing, Horimohini went away. Evening fell.

This time Gurudas had brought a ream of foolscap paper from Calcutta. It was cheaper there, and available at even lower prices if bought by the ream. He had nearly exhausted his older notebooks. He had to scribble copiously – scratch out bits, make changes, there was new information every day. And yet he wasn't even done with the first letter, 'Aw'.

Gurudas got down to work calmly. Some of it involved reading. He had avoided reading the newspapers all this time, but now he had to scan a couple of Bengali dailies every evening at the public library. And he left no Bengali book he could get hold of untouched. Happening to read Rabindranath's *Ghare Baire*, he was astounded. Could the Bengali language actually work this way? This was not Hutoom, this was Kalidasa. Not even Kalidasa, something else altogether.

His notebook and pencil were always in his pocket. He took voluminous notes. Most of them would not prove useful, but who could predict what would?

The Bengalis' forms of self-expression became the subject of his discoveries. He listened closely when his wife, son or daughter spoke; with so much interest that he often did not grasp the content and forgot to answer. What he wanted to know was not what they were saying but how they said it. When the younger students raised an uproar during the lunch break at school, he lurked unobserved behind them. At the market he kept his ears peeled for rural dialects. When he went home on holiday, he sought out Muslim peasants and engaged them in needless conversations – they had a unique way of speaking.

And he had to go to Calcutta during the longer vacations. He learnt the Greek alphabet, took help from a priest at St Xavier's School to understand the rules of Latin grammar, even visited madrasas for Arabic and Persian. Hardly any books were available in the provinces – for this too he had to visit Calcutta.

How did he afford all this? Cheap boarding houses and pice hotels, yes, but still? Gurudas had made arrangements, getting rid of another acre of land, this time without telling his wife. He didn't know anyone in Calcutta particularly well, feeling beleaguered if he had to speak in English. Nor did his soiled clothes evoke respect. He had to discover everything he needed all by himself, with the help of that eternal quality – effort, the capital that god had endowed every human being with. Effort, endeavour, waiting, patience. It took him four hours to do an hour's work – he was lighting rows of fireflies as he pushed through the darkness. But there were lights at every street corner – like signals for trains in the blackness of night.

Summer holidays once more, the monsoon once more. The rains were torrential that year. Earthworms burst through the kitchen floor in July. Leeches in the front yard. Snakes here and there. On some nights water streamed through gaps in the tin roof – having found dry spots for the children to sleep, the parents stayed up all night. After seven days of incessant rain, Gurudas opened his safe one day to get the shock of his life. Instead of his best books, what he saw were millions of termites wriggling about. Fifty pages of Suniti Chatterjee's book were missing, the third volume of the *Mahabharata* was in shreds, the Sanskrit dictionary from his father's time crumbled in his hands when he picked it up. The day passed battling the termites – he poured in four annas' worth of kerosene.

Immediately after this accident a ray of hope emerged; marriage for Shibani suddenly seemed a likelihood. The groom was from Barishal, recently posted here at the Khulna steamer station. The groom's family approved of the bride, and made no demand for dowry – only the cost of the wedding, and accoutrements for the bride. This was no cause for concern – Horimohini still had some ornaments left.

The wedding would not take place before March, but Bhabani was overcome with joy when she heard. At long last she would be able to visit her mother. She lived in a large family, surrounded by her in-laws, in Madaripur – she didn't even have the chance to visit her own family during Durga Puja.

Shibani ran up a fever after the rains. When the fever didn't go down even after a week, Gurudas sent for the ayurvedic doctor. He prescribed plenty of red and black pills – but to no avail.

On the twenty-first day the official assistant surgeon turned up. His fees were four rupees, and he stomped about in boots. Typhoid, he said after examining the patient. Give her nothing but glucose. Pour water over her head morning and evening. Here are the medicines. Note down the temperature at four-hour intervals. Inform me after three days.

The medicines were bought with borrowed money. The doctor came once a week – paying his fees was a near-impossible task. Milk and fish were stopped; Horimohini's deity was given a quarter of her regular rations.

Shibani lost weight, the fat disappeared from her cheeks, her discoloured teeth grew bigger and uglier. Then came the day when her hair had to be cut on the doctor's orders. Her scalp needed water, the more the better. Horimohini poured water over her daughter's head every hour, but Shibani was delirious.

When she died, her limbs had withered away to resemble sticks, her breast was like a seven-year-old boy's chest. And the sixteen-year-old girl used to be so healthy, full of grace. The ornaments put aside to pay for the wedding were used to clear the debt to the doctor.

Gurudas returned home at ten at night after the cremation. It was the end of February, winter was on its way out. He felt rather cold – wrapping a shawl around himself, he sat down next to his wife, who was slumped on the floor. The night passed in the same position.

A long night, but the sun rose finally. Horimohini had fallen asleep, while Nobu was curled up on the floor in the cold. Covering his son with the shawl, Gurudas carefully slipped a pillow beneath Horimohini's head. Then he went out, spread a mat and sat down with his notebook. This last one had also been made by Shibani. For a moment, all the letters blurred. Wiping his eyes on the end of his dhuti, he set down more letters next to the blurred ones.

Five more years passed, the dictionary was in its seventh year. He had done twenty-four letters and was up to 'Thaw'.

The words no longer flowed. What had started as an extraordinary, thrilling joy had turned into work now. Work, duty, responsibility, compulsion. The madness of discovery was gone, the excitement of gathering material had dissipated. He had an enormous quantity of information at his disposal now, the roads were familiar. It was time to work, it was time for nothing but work. Daily work, weekly work, monthly, annual, continuous. No likes, no dislikes, no reluctance either. This was an immaculate world, where the individual's angularities were dead.

That year saw the fruition of a long-drawn-out effort on the part of Jagattarini School – the government finally approved grants. Teachers' salaries were increased; Gurudas's monthly earnings leapt to fifty-five rupees – it could even rise to seventy or seventy-five eventually. In that same year Nobu, or Nobendu, vaulted over the hurdle of the matriculation examination. Not just that, he got a job almost immediately. A job with the railways, as his mother had hoped.

A few months later there was tragic news: Bhabani had become a widow. And within two months she appeared in her father's yard with close-cropped hair, dressed in widow's garb and holding three children by the hand. Her late husband's parents were no longer willing to shoulder the burden of their daughter-in-law, without whom they couldn't survive for a moment once upon a time. 'They are not as well off as before, my brothers-in-law have several children, and he didn't leave anything for us, baba.'

Her father said, 'Don't worry. Nobu has a job now. I'll look after all of you.'

Gurudas went to Calcutta during the summer holidays that year – after a gap of two years. He couldn't postpone things any more, it was time to find a publisher.

In his canvas shoes, holding a dusty umbrella, he scoured the summer pavements from Goldighi to Hedua with his manuscript stuffed into a tin trunk. Finally he came across Bharat Press in a lane off Sukia Street. They published old Sanskrit and Bengali books, and were inclined towards dictionaries. But the proprietor, Bipin-babu, said, 'We cannot judge how good your dictionary is. If you can get a recommendation from someone important, we'll think about it.'

'Such as? Whose . . .' Gurudas was too embarrassed to utter the word recommendation.

Bipin-babu mentioned three or four names. The very first one was that of the vice-chancellor of the university.

Gurudas arrived at this gentleman's house the next day. About a dozen people were waiting in a small room. As the day progressed, the crowd of people gathered for an audience grew to fill the open space in front of the house. Dhutis and Western suits, Madrasis and Punjabis, even men in saffron robes. Some paced up and down, some leant against the railing, some peeped over the swing door before ducking behind it. Young men, old men, women, helpless faces, grave expressions – but all of them similarly afflicted by the need to seek help. The clacking of typewriters, the ringing of telephones, the bustle of orderlies and clerks – it was impossible to tell who had got an audience and who was waiting in despair. From seven the clock moved on to eleven – there was no hope of a meeting today.

Gurudas slipped while getting off the tram on the way back, injuring himself. Putting tincture of iodine on his bruises, he rested on a plank in the boarding house all day. When he awoke the next morning, his hips were aching. But still he got into the second-class coach of the tram with his trunk.

No luck that day either – four hours passed, alternately sitting and standing. Four successive days went by this way.

On the fifth day he arrived even earlier, in case he could get in before anyone else. He discovered only two people there before him. A man of dignified appearance walking across the yard stopped suddenly on seeing him.

'What's the matter? Here again?'

'I had to come again, because . . .'

'You haven't met him yet? I've been seeing you every day. Well, what do you need?'

'I have composed a dictionary of Bengali. It's about this dictionary . . .'

'Oh, a dictionary? Of Bengali?' The man surveyed Gurudas from head to toe, not omitting his tin trunk. 'You've actually brought your manuscript?'

'Just . . . in case he wants a look . . . if he has the time.'

'Very well, sit down. Go straight in as soon as he arrives. Through this door here – there's nothing to be afraid of.'

He really did get an audience, along with a slip of paper with the words, 'I endorse this book for publication', accompanied by a signature.

Five hundred copies of each of several slim volumes would be published, each costing one rupee. The books would not be bound. Half of whatever was left over after paying for costs would go to the author, but if expenses were not recovered within a year the writer would recompense the publisher.

These were the terms of the contract. Bipin-babu kept the manuscripts for the first four letters, 'Aw' through 'Dirgho-ee', and Gurudas received the proofs within a week of returning to Khulna.

Six volumes were published in a year; the vowels were done. But Bipin-babu welcomed him sombrely the next summer. 'The books aren't selling at all. There they are – see for yourself. An entire dictionary is available at ten rupees, who's going to pay six for just the vowels? And who cares for so many details? I couldn't cover my costs, but I know you cannot recompense me. I can absorb this loss, but if you want to publish further you'll have to pay half the costs. If the books sell, I'll recover my costs first, plus thirty per cent commission. The rest of the money will be yours.'

'Half the costs? How much?'

'It takes between two hundred and two-fifty to print each volume. You'll get bills.'

Gurudas left another six volumes of his manuscript with the printer. For each volume being printed, he sold half an acre of land. Eventually nothing but the homestead was left, and then that was sold too.

By then ten more years had passed. Gurudas was almost through with 'Baw'; all the letters up to 'Dontyo-naw' had been published. Meanwhile his hair had greyed, he wore thick lenses in nickel-framed glasses – but despite the spectacles everything seemed blurred at night. Horimohini was suffering from arthritis, she couldn't do the household tasks any more. The entire family was under the care of the lean, indefatigable Bhabani. She paid a little extra attention to her father, offering him whatever she could – a little milk or fruit, or some juice. When she had a few moments to spare, she leafed through his dictionary. Gurudas had taught her, the first child of his youth, a little Sanskrit and Bengali. She knew her grammar, and had even picked up proof-reading skills. There were times – perhaps on the morning of a holiday – when Gurudas sat outside the house, writing, while Bhabani sat beside him, turning over the pages of books, not talking. They never spoke – but they were happy, both of them.

Nobendu now had a salary of seventy-five rupees. He lived in Calcutta, his job was to check tickets on trains leaving from Sealdah Station. His days passed travelling on trains, but he rushed home whenever he could, and he handed over a reasonable sum of money to Gurudas every month. It was thanks to him that they survived even with Bhabani's three growing children. Gurudas could afford to go to Calcutta from time to time, and Horimohini did not come to know that they didn't own any land any more, that they actually had to buy all their provisions now.

Horimohini busied herself in finding a match for her twenty-seven-year-old son. Nobendu wasn't willing, he said he was trying to get the post of stationmaster – it would be better to marry after he had settled down. Actually, it was the state of the family that had made him reluctant to add to his financial burden. But Horimohini insisted, and he was married in May.

Along with new quilts and sheets, a painted box of toiletries and the fragrance of cream and scent, the new bride also brought a wave of joy into the house. A beauteous girl of fifteen. A little pain was unavoidable too; reminded of Shibani, Horimohini wiped her eyes covertly.

Nine months after his wedding, Nobendu slipped while trying to climb into a moving train and fell on the tracks. When he was pulled out his heart was still beating in his mangled body, but not long enough to make it to the hospital.

His wife was seven months pregnant at the time. She fell unconscious when informed, and delivered a premature, dead baby four hours later. She never succeeded in getting back on her feet; overcome by childbed fever, suffering for six months, she finally vanished into the shadows like an insubstantial shadow herself.

Gurudas received 1,500 rupees from Nobendu's provident fund, and another 2,000 rupees as 'compensation'. And a few months later, just before Durga Puja, the war between Germany and England broke out.

From 'panchambahini' – fifth column – to 'anubidaran' – splitting the atom – Gurudas collected many new words during the six years of the war. These would have to be added to the appendix. But his work didn't progress significantly during this period, he only got as far as the Bengali letter 'Law'. Nor could he publish beyond the Bengali letter 'Raw'; printing had become four times as expensive and paper was hard to come by. Meanwhile, the landlord suddenly demanded seventeen rupees as rent for the house for which Gurudas had been paying seven and a half rupees all this time. The price of rice vaulted from four rupees per maund to forty. Kerosene became too expensive for lanterns. And his eyes began to trouble him. The doctor said he had developed a cataract in one of them and that surgery was necessary. This meant a trip to Calcutta and a cost of about 150 rupees. He dismissed the proposition as soon as he heard it – it was more important to remain alive, even if on only one square meal a day.

They survived on Nobendu's 3,500 rupees. Gurudas dipped into it to pay for Bhabani's daughter's wedding, which cost about 500. Despite controlling his expenditure strictly, the rest melted away during the war years like ice put out in the sun. He had returned his daughter-in-law's jewellery to her father.

It was during the war that Horimohini learnt that they no longer owned a home of their own. But she was not perturbed – she had lost that ability. She had turned inert after her son's death – almost deranged. She seldom spoke, just eating her meals and staying in bed most of the time, and suffered from her arthritis. Her teeth had fallen off, she was an old woman now.

Bhabani stood like a pillar, resilient. Her sons Amal and Bimal were in school. The elder one passed his Matriculation examination and joined Khulna College, where Gurudas intervened with the principal to ensure that he would not have to pay any fees. Bimal gave up his studies suddenly and, applying his own judgement, got a job at the ration shop, where he learnt to pilfer. When the sixteen-year-old's mother found out, she used a piece of wood to take the skin off his back.

Gurudas was penniless when the war ended. His salary and allowance at the school amounted to sixty-three rupees, but because of his age the authorities were pleading with him to retire. After much begging, he secured an extension of two years – he would have to leave after that.

But suddenly the problem of employment became a trivial one. Rivers of blood began to flow across the country, which then became independent. Khulna was allotted to Pakistan. After waiting and watching for a while, Gurudas decided to leave with his family.

It's best not to talk about how the journey was made. Partly on foot, partly by train, occasionally on a boat across a river. Their belongings (such as they were) were left behind; they took only absolutely essential clothes, a few utensils and his case of books. The published copies, handwritten notes, and . . . and virtually nothing else. All those books he had collected with so much effort since childhood had to be left behind.

Although they were unencumbered, the journey was not an easy one. He had grown old, his vision was dimmed. His wife hobbled. Amal and Bimal actually had to carry their grandmother at times – but how far can you walk bearing the weight of a heavy old woman? They had to pause for rest beneath trees, while Horimohini shrieked with arthritic pain. Rain. Sun. Dust. Droppings. Flies. And hordes of helpless people. Two babies were crushed to death by the crowd at Ranaghat Station.

It took ten days to get to Calcutta. They passed a week at Sealdah Station, eating nothing but puffed rice, and were then transferred on a lorry to a camp at Bongaon, where they were served a lump of rice and daal at two every afternoon. Gurudas recovered a little on this diet, but there was no respite from Horimohini's cries of pain.

Finally the lord took pity on her. Cholera broke out at the camp, and her heart gave way after she had emptied her stomach out several times. They could not cremate her themselves; government officials gathered bodies wholesale and took them away in a black vehicle.

Two months later they were given shelter at a refugee colony near Kanchrapara. Rows of one-room bamboo shanties, with a little space to cook in. A pond nearby, a tube-well for fresh water at a slight distance. Still, Bhabani set up a household despite the limitations. Amal got a job at a nearby mill, which helped them survive. Bimal went astray, spending all his time outdoors, smoking and watching films, though no one knew how he got the money for it.

Gurudas pulled out his notebooks again. One eye was clouded over with a cataract, the other had dimmed too. Every moment of daylight was priceless. He went outside as soon as the sun rose, while Bhabani brought him a cup of tea and a little puffed rice. She had to have her tea with her father – he insisted on it. Gurudas had discovered tea towards the end of the war. It provided energy, and suppressed hunger too. Starting with the first light of day, he worked till the last rays of the sun faded. He sat cross-legged, his notebooks on a small stool, and just two or three books open around him – whatever he had been able to salvage from Khulna. When his back ached, he placed a book beneath the small of his back and lay down for a few minutes. It brought relief.

The next month Bhabani made him a bolster. And that same day he wrote a postcard to Bipin-babu at Bharat Press.

The reply came two days later. Bipin-babu had asked after him, expressing pleasure at hearing from him after such a long time. Demand had picked up for his dictionary recently, the previous editions had almost sold out. It was necessary to publish the subsequent volumes now. The money realized from the sales of the earlier volumes would be enough to publish the new ones – Gurudas would not have to pay any more money. Bipin-babu would be obliged if Gurudas could inform him when the new manuscripts would be available.

After a few more letters had been exchanged, Bipin-babu agreed to provide a monthly 'assistance' of fifteen rupees. Gurudas saved some of it to get some new books all over again. Several volumes were published in succession over the next two years; he got as far as the letter 'Dontyo-shaw' meanwhile.

The following year Gurudas finished his dictionary, while it took another two years to publish all the volumes. He had to read everything in print once more: the corrigenda, the appendices, everything. The *Great Bengal Dictionary* was complete in fifty-two volumes. It had taken him thirty years. He was a young man of forty when he began – now the hair on his head was white, his back was bent, his cheeks were like crevices, the veins protruded on his skin. He was blind in one eye and had marginal vision in the other.

Gurudas took to his bed a few days later. The task for which he had conserved the last drops of his energy had been completed; he no longer needed it. He recalled Shibani, Nobu and Nobu's wife. He recalled his wife. 'Don't perform my last rites, Bhabani,' he told his daughter. 'I don't believe in any of it.'

But he suffered along and incessantly. Death was not at his beck and call.

Meanwhile, there were murmurs in Calcutta about his dictionary. One Gurudas Bhattacharya had apparently composed a dictionary – an outstanding achievement. Word spread – to the university, to literary gatherings, to newspaper offices. Those who bought the dictionary praised it, those who didn't praised it even more.

Eventually a young journalist appeared in a jeep one day, accompanied by Bipin-babu from Bharat Press. Gurudas did not speak much – he had no strength. Covering her face, Bhabani answered all their questions in a soft tone. A sensational report appeared in the next day's paper, peppered with magnificent words like sacrifice, dedication and devotion.

And so Gurudas became famous.

It was the fifth year after Independence. The government had announced literary awards. Someone in the committee proposed Gurudas for an award. Gurudas Bhattacharya? Oh, the dictionary. Well . . . well, one has to admit he has accomplished a mammoth task, written thousands of pages. And we hear he's in financial difficulties, eking out an existence in a refugee colony – it would be a splendid gesture. Something that would capture the popular imagination. You've seen how *Swadeshi Bazaar* has praised him, haven't you?

Gurudas was chosen to receive the award.

In reply to the official communication, Bhabani wrote that her father was ill and unable to visit Calcutta in any circumstances.

One of the younger ministers said, 'Very well, let us go to him. People will approve.'

Therefore an enormous car drew up at the Kanchrapara refugee colony at ten o' clock one morning, escorted by a jeep. A minister of the independent state emerged from the car, accompanied by two high officials and two orderlies in shining red uniforms. The same young journalist, a government clerk and a photographer with a camera jumped out of the jeep. The car could not come up all the way to the door. As children and women watched with bulging eyes, they walked along the narrow path between rows of shanties to Gurudas's hut. The tiny space was suddenly filled with people.

There was no room to sit – the ceremonies were conducted with everyone on their feet. The minister said a few words. A silk shawl, a bouquet of flowers, and 100-rupee notes tied with a silk ribbon, amounting to 5,000 rupees, were placed on Gurudas's bed. The cameras clicked, Gurudas's weak eyes blinked at the flash-popping bulbs.

He lay still on his back, his hands gathered at his chest. His expression did not betray whether he was aware of what was going on. But when the guests had moved away from his bed, when their demeanour suggested they wanted to leave but were staying back only out of embarrassment, Gurudas spoke clearly but faintly. 'Turn me on my side, Bhabani. This is very funny, but if I laugh I will be insulting all these people. Make me face the other way.' The eye with a cataract was still, but laughter flashed in the other one for an instant. Bhabani turned him over on his side carefully.

He died the same afternoon. His grandsons and the young men from the neighbourhood took him to the crematorium draped in the same silk shawl and covered with the same flowers.

He had made a single statement before dying. 'Keep the money, Bhabani, it'll prove useful for you.'

MANIK BANDYOPADHYAY

Prehistoric

Bhikhu had suffered greatly throughout winter. In mid-June the gang was caught during an attempt to rob Baikuntha Saha's business establishment in Basantapur. Bhikhu was the only one among the eleven who had managed to escape, despite a jab from a spear in his shoulder. Making it overnight to the dilapidated bridge ten miles away, he had hidden all day in a clump of reeds with half his body buried in the mud. A journey of another eighteen miles the next night took him to Prahlad Bagdi's home in Chitalpur.

Prahlad refused him sanctuary.

Pointing to Bhikhu's shoulder, he said, 'That's not a minor wound, my friend. It will get inflamed. What will happen to me if people come to know? If only you hadn't committed the murder ...'

'I feel like murdering you, Prahlad.'

'Not in this life, pal.'

The forest wasn't far away, about five miles to the north. Bhikhu had no choice but to take shelter there. Prahlad personally chopped off bamboo sticks to make him an elevated platform on the branches of sinjuri trees inside a dense and remote part of the forest, even covering it with palm leaves. 'All the tigers and other animals are higher up in the hills because of the rains. You'll be comfortable here unless a snake bites you.'

'What'll I eat?'

'What about all the chira and gur I gave you? I'll bring you a meal every other day, people will suspect something if I come every day.'

Bandaging the wound with leaves and vines, Prahlad left with assurances of returning. At night Bhikhu developed a fever. The next day he discovered Prahlad was right: the wound had indeed become extremely painful. His right arm had swollen abnormally and he couldn't move it any more.

Soaked to the skin, enduring the infestation of mosquitoes and other insects, detaching a leech from some part of his body every hour, and suffering continuously from a high temperature and pain, Bhikhu somehow survived two days and nights on the constricted platform in a forest that even tigers refused to inhabit during the monsoon. Getting drenched when it poured, finding it difficult to draw breath in the damp, humid heat when the sun was out, tormented by insects round the clock, he had not a moment of peace. Prahlad had left him a few local cigarettes, but the stock was exhausted by now. He still had enough of the flattened rice for three or four days, but no jaggery. And though he had run out of the sweetener, the red ants that had been drawn by it to the bamboo platform were still gathered there. Bhikhu bore the brunt of their disappointment all over his body.

Wishing death for Prahlad, Bhikhu continued to battle for life with all his might. Even the water in his pot ran out on the morning Prahlad was supposed to come. Having waited till the afternoon and unable to bear his thirst any longer, Bhikhu had to endure indescribable pain in fetching half a pitcher of water to drink from a distant canal and returning to his platform. When he couldn't stand his hunger any longer, he chewed some of the flattened rice to fill his empty belly. With one hand he kept exterminating ants and insects. Capturing leeches, he attached them to the skin around his wound to suck out the poisonous pus. Catching sight of a green snake poking its head out between the leaves of the sinjuri trees, he sat poised with a stick for two full hours, beating on the leaves and bushes around him thereafter at regular intervals to get rid of snakes.

He wouldn't die. He refused to die. Even in a condition in which forest animals would succumb, he, a human being, would survive.

Prahlad had been visiting his in-laws in a neighbouring village. In a stupor from all the drinking at a wedding there, he didn't come the next day either. It didn't occur to him to wonder even once in three days how Bhikhu was getting by in the forest.

Meanwhile Bhikhu's wound was beginning to rot, with pus oozing from it. His entire frame seemed swollen now. The fever had gone down a bit, but his body was stricken by an unbearable pain that had overpowered him, making him all but comatose. He no longer experienced hunger or thirst. The leeches kept sucking his blood, swelling into balls and falling off of their own accord. A jerk from his foot sent his pitcher of water crashing to the ground, the flattened rice in the bundle went bad in the constant rain, and at night jackals attracted by the stench of his wound began to frequent the area around the platform.

Finally returning from his in-laws, Prahlad went to check on Bhikhu in the afternoon and shook his head gravely. He had brought along some rice and fish and vegetables for Bhikhu, but now, sitting beside him in the darkness, he ate it all himself. Then he left to fetch his brother-in-law Bharat and a small bamboo ladder.

Laying Bhikhu on the ladder and using it like a stretcher, they took him home and made a bed for him with straw and hay on the platform fixed halfway up the wall.

And so strong was Bhikhu's survival instinct that this refuge was all he needed to gradually conquer death after a month spent in a moribund state without treatment and more or less without care. But his right arm did not recover, withering like a dying branch on a tree and becoming entirely useless. Initially he could move it with great effort, but eventually this became impossible too.

Once the wound had healed, whenever there was no visitor at home Bhikhu began to climb down the ladder with the help of his one good arm, and then, one evening, did something.

Prahlad was not at home, he was out drinking with Bharat. His sister had gone to fetch water. Entering the room to put her son to bed, Prahlad's wife began to beat a retreat when she saw the look in Bhikhu's eyes, but he grabbed her arm.

Still, Prahlad's wife came from a militant clan, and it wasn't going to be easy to overpower her with his left hand alone and lacking full strength in his body. Freeing her arm with a jerk, she left with a volley of abuse, and told Prahlad everything when he came home.

Drunk on hooch, Prahlad considered it his duty to kill such an ungrateful man. After delivering a blow on his wife's back with the thick bamboo stick in his hand, he was about to split open Bhikhu's skull with it when he realized despite his drunken haze that the task might be his sworn duty but was utterly impossible. For Bhikhu was brandishing a sharpened chopper, held firmly in his left hand. There was an exchange of obscenities rather than a killing.

Eventually Prahlad said, 'I've spent seven rupees on you, hand it over and get out of my house.'

'I had a gold chain, you've stolen it. Return it, I won't go till you do.'

'Who the hell knows anything about your chain?'

'Return my chain, Prahlad, I'm warning you. If you don't I'm going to slit your throat right now like that Saha's. I'm telling you straight. Give my chain back and I'll leave at once.'

But Bhikhu didn't get his chain. With Bharat arriving in the middle of the dispute, Prahlad had no problem overpowering Bhikhu with his brother-in-law's help. Weakened and crippled, Bhikhu couldn't do anything more than sink his teeth into Prahlad's upper arm. Prahlad and his brother-in-law beat Bhikhu to a pulp and threw him out of the house. The nearly healed wound began to bleed again and, wiping the blood with his hand, Bhikhu left, gasping for breath. While no one got to know where he went, in the dead of the night there was a huge commotion in the neighbourhood when Prahlad's house went up in flames.

'It's all over, it's all over,' Prahlad wailed, 'the devil got into my house, everything is finished.'

Still, the poor man could not utter Bhikhu's name for fear of being questioned by the police.

The second phase of Bhikhu's primitive, uncivilized life began that night. There was a river flowing past Chitalpur – after setting fire to Prahlad's house Bhikhu had stolen a fishing boat and set himself adrift on its currents. He had no strength to row; all he could do was use a flattened bamboo pole to steer the boat straight ahead. But he had not made much progress by morning, since he had been forced to rely only on the currents.

Bhikhu was worried that Prahlad might let slip his name to avenge the burning down of his house, being too upset to think of the trouble this would get him into. The police had been trying to capture him for a long time, and after the murder in Baikuntha Saha's house they had intensified their efforts rather than diluting them. If Prahlad informed them of his whereabouts they would search the entire area immediately. But Bhikhu was desperate, he hadn't eaten since the previous evening, and the thrashing he had received from two able-bodied young men had left his feeble body wracked with pain. Reaching the subdivision town at dawn, he moored his boat at the landing stage. Taking several dips in the water to wash off the bloodstains, he entered the town, his hunger drawing a film of darkness over his eyes. He didn't have even a paisa to buy himself something to eat. To the first man he met on the way to the market he held out his hand and said, 'Two paise. Please.'

Perhaps Bhikhu's wild, matted locks, the filthy rag tied around his waist and his withered, rope-like arm stirred the stranger's charitable instincts. He handed over a paisa.

'Just one, sir?' said Bhikhu. 'One more, please?'

'Oh one isn't enough for you?' The man flew into a rage. 'Get away from me.'

For a moment it seemed Bhikhu was going to swear at the man, but he controlled himself. Contenting himself with a glare from his bloodshot eyes, he bought whatever food he could and began to wolf it down.

This was how he learnt to beg.

Within a few days he learnt the techniques of the most visible department of this ancient profession, quickly mastering the gestures and language of supplication. He didn't clean himself at all any more and his matted hair was now gathered in clumps on his head, with a number of lice families increasing the strengths of their clans in it. Occasionally Bhikhu scratched his scalp with both his hands like a madman, but he didn't dare cut the extra hair. He had begged his way to owning a ripped coat, which he wore even in the sultriest of weather in order to conceal the wound in his shoulder. The withered arm was the most powerful advertisement for his business, which he couldn't afford to keep covered. So he had cut the right sleeve off. He had also acquired a tin mug and a stick.

Bhikhu took up position beneath a tamarind tree near the market and begged from morning to evening. In the morning he ate a paisa's worth of puffed rice. At lunchtime he stole into an abandoned garden at some distance from the market and cooked a pot of rice on a brick oven beneath a banyan tree, along with some fish or vegetables in an earthen pan. After a full meal he leant back against the tree and smoked luxuriously. Then it was back to work under the tamarind tree.

All day long he moaned and gasped in rhythm, chanting: just one paisa, baba, god will give you if you give me, just one paisa, baba . . .

Like many ancient sayings, the adage 'Be not a beggar ever' is also untrue in reality. Between 1,000 and 1,500 people passed Bhikhu during the day, and on average one out of fifty gave him one or half a paisa. Despite the preponderance of the half-paisa coins, Bhikhu earned at least five to six annas every day, and usually closer to eight annas. It was market day two days a week, when his income doubled to at least a rupee.

The rainy season had ended, and white kans grass had sprouted to a height on both banks of the river. Bhikhu had rented the dilapidated shanty with only a roof and no walls near Binu the fisherman's home close to the river. He slept there at night. He had gathered a worn but thick quilt used by someone who had died of malaria, spreading it at night over a bed of stolen straw and hay. His occasional efforts to go into the town and beg at people's homes had yielded some scraps of cloth, which he had bundled together to use as a pillow. When the night or the moisture-laden breeze turned chilly, he used one of those pieces of fabric to cover himself.

A life of contentment and two square meals a day restored Bhikhu's former physique. His chest expanded, and the muscles on his arm and back rippled visibly every time he moved. But being forced to suppress his strength gradually made him arrogant and impatient. He still begged using the same lines as before, uttered in a voice of pleading desperation, but now he flew into a rage when a passer-by declined to give him alms. If the road was empty he hurled obscene abuse at the pedestrian indifferent to his demand. When he went to buy something, he threatened to beat up the shopkeeper if he didn't give Bhikhu a little extra. When the women went down to the river to bathe he stood nearby on the pretext of begging. He was pleased if they were frightened, refusing to go away when asked to and baring his teeth in an insolent smile.

At night he tossed and turned on the bed he had made for himself.

He couldn't bear this dull existence, devoid of the company of women. His heart cried for the days from his wild, eventful former life.

That was when he would swallow hooch by the gallon and raise hell everywhere he went before tottering off to spend a tempestuous night with a woman. Sometimes he would join his gang to plunder a family

home, killing or maiming everyone and robbing all the money and jewellery before disappearing overnight. Was there anything more rousing
than witnessing by the light of torches the indescribable expression on the
wife's face when her husband was trussed up and murdered before her
eyes, or the mother's piteous screams when blood spurted from her son's
body? Even being on the run from the police and moving from one village
to another and into the forest was a source of joy. Many of the others in
his gang had been caught several times and been to jail, but the police had
never captured Bhikhu more than once. He was sentenced to seven years
in jail the time he joined up with Rakhu Bagdi to abduct Sripati Biswas's
sister in Pahana, but they couldn't keep him in there for more than two
years. He had vaulted over the wall and escaped one rainy evening. After
this he had sneaked into homes all by himself to steal money, he had
clamped his hand over the mouths of solitary housewives by the pond to
take away their chains and bangles, he had gone to Hatia with Rakhu's
wife across the sea in a boat from Noakhali. Having abandoned her after
six months in Hatia, he had lost count of the robberies he had committed
far and wide with three separate gangs that he had started. And then just
the other day he had slit Baikuntha Saha's brother's throat with a single
flick of his knife.

Just compare the life he had then to what it had become now.

The man who used to enjoy killing human beings vented his frustration
today by taunting passers-by who did not give him alms. His physical
strength was intact, it was just that he had nowhere to apply it. So many
shopkeepers tallied their accounts in the dead of night with the day's takings piled up in front of them, so many women were alone at home
because the men of the house were travelling, but instead of leaping into
their midst with threats and a sharp weapon and becoming rich overnight,
he only lay in silence in Binu's dilapidated shanty.

Bhikhu's regret knew no bounds as he stroked his right arm. Despite
being in possession of indomitable courage and a strong body amid the
sea of weak and fearful men and women in this world, he was all but dead
because he lacked an arm. Could anyone have such ill fortune?

Still, he could endure this particular wretchedness, for which regret
would suffice. But Bhikhu could not bear to be alone any more.

There was a woman who begged at the entrance to the market. Not very old, and with a firm body. But she had an ugly, pus-filled wound running down one leg from the knee to the foot. It was this wound that enabled her to earn more than Bhikhu, which was why she didn't treat it.

Bhikhu sat down beside her sometimes. 'It won't heal, will it?' he said.

'Of course it will,' she said, 'just needs medicine.'

'Do it then,' Bhikhu said eagerly, 'use the medicine. You won't have to beg once it's healed. You can be my woman.'

'That's if I agree.'

'Why not? Why won't you agree? I'll take care of your food and cloth-ing, you'll live in comfort, no need to work. Why will you say no?'

She wasn't one to be taken in easily. Tucking some tobacco leaves into her mouth, she said, 'And when you kick me away in a few days how will I get my wound back?'

Bhikhu vowed lifelong devotion and tried to tempt her with promises of luxury. But she refused. Bhikhu returned in disappointment.

Meanwhile the moon rose in the sky, the tides flowed in the river, the advent of winter brought a drunken feeling. There was no longer any fruit in the banana orchard next to Bhikhu's shanty. Binu bought his wife a silver girdle with the money made from selling bananas. Drunkenness intensified with the palm juice toddy. The heat of Bhikhu's lust smothered his revulsion, and he could control himself no longer.

One morning he went to the woman beggar immediately on waking up. 'All right,' he said, 'come with me, never mind the wound.'

'You couldn't come earlier?' she said. 'Go to hell now.'

'Why? Why should I go to hell?'

'You think I've been sitting here waiting for you? I'm with him there.'

Looking over in that direction, Bhikhu saw a crippled, bearded beggar, as strongly built as him, sitting at a little distance. Just like Bhikhu's arm, the beggar's right leg was withered too, and he made sure to hold it out with a flourish while he invoked Allah's name to ask for alms.

An artificial wooden leg lay next to him.

The woman beggar said, 'What are you sitting down for? Get out of here, he'll kill you if he sees you, I'm warning you.'

'Fuck it,' said Bhikhu, 'all the bastards are trying to kill me. I could take care of ten like him once, did you know?'

'Then go take care of him,' she said, 'why are you sitting here?'

'Leave him. Come away with me.'

'Don't you want a smoke also? Remember when you saw my wound and said no? Why should I want you now, you worm? Why should I leave him? Do you earn as much as him? Do you have a house? Fuck off or I'll curse you.'

Bhikhu retreated temporarily, but didn't give up. He sidled up to her whenever she was alone. Trying to get intimate, he said, 'And what's your name?'

They were so lacking in identity that they hadn't even found it necessary to find out each other's names.

She laughed, exposing her blackened teeth.

'Back? Go try with that old hag there.'

Bhikhu squatted on his haunches beside her. Since many passers-by offered rice instead of money, he had a bag slung around his shoulder nowadays. Reaching into it for a banana, he put it in front of the woman. 'Eat this. I stole it for you.'

She peeled and consumed her suitor's offering at once. Pleased, she said, 'You want to know my name? They call me Pachi. Pachi. You brought bananas, I've told you my name. Now fuck off.'

Bhikhu showed no signs of leaving. He wasn't sophisticated enough to be pleased by learning her name in exchange for a large banana. He remained squatting in the dust, conversing with Pachi as long as he could. Those who did not belong to the same class would not have called their dialogue a conversation, they would assume these two were swearing at each other.

Pachi's companion was named Bashir. Bhikhu tried to strike up a conversation with him too one day.

'Salaam, mian.'

'What are you hanging around here for?' said Bashir. 'Salaam, mian indeed. I'll smash your head in with my stick.'

Volleys of invectives followed from both sides. Because Bhikhu had a stick and Bashir had a rock, an actual fight did not ensue.

Bhikhu said before returning to his spot beneath the tamarind tree, 'Just you wait, I'll finish you off.'

Bashir said, 'Talk to her again and I swear by the lord I'll bash your head in.'

*

It was around then that Bhikhu's earnings began to drop.

The street he begged on didn't see new pedestrians every day. The number of people passing by for the first time dwindled in a couple of months. The rest had given Bhikhu money once, they felt no need to continue. There was no lack of beggars in the world.

Bhikhu was barely eking out a living now. Unable to save any money from his earnings except on market days, he began to fret.

It would be hard to live in the unwalled shanty in winter. He simply had to get a place with walls on all sides. Without somewhere to stay and enough to eat, no young woman beggar would agree to live with him. But his income was shrinking in a way that suggested he might not be able to feed himself this winter.

Bhikhu had to find a way to increase his earnings, but he could see no means of doing so as long as he stayed here. There were no opportunities to steal or rob or to work as a daily labourer, and it would not be possible to take money from anyone without actually killing them. But he did not want to leave Pachi behind and move elsewhere. Bhikhu grew rebellious against his fate. Binu's happy family life next door to his shanty tormented him with jealousy. On some days he itched to set Binu's house on fire. Wandering around the river like a madman, he felt he wouldn't be satisfied unless he possessed every morsel of food and every woman in the world.

Bhikhu spent some time wallowing in his discontent. Then, packing all his valuables in a bundle one night, and securing his money in the clothes he was wearing, he left his shanty. He had found a long iron stick beside the river earlier whose tip he had sharpened to a point with a rock. He took this weapon along.

The sky was twinkling with stars in the absence of the moon. Serenity prevailed over god's world. Bhikhu experienced an inarticulate elation as he went out into the deserted midnight world after such a long time with a horrific plan in his head. 'If only the lord had taken the left and spared the right,' he muttered to himself.

Walking half a mile along the river, he entered the town along a narrow path. Passing the market on his left, he took a series of lanes to the other end of town. The main road to the big city led out from this point. The river had wound its way here and ran alongside the road for a mile before changing direction again to the south.

For some distance along the way, a building or two was to be seen at intervals on either side of the road. Then the rice fields and stretches of fallow land taken over by wild trees appeared. A group of wretched people had cleared some land next to a stretch like this and set up the poorest of poor habitations with six or seven huts, one of which was Bashir's. He rose at dawn every day and clattered his way to town on his wooden leg to beg, returning in the evening. Pachi lit a fire with leaves and cooked, while Bashir sat and smoked. At night Pachi bandaged her wound in rags. Then the two of them lay down on their bamboo cot and chatted in their jagged and hideous way of speaking till they went to sleep. A fetid, rotten stink rose from their nest, their bed and their bodies, penetrating the thatched roof and merging with the air.

Bashir snored. Pachi mumbled.

Bhikhu had followed them home furtively one day to find out where they lived. Now, stealing his way to a spot behind their hut, he stood cautiously in the taro bushes for some time, listening closely through the gaps in the fence. Then he walked round to the front of the hut, where Pachi had not locked what passed as the door. Moving it aside silently, Bhikhu took his weapon out of his bundle and gripped it firmly. He entered. There was faint starlight outside, but even this was missing inside the hut. He couldn't spare a hand to light a match, and, standing in the darkness, Bhikhu realized he couldn't possibly gauge the current location of Bashir's heart. He would deliver the blow with his left hand, and if it didn't land in the right place Bashir would have the opportunity to make an uproar, which would only lead to trouble.

After a few moments' thought, he moved close to Bashir's head and, with a single movement, thrust the pointed tip of the stick some two inches into his crown. It was impossible to tell in the darkness whether the assault had proved lethal. So Bhikhu did not feel reassured even though he knew the weapon had penetrated the head. Now he grabbed Bashir's throat and squeezed with all his might.

To Pachi he said, 'Shut up. If you scream I'll kill you too.'

Instead of screaming Pachi only moaned in fear.

'Not a peep out of you,' Bhikhu continued, 'don't make a sound if you know what's good for you.'

He released Bashir only after he felt the body turn still.

Drawing a breath, he said, 'Turn on the lamp, Pachi.'

By lamplight he gazed at his own exploit with great pleasure. He was bursting with pride at having finished off an able-bodied man with just one good arm. Turning to Pachi, he said, 'Did you see who killed whom eventually? I warned him so many times, listen to me, leave her alone. But that made him angry, he threatened to bash my head in. Go ahead, mian, bash my head in now.' Bowing mockingly to Bashir's corpse, Bhikhu threw his head back and roared with laughter. Then, flying into a sudden rage, he said, 'Why do you stand there like you're struck dumb? Talk, you bag of bones, you bitch. Or should I finish you off too?'

'What do you want to do now?' Pachi said, trembling.

'Watch me. But first, where's his money?'

After much effort, Pachi had recently discovered the location of Bashir's secret stash. She pretended ignorance at first, but when Bhikhu grabbed her hair she had no choice but to tell the truth.

Bashir's lifetime savings were not small, amounting to over a hundred rupees in coins of various denominations. Bhikhu's murders had earned him more from each victim in the past, but still he was pleased. 'Pack whatever you want to take, Pachi,' he said. 'Then we'll leave while it's still dark. The moon will be up soon, we'll walk by its light.'

Packing her things, Pachi stood up, took Bhikhu's hand and limped out to the road. Looking at the eastern sky, Bhikhu said, 'The moon will be up soon, Pachi.'

'Where are we going?' Pachi said.

'To the district town. We'll steal a boat at the river. By day we'll hide in the jungle in front of Sripatipur and reach the town at night. Hurry up, Pachi, we have more than two miles to walk.'

It was painful for Pachi to walk with her wounded leg. Coming to an abrupt halt, Bhikhu said, 'Isn't your leg hurting, Pachi?'

'Yes, it is.'

'Should I carry you on my back?'

'How will you manage?'

'I will. Come.'

Pachi clambered on to Bhikhu's back, slinging her arms round his neck. Leaning forward under her weight, Bhikhu walked briskly. The rice fields on either side lay inanimate in the pale light. The moon had risen in the sky behind the distant trees in the village. A quiet silence reigned over god's world.

No doubt the moon and this earth have their own histories. But the serial darkness that Bhikhu and Pachi had collected from their mothers' wombs and secreted within themselves when arriving on earth, the darkness which they would also secretly leave within the flesh-and-blood beings of their children, is a prehistoric one, which the light of the earth has never reached and never will.

ASHAPURNA DEVI

Deceiver and Deception

Trying to test the coldness of the icy body of someone who had died a short while ago, or perhaps earlier, Barin discovered his own fingers to be incapable of sensation. Only his numb hand trembled uncontrollably.

The trembling was not just with grief, but in fear.

And yet, it was grief that should have assailed him at this terrible moment. Or perhaps not, for the sensation that freezes the heart following the realization of death is nothing but fear. Fear! After fear came the awareness of what had happened, the sorrow, and then the mourning. Much later. Hour by hour, day by day.

But for now, Barin was in the grip of the first sensation. Frozen by a violent panic attack.

Chitra was dead.

This was the gift she had chosen for him today. Chitra had blown a small matter out of proportion. Chitra had killed herself.

This was beyond belief.

Was it really Chitra who was lying there in disarray on the bed, the blood drained from her face?

This house, this room in this house, all of it belonged to Barin. But was the man who stood in the middle of the room, who had come home without a care in his heart, calling out his wife's name, actually Barin?

The dressing table they had been gifted at their wedding lay along the wall, beckoning Barin irresistibly, but he didn't dare glance at it. What if he discovered that it was indeed Barin in the mirror? Oh god!

Forcing his eyes away from the mirror, which was drawing him like a magnet, Barin stared at the opposite wall. The one on which a calendar was hanging.

But then the calendar was a dreadful reminder too. His head reeled as he looked at it.

He couldn't forget the date.

Should Barin lose his memory? Should he forget how to tell the date? Because if he did neither, it would be obvious at once that it was 11 August, Chitra and Barin's wedding anniversary.

And then?

What would the calendar tell him after that?

Barin knew already. He knew that, as its pages blew in the wind, the calendar would announce without hesitation, this is the day on which Chitra died.

And all their friends and family, on both sides, would whisper in disbelief, 'Have you heard? Chitra took poison on their wedding anniversary.'

Suddenly Barin experienced a profound sense of disgrace, surpassing his fear.

Yes, disgrace.

Did Chitra have to humiliate him like this, just because she was angry?

Did Chitra have to heap such ignominy on Barin? Why had she left him as the accused standing trial in the court of public opinion?

Why? Why?

What was Barin's crime?

Had he ill-treated Chitra?

Not at all. Not particularly, anyway.

Chitra had wanted to invite her family to tea on the occasion of their wedding anniversary. She had said, 'We haven't asked them in our entire life, this one time on our wedding anniversary . . .'

Had Chitra sensed Barin's mood last night and said cautiously, 'I really want to ask them . . .', by now the house may have been filled with conversation, redolent with the aroma of cutlets being fried.

Because that was what Chitra had specifically said, 'Some tea and cutlets . . .'

But Chitra had said none of this last night. Meaning, Chitra had not waited for a suitable moment to speak, nor had she gauged Barin's mood. She had unceremoniously asked him to buy some meat for the cutlets when he was on his way to the market in the morning. And had added, 'We haven't asked them in our entire life . . .'

That phrase. 'Entire life.'

It was like a firecracker going off in Barin's head.

He had forgotten the occasion, forgotten the date. The words had slipped out of his mouth, 'I don't have the money to feed the hordes with cutlets.'

Yes, Barin had said this. There was no denying that it had been a horrible thing to say, though it wasn't a lie. Chitra's parents, her unmarried brother and sister, her two married sisters with their husbands and children, and her brother and his wife – seventeen or eighteen people in all. With prices going through the roof.

And so the words had slipped out.

But then Barin had tried to effect a truce. He had said, hadn't he, 'All right, let them know. I'll get out of the office early . . .'

'No,' Chitra had said.

This familiar, inflexible attitude of Chitra's had opened up a wound and rubbed salt into it. He knew, he had always known, that once Chitra was angry, she wouldn't heed anyone's request.

Still Barin had persisted, 'Don't go to the trouble of cooking at home, you make the tea, I'll leave the office early and go to the Great Eastern Hotel to . . .'

'No,' Chitra had repeated.

Barin had realized there was no hope.

She had always been stubborn.

But, penitent because of the occasion, Barin had tried to sweep her resistance away, saying, 'Come on, don't be so angry. Don't you even get a joke? All right now, you send Bhuban with a note, I'll make all the arrangements . . .'

Chitra had said, 'Don't bring any food, it'll all go to waste. I'm not asking anyone. I may not even be here myself.'

Not be here. Not be here myself. So this was what you meant.

Chitra had remained true to her word. She had told her husband of her intention to die.

But Chitra?

So vengeful? Such extreme cruelty?

Yet . . .

Barin's eyes smarted, but today it was Chitra who had labelled him 'cruel'.

But it wasn't as though nothing like this had ever taken place between them.

It had happened many times.

It had taken place, they had stopped talking to each other for a few days, then they had made up too. But not this time.

Today, Chitra had stopped talking to him forever. There would be no opportunity to make up. Not in this life.

The enormous mirror on the dressing table seemed to have acquired a form of its own to glare at Barin. He could feel its gaze. Even without looking into it, Barin knew that a woman named Chitra lay on the bed opposite it, her face blanched, while a man stood like a beaten dog at a distance, his name Barin Bose.

A name that would appear in every newspaper tomorrow. Belonging to someone who would have to say over and over again as the first witness, 'I came home early from the office because I wasn't feeling well (which was the reason he'd given at work). Instead of calling out for the servant, I opened the door myself with my latchkey. I had meant to go to bed without disturbing Chitra. But when I entered, I found her lying this way. Yes, exactly like this. I called out to her repeatedly, there was no reply. When I touched her I found . . .'

Like a gramophone record he would have to repeat the same statement flawlessly. To the doctor, to the family, to the neighbours, to the police.

Then he would have to say, 'No, we hadn't quarrelled or anything. We never really quarrelled during the eight years of our married life.' But Bhuban might spill the beans. Maybe he would blurt out, 'There was a big fight in the morning. Dada-babu left for work without eating his breakfast . . .'

He would have to have a ready-made response to this if he had to play the role of first witness.

Oh lord, why did Barin have to come home early? What if he hadn't!

Bhuban would have played this role if he hadn't come home early. Even after prolonging his afternoon nap as long as possible, when Bhuban would realize that no wake-up call was forthcoming, he would himself go looking for Boudi.

He would call her name, repeatedly, as Barin had. Then, just like Barin, he would have turned cold with fear, and he would have gone shrieking to fetch Aruna from next door. Aruna visited often. Chitra's only friend in the neighbourhood, she would have come running.

It was Aruna who would have said, 'Inform her family at once . . .'

They lived about ten minutes away, they would have come running too.

There would have been a phone call to Barin's office, 'Come home at once . . . Chitra has suddenly . . .'

Rushing home in panic, Barin would have discovered his home filled with people. The doctor, the police, the first witness being examined.

But wait, why not make just this happen? Everyone must be busy in their respective flats on this desolate afternoon. Would anyone have noted when Barin-babu from Flat No. 3 on the ground floor had arrived, and when he had left again?

No one.

Barin hadn't run into anyone.

He retreated slowly – out of the room, into the passage.

The door to the pigeon coop that was the servants' quarter was closed, which meant Bhuban had shut it so that his siesta wasn't interrupted.

God's grace was endless.

Yes, Barin could sense it now.

He went out of the flat, shutting the door behind him. Bhuban would open it when the maid arrived in the evening and rang the bell.

Chitra did it usually, complaining angrily, 'I have to open the door while Bhuban-babu sleeps.'

She would not complain today.

She would not leave her bed today. Woken up by the maid's impatient ringing of the bell, it would be Bhuban who . . . Barin stepped on the road.

Lowering his head and hunching his shoulders, he strode away quickly before he could be spotted. Only after putting some distance between himself and the house did he take a deep breath. He felt himself delivered from a terrible danger. Barin couldn't remember that the danger was actually waiting on the bed in his room, ready to pounce on him as soon as he went back in.

He breathed deeply, despite the scorching afternoon sun. He seemed to have earned himself a new life.

Then he began to plot with extraordinary skill, like a practised murderer.

Everyone at the office knows I left at exactly one-thirty. I cannot wipe out the evidence. I will have to lay out my subsequent actions perfectly.

Barin was feeling too ill to return home. So he had got off the bus near his cousin Rama's house, who lived close to his office. He would say, 'I'm feeling very sick, so I thought I'd rest here for a while. I have a terrible headache. Do you have a pill or something? Women always do. Chitra always . . .'

Barin boarded a bus that would take him back towards his office.

It was 11 August, but there was no sign of rain. Clouds and rain were like a cover. The sharp gaze of this scorching afternoon sun was cutting into Barin's body like a knife. What if someone had seen him? Maybe he had been spotted taking a bus near his house. Someone might see him now on the bus going back to his office.

If only men could draw a veil over their heads just like women.

Rama-di's house exuded wealth. It was replete with ways to rest in comfort. Chilled water from the fridge, rooms with thick curtains on the windows, air-conditioning, soft mattresses, anything you wanted. Sleeping pills? But of course. A rich man's wife cannot sleep as soon as she goes to bed. Chitra herself found sleeping difficult, and she was only the wife of a clerk.

Maybe that was the cause of her irritation.

Chitra's nerves were perpetually frayed. Maybe this was the reason.

But still Barin had never imagined Chitra betraying him in this way.

Rama-di said, 'My goodness, really? But I must say you've done the wise thing. Thank goodness you used some common sense.'

Then Rama-di busied herself arranging for her younger cousin to rest in comfort.

There was affection, of course, but also her organizational abilities, which were exemplary.

She was even about to ring the doctor, stopping only because of Barin's vehement protests.

Rama-di relinquished her own room, settling Barin on her bed and going out.

Barin had a host of objections to this air-conditioned room. Chilled water from the fridge, and then this. Despite his being suscep-tible to cold. But he had no choice but to lie down at Rama-di's insistence.

After he was left alone, Barin tried to picture once more the scene he had left behind. Again his reasoning was overcome by a wave of fear. He tried his best to convince himself that no one named Barin had been any-where near Manoharpukur a short while ago. Because of a headache he had left the office early to rest at his well-off cousin's house.

He seemed to be catching a cold.

Let him catch one, it would work in his favour. Getting a fever would be even better.

But why had the world turned so silent? Why was there no message from anyone? Barin was waiting, he couldn't sleep even after taking a sleeping pill.

But then why should the news be delivered here? No one knew that Barin was at his cousin's house, on this soft bed in this air-conditioned room, counting the minutes.

They were bound to ring Barin at his office. Which was when they would be told he had been feeling unwell, and so . . . Oh, please let Barin develop a virulent fever. Let him lie unconscious for three or four days. All the terrible agony would have abated by then. Who would interrogate an unconscious patient? Who would tell him, 'Go to the crematorium, do the rituals for Chitra'?

Who knew whether he would get a fever in natural course? It was unlikely. But Barin could feel a dreadful fever coming on. He could not shoulder all these responsibilities. Let his brother-in-law take care of everything, he was a capable man.

Not just three days – let Barin languish in his fever much longer, let the intensity of the grief in Chitra's family be lessened, and along with it the curiosity among his own family.

Let everyone's sympathy be directed at Barin. Let them tell one another, look at god's ways. While Chitra was going on her final journey, Barin was lying sick in bed.

If there's anyone named god, all he has to do is give Barin a high fever. A hundred and four or five or six degrees.

Of course there was someone named god. How else could Barin have travelled all this way without running into anyone he knew?

Had Rama-di checked what time Barin had come? Surely not. Even if she had afterwards, he would be able to confuse everyone.

But why was Barin not feeling any pain after Chitra's death? Why did he not feel any grief?

Why was Barin breathing a secret sigh of relief at having been saved?

Was Barin a monster then?

Certainly he was a monster.

How else could he have 'woken up' later in the evening and taken his place at the dining table in Rama-di's house for a cup of tea? How could he have eaten all those snacks? And, how strange, he had even felt hungry as he ate!

Was it possible to lose one's identity in the process of acting? How did Barin manage to laugh and joke with his cousin? How could he actually feel pleased when she said, 'Never mind the bus now, I'm asking Mahadeb to bring the car round to take you home'?

A wonderful arrangement!

The acting would be perfect in every way.

And there would be proof that Barin had been really ill, not even able to return home on his own.

But did Barin himself know what a monster he was? He realized it only when he saw, on getting out of the car, that the area in front of his flat looked the same as on any other day. The boys were playing in front, no cars were lined up outside the door, and Chitra stood in the iron-grill-fronted veranda, dressed in a lovely sari, her hair done up.

The sight infuriated Barin. Chitra had turned him into a performing monkey. She had betrayed him in the most insidious way. She had deceived him utterly.

This was why Barin had felt no pain, this was why. Chitra had not died.

His heart as bitter as when the sky makes all the arrangements for a nor'wester, only for the clouds to disperse, Barin went up to his door.

So she had just taken a pill to sleep like the dead. Sleeping so soundly that she couldn't wake up even when a man had all but frightened himself to death because she wasn't responding. Shame on her!

SUBODH GHOSH

Unmechanical

Bimal's obstinacy was as inexhaustible as the lifespan of his taxi, an ancient Ford of prehistoric structure with signs of hideous poverty written all over it. Only someone who simply had no choice or had never seen a motor car in his life would go anywhere near Bimal's taxi.

But although ungainly in appearance, this taxi of Bimal's was rather wondrous when it came to performance. What was impossible for a large, much-used vehicle was child's play for it. While almost all other cars were unwilling to ply on nights of torrential rain along the decrepit and dreadful roads running through forests in this remote area around mica mines, Bimal's aged taxi stepped up to the task fearlessly. Still, it was summoned out of necessity only when everyone else had refused, not before that.

Bimal's Ford usually stood dozing with the burden of its senility amid the rows of shiny young new models in the taxi rank. It was truly an eyesore. Patched hood, broken windshield, dented bonnet, soot-covered curtains, and tyres with rubber strips all over them – an exquisite beauty. Setting foot on the running board made it yelp like a dog someone had stepped on. The seats were so splotched with deep oil stains that a well-dressed person would not deign to occupy them even if someone begged them. Closing the doors was quite difficult, and even if they could be closed, opening them again was next to impossible. Sitting in the car meant being struck on the face by Bimal's homespun towel, a couple of filthy undershirts and a greasy shawl, all of them hanging from a rope strung overhead.

Every rickshaw moved to the edge of the road in trepidation as soon as they heard the distant war cry of Bimal's vehicle. Even the boldest cyclists quaked at the prospect of overtaking Bimal's taxi. In the darkness of the night a one-eyed monster could sometimes be spied in the distance, charging towards you with a grotesque roar – you had to conclude it was Bimal's car. One of the headlights had achieved nirvana. The loose joints holding the body together could explode any moment into a hundred fragments and be expelled in all directions.

Bimal's vehicle was the one to kick the most dust, provoke the oxen and emit ear-splitting sounds. But no one dared say anything to him about this. He would snap back, 'Does sir never get his hands dirty, does he never shout or run? Is it only my car that's at fault?'

There was no counting the taunts and adjectives showered on this vehicle – old crock, hobbling duck, blind bull. But Bimal had given it a loving name – Jogoddol. The rock that presses down on the entire universe. This was how he addressed it; during the long years of his busy, beleaguered work life, this mechanical beast had been his companion, a friend who had given him service, his breadwinner. One might have doubts as to whether Bimal ever got a response when he called his taxi by its name, but that was because it was difficult for a third person to gauge. Bimal, however, could interpret each of Jogoddol's desires, demands and disappointments at a glance.

'Very thirsty, aren't we, Jogoddol? Is that why you're panting? Just a minute, my boy.' Parking Jogoddol in the shade of an enormous banyan tree by the side of the road, Bimal fetched cool water from a well nearby in a bucket and poured it into the open mouth of the radiator. Glugging down four or five bucketfuls, Jogoddol calmed down and resumed its journey.

Bimal was both the owner and the driver of this taxi. Not just at present, but for fifteen consecutive years. The ancient Jogoddol stood in a corner of the taxi rank in all its misery and decrepitude. Leaning back on the smooth grey bonnet of the latest model standing next to it, Pyara Singh sniggered at Bimal, 'Enough, Bimal-babu, time for your old lady to retire.'

'Hmm, and then maintain a glamorous whore of the latest model as you have done,' Bimal retorted. Pyara Singh realized it was pointless to continue the conversation. Anything he said would infuriate Bimal, whose anger was quite wild.

A country fair was held on the day in the month of Kartik when the full moon would appear, twelve miles from here, near a temple with an idol of the god Narasimha. Passengers crowded the taxi rank, quickly filling the taxis, which promptly raced off. Old Jogoddol alone remained, gasping for breath. Who would take a ride in this vehicle of prehistoric shape and mythical appearance?

Gobindo came up to express his sympathy. 'Not a single passenger, Bimal-babu?'

'No.'

'What to do then?'

'I'll take revenge in the evening. Double the load. We'll see what happens.'

'How long can you go on with business this way? Best not to waste any more time, just swap Jogoddol for Maganlal's car in Jharia, top-class six-cylinder sedan.'

'Forget it, who'll go to so much trouble?'

'You call this trouble? And this daily pressure of quietly doubling the load, that's not going to cause any trouble?'

'Never mind all that, here, have a smoke.'

Gobindo lapsed into silence. Bimal never did tolerate anyone else discussing Jogoddol. It was best to shut up, or Bimal might swear at him any moment.

Instead of paying attention to meaningless suggestions, Bimal went off to get a canister of water – and then, using a syringe, proceeded to clean up the mud stains and dust in which Jogoddol was covered. Crawling underneath the vehicle, he turned on his back to spray water on the underside, checking carefully whether the smear of cow dung on the tyre rod was gone, rubbing the spherical bottom of the differential till it shone. He rose to his feet again to inspect his taxi – oh, how old the hood was, it had cracked in two places to display a pair of large openings.

'I have no choice, Jogoddol, make do with patchwork this time. I'm promising you a new Rexine hood if we get a couple of lucrative reservations during Durga Puja.'

Jogoddol's toilette didn't end there. Rummaging in his pocket, Bimal fished out the only coin in it to get some kerosene and busied himself polishing the rusted bolts.

Gour turned up and said, 'What's this Bimal-babu, whitewash for a ruined temple?'

With an ugly grimace Bimal snarled, 'Get out of here, who asked you to come here to yap?'

Bimal just didn't understand why everyone wanted to poke their noses in his private affairs.

'Private!' Pyara Singh rolled with laughter. 'Is your taxi a woman in your family?'

Business was on the verge of collapse, but Bimal was adamant. A peculiar bond with his hideous, aged vehicle had dulled his commercial instincts. How else to explain a notoriously bloodsucking miser like Bimal – who had fasted the entire day in Dhanbad, where food was more expensive, so that he could go to Gaya the next day and eat twice as much cheaply – lavishing his money on this taxi, which was a complete waste.

Mad Bulaki had also displayed a similar blind affection for a damaged tin tub. He would get drenched in the rain, but carefully protect the tub with an umbrella.

As evening arrived, a couple of Petromax lanterns were lit in the shops. A mass of smoke from the clay oven in the sweet shop deepened the darkness. Even the traffic policeman nearby was looking wistful. A group of farmers was approaching with cloth bundles – passengers from the hinterland. It was an auspicious hour to travel.

Bimal called out loudly – it wasn't so much a voice as a megaphone – 'Come on, come on, Ramgarh, Ranchi, Nayasarai, Mazudganj, Chitrapur, Jhalda. Discounted rate, discount.'

The offer went from their ears to their very hearts. Discount. But there were fourteen of them. Bimal stuffed all fourteen into old Jogoddol's belly, which could usually hold six. The spitting image of a kangaroo's pouch – there was no way to tell from outside how many souls were concealed within. Bimal spun the starting handle swiftly, two or three turns were all it took. Like a crazed lion, aged Jogoddol roared loudly, making the bottles of red drinks in the paan shop vibrate and give out tinkling sounds. Overwhelming the entire market with the lamentation of its horn, like the howl of a nor'wester, Jogoddol left the taxi rank and disappeared down a road on the right.

Now this was a car! The paan seller said, 'What a strange beast Bimalbabu's taxi is!'

This, in brief, was Bimal's daily routine.

The entire world had conspired against Jogoddol. This suspicion was entrenched in Bimal's head. The more he saw, the more he was surprised – why, even the birds flying overhead deposited their excreta on Jogoddol. When they had finished their paan, pedestrians didn't hesitate to rub the lime off their fingers on Jogoddol's body before making off. There were twenty-seven other vehicles of varying quality in the taxi rank, nobody dared be so disrespectful towards them. Whom had Jogoddol harmed anyway?

'Jogoddol!' Bimal called the name softly, his voice dripping with affection. All his tenderness was directed towards protecting Jogoddol from the collective cursing and constant humiliation, like an amulet might.

'Not to worry, Jogoddol. There's you and there's me.' Throwing the gauntlet down daringly, Bimal took long, reckless drags on his cigarette, seemingly preparing for a fightback.

There was an occasional stormy day, there were unexpected illnesses and repairs, forcing every one of the other vehicles not to show up for work now and then. But Jogoddol's presence was even more regular and certain than the sunrise. This too could be a cause for jealousy among fellow taxi-drivers. At least, that was Bimal's belief. A doddering geriatric who could leap and wrestle and do sit-ups effortlessly every day was bound to attract the envy of youngsters.

Bimal was perpetually swollen with unwarranted pride about Jogoddol, who had been his steadfast companion through pleasures and indulgences and crises over the past fifteen years, who had fulfilled his needs with single-minded service. People made such strange demands of Narasimha – grant me beauty, grant me glory. Bimal placed an offering of flowers and sugar crystals worth two paise at the deity's feet, uttering a silent prayer, and made a small request. 'Let Jogoddol not break down, do not rob me of my companion at this age, my lord, I beseech you.'

'The man is a machine himself,' they said at the Bengali Club. 'Imagine thinking of nothing but his motor car day and night for fifteen years. No human is capable of this.'

Bimal himself confessed he found the smell of petrol sweet and intoxicating.

'I'm a machine myself. Well said, Bengali Club.' A pleased Bimal smiled to himself. But his regret was that the Bengali Club hadn't realized that

Jogoddol was just like a human being. Even in this competitive market, amid this crowd of predatory creatures, it was good old Jogoddol who made sure he earned a couple of rupees at the end of the day. And how little fuel it consumed, racing twenty-two miles on a gallon! Jogoddol seemed to realize that Bimal was poor. Like an Arab stallion it galloped recklessly along the road to Ranchi. Its stamina, its speed, its load-bearing capacity – bravo! Bimal clutched the vibrating steering wheel with both hands while holding it steady with his chest. He could feel the thrill of Jogoddol's impudent ebullience. The icy January wind sliced the skin open like a steel knife. Bimal tugged on the muffler wrapped around his head to cover his ears. He was getting on in years, and was often overcome by the cold.

The road began to slope upwards as it wound around a hill. Jogoddol had traversed this serpentine uphill journey many times like a furiously growling cheetah who would brook no obstacle. That day too, secure in his faith, Bimal floored the accelerator. Jogoddol lurched forward fifty feet and then emitted a metallic groan, as though all its ribs had been displaced. Bimal listened to the sound with close attention. No, he wasn't mistaken. Jogoddol's piston had snapped.

A few days later, a bearing broke down unexpectedly, after which there was a new ailment every day. If it wasn't one thing it was another: today a torn fanbelt, tomorrow an oil blockage in the carburettor, the day after a short circuit from non-functioning plugs.

Was the mountain of faith tottering? Bimal had been uncharacteristically dejected for several days, rushing about madly. Jogoddol too had broken its own rule, failing to appear occasionally in the taxi rank. Bimal's heart trembled in anxiety – was Jogoddol really going to call it a day?

'No, Jogoddol, I'm here, don't worry, I *shall* make sure you recover,' vowed Bimal, seasoned automobile mechanic that he was.

He ordered genuine spare parts from Calcutta – a new battery, distributor, axle, piston. He began to spend unstintingly, wiring for overnight delivery when necessary, staying up nights to tinker with the taxi, change parts, pour in fresh oil and water. Jogoddol was unwell, and Bimal was in a frenzy. Running out of money, he sold his watch, his utensils, even his plain wooden cot.

Everything was gone, but so what? Jogoddol, his friend for fifteen years, would recover now and be happy. Bimal had done so much – with a new hood, and fresh paint and varnish, how handsome his taxi would look. His fancies seemed to be chuckling with joy in his head.

In the dead of night Bimal lifted his lantern to take a look at Jogoddol before closing the garage. His eyes brimmed with happiness. How marvellous Jogoddol was looking. Bimal's unceasing toil over the past few days had transformed Jogoddol's appearance; the vehicle was looking like a powerful, muscular wrestler, ready to leap into the ring at a single gesture. Bimal washed his face and hands and went to bed. He had toiled hard these past few days, but how comforting it was to reflect that Jogoddol had recovered! How astonished everyone would be, how they would burn with envy, when he entered the taxi rank tomorrow with Jogoddol, loudly tooting the new horn.

Bimal woke up suddenly. It was almost dawn, but still the darkness was impenetrable. It was raining torrentially. He sat up with a start; what if Jogoddol was getting drenched? The tin roof of the garage was so old, who knew how many holes it had! It would be disastrous if the rainwater seeped into the engine. The brand-new polish would also be damaged.

Entering the garage with a kerosene lamp, Bimal almost screamed in despair. Water was dripping from the roof directly on the engine. He ran into his room to fetch his raincoat, bringing his sheets and blankets too.

Wiping down the wet bonnet, Bimal put the blanket on it, and then the raincoat. Covering every inch of the vehicle with sheets, he crept inside, curling up luxuriously on the new, soft seat. An avalanche of sleep seemed to descend on his eyes.

The story of the next day? An eager crowd surrounded Jogoddol at the taxi rank, as though a miracle had taken place. Voicing their admiration, the audience gazed at Bimal's handiwork as a mechanic. On his part, Bimal laughed long and loud several times, but the laughter wasn't pure, it was murky with traces of anxiety.

Why? There was an ache in Bimal's heart, a spreading doubt. It was true Jogoddol was moving again, but where was the high, powerful roar that used to emerge on starting the engine, where were the arrogant snorts and the pace of the wild deer?

Driving Jogoddol to a field some distance from the town, Bimal conducted a thorough examination.

'Now, my boy, it's time to spread your wings like a flying horse, Jogoddol.' Bimal pressed down on the accelerator.

First, second, third – Bimal shifted through all the gears. Finally, he lost his head in anger. 'Move, or I'll give you a kick.'

Jogoddol limped along, gasping like a worn-out old man.

'Doesn't understand loving words, doesn't understand requests, bloody heap of iron, a piece of junk.' Bimal actually delivered a couple of mighty kicks to the clutch.

His fury kept increasing, that infamous wild rage of his. He would extract an answer today, once and for all. Did Jogoddol intend to move or remain immobile? Enough of appeasement.

Had Bimal gone quite mad with rage? He rolled seven or eight enormous rocks up to his taxi, his khaki shirt bloated with perspiration. One by one he loaded the rocks into the vehicle. Now this was a load! And Jogoddol would have to bear this burden today, Bimal would find out if the taxi still had its old power, or whether it was spent forever.

'Move!' Jogoddol moved, but every joint screeched in protest. No, Jogoddol could not carry this weight.

Now Bimal was sure. Jogoddol was in the grips of death. The truth could no longer be doubted. Such a stout heart, but it had withered away. The god of death was calling, there was no escape now, the sun was about to set. Bimal had spent his last penny, but Jogoddol had not survived.

Now it's just me . . . an exhausted Bimal hummed in his head. But I am almost done for too. My hair has greyed, my skin clings to my bones like leeches. The day when I too will be among the rejects, panting and limping like Jogoddol, is not far away.

Lighting a cigarette, Bimal stared at Jogoddol. A desolate feeling of regret seemed ready to burst out of him. 'Looks like Jogoddol will be the first to go. And then it will be my turn. Go, Jogoddol, I bid you farewell without rancour. You took care of me for a long time, how long can you go on? Leave me to my fate.' An unprecedented event took place: two warm teardrops trembled in Bimal's eyes. Bimal, who was usually as dry and cold as a steel bullet.

Returning to the garage, Bimal parked Jogoddol beneath a tree outside and got out. He didn't look back, going into the yard and setting two bottles of toddy on the ground in front of him.

He had barely taken a sip when he heard someone calling his name. 'You there, Bimal-babu?' It was Gobindo. He entered, followed by a Marwari man, a trader, who greeted Bimal.

'Which brand of car are you an agent for?' Bimal asked. Introducing the stranger, Gobindo said, 'He isn't an agent, he's here from Calcutta to buy scrap iron. You have all those broken-down axles and rims. Negotiate a price and let him take them.'

Bimal gazed steadily at both of them. The phantom of destiny was here with a demand for what he wanted the most, holding out his begging bowl. He wouldn't leave without the finest alms. Bimal understood.

'Yes, I have scrap iron, lots of it, how much are you paying?'

'Fourteen annas a maund,' the trader answered eagerly. 'It's wartime, here's your chance to get rid of everything.'

'Yes, yes, I will. That car of mine too. It's useless.'

All that a bewildered Gobindo could say was, 'What are you saying, Bimal-babu?'

Bimal came to his senses after a spell of sleep. It was still night, so he finished the second bottle too and went back to sleep.

Now it was nearly dawn. Bimal kept waking up. There was just the one sound spilling over from the noise of the waking world outside – bang clang clanggg. The trader's people had appeared before sunrise to break Jogoddol into pieces and haul them away.

Grief and drunkenness. Jogoddol's ribs were falling off one by one. Bimal's consciousness was spiralling down an endless whirlpool of silence into the depths. Only to lose all weight and float up to the surface the next moment. And through it all Bimal could hear the sounds, bang clang clanggg. Some people were digging a grave for a dead and dismembered Jogoddol. Bang clang clanggg, the sounds of spades and crowbars.

NARENDRANATH MITRA

Organic

'. . . therefore we have to examine the basis and the accuracy of the commonly accepted ideas on heredity. From physical structure to mental abilities and proclivities, how much is passed on by parents and ancestors to descendants? And how does the influence of the environment – the climate, family education and practices, the company of friends – modify heredity and control the course of life? . . .'

Switching off the radio, Karabi said with a gesture of annoyance, 'Same old lecture again. Here I was hoping for some nice music, but . . .'

Lying back in the deckchair, her friend Basab Mukherjee the doctor was smoking quietly. Suddenly he said, 'Oh did you turn it off?'

'Obviously,' replied Karabi. 'Do you want to hear ridiculous lectures by unknown people?'

'You can't tell for sure whether it's ridiculous. The man isn't exactly a non-entity, though. He's a university scholar, a professor at a college here . . .'

Karabi was deflated, but didn't abandon her argument. 'What if he is a scholar,' she countered. 'And just because he's a professor . . .'

'That's not all,' said Basab, 'I do know Mriganka Majumdar quite well.'

'Ah, I see now,' responded Karabi. 'So that's why you were listening to the talk with such attention. It's true, I too love listening to my family or friends on the radio or on the phone.'

She was about to turn the radio on again when Basab stopped her. 'What's this, are you turning it on again? No, don't.'

Now I said in irritation, 'But why? Didn't you say it was your friend the professor?'

'But I didn't say we have to listen to the lecture in its entirety. And besides, I don't care to listen to my friends on the radio – I don't have an ear like your wife's.'

'Of course you don't,' I smiled. 'You can at best tuck a leather stethoscope into your own ear, but how will you have a jewel-bedecked organ like my wife's?'

'That's true,' Basab smiled as well.

'Then you don't want to listen to your friend's talk?' asked Karabi.

'No, I don't,' replied Basab. 'I don't enjoy these talks of Mriganka-babu's at all. He should realize how much they hurt Sudatta, how much she suffers. The reaction that these speeches . . .'

Karabi's curiosity appeared not just in her voice but also on her face. 'Who's Sudatta?'

Basab looked embarrassed at his impulsive statement.

'Sudatta is Mriganka-babu's wife,' he said gravely.

'Then why should she mind listening to her husband's lecture?' enquired Karabi. 'Really, the things you say!'

'That's true,' I said, trying to lighten matters. 'Even a meaningless talk by one's husband and a tuneless song by one's wife are still sweetest to each other's ears.'

My joke fell flat, for Basab still looked solemn. Ignoring what I had said, Karabi looked at Basab. 'What's the story, Basab-babu? Of course, if it's confidential . . .'

'Very confidential,' said Basab with a smile. 'I might have been able to satisfy your curiosity to some extent, but it's difficult to tell you.'

'It needn't be,' said Karabi. 'My nerves are no less strong than anyone else's.'

'Women always think and say that at first,' Basab smiled again. 'But what happens eventually . . .'

Impatiently Karabi said, 'We'll wait for the end to see what happens eventually. But if you do want to tell us, please start at the beginning.'

Flicking the ash from his cigarette, Basab said, 'Very well then, listen. But from the middle, not the beginning. Because not even I know how it started . . .'

All this happened during the riots. The dispensary was not particularly crowded that day. Most of my patients were Muslim, who couldn't visit the Hindu neighbourhood because of the aftermath of the riots. Nor was it safe for me to venture into their area. But groceries wouldn't wait for riots to end. And buying them needed money. I was quite upset. Normally there would be a crowd of patients till nine or nine-thirty at night, but that evening the dispensary was emptied out by eight o' clock. The few patients from the neighbourhood who did turn up usually received their treatment out of courtesy. Sending them on their way, I was thinking of leaving when a taxi suddenly stopped with a loud noise in front of the dispensary. Sensing the arrival of a patient, I sat up eagerly, tidying my desk in a flash. The visitor had entered by then.

He looked familiar. Hesitating, I said, 'Take a seat, please.'

Taking a chair, the handsome, well-built man of twenty-seven or twenty-eight said, 'I don't think you recognize me. We had studied at Scottish together for a couple of years.'

'Oh yes,' I said, 'I remember now. Your name is . . .'

'Mriganka Majumdar.'

'It's been a long time,' I said.

'It has,' he agreed. 'Look, I'm here to see you for a special reason.'

I looked at Mriganka-babu. Tall, strong, fair of complexion, with a broad forehead and back-brushed hair. I didn't see any signs of illness. But then ailments are not always visible at first sight. Not even to a doctor.

'Tell me.'

Glancing around the dispensary, Mriganka-babu said, 'It's absolutely confidential.'

There wasn't another soul in the dispensary. Across the partition dividing the room, Ramesh the compounder was nodding off on a stool in front of the medicine cupboard. Haridas the servant was not nearby either. He was probably chatting at the paan and cigarette shop down the road.

'You can tell me here,' I said. 'And if you're uncomfortable here, we can go into the cabin next door.'

Glancing in turn at the door leading into the cabin and at the taxi waiting outside, Mriganka-babu said, 'My wife is in the taxi.'

I had already realized that there was a lady in the vehicle, but pretending that I had only learnt this now, I said, 'Oh please bring her inside.'

'I will if necessary,' he said.

'Would you like to go into the cabin then?' I asked.

'No need, I'll tell you here,' he responded. 'She's in the family way. But we don't want it. You understand?'

'I do,' I said. 'How long?'

'Slightly advanced stage,' he said. 'Fourth month.'

'Quite advanced,' I said, 'not slightly. There's nothing to be done now. And besides, if you don't mind, why are you even considering this option? Do you have other children?'

'No.'

'Well then? And besides, it's best to be careful about these things beforehand.'

'We did take precautions.'

'Did they fail? But how can you not even allow a child or two to be born? How old is your wife?'

'Twenty-three or so,' he said.

'It's best to have a child at this age,' I told him.

'I know,' said Mriganka-babu, 'but I simply cannot persuade her.'

Surprised, I said, 'I don't understand why women do not care for motherhood these days. If you'd like to bring her in here, I can try to explain things. And besides, there's nothing to be done now. No reasonable person will agree.'

'Other doctors have said the same thing,' said Mriganka-babu. 'Very well, why don't you try to convince Sudatta? I don't want anything like this at all. I know very well how high the risks are. But still she won't listen.'

Mriganka-babu fetched his wife from the taxi. Tall, slim, fair and beautiful. She seemed quite healthy, displaying no sign of fatigue or tiredness even in this condition. I could not understand the reason for her peculiar demand.

'Come into the cabin here,' I said.

The lady looked pleased. As though she had received promising news.

All of us entered the cabin, sitting side by side on the padded bench.

Before I could speak, the lady said, 'You're willing, then. Can you do it?'

'No one can,' I shook my head. 'Why are you even considering such an impossible step?'

Sudatta seemed to pale for a moment, but the very next moment she said in agitation, her face reddening, 'Look, I haven't come to you for a moral lecture. Several doctors have given me the same lecture over the past month and a half. Tell me whether there's a way or not. Doesn't matter how much it costs . . .'

Offended at hearing a beautiful, educated, well-bred woman say such things, I said, 'It isn't a question of money. Let's put aside the question of ethics too for now. But when there's a risk to your life . . .'

'Risk to my life!' Sudatta wailed helplessly. 'You have no idea how I'm dying every moment. My stomach turns continuously, I feel nauseous all the time. It's like a thousand thorns in my flesh. I cannot stand it, I simply cannot. Please save me. Rescue me from this filth. I shall be grateful to you forever.'

I looked at Mriganka-babu in surprise. He looked in silence at his semi-hysterical wife.

It was Sudatta herself who spoke a little later. 'Explain to him, explain everything. There's no need to conceal anything.'

'But disclosing everything will not change medical science, Sudatta. We disclosed everything to the other doctors too,' said Mriganka-babu.

'Tell him too. I'm sure he can offer us a solution.'

Mriganka-babu indicated that I should accompany him into the next room. Sudatta remained in the cabin.

Hesitating a little, Mriganka-babu finally told me briefly, 'My wife was in Lahore during the riots in north India.'

'With a relative?' I asked.

'Yes, that is where the whole terrible thing took place. We managed to rescue Sudatta from a small princely state about three months later. But she simply cannot return to a normal state of mind – all she does is visit one doctor after another. And yet I know very well that in this condition there's nothing that doctors can do, or should do.'

'No,' I nodded. 'We must explain things to her and calm her down.'

'Of course,' said Mriganka-babu. 'I have tried my best. What else is it but an accident? We must wait for the proper time.'

'Why don't you send her to her parents?' I asked. 'She might be at peace there.'

'Her parents are dead,' said Mriganka-babu. 'She has a distant uncle and aunt. I did force her to go to them, but she came back in a day or two. They know everything, and they're not willing to shoulder the responsibility.'

'I have bothered you unnecessarily,' said Mriganka-babu, rising to his feet. 'Your fees ...'

'Absolutely not,' I told him. 'I'd have liked to have helped you, but in this condition ... However, if you need me later ...'

'Certainly,' said Mriganka-babu. 'We will definitely need your help, we'll have to arrange for a hospital when the time comes. I don't know many people here ...'

'That won't be a problem,' I assured him. 'I know the people at Carmichael particularly well. All the arrangements will be made there. Don't worry.'

'Thanks very much,' Mriganka-babu responded. 'Why don't you visit us at home one of these days? My house is on Beadon Street. I'd be delighted if you came. Those college days really were the best, you know.'

'You're right,' I said.

Pausing, Basab glanced at Karabi. She was leafing through a magazine in silence. But I had no doubt that she was as keen as before on listening to the rest of the story. 'And then?' I asked.

Lighting another cigarette, Basab continued, 'I met them several times over the next five or six months ...'

The better I got to know them, the more my respect for Mriganka-babu grew. To tell the truth, I did not hold the so-called good boys of college in high regard. I believed that the attentive students and the first-class degree holders were in reality quite third-class. Mriganka-babu changed my view-point. His own subject was chemistry. But his interests were not limited to chemistry – he was eager to know about the other branches of science too, as well as literature, politics and sociology. However, what attracted me most was not his erudition but his amiability, courtesy and civility. I was particularly pleased to see the ease with which he had accepted the accident that had taken place in his wife's life. Whatever I may say, I am not sure whether I could have accepted it had it happened to me.

Mriganka-babu told me one day in the course of conversation, 'You must have been surprised by our behaviour that evening. I knew it could not be – I was not willing to take the slightest risk. But what could I do, I simply could not persuade Sudatta. It was to get you to see her that ...'

'I realized as much,' I said. 'Or else someone like you would never have made such a strange proposal . . .'

When she reached an even more advanced stage, Sudatta finally desisted from her attempts. She too realized that there was no choice but to wait for the inevitable – no one would help her, no one would be able to help her.

But although she had stopped trying, the whole thing continued to bother her. One day she said with great indignation, 'I no longer have any faith in your medical science.'

I was silent, not inclined to defend the medical sciences. Mriganka-babu had told me in great detail how much his wife was suffering. Sudatta could not shake off a constant feeling that she was impure and infected. She trembled even in her husband's ardent embrace, or turned stiff. Mriganka-babu felt a certain stiffness too in response to his wife's behaviour, but his patience was infinite, and his scientific tolerance astounding. There was no limit to his efforts to bring his wife back to normal. Earlier, Mriganka-babu did not like going to the cinema or the theatre, considering them harmful for his work. Sudatta would go with other friends and relatives. But after the incident, Mriganka-babu himself became her companion. Not that Sudatta wanted to go out very often, preferring to stay holed up inside the house day and night. But it was I who had suggested not leaving her by herself. It would be better to be out and about at this time, so that she got some sunlight and fresh air. She had to be kept cheerful.

Of course, Sudatta did not take any of this advice. On the contrary, she subjected her body to as many hardships as possible. She didn't bathe or eat on time, torturing herself in different ways. Her objective was obvious.

One day Sudatta asked, 'Can't something be done so that this thing inside me is destroyed on its own, Basab-babu? I cannot endure this any more.'

I could make out that she would send for me sometimes precisely to say such things, to discuss such possibilities. Mriganka-babu was also keen that I visit them, and that Sudatta talk about these things with me. This would help her find an outlet for all the hatred and abhorrence bottled up within, while offering her some satisfaction and relief.

Then there was a new development. Mriganka-babu told me the story.

A distant aunt of his used to live in Varanasi. Visiting Calcutta to have her eyes treated, she stayed at Mriganka-babu's house for some time. I arranged for her to be admitted to the Medical College. She had cataracts in both her eyes and would need an operation. Mriganka-babu's aunt not only had bad eyesight, but was also hard of hearing. She had not heard of the riots or of the crisis in Mriganka-babu's life.

But however weak her eyesight might have been, Sudatta's pregnancy did not escape her notice.

'How many months? Have you done the ceremonies?'

'We don't believe in these rituals, Pishima,' Mriganka-babu told her, shaking his head.

'Why should you?' she said. 'Godless Christians, the whole lot of you. Do you know what happens if you don't do the rituals? The child grows up greedy, drools all the time. You won't be able to take it in your arms, your clothes will be ruined. Do the ceremonies while there's still time. Give her whatever she wants to eat. You're not feeding someone else's daughter – your own child who's living in her womb will taste all this good food through its mother. But then it's like father, like son. You're as much of a miser as my brother is.'

Mriganka-babu's father had lived in Calcutta for some time, only going back to his family home in the village once things had quietened down. All his property was over there, and he had to look after everything himself.

It was Mriganka-babu's aunt who made all the arrangements for the rituals, bullying her nephew into getting whatever was necessary. She made the sweets herself, bought new saris, and presented everything to the mother-to-be.

Out of her husband's aunt's sight, Sudatta threw everything into the drain. Summoning her husband she said, 'Maybe Pishima has no idea, but why must *you* humiliate me?'

And then she began to cry into her pillow, refusing to bathe or eat or go out.

Mriganka-babu's aunt stayed in hospital for nearly a month after the surgery. 'Tell me if you'd like me to stay longer,' she told Mriganka when leaving. 'Someone should be with her at this time.'

'I don't want to hold you back, Pishima,' said Mriganka-babu. 'Don't worry, I'll get a nurse.'

A little upset, the aunt said, 'Very well, let me know once it all goes off well. Don't forget to send a postcard telling me whether it's a boy or a girl. May the god Bishwanath send you a son. I'll send offerings to his temple. The boy will be named Bishsheshwar.'

'It's almost time for your train,' Mriganka-babu told her. 'Better finish your packing.'

Another family of tenants lived on the ground floor of Mriganka-babu's house. Husband, wife and mother-in-law. The wife had not had a child. Several doctors had been consulted, many vows made at different temples. Amulets and lucky charms adorned her wrists and throat. Sometimes she told Sudatta, 'What are all these Western ways of yours, didi? A precious jewel is coming your way, and I don't hear a sound out of you. Winter's coming. Get some clothes and socks ready. You'll be in trouble afterwards.'

'We don't need those things,' Sudatta said in an attempt to avoid her.

'What do you mean you don't need them?' said the woman. 'Maybe I haven't had a child of my own, didi, but that doesn't mean I don't know anything. My three sisters have thirteen children between them. If you don't get some swaddling clothes ready now, it will be very difficult later. Very well, if you're not up to it, get me the wool, I'll knit them for you, you won't have to worry about a thing. People desperate for a baby don't get one, and you ...'

When Sudatta didn't get her any wool even after this, the woman got her own husband to get some and began to knit socks and caps.

'This is the limit,' Sudatta told her husband. 'Better tell them everything. Let the entire world know – it's horrible, horrible, I can't take this any more ...'

But Mriganka-babu could take it. I never saw his patience crack in the slightest in his conversations and behaviour with his wife.

Eventually it was time. As you know, I was the house surgeon at Carmichael for some time. They still hold me in high regard. There was no problem. A cabin was booked for Sudatta, and two nurses were engaged. I requested Dr Bose from the ward to take special care of her. Still Mriganka-babu said to me, 'I would be grateful if you were present ...'

'There'll be no need,' I told him with a smile. 'Still, I will make enquiries to the best of my abilities. I'm also making arrangements to be informed on the phone immediately after the delivery.'

Even Sudatta smiled at her husband's anxiety. 'There's nothing to worry about, don't fret so much . . .'

The smile on Sudatta's face appealed to me very much. So did her way of reassuring her husband. She herself appeared to be confident. At long last, there would be a release from anxiety, worry and discomfort. All the arrangements had already been made with the hospital authorities. After the delivery, the nurse would take the child away, and then hand it over to the sweeper or someone like that, or else to an orphanage or something. The hospital would make all the arrangements – Mriganka-babu would not have to be involved. They did get such cases here from time to time. The nurses knew what to do – they only had to be paid. The money was never wasted.

'But whatever you may say, Basab-babu, I'm not happy about this,' said Mriganka-babu. 'I have never knowingly resorted to lies. And now I have to be involved in this deception.'

'What's the alternative?' I said.

'Don't pay any attention to him,' Sudatta said firmly. 'No better arrange-ment could have been made.'

The nurse rang me from the hospital. Sudatta had given birth to a son in the early hours of the morning. Mrs Majumdar hadn't suffered too much. The child was well too – quite a healthy child.

I gave the first half of the news to Mriganka-babu.

'Let's pay Sudatta a visit,' he said.

I was a little irritated. Why draw me into this? 'I'm busy till one in the afternoon,' I said.

'Very well, we'll go at one then.'

We arrived at the hospital together, parting the curtains to enter Mrs Majumdar's cabin with the nurse. Both of us paused as soon as we crossed the threshold. A nurse was sitting on the stool, holding the baby – wrapped in an expensive towel – in her arms. And Sudatta was gazing at her child. Her eyes held no loathing, no antagonism, not a single sign of discomfort or unhappiness. A deep sense of peace and satisfaction had turned her expression entirely natural, beautiful and tranquil.

But she was flustered when she saw us. The blood rose on her wan, exhausted face. The next moment she scolded the nurse, 'Take him away. Who asked you to bring him here?'

The nurse stared in surprise for a moment before leaving with a chuckle. I was looking at Sudatta, and had no opportunity to observe any change in Mriganka-babu's demeanour. I saw no contortions on his face when I turned to him.

A little later he asked his wife lovingly, 'How are you, Sudatta?'

It took some time for Mrs Majumdar to regain her composure. Lowering her eyes, she said, 'Very well.'

'I was so scared,' said Mriganka-babu.

After a silence Sudatta said, 'There was nothing to be scared of.'

Mriganka-babu seemed to smile. 'No, I'm relieved now.'

We went out of the room after a while. Suddenly Mriganka-babu said, 'Cancel all the arrangements, Basab-babu. We'll take him home.'

'What!' I was astonished. 'How is that possible? And why should Mrs Majumdar agree? Don't try to do this, Mriganka-babu, don't complicate things further.'

Lighting a cigarette, Mriganka-babu said, 'There's nothing complicated about it. Motherhood is the simplest thing in the world, the clearest.'

'What are you saying?' I protested. 'Motherhood doesn't exist in a vacuum these days. Society, respect, superstitions, the sense of convenience and inconvenience – all these things are connected with it. The mother's love that you saw on Mrs Majumdar's part might just be temporary, merely physical.'

'All love is,' said Mriganka-babu with a smile.

He paid no heed to my objections and cancelled all the arrangements made with the nurses at once.

'But Mrs Majumdar . . .' I said.

'I'll manage everything,' said Mriganka-babu. 'Don't worry.'

He sounded more than a little annoyed.

'Why should I worry?' I told myself.

Mriganka-babu took his wife and son home a week later. I heard that Sudatta had objected strongly. But Mriganka-babu had paid no attention. 'Are you mad?' he had said. 'Maybe he isn't as beautiful as you, a bit on the dark side, but that doesn't mean you will leave your own son behind.'

Mriganka-babu telephoned me after they had reached home, saying, 'It's all sorted. I'm sorry to have troubled you so much . . .'

'Not at all,' I said.

A patient of mine, a labourer, was in my dispensary at the time, accompanied by his wife and two children. The elder one was a boy. The labourer was there to have his wife treated. I prescribed medicines. When the elder child saw that his younger sister had climbed on her mother's lap, he made the same demand. The husband took him on his own lap.

'Your son loves you, doesn't he?' I asked.

'Yes, Daktar-babu,' he answered. 'He follows me about everywhere.'

I smiled to myself. The boy was his wife's son from her first marriage. He had been my patient for a long time – I knew everything about them. He had married his present wife after her first husband died. The boy used to be in her arms all the time – and now he had happily abandoned her lap to sit on my patient's. It was all a matter of habit, of practice. Considering Mriganka's willpower, nothing was impossible for him.

I didn't keep track of Mriganka-babu for a year after this. They did not try to keep in touch either. I had chosen to maintain a distance. My company might not have been preferable or pleasant.

But about a month ago, Mrs Majumdar suddenly rang me and said she was ill. She would be extremely obliged if I could visit her at home.

'Very well,' I said. 'But where's Mr Majumdar?'

'He's out of town.'

I had a call to make in Haripal Lane nearby. By the time I was done there it was one-thirty in the afternoon, after which I went to Mriganka-babu's house.

Their old retainer Amulya had known me since last year. With a smile he said, 'Come in, Daktar-babu, you haven't been here in a long time.'

There did not appear to be anyone severely ill at home. I followed Amulya upstairs. Mriganka-babu and his family had rented three rooms in this building. One of these was his library, a second one was the drawing room, and the inner room – the largest of the three – was where Sudatta's universe was located. I saw that the doors to the two other rooms were padlocked.

Sudatta came up to the door when she heard me. 'I thought you wouldn't come.'

She seemed to have become more beautiful – her earlier restlessness had disappeared. Her face was serene and solemn, but there was a hint of melancholy in her eyes.

'What are you ill with?' I asked.

'Must you ask about illness the moment you step in?' she smiled.

'No one summons the doctor in wellness,' I said.

Sudatta did not answer.

A child of about a year was asleep in a cradle inside the room. 'I hope your son's well,' I said.

'Yes, there's nothing wrong with Bishu,' Sudatta said.

'Bishu?' I asked.

Blushing a little, Sudatta said, 'We took Pishima's suggestion. His name is Bishsheshwar.'

Taking the padded chair, I said, 'Very nice name. So no one's ill. I was worried when I heard. Glad everything's well. Did Mriganka-babu leave town suddenly?'

'Yes, he's gone to Nagpur. Apparently a new variety of guinea pig has appeared there. He wants to collect a few specimens.'

'Guinea pig!' I exclaimed in surprise. 'What does he want with guinea pigs!'

Sudatta replied, 'He needs them for his cross-breeding experiments.'

'Cross-breeding!' I said.

Sudatta looked into my eyes. 'Yes, biology is his main subject now. Heredity . . .'

Suddenly she said, 'I can't take it any more, Daktar-babu.'

I tried to smile. 'When you've married a scientist, these little nuisances . . .'

'Nuisance!' Sudatta said sharply. 'Is a scientist's wife not human, Daktar-babu? Is she a rat or a guinea pig?'

Sudatta told me the entire story. Pointing to the locked rooms, she said, 'Both those rooms are now full of biology textbooks and bottles stuffed with worms. He probably wanted to put Bishu in one of those bottles too, but maybe you don't need so much care when testing for the effect of the environment on human beings.'

I was flabbergasted. 'What are you saying?'

Sudatta explained that she had tried her best to have Bishu sent away.

But Mriganka-babu had refused. Who gives away one's own possessions? Bishu was nothing but an object for Mriganka-babu – an ingredient for his experiments. But Sudatta could not bear to see all this. Mriganka-babu had arranged for expensive toys, clothes and food for Bishu. He enquired after the child at least three or four times a day, took him in his arms, kissed him too. Then he stopped abruptly to inspect Bishu and take notes. How was Sudatta to endure the look in his eyes when this happened?

I didn't know what to say. After a silence, I rose. 'I'm in a hurry today, Sudatta-debi. For now . . .'

'No, stay a little longer,' she stopped me. 'I have something else to tell you.'

'What?' I said in surprise.

Sudatta was silent for a few moments, hesitating a little. Then suddenly she said, 'Look, this time too I want . . . It's not as advanced as last time. Surely you can help me this time.'

Startled, I asked, 'What are you trying to tell me?'

Sudatta had been speaking with her eyes on the floor all this time. Now she looked at me directly. The same frenzied look in them. As though she couldn't tolerate it this time either. Today too her entire body was shaking with an unknown hatred and repugnance.

Like last time, Sudatta looked at me directly. 'I'm sure you know what I want. I don't wish to provide material for your scientist friend's comparative studies.'

Basab stopped, lighting a cigarette. I was about to speak when Karabi jumped up and turned the radio on quickly. Neither a talk nor a story, but a song.

On a music request show.

'Thank goodness!' she said.

SATYAJIT RAY

Pikoo's Diary

Im writing a diry. Im writing a diry in my blue new blue notebook. Im writing in my bed. Dadu writes a diry every day too but not now because he fell sik. I know the name of the sikness and the name is coronany thombosi. Baba doesnt write a diry. Ma doesnt either not even dada only dadu and I. My notebook is bigger than dadus. Onukul got it he said it was twenty paise ma gave him the money before. Ill write in my diry every day when theres no school. Theres no school today its not Sunday only its a holiday because strike. We often have holidays because strike thats why so much fun. Luckily the notebook is ruled so my writing is straight. Dada writes straight without rules on the page and baba of course but baba has no holidays. Dada also. Ma also. Ma does not work in office only at home. She is not home now she has gone out with hitesh uncle she said she will bring me a gift from new market. Ma gives me many gifts these days. A pencil sharpener then a ristach its always 3 o clok on it, a hokistik and a ball. Oh and a book grim fairy tales it has lots of pictures. God knows what she will bring today maybe airgun or something thats what she said lets see. Dhingra shot a magpai with an airgun I will also aim and go bang at a sparrow it sits on the railing every day it will just die. Last night there was a bom so loud baba said bom ma said no firing maybe it is the police baba said no bom lots of bangs these days through the widnow. Car horn must be hitesh uncles i know he has a stendad heral then ma is back.

Ma brought airgun yesterday from new market hitesh uncle gave it he said this is from me pikoo-babu not from your mother. Hitesh uncle bought a ban for his ristach I said its a tisot he said no tiso the t is silent so. My airgun is very good I have many pelets in a large tin more than hunred. Hitesh uncle taught me I fired just like that in the air onukul jumped in fear. The sparrow didnt come yesterday not today also hes notty but he will definitely come tomorrow and I will be ready of course. Baba said why a gun when he came home ma said so what baba said you have no sense ma said why are you shouting as soon as you have come home baba said no baba yes baba spoke in english ma also in English, ma very fast just like the movies. I have seen jeri luis clin istwud another hindi movie with miludi no fighting in it ono the ink is

I filled my pen with babas green ink which is quing with a dropa ma used the same dropa for medisin when she had a cold. Today I am writing my diry at babas desk. The phone went kiring kiring just now I ran up and said hallo oh it was baba baba said is that pikoo i said yes baba said is ma not home i said no baba said where is she i said ma has gone with hitesh uncle to watch a film a film for grown ups so she is not home. Baba said I see and put the phone down with a kerak sound I heard it. Then I dialled one seven four and they told me the time I hear it sometimes I cannot tell what rubbish they say. The sparrow came today. I was waiting with airgun by the widnow the sparrow did come and I went bang and the pellet was in the wall I saw a hole in Dhingras wall. The sparrow flu off in gret fear. Yesterday on the roof dadas aim terrific aim he put an empty pot of curd the smallest pot on the tank then from a long way off bang and the pot was in pieces some of the pieces even fell on the road what if they hit someone on the head I said. Dada is much older twelve years so terrific aim he goes to college I go only to school. He goes out every day I stay at home only movies sometimes and I have seen one CLT. Dada came home very late last night so baba scolded him loudly and he also spoke loudly I woke up so loudly I could not finish a luvly dreem. I was going very fast on a horse galoping Dhingra could not catch me and hitesh uncle gave me a new gun a revolver and said this one is called fiso and dadu was a cowboy he was saying come dadubhai let us go to victoria memoria and that was when I woke up. Bathroom now.

There was a parti at home last night but not my birthday but just like that a parti. Everyone came only grown ups so I did not go but I peeped in. Only babas friends and mas friends and not dadas friends though. Dada isnt here since yesterday or maybe the day before I dont know where he is. Dada is in politis so baba keeps saying hopeless ma also. Ma says dont go so I dont go to partis but I had three sosages yesterday and a cocacola. There was a white man he laughs very loudly ho ho ho ha ha ha and a white lady. And mister menun and misses mennun and another man must be a sikh I could tell from his turban. Once I heard from my room everyone laughing very loudly. Once ma came into the room and went to the bathroom and looked into the mirror once and another time another lady went into the bathroom and misses menun whose sent was very strong a new sent ma doesnt have. Then ma came again and said what darling you are awake go to sleep I said I am afraid by myself ma said afraid of what silly boy go to sleep its eleven close your eyes you will sleep at once I said wheres dada ma said enough go to sleep then she left. But baba didnt come into the room baba these days baba and ma quarrel a lot in english and sometimes in bangla. But no fights in partis so partis good only drings and one day someone vomited ma said he was sik but onukul said dring. Our frij is full of it and when the bottle is empty its used for cold water and when it smells ma scolds sukhdeo says in hindi not washed properly. And sukhdeo says why does he call ma memsaab is she a white lady and is she a forener its very funny. Then I went to sleep no one knows when sleep will come dadu says dying means long sleep and only dreems and whatever you want to see dreems only.

I hide my diry no one knows the place where I hide it. Thats our old gramophone you have to wind it up by hand no one plays it any more becos the new one is electric and long play so no one plays the old one so my diry is in there and thats why no one knows I write a diry. I write a lot so my fingers hurt a bit so when ma was cutting my nails I said aah ma said whats wrong diz it hurt I said no or else ma would find out I write a diry. Dadu said dont show your diry to anyone he writes it and reads it himself only he no one else. I have twenty two pellets left I counted but the sparrow is very notty he didnt come back. I only fire at the tank on the roof there is a ting sound and small round marks on the tank so Im thinking of shooting pijuns they sit quietly and walk and dont fly much. Dada has not been home for five days so his room is empty and there is a shirt on the rack its white and blue pants and all his books. Yesterday when I was blowing a bubble a large one I clearly heard a horn and I said hitesh uncle and ma said why dont you go to dhingras house its dhingras holiday too. I said dhingra keeps pulling my sideburns near my ears it hurts I won't go so ma said then roof with your airgun I said then Ill shoot at pijuns ma she said very bad why should you do that fire in the air now go I said huh what will I aim at in the air then ma said then why dont you go to onukul then I said onukul only plays cards and the doorman and sukhdeo and another man they all play cards so im not going anywhere. Then ma slapped me so hard I hit the bedpost. I cried a bit but not much and then ma went off I cried a bit more but not much then I wondered what to do now. Then I thought lets see whats in the frij I found two sweets and one krimrol from trinka I ate all of it then straight from the botl I didnt pour it into a glass. Then I saw an illustrated weekly on baba's desk but no good pictures only a donel duk. Then I ran into the veranda and did a little haijum over a stul the first one was smal so very easy but I scraped my leg against the big one so I saw there was a small cut a little blood so to the bathroom there is dettol there dettol doesnt hurt but tinaraidin does so I put dettol. I ran off at once and saw a jet plen go by very fast when baba went off in a jet I went to dumdum and baba brought an electik sheva from london for himself and two pairs of shoes for me and an astonot it was a toy but very large ronida broke it. Now let me do some sums.

I'm writing my diry again today. Ive run out of pellets and why couldnt I hit the pijun the gun must be lousy I think I will throw it away then. I found a machboks in dada's drawer today he must be smoking otherwise why machboks. But dada hasnt returned god alone knows where he is or maybe even god doesnt know. Now if ma also leaves Ill be in trouble last night ma told baba she will leave I had napped in the afternoon so I was awake but I kept my eyes shut tight so ma thought pikoo is sleeping and baba also so they were talking very loudly. Now only dadu and I are at home onukul must be playing cards so there is no one at home only dadu and I. Dadu lives downstairs his doctor benazir said coronany thombosi so no climing stairs. So dadu has a bell when it goes ding ding ding everyone can hear. So today I heard him ringing it I was spiting through the window thoo thoo thoo so it goes a long way that was when I heard ding

ding ding and I knew at once it was dadu then I spited four times more one went over the wall and then I thought dadus calling let me go. I found dadu lying quietly in bed but not sleeping so I said whats the matter dadu but he didnt speak he kept looking at the seeling at the fan its a usha fan the others are all gec and then the telephone rang again so I ran up it had rung several times I said hello and I heard in hindi is mister sharma there I said in hindi theres no sharma here wrong number and put the phone down with a kerak sound and then I was panting because I had been running so I lay down on the sofa and put my feet on it since ma wasn't home and as soon as I did I saw they were dirty but ma wasn't home. And now I'm writing my diry in my bed and there are no pages theres no one now only dadu and I and a fly that keeps returning its botharing me very notty fly and thats it pages over diry over all over.

GOURKISHORE GHOSH

Sagina Mahato

Basanda, Dinda, Karabi-di, Sarat-da – I had no problems telling their stories. Then why do I find myself stumbling repeatedly in Sagina's case?

I have been trying to tell Sagina's story for three years now, but I simply cannot do it in a way that makes me happy. And yet, if I were to leave him out, that would mean omitting the brightest of them all.

Every time I think of Sagina, I am reminded of that bone-rattling morning of December 1944.

The station in the Himalayan foothills was shrouded in dense fog that day. Hardly had I got out of the stifling third-class compartment of the *Darjeeling Mail* and set foot on the platform when I felt someone had severed my legs with an icy saw. I had no idea the cold could bite so fiercely.

My luggage was minimal. Gathering my bag, I asked the first porter I saw, 'Do you know Sagina?'

Surveying me carefully, he walked away without answering.

I had no money to speak of. Nor had I eaten since the afternoon of the previous day. Most of the night had been spent on my feet in the train. Add to that the unbearable burden of this cold. I felt I'd die if I couldn't get something hot inside my belly at once, or thaw my hands and feet near a fire.

I knew only two people in this unfamiliar, friendless area. One was comrade Cuzimon, a friend of mine. And the person I was here to visit, Sagina. I had met him for the first time in April that year, at a workers' conference in Jharia. It was Cuzimon who had brought him.

There was no chance of meeting Cuzimon here. He lived in Kurseong. So Sagina was my only hope.

But where was he? Everyone I asked averted their eyes and went away.

I even went into the station office to ask some of the railway officers, who snarled back at me, 'Who Sagina, we don't know any Sagina.'

Left without a choice, I went out of the station and into the market. Sipping a cup of tea in a small tea shop, I asked a passer-by, 'Where's the loco shed of the mountain railway?'

From him I learnt it was some distance away. I would have to walk along the narrow hill track till I got to a minor station ahead. A turn to the right would lead me to a small market. I would have to pass through it to arrive at the loco shed a little further away. On the bank of the Mahananda.

The sky looked like it would rain any moment. There were strong gusts of wind as I walked along. Two engines chugged past me, pushing several carriages on their way to the hill station. Two locals were perched on the buffer of the engine in front with buckets of sand, conversing at the tops of their voices. Mountains of oranges were scattered about. There was much shouting everywhere. Several buses stood close together, stuffing passengers into their bellies. Drivers from the hills sped past them at the wheels of trucks and cars. I was in no mood to look at any of them. What if I could not locate Sagina?

I found myself having walked a long way. I was enjoying the walk, for it had warmed me up inside. Here we were at the station they'd mentioned. That must be the road I would have to take. Yes, this was the market.

Barely had I taken a step or two in that direction than I saw that a terrible fracas had broken out outside a tea shop. A woman was thrashing a man with a broom, and he in turn was kicking and punching her. A crowd had gathered around them to enjoy the entertainment this provided. I was terribly flustered. Suddenly the commotion increased, and the sharp sound of whistles began to fly through the air. I was astonished to find out what had happened. Unable to withstand the blows from the broom, the man had grabbed the woman's sari and tugged on it so violently that she had been disrobed and was standing there flabbergasted. Thrilled with this unexpected climax, the audience was whistling its joy.

Suddenly, Sagina arrived from nowhere. In a flash the whole scene collapsed.

'Fucking son of a bitch,' said Sagina, and lifted the man in the air by his neck. It was like a rat dangling from a tiger's paw. Sagina slapped him with his other paw. Blood began to trickle from the corner of the man's lips. Then Sagina flung him away like a ripped sack and, turning to the gathering, screamed like a maddened gorilla, 'Fuck off, all of you!'

The show was over in a matter of seconds. The place emptied out.

The woman entered the tea shop to put her sari back on. Sagina sat down next to her. The other man rose to his feet and I, too, sat down at one side, feeling as though I had just watched a scene from an English film.

Sagina frowned at me, whereupon I said, 'I'm here from Calcutta, comrade Sagina.'

All he said was, 'A comrade from Calcutta? Okay, we'll talk later.'

Then, ignoring me entirely, he asked the woman gently, 'Who are you?'

'Lalita,' she said with a smile.

Finally Sagina's round face, with its perpetually hard expression, seemed to soften. Suddenly he tilted her face upwards with a crooked finger beneath her chin and gazed at her, spellbound.

'You're very pretty,' he said.

Lalita giggled. I looked at her carefully. Yes, she was pretty all right.

'Who's that man?' Sagina said.

'My enemy,' said Lalita.

Then she dissolved in giggles again.

The man had been standing outside.

Now he roared, 'She's my woman. Ran away from home.' Turning to Lalita, he said, 'Just you come home. I'll show you who your enemy is. I'll bury you alive.'

His face was a fiery red with anger and humiliation. Lalita snuggled up to Sagina. Then she spat contemptuously in the man's direction.

Sagina gripped her arm lightly.

Glaring at the man, he said, 'Get out of here if you care for your life. As long as you're alive there'll be plenty of women.'

The man stared at them in turn like a wild beast. Then he left without a word.

Chuckling, Sagina looked at Lalita. 'Happy? Your enemy is gone. Now tell me where you want to go.'

Lalita went off into peals of laughter and then said, 'How should I know?'

A smiling Sagina said, 'Now that your enemy has run away you can go wherever you want to.'

Lalita stared at him in surprise. But only briefly, after which a naughty smile appeared on her face. She rose to her feet, still smiling, adjusted her clothes and moved towards the door.

Sagina grabbed her hand. 'Very good answer. Come, let's find you an address.'

As he made to leave I said, 'I'm here from Calcutta, comrade Sagina. Comrade Mitra has sent me to meet you.'

He had forgotten all about me. In fact, he seemed to be seeing me for the first time.

'Oh yes, Calcutta comrade, that's fine. We'll talk, yes. But later. You can see I'm busy now. We'll meet tomorrow or the day after.'

Seeing him move towards the door, I grew desperate. My belly was rumbling with hunger. Locating Sagina had already exhausted me. It was afternoon, evening would follow, and then the night. Where was I to stay? If I let him go now would I ever find him again?

Irked, I said, 'It's an important matter, comrade, I'm here on union work. I've come to meet you, where should I stay?'

Sagina surveyed me from head to toe and burst into laughter.

'Oh wonderful, you don't have an address either, just like her! Fine then, you come with me too. We'll work something out.'

By now I was beginning to realize this wasn't going to be easy. The party had instructed me to work with him. Sagina had a formidable influence in this area, Cuzimon had reported. If we could exploit his standing, our party would enjoy exclusive dominance here.

I had just seen an example of the power he exercised in this region. It had bewildered me.

And yet I was so happy before actually setting eyes on Sagina. For the first time I was going to comply with the orders issued by a labourer.

No matter how much we cried ourselves hoarse talking of the leadership of the proletariat, I had always seen that it was the upper classes who retained control. Just as the labourers in mills and factories followed the orders of the rich owners, so too were trade unions subservient to the gentlemen comrades.

The books had taught me so much. Only the destitute could usher in the revolution, for they were desperate and had nothing to lose. And so workers were the finest soldiers of the class struggle. The red flag would flutter all over the world one day under their leadership.

But when I began working with the Labour Front, I found that the middle class had sole claim to leadership. The same petite bourgeoisie whom the party literature had trained us not to trust – because apparently they are the most opportunistic, not hesitating to switch sides, and are the first to desert the party during the revolution to suck up to the owner class – and whom I had learnt to hate was now turning out to comprise the entire leadership of the labour movement.

I was born in a middle-class family. By birth I was a member of the opportunistic petite bourgeoisie, which was why I had nowhere to hide my shame. I used to die of remorse at not having been born into hallowed generations of labourers.

And so I had come over to meet Sagina at the first opportunity. To my own place. My own home. I had decided to correct the mistake of my birth by training with Sagina.

But was this what Sagina was really like? My middle-class mind was saying, so you've fallen into the clutches of a debauchee.

The three of us were walking across one slum after another. Sagina and Lalita in front, me behind them. From the back Sagina looked like a huge demon.

He was a giant, as tall as he was broadly built. Like a gargantuan mound of flesh on the move. He was dressed in a dirty, oil-stained, ragged shirt and tight trousers of the kind hill men wore. Next to him was the beautiful, slender Lalita. They were talking incessantly and laughing, leaning against each other every now and then.

They stopped outside a dilapidated hut beyond the loco shed.

'Gurung, ey Gurung,' Sagina shouted hoarsely.

An old man came out.

'Call Daiburi.'

Gurung went back in and sent an old woman out.

'Keep Lalita with you,' Sagina told her. 'I'll talk to the doctor and get her a job at the hospital.'

To Lalita he said, 'You can stay here now. We'll see about other arrangements later.'

Lalita disappeared with the old woman inside the hut, still laughing.

Lalita had been taken care of, perhaps Sagina would make some arrangements for me now. I had made up my mind meanwhile – I would spend the night here and leave for Kurseong next morning. It didn't look like I'd be able to get along with this fellow. I'd have to talk it over with Cuzimon.

Turning to me, Sagina said, 'Come, let's go to my shanty.'

And where might that be? How was I expected to run around on an empty stomach?

'How about informing comrade Cuzimon on the phone?' I said.

Sagina looked at me. 'You know Cuzimon?'

'Yes, he's a friend of mine,' I said.

'All right,' said Sagina, 'let's go to the station then. We can ring him right now.'

Finally it seemed Sagina had acknowledged me. On the way to the station he asked me about three or four of the top leaders.

'Do you know comrade Mitra?'

'I do,' I said.

'Comrade Mukherjee, Banerjee, Sen, Husain, do you know all of them?'

'I do,' I told him.

Sagina levelled a long glance at me, as though sizing me up again.

'Then it's fine,' he said.

Anyone whom Sagina ran into on the way to the station had a cordial chat with him. And yet when I had asked everyone I saw about him, none of them had responded. Most peculiar.

It took half an hour to reach the control room. One or two of the officers at the station looked away grimly when they saw Sagina. He didn't even throw them a glance, and went directly to a white-skinned officer.

'Salaam, Antony sahib,' he said.

'What is it Sagina,' the officer said in irritation.

Sagina laughed. 'I just greeted you, but look at you, you're angry.'

The officer grew angrier. 'Don't fool with me, Sagina, what is it you want?'

Now Sagina lost his amiability.

'I want to make a phone call. Connect me to the Kurseong loco office.'

'Go away,' said the officer, 'can't do it.'

'Just look at his cheek,' someone commented from the back. 'Does he think it's his father's property?'

'I don't have all the time in the world either, sahib,' said Sagina. 'It's important. Connect me quickly if you don't want trouble.'

Now the entire roomful of railway officers flew into a rage, asking Sagina to get out in different languages. How dare a minion throw his weight around? Was everything a joke? It was time to report him upstairs. The company was useless, it actually patronized these louts instead of sending them to jail.

'You, get out of here,' one of the officers snarled at me.

Sagina let them spew their invective without protesting. He didn't seem even remotely perturbed. Going up to Antony, he said, 'All of you are heavyweight officers who forget the past easily. How quickly you've forgotten what happened in Bastibazar! But never mind, I don't want to bring it up.'

Suddenly spotting someone outside, he said loudly, 'Ey Bahadur, come here.'

A face peeped in at the window.

'Are your people ready?' Sagina asked.

'Of course,' the man answered. 'But why?'

'One sahib and three Bengalis have to be fixed.'

With a wide smile the man said, 'Very well. When?'

Surveying the room, Sagina said, 'Come to Bastibazar in the evening, I'll let you know.'

'All right.'

Now Sagina said, seemingly to himself, 'Looks like we'll get some work done now.'

The occupants of the room seemed to have lost their voices. A flabbergasted Antony stared at Sagina.

'Maybe you'll connect me now, sahib,' Sagina said.

Antony picked up the phone without a word. A little later he said, 'Hello Kurseong, loco office please,' and handed the receiver to Sagina, who began to shout into it.

'Hello, Cuzimon sahib? Yes, it's Sagina. Some chap from Calcutta is here. Says he knows you. Of course, talk to him.'

Handing me the receiver, Sagina said, 'Talk to him.'

Cuzimon was delighted to talk to me. 'Stay with Sagina for now,' he said. 'I'll be there the day after tomorrow. We'll chalk out a programme then. Give the phone back to Sagina.'

I heard Sagina say, 'All right, don't worry about him. Yes, come the day after tomorrow. All right. All right. Ha ha ha. Don't worry. Who? The general manager, ha ha ha. Excellent. We'll change the world, senior manager, junior manager, all the bastards will turn dark-skinned. No more exploitation. Yes, we'll talk about these things later. Woman? Oh ha ha ha, you mean Bhukhan's wife. She's run away. Drove me up the wall before she left. It's been two months. No, it wasn't her fault. Went home drunk one night, gave her a few slaps. Woke up in the morning to find the bird had flown. I regretted it. But listen, I'm a man, am I not? So I'll find a woman. Ha ha ha. You've done wonders, wonders. All right. All right.'

Sagina put the receiver back in its cradle noisily. He was beaming with joy.

'Good morning, sahib, good morning. Come, comrade.'

Slapping my back with his big palm, he guided me out.

A number of thoughts ran through my mind on the way back with him to his quarters. As I had just seen, Sagina always took the direct approach. No need to be perturbed if the officer doesn't let you make a phone call, just beat him up. Since he had been born a man, he needed a woman. No need to grieve over someone who had left him, he would always find another one.

Not *would* find, had found already. I remembered that morning's incident. Sagina had got rid of Lalita's husband and deposited her in an old woman's house.

This was the man I would have to build the party around. I had never believed in bookish theory. I knew the Marxist analysis of morality and immorality. But still, all that I had seen this man do ever since I had come into contact with him had left me with a niggle of doubt.

With a broad smile, Sagina said, 'Time for some food and drinks, comrade. Your arrival here is a matter of great joy.'

What Sagina had by way of a home comprised a single room. But I had not anticipated how hideously he maintained it. I had no bedding of my own. I slept on Sagina's bed, next to him, wrapped in his foul-smelling blanket.

The only door to this brick shack was closed to keep the cold out. There were no other openings. Five of us were in the room, with a fire burning in an earthen basin in the corner for warmth.

Sagina had drunk copiously, and his alcohol-laden breath hovered over my nose. The smells, the smoke from the fire, our exhalations – all of them circulated in the room, unable to escape. The humid, distressing environment led me to believe I might choke to death.

I could also tell how privileged my discomfort was. It was nothing but the snobbery of the petite bourgeoisie. I died of shame every time the thought occurred to me. This was my real home, the dwelling of a genuine labourer. I was here precisely because I would never otherwise have the chance to live in such a place. Why this uneasiness, then? Why couldn't I settle down? Why was I unable to sleep soundly like Sagina and the rest of them? Admonishing myself, I tried to get some sleep.

Suddenly I saw Sagina sitting up in the shadowy darkness. He shook me till I was fully awake.

'Comrade.' He gripped my hands. 'Forgive me, comrade, I'm a sinner.'

I realized he was in a drunken haze in the middle of the night. Trouble.

'I'm telling you the truth, comrade, I was going to do something bad. Forgive me.'

I was annoyed by now.

'We'll talk tomorrow, comrade,' I said. 'Go to sleep.'

'All right,' said Sagina. 'But listen, comrade. When I saw you for the first time I thought, this bastard is a spy. I decided to kill you and throw you into the boiler of the engine.'

Good grief! I began to sweat in terror at what he had just said.

'And then?'

'And then,' Sagina said, 'I found you talking to Cuzimon. I realized you're a real brother. I was filled with regret at not believing you. Forgive me, comrade.'

To tell the truth, I passed the rest of the night in great fear. The same Sagina next to whom I had lain down with so much trust now appeared to be the god of death.

Meanwhile he had sunk back into deep sleep, not before assuring me repeatedly that he had realized his mistake, that he had accepted me as a comrade. But I had not overcome my fear. I spent the night as though a snake were lurking under my bed.

After this I spent an entire year with Sagina. Cuzimon had not exaggerated. Sagina's power over this region could not be obstructed. The workers of the hill railway knew no one but Sagina, acknowledged no one but Sagina either.

These labourers had been made to face tremendous oppression from the foreign owners of the railway company. It was a cold land, a land of rain. But their living quarters were woefully dilapidated. Every year the roofs let in rainwater and icy winds through the cracks. Countless workers had died of illnesses. Still the owners had not remedied the problems. There had been countless petitions and requests, but the company rejected them every time.

This regime of injustice had flourished for a long time, before Sagina appeared on the scene. He brought the workers together, their unity growing stronger by the day in the face of the white and Anglo-Indian officers' tyranny and Bengali clerks' mischief.

I learnt of these things at the various gatherings of Sagina's people, from several of them, in fact, separately. Most of these gatherings were drinking sessions, each of them like capitals of Sagina's extensive kingdom. No one in the world dared flout the commands that he issued there. They were followed with the certainty of sunrise and sunset.

'How many stories do I tell you, my friend? Shameful stories, all of them – those bloody white men kicked us around all the time.'

Old Gurung would tell stories of bygone days. Swaying drunkenly, he would put his arm around me intimately, fill my glass, and say, 'Drink up.' And then his stories would flow.

'Yes, they used to kick us. The men, the women too. They kicked us when we were wrong, and also when we were not. The bastards' boots would always be trampling over us. Yes. Many of our friends were killed. What could we do but let ourselves be kicked? And those fucking officers would take our wives and daughters to their bungalows. The junior officers, the inspectors and ticket checkers, they did the same thing. What could we do, the bastards were all white men. Fine, kick me, take my wife away, my daughter, my sister. But not my job. What were we to do, we had no leader? We couldn't say a word, out of fear. Yes, we were poor, we were labourers, we were workers. All they did was to kick us. I'd have done it too if I'd been a white man or an Anglo-Indian. And if I'd been a Bengali clerk I'd have also lined my pockets at the expense of the poor. All right then, kick us. We had no organization, no leader. What could we do? Today the sahib kicks me, the other fellow laughs. Tomorrow the sahib kicks the other fellow, I laugh. Yes, that's the truth. The complete truth. What could we do? If I tried speaking to the officers every other fucker would run away. No one would help. I could grab the bastard and beat him up. But that would be the end of my job.'

This was the state they were in when Sagina appeared amid them. He came directly as their leader. And he proceeded to beat up people immediately, starting with the labourers.

'Fucking sons of bitches!'

This was Sagina's slogan initially. Beat up any of the bastards who wouldn't join the organization, who would allow themselves to be thrashed by white men without protesting. And if any fucker turned out to be a traitor, kill him. If any son of a bitch allowed his wife or daughter or sister to go to the officers' homes, throw him off the hill.

This was how Sagina made his entrance. All the workers joined him in a couple of years. And then the game changed. 'Yes, my friend.' Gurung tipped his head back and emptied his glass. Then he paused for breath before resuming.

'Yes, my friend, the game changed. If the sahib kicked me, I kicked him back. What could I do, leader's orders. Beat up the bastards if they beat us up. What were the sahibs going to do? Sack me? Hah, if they did all the workers would stop working. What could we do, leader's orders. And if the wheels stopped rolling so would the company. Ha ha ha. If the wheels stopped rolling so would the company. Four times they suspended me, sacked me. The wheels stopped. And then? They were forced to give my job back to me. And then? The bloody beating up stopped entirely. All this was Sagina's doing. Sagina is a leader. Our captain.'

At this moment Sagina entered amid a cacophony of voices, accompanied by several others.

'Come my friend, have a drink,' Gurung jumped up and shouted.

Sagina seemed to throw his enormous frame on the bench next to me. He slapped me on the back.

'Aaaah, comrade,' he said, 'so you're drinking. Ha ha ha. This one's become one of us. But something's missing. Comrade needs a woman. Is he a man or not? Anyway, not to worry, you'll get one.'

To console me he called out to a man nearby, 'Got anyone, Bahadur, someone good you can give our comrade?'

Bahadur looked at me and laughed.

'Not difficult,' he said.

'All right then,' Sagina commanded, 'let's drink to our comrade.'

We had converted what used to be 'Sagina's Gang' into a workers' union. We had got ourselves an office, where I was the office secretary, Sagina the president and Cuzimon the secretary. There was an executive committee too. But effectively Sagina was the all-in-all.

With great effort we had managed to instil some discipline. The company had recognized the union. Physical violence had gone down, and the wheels no longer stopped rolling at the drop of a hat. The company had given the president, secretary and office secretary first-class passes. They even provided a halting allowance in case of meetings at the headquarters. Sagina was acknowledged formally. They had wanted to increase his salary, but he had said no to their faces. 'Raising my wages alone won't help anyone,' he had told them, 'raise everyone's.'

We had presented a memorandum to the company two months ago, demanding new quarters for the workers and renovation of the old ones. We had also demanded basic wages of twenty-five rupees, an increase in the dearness allowance amounting to fifty per cent of the basic wages, overtime, holidays and improvements in educational and medical facilities.

The company used various pretexts to procrastinate on these matters. Letters went back and forth, with a mountain of them piling up in our office.

Sagina scoffed at us every time he saw the letters. He didn't believe in such methods.

'You can feed the tiger all the milk you want, it will still suck out blood. Those bastards will never consider us the boss without a taste of their own medicine.'

He burst into laughter every time I tried to explain the principles of trade unions. 'Six months have gone by,' he said. 'We asked the company for food. And what did we get? These letters.'

Contemptuously he overturned the pile of files holding the correspondence.

'This exchange of letters will lead nowhere. For six months you've been pecking away at your letters and replying to them, and the bastards are doing the same thing. What are we getting out of it? This new way of doing things that you people have won't get anything out of them. We have to go back to the old ways. Beat the fuckers up, jam the wheels again. Then they will accept us as the boss. Call for a meeting.'

The executive meeting was held first, followed by the general meeting. It was decided at both to serve an ultimatum to the company. We would resort to extreme steps if our demands weren't met within a month.

There was great elation among everyone the day we sent the ultimatum. The brewery filled with Sagina's companions, with the drinking going on late into the night, complete with celebrations and merrymaking.

Suddenly Sagina ushered me out of the place. I had been living in the union office ever since it was set up.

'Look, comrade,' Sagina said, 'those who have food to eat at home can wait out the delay, they can be patient. But how will starving, half-clothed labourers be patient? Give food, give clothes, get work out of them. No one will create trouble. But without food, just promises and talking serve no purpose. It's time for the final battle. And then an outcome. There's no other way.'

We had reached the office. It consisted of two rooms, one functioning as the office and the other as my bedroom.

Pushing me into my room, Sagina said, 'Well, do you like her?'

I found Bahadur sitting on my bed with a woman of about nineteen or twenty. She was quite pretty, a lot like Lalita. She was smiling at me. My drunken haze vanished at once, and my heart began to flutter. I felt my face and ears turn warm.

Bahadur winked. 'Hot stuff!'

Sagina and he burst out laughing at my bewildered state. It was infectious, and the woman started to laugh melodiously too, the song spreading across the room.

I came back to my senses at once. The veneer of destitution that I'd covered myself with over the past year was peeled off ruthlessly by the ghost of the petite bourgeoisie. Before I knew what I was doing, I found myself running furiously along the street. For a moment it felt as though Sagina and Bahadur had given chase, laughing. It felt as though the woman's melodious laughter was pursuing me too. Some people seemed to be shouting, 'Comrade, comrade!'

I didn't stop till I was on the bridge over the Mahananda. I gasped for breath, holding the railing. The chilly wind brought some comfort to my eyes and ears and face. An erect peak of dense darkness stood in the distance. The Himalayas. What lay directly ahead was shrouded in darkness too, the Sukna Forest. The silver ribbon of the Mahananda lay below and a star-filled sky above. There was a multitude of fireflies and the unending chirping of crickets. Amid all this the young woman's beautiful, innocent face kept floating up before my eyes.

Suddenly it occurred to me, it was true, why exactly had I run away? The woman's face and sweet smile were drawing me. By the time this attraction made me retrace my steps, dawn was not far away. Even when I reached home I paused for a long while outside the door. My heart was beating fit to burst. Then, summoning up courage, I opened the door lightly, only to find no one inside. Disappointment gnawed at me like a rat. I was a fool, I was a coward, I was a petit bourgeois.

I remember being admonished by Sagina for behaving the same way on another occasion. 'You're a good-for-nothing,' he said. 'How are you going to subdue these formidable sahibs when you run away at the sight of a woman?'

The next day Cuzimon arrived from Kurseong, where the regional head-quarters of our party was at the time. He was the head of the local branch.

'The train for Calcutta leaves soon,' said Cuzimon, 'get ready at once, we have to go to Calcutta, urgent summons.'

We went off in search of Sagina at once, discovering a volatile situation at the brewery.

Wangdi, the unit secretary of Kurseong, was present. He was speaking agitatedly and Sagina was listening with attention.

From Wangdi we learnt that things were coming to a head. For quite some time we had been receiving complaints against an officer named

Burne, a real scoundrel. He was the assistant foreman in the carriage shop. He took bribes, troubled the workers in as many ways as possible, harassed women. The union had complained formally to the company against him, but it had not helped. We had demanded that he be transferred, warning of possible unrest because of his behaviour. The company had paid no attention. As a result his impudence had grown by the day.

Last night Burne took advantage of a worker named Namgil's being on night duty to sneak into his home. Namgil found out and came back. Discovering the white man naked in his wife's bed, he thrashed him within an inch of his life. Burne was alive but his limbs were broken, crippling him.

'Then the police came,' Wangdi said. 'They arrested Namgil and put him in jail. Now what should we do?'

'Go on strike. Stop work. What else do you suppose?'

Everyone was shouting in unison, Sagina too.

'Stop work,' he said, 'then we'll see.'

'It's a bit illegal, Sagina,' said Cuzimon. 'I think we should send a telegram to the general manager to inform him of the situation. We can demand that the case against Namgil be withdrawn, pending investigation. Let him be released now.'

Sagina shouted Cuzimon down.

'Forget it, my friend,' he said. 'You're a good man, educated too, but a fool. Why should we go to the general manager? What have we done that's wrong? A wild beast has tarnished my honour, I have beaten him up. How is it my fault? The bastards have the police on their side, so they caught me. Now we have to show our strength too. If work stops tomorrow the general manager will acknowledge we're the boss and come to a compromise.'

Cuzimon tried to explain things to Sagina in many ways. 'The age of physical might is over, comrade,' he said. 'You can win a battle or two this way, but you won't win the war. You'll have to follow the principles of trade unionism if you want victory.'

Sagina taunted Cuzimon openly. 'Wars are not fought with paper and ink, my friend, you need weapons. I've been watching your paper-and-ink war for the past six months. I've seen the outcome too. Now you watch my war with weapons. And watch the outcome too.'

Slapping the table, Sagina said, 'Friends, any bastard who attacks our stomachs and our honour must be attacked back. Work in the carriage department will stop tomorrow. If that doesn't lead to a solution, work will stop on the entire line from the day after.'

Everyone exploded in joy at this. Their eyes began to blaze.

Cuzimon and I went out. He didn't speak for some time, walking in silence. Finally he said, 'It won't be right to leave this place now. Let's wire Calcutta.'

Eventually the whole thing became exceedingly complicated. The strike spread through the entire line.

It was wartime. The hill station was an important holiday destination for English soldiers, which the company tried to take advantage of at first, resorting to an authoritarian policy. The union was declared illegal, and arrest warrants were issued for us. Packing me off to Calcutta, Sagina went underground with his followers.

But his organizational skills were extraordinary. He continued to run the strike from behind the scenes. None of the workers reported for duty, and the company couldn't run a single train.

There were regular meetings in the party high command about this. Sagina's sudden declaration of a strike had put the party in a slightly difficult position. Because our rulers were engaged in a battle against fascists we had chosen to support them, and were directing the labour movement accordingly. We were pressuring the government to accept a progressive labour policy.

That was when Sagina created trouble. Although he was not a member of our party, and neither cared nor wanted to care about it, effectively we ran his union as our own.

Now the party slapped notices on Cuzimon and me, demanding explanations for Sagina's exploits. We were at the receiving end of rebukes from the leaders for having allowed this to happen. We had little to say in our defence. Still, I argued that it was primarily the company that was responsible for the chaos. Cuzimon and I had put in six months of hard work to create a healthy environment for the trade union, but the company had made no effort to maintain it. Anarchy was inevitable unless the inhuman conditions in which labourers spent their days were improved. Workers wanted food to eat, they would have to be given food. How could starving workers be expected to be patient?

I could tell I was parroting Sagina's lines. It was also evident that the party leaders were not satisfied. When the freedom of the workers of the world was jeopardized by fascism, whether Sagina's followers were getting enough to eat or not was no concern of theirs. We were fighting for an ideology, while Sagina and his people were far too involved in material things like hunger. It was quite natural for the leaders to be furious.

It was decided at a secret meeting that the party would have to establish its authority over the union. Or else it could not be run according to party policy. I laughed to myself when the decision was revealed to me. No one but Sagina could sink his teeth into the situation there.

But the party actually achieved the impossible. When the company could not run the trains despite its best efforts, it turned to us for help. A series of meetings between the upper echelons of the party and the company took place. An agreement was signed. On the advice of the party, the company withdrew all cases and recognized the union once more.

What was even more astonishing was that the post of a labour welfare officer with a fat salary was created. And the company agreed to appoint not an Englishman, not a clerk, but a genuine worker trusted by all the labourers. It was a triumph for the workers.

My chest swelled with the pride of victory. All my respect was directed towards comrade Bijan Dutta, the lawyer who had drawn up the agreement.

All that the company would do for the betterment of its workers would have to be done according to the advice of the labour welfare officer. The workers would elect the person who would hold this post. The company wouldn't be able to interfere or play games.

There was a huge gathering of workers in the large field in Bastibazar. I have a bright memory of the day. Comrade Dutta chaired the gathering. He was accompanied by his sister, comrade Bishakha Dutta. The party didn't have another comrade as beautiful as her. She positively lit up the stage. Next to her was Sagina, seated like a victorious hero, his head held high. Bishakha leant towards him, whispering constantly. Sagina's elation could not be contained.

Comrade Dutta's speech ran for an hour and a half, during which he heaped copious praise on the determined attitude of the workers. Over and over again he declared his respect for Sagina's leadership, personality, strategy and self-sacrifice. The place exploded in cheers and applause. Our ears rang with shouts of 'Long live comrade Sagina!'

Comrade Dutta said, 'This victory isn't Sagina's alone, it's a victory for the unity and organization of workers. No group of workers anywhere in India has extracted from the owners what the railway workers here have, on the strength of their organization. Is there another place where the labour welfare officer has been appointed on the basis of workers' votes? Comrades, you have to elect someone to this post now.'

The clamour died down as comrade Dutta returned to his seat. You could hear a pin drop in the silence. It appeared no one had quite understood. Bishakha rose to her feet, like a flaming torch.

Her voice emerged in a low, musical timbre. 'Sagina. In my view comrade Sagina is the most suitable person for this post.'

'Sagina! Yes, Sagina!'

The name reverberated through the tumult of voices. 'Long live comrade Sagina!'

Picking up a giant garland from the table, Bishakha Dutta put it around Sagina's neck. Bahadur, Wangdi, Namgil, Gurung and several others I didn't know rushed to the stage. They hauled Sagina up on their shoulders and began to dance.

The celebrations went on all day. Comrade Bijan Dutta and Bishakha went off to Kurseong in the evening. Before leaving they told Sagina and me to meet them there the next morning. Cuzimon left with them.

In Kurseong we put up at comrade Dutta's house. Bishakha welcomed Sagina warmly and escorted him in. Cuzimon came in the afternoon; the Duttas had invited him to lunch too.

The conversation during lunch was about work. Comrade Dutta explained to Sagina the importance of his new post. It involved a great deal of responsibility, with the entire welfare and future of the workers being in Sagina's hands. He would be given spacious living quarters, as large as those of the Englishmen. Sagina should now make it clear to the company that workers were no less important than the sahibs. He would have to run an office too, but he shouldn't worry about that, for comrade Dutta would send him an excellent secretary from Calcutta.

I found Sagina looking rather serious after lunch. He was thinking hard, and didn't speak to us.

The general manager's bearer appeared with a letter and handed it to comrade Dutta. He read it and beckoned to Sagina.

'You'll have to meet the burra sahib tomorrow, comrade,' he said. 'Your appointment will be finalized.'

'That's good.' Sagina nodded absent-mindedly.

Comrade Bishakha emerged from her room, all dressed up.

'Is your work done?' she asked. 'I'm going to the hill station.'

'Carry on,' said comrade Dutta.

'Will you go with me?' she asked Sagina at once.

Sagina's face finally brightened.

'Of course,' he said with a smile.

They returned around nine at night. I was astonished, I really couldn't recognize Sagina. He was wearing a clean suit with a tie, and new shoes. I hadn't realized over the year gone by how handsome he was. Sagina appeared to be a new creation of comrade Bishakha's. His moodiness of the afternoon had disappeared, he was brimming with good cheer now, looking positively animated.

'I presented these to our hero, comrade Sagina,' Bishakha told her brother, 'so that he can stand before the white man tomorrow as an equal.'

Comrade Dutta was surprised, but he seemed rather pleased at Sagina's transformation.

'They suit our comrade very well,' he said.

Bishakha was bubbling. She adjusted Sagina's tie, which he was unused to wearing. In great happiness she said, 'He's a new man, isn't he?'

Sagina guffawed in his characteristic way. His familiar laughter, capable of shaking walls and roofs.

I was in Siliguri for two months after Sagina became the labour welfare officer. At first he used to visit Siliguri often, accompanied by comrade Bishakha. Then she decided to stay in Kurseong for some time, which suited Sagina, for she acted as his secretary. Possibly she taught him some manners too. Then his visits became infrequent. Perhaps his work was becoming more intense.

I was abruptly despatched from Siliguri to Lalman. Before leaving I sent a memorandum to Sagina's office based on the various requirements and demands of the workers. He informed us that he would secure these for the workers.

But before he could concentrate on his work properly, Sagina began to get invitations from various places. His name spread by word of mouth, and so did stories about his exploits. Madras, Gujarat, Bihar – he was invited everywhere. He was given elaborate receptions in Kanpur and Ahmedabad, in Jharia and Tatanagar. I was told Bishakha went with him to almost all of these places. Sagina was elected vice-president of our All India Workers' Union.

Sagina was out of Siliguri for six years.

And in this period factionalism began in the union. Cuzimon used to write to me now and then, sounding rather perturbed. Everyone knew the labour welfare officer was one of our people. The workers' grievances were piling up. It was no use complaining to the company, for they only pointed to Sagina's office. But where was Sagina?

Cuzimon was fed up with writing to the party office about this. The reply was that comrade Sagina had been assigned to other tasks in the greater interest of the party. He was organizing workers across the country.

Eventually the single union split into three. One of them remained under Cuzimon's control, however, and it effectively turned into the labour front of our party. The other two factions went under the control of other parties.

All kinds of accusations against Sagina began to surface. Even Gurung, Bahadur, Wangdi and the others turned into his enemies.

Meanwhile clashes broke out between the rival unions. When things became dire, the party instructed me to go to Siliguri. Cuzimon had left the party and the fifth column had infiltrated the union. They wanted to engineer a strike, which had to be stopped.

I was stunned when I returned to Siliguri. The office had been wound up and we had no supporters to speak of. I went to Kurseong to find Cuzimon a broken man.

'All the work we did here has been destroyed,' he said, 'utterly destroyed. It's all broken into pieces. Who'll put them back together?'

'Why, we have Sagina,' I said. 'We'll bring him here, if anyone can do this, it's him.'

'Once upon a time he could have, but even he can't do it now,' Cuzimon said hopelessly. 'We've finished with him.'

I didn't understand Cuzimon. What did he mean, we had finished with Sagina?

Cuzimon explained.

'We finished with Sagina at the Siliguri conference a year and a half ago. I had doubts at that time, comrade. Why had the company accepted our demands so easily? Then I reasoned, it was wartime, perhaps the company had buckled under pressure from the government. But I realized my mistake a few months later. You left, after which the party began to put pressure on me to turn the union into its wing. To turn the union members into party members. The party wanted a stronghold here. But the more I said the union would collapse if we tried to do this, that worker unity would suffer, that their collective strength would be compromised, the less they listened. One day there was a summons from Calcutta. I went. Comrade Dutta asked casually whether Sagina's influence was on the rise or on the wane. I didn't read between the lines, and said vehemently that keeping Sagina out of Siliguri all this time had been a mistake. People were saying things against him. Naturally, his hold over the people was weakening.

'You know what comrade Dutta said?' Cuzimon continued.

He waited a while for me to respond, and then answered his own question. 'He said, the party will operate there, but Sagina will not. You must build the party.'

Cuzimon paused again.

Then he said, almost to himself, 'What couldn't have been achieved by sending Sagina to jail was accomplished by turning him into a hero. But what did we gain?'

Cuzimon was my friend, a dedicated party worker. But honestly, I didn't believe him. Was this even possible?

For five days I went around everywhere in Siliguri. All the old friends gathered at the brewery, only Sagina was missing. I was told he was in Bombay, where he had been sent to attend an international labour conference.

'Going on strike will finish you unless everyone's united, my friend,' I told Gurung. 'But the union is broken. Where's your leader?'

Gurung was high on liquor.

'What do we do?' he said. 'He was a fucking leader, but he became a fucking agent. He's a white man now. Big house. Shows off his wife. What do we do? We'll die of starvation, but we'll make sure the wheels stop rolling.'

'Yes, we will!' screamed the drunkards in violent rage.

I went to the station the next morning to find Sagina there. In full Western regalia.

He called out to me. 'You here, comrade? Where did you spring from?'

'I live in Lalmonirhat these days,' I told him. 'I've been here for about ten days.'

He took me into the restaurant. 'What's happening, comrade?' I asked.

I hadn't expected to meet him now. Perhaps it was destiny.

Sagina said he had run away from Bombay.

'I don't care for these things,' he said. 'All these meetings, useless stuff. What's the use of talking so much? Organize, take power into your own hands. Only then will the bloody owners accept the worker as the boss. Right?

'And as for you,' he said, 'what are you doing here?'

'Don't you know there's going to be a strike in your company?'

'A strike!' Sagina was astonished. 'When?'

'There's a meeting in Bastibazar this afternoon. They'll decide there.'

Sagina was lost in thought.

'You didn't know?' I asked again.

'I'd have to be here to know,' he said. 'All this travelling has been disastrous. But the right action is being taken, the wheels need to stop again. The fucking company is an out-and-out cheat. It's been a year and a half and they can't get cement! They're supposed to build quarters for the labourers, apparently there are no contractors! Just giving us the runaround, bloody liars.'

Sagina leant towards me.

'Look, comrade,' he said, 'I've realized all this welfare business is just fraud. I can't do this any more, my friend. Will all workers benefit if I live in a fancy house? Nonsense! This is wrong. Give the same quarters as mine to everyone, give them good food, get all the work you want out of them. No one will create trouble. But I will put my blood, sweat and tears into my labour, and you will fucking give me dry words and false promises in return? This can't go on all your life. It's right to shut the wheels down. But who will do it?'

I conveyed the developments to Sagina, and gave him detailed descriptions. 'There's no union,' I told him, 'only fights. This is the situation in which they're going in madly for a strike.' I gave him all the news, except the things Cuzimon had said, and the opinion of him that Gurung and the rest of them had been airing.

When he had heard me out, Sagina said, 'Then we can't stop the wheels right now. The organization has to be strengthened first. All right comrade, you come back here then. We have to build the old union again. I'll come too. This bloody job is not for me.'

I was very happy to hear this.

'Let's go to Bastibazar then,' I said, 'to the meeting. You must speak. Everything will be all right if they have you again.'

'Yes, let's go.'

'Where's that comrade of yours?' I asked.

'Who?'

'Comrade Bishakha,' I said.

Bursting into laughter, Sagina said, 'Oh she has other gentlemen. How long will she be with a labourer? She's gone away as well. Let her go. If I live there will be other women.'

At the Bastibazar meeting I realized how right Cuzimon was.

Sagina had told me he would arrive in time for the meeting. But when I went there around sunset he was not there yet. A new hope had been born in my heart. There was nothing to fear now that Sagina had realized how things were, now that his infatuation had faded. His iron personality would end all anarchy. He would rebuild this crumbling organization.

I knew the party wouldn't tolerate my thinking. But then the party leaders knew neither this area nor these people. They had made a mistake in removing Sagina, which I would rectify.

There was a commotion early on during the meeting, and the temperature kept rising. They couldn't agree on anything and were getting angrier as a result, showering choice abuses on one another.

Suddenly Sagina arrived on the scene, dressed in a suit and a tie. But the shine had been taken off his clothes. His eyes and expression suggested he had been drinking. His hair was dishevelled. Must have been moving around town all day.

Before I could go up to him he went to the table where the speakers were seated.

The uproar died down at his appearance. The meeting was silent.

'What's going on, my friends?' Sagina asked loudly.

Silence.

'What's the meeting for?'

Suddenly Bahadur screamed, 'Get out, you fucking traitor. Get out of here.'

You had to see Bahadur's eyes to believe how they were glittering with malignance. They were like daggers of revulsion. I shuddered. This was the same Bahadur who used to be Sagina's most faithful follower, who had followed his instructions one night to bring a woman to my room.

He had barely stopped when everyone else began attacking Sagina with hatred and loathing. Sagina was flabbergasted.

It was evident he couldn't believe his eyes. Nor could I.

'Fuck off! Goddamned agent! The son of a bitch has become a sahib now.'

'Look, you bastard!' Gurung went up to Sagina, trembling with rage. 'Look at us you bastard, see the state we're in. No food, no clothes. And you're an Englishman now. Spit on the bastard, all of you.'

Gurung directed a gob of saliva at Sagina's face.

'My friends, my brothers,' Sagina cried out. His voice was drowned in the noise.

'Beat the fucker up,' someone screamed. 'Kill him.'

In moments the frenzied crowd pounced on Sagina, who gasped under an unstoppable avalanche of punches and kicks. Several times he tried to get to his feet, to say something. But it was futile. He could neither lift his head nor make a sound under the inhuman beating.

My blood froze in fear. Never having seen rage and hatred in such naked form, I was trembling uncontrollably. Suddenly Sagina screamed, a heart-rending cry. A voice inside my head said 'run'. I ran, losing all my bearings.

Nakchhedi, the owner of the brewery, was a close friend of Sagina's.

It was nearly nine at night by the time he, I and six or seven youngsters from the party returned to Bastibazar. Because we were in the Himalayan foothills, it felt like midnight. Sagina was lying on his back in the open field. Alone. His suit and tie were shredded. His face and nose were swollen, there were wounds in his head and bloodstains all over him.

No, Sagina wasn't dead. We carried him to the brewery, where he recovered consciousness two or three hours later. He didn't emit a single groan of pain.

Nakchhedi gave him a bottle of liquor, which he emptied down his throat. Then he sat there, panting and heaving.

A little later he said haltingly, 'They beat me up. Mercilessly. They were right to do it. I betrayed them. I have understood.

'But comrade,' Sagina grabbed my arm, 'I was trapped in a giant swindle. Which I didn't realize. It's true, all I did under the pretext of helping workers was to have a good time. I was a dancing monkey. I regret it.'

Those were his last words. The next day his body was found beside the railway line in Sukna Forest, cut into two parts. Some said he was murdered, others said he had killed himself.

SAMARESH BASU

Aadaab

Shattering the silence of the night, the military patrol car completes a circuit around Victoria Park.

A curfew as well as Section 144 has been clamped on the city. Hindus and Muslims are rioting. Frontal assaults are raging – with cleavers, spears, daggers, even sticks. And secret assassins are spreading everywhere, striking under the cover of darkness with intent to kill.

Criminals are out on looting expeditions. The scourge of death on this dark night is making their euphoria wilder. Slums are on fire. The dying screams of women and children have made things even more terrible. Armed vehicles are ploughing into them, the soldiers firing indiscriminately to maintain law and order.

Two lanes converge at this point. The dustbin has upturned at the spot where they meet, parts of it broken. A man crawls out of one of the lanes, positioning himself to use the dustbin as a shield. Lacking the courage to lift his head, he lies inert on the ground for some time, keeping his ears peeled for the indistinct cries floating in from the distance. The sounds aren't clear. Is it 'Allahu Akbar' or 'Bande Mataram'?

Suddenly the dustbin moves slightly. All his nerves begin to tingle. Clenching his teeth and tensing his limbs, he waits for something terrible to happen. A few moments pass. There is stillness everywhere.

Probably a dog. The man pushes at the dustbin to drive it away. There is no response for some time. Then the bin moves again. This time there is curiosity mingled with his fear. He lifts his head slowly ... and so does another man on the other side of the bin. Two creatures, frozen, a dustbin between them. Their hearts have all but stopped beating. Two pairs of eyes, probing, the look in them a mixture of dread, suspicion and anxiety.

Neither can trust the other, each of them considers the other one a murderer. Their eyes locked on each other', both wait for an attack, but even after some time there is no aggression from either. Now a question arises in both their minds. Hindu or Muslim? Perhaps the answer will lead to a fatal outcome. So neither of them dares ask the other one. Nor can they flee, for fear of being jumped on with a knife.

After several minutes of discomfort and doubt, both become impatient. Finally one of them blurts out the question. Hindu or Muslim?

You first, says the other man.

Both are unwilling to state their identity. Their minds are swayed by suspicion. The first question is buried. It gives way to another. Where are you from? asks one of them.

Across the Buriganga, in Shubaida. You?

Chashara, near Narayanganj. What do you do?

I have a boat. I ferry people. You?

I work at the cotton mill in Narayanganj.

Silence once more. Each of them tries to covertly scan the appearance of the other. They try to gauge how the other one is dressed. The darkness and the shelter of the dustbin make this harder. Suddenly a commotion breaks out nearby. Manic screams from two groups of people can be heard. Both the millworker and the boatman become alert.

Seems to be nearby. The millworker sounds terrified.

Yes, let's get away from here. The boatman's voice holds the same note of fear.

The millworker stops him. Don't move. You want to die?

The boatman is overcome by suspicion again. What if the man is plotting something? He stares into the millworker's eyes. The millworker has been looking at him too. As soon as their eyes lock he says, sit down, stay as you are.

The boatman's heart leaps into his mouth at this. Is this man not going to let him escape? Suspicion gathers in his eyes. Why? he asks.

Why? The millworker's voice is muffled but sharp. What do you mean, Why, do you want to get killed?

The boatman doesn't care for this manner of speaking. He considers the possibilities, even the impossibilities, and comes to a firm decision.

What do you think? You expect me to keep hiding here in this dark lane instead of leaving?

His obstinacy makes the millworker suspicious too. I don't like your intentions, he says. You didn't say whether you're a Hindu or a Muslim. What if you fetch a group of your people to kill me?

What do you think you're saying? Forgetting where he is, the boatman shouts with rage and regret in his voice.

What I said is right. Sit down. Can't you understand what's going through my mind?

There's something in the millworker's voice that reassures the boatman.

I'll have to stay here alone if you go.

The uproar in the distance dies down. A deathly silence descends again. Every moment seems to pass in expectation of death. Two living beings on two sides of a dustbin in a darkened lane reflect on their own predicament, their homes, their wives and children. Will they be able to go back to their families alive? Will their families survive, for that matter? Like a thunderbolt from the sky, without any warning, the riot has erupted in their lives. There they were, strolling around the market, laughing and talking with others – and in a moment it had turned to murder and violence, rivers of blood. How can people turn so cruel in an instant? What an accursed race we are! The millworker sighs. The boatman echoes him.

Want a bidi? Taking a cheap cigarette from his pocket, the millworker offers it to the boatman. Accepting it, the boatman squeezes it gently out of habit, waves it in the air near his ear a few times and then clamps his lips on it. The millworker is trying to light a match. He hasn't realized that his shirt has become wet, and with it the matchbox. The sound of the matchstick being scraped against the box is heard repeatedly, but there is barely a spark. Disgusted, the millworker tosses the stick away.

Bloody matchbox is soaked. He takes another stick out of it.

Impatient now, the boatman leaves his position to crouch next to the millworker.

It'll work, give it to me. He practically snatches the matchbox from the millworker's hand. And, after a couple of attempts, he actually manages to get a matchstick alight.

Subhan Allah! Come on now, light up quickly. The millworker jumps out of his skin, as though he's seen a ghost. The cigarette slips out as his jaw slackens.

So you . . . ?

A gust of wind blows out the matchstick. Two pairs of eyes widen in suspicion again in the darkness. The owner of one of them says yes, I'm a Muslim. So?

Nothing, answers the millworker. But . . .

Pointing to the bundle under the boatman's arm, he asks, what's in there?

A couple of shirts for my son and a sari for my wife. You know it's Eid tomorrow, don't you?

You aren't hiding anything else? The millworker cannot shed his suspicion.

You think I'm lying? Check for yourself. The boatman offers his bundle to the millworker.

No, there's nothing I want to check. But you know the times we live in. You tell me, is it safe to trust anyone?

That's true. Er . . . you don't have anything, do you?

Not even a needle, I swear to god. All I want is to go back home safe and sound. The millworker gives his clothes a shake to demonstrate.

The two of them sit down again side by side. Lighting their cigarettes, they smoke in concentrated silence for some time. Can you tell me . . . The boatman seems to be addressing a close friend now. Can you tell me what all this killing and maiming is for?

The millworker keeps in touch with the news, he reads the newspapers. Hotly he says, it's that League of yours that's to blame. They're the ones who started all this, calling it a protest.

I don't understand any of it, the boatman retorts harshly. All I want to know is, what's the use of this fighting? Your people will die and so will ours. What will the country gain?

That's exactly my point. What do you suppose the country will gain? A big zero. He makes a circle with his fingers. You will die, I will die, and our wives and children will be out on the streets begging. They chopped my brother-in-law into four pieces in last year's riots. So my sister became a widow and now I have to look after their children too. The leaders lie on their soft beds in their mansions and issue orders and we poor bastards have to die.

We aren't humans any more, we've become dogs. Only dogs bite one another. The boatman wraps his arms round his knees in impotent rage.

Exactly.

Who cares for us? Where's the food going to come from now that we have a riot? You think I'll get my boat back? Who knows where they've sunk it? Rup-babu is the landowner in our area, his manager used to travel in my boat to the island in the middle of the river once a month on work. The landowner was as generous as the lord, I'd get five rupees as tips and five as the fare, ten in all. I could buy food for the entire month. And the man who rode in my boat was a Hindu.

About to respond, the millworker stops abruptly. The clomping of heavy boots can be heard. There's no doubt that the marchers are coming into the lane from the main road. The two of them exchange terrified glances.

What should we do? The boatman grabs his bundle.

Let's run. But which way? I don't know my way around the city.

Doesn't matter which way, says the boatman. We're not going to sit here and get beaten up by the police. There's no trusting the swine.

Yes, you're right. Which way, then? They're almost here.

This way.

The boatman points towards the southern end of the lane. If we can make it to Badamtali Ghat, he says, we'll be safe.

Lowering their heads, they race out of the lane, not pausing till they reach Patuatoli Road. The deserted tarmac is glittering under the electric lights. They stop for a moment – there's no one lying in ambush, is there? But there's not a moment to lose. A quick glance up and down the road, and they rush off again towards the west. After they have travelled some way, they hear hoofbeats behind them. Turning, they see a solitary horseman approaching. There's no time to think. They duck into a narrow alleyway on the left used by toilet cleaners. In a moment, an Englishman on horseback gallops past them holding a gun. Only when the sound recedes in the distance do they leave the alley for a cautious peep.

Stay close to the houses, the millworker says.

They move forward swiftly and fearfully along the edge of the road.

Stop, the boatman says softly. The millworker halts abruptly.

Come this way. Taking the millworker's hand, the boatman leads him behind a paan shop.

Look.

Following the boatman's direction, the millworker's eyes stop at a lit-up building about a hundred yards away. A dozen policemen with guns are standing like statues in the veranda adjoining the building. And an English officer is speaking continuously through a mouthful of smoke from his pipe. Another policeman is holding the reins of his horse on the road in front of the building. The horse is stamping the ground restlessly with its hoof.

That's Islampur police station, says the boatman. There's a lane near it, it leads out of the street and goes to Badamtali Ghat. We can take it.

The millworker looks terrified. But how will we get there?

I suggest you stay here, reaching the Ghat is of no use to you anyway, says the boatman. This is a Hindu stronghold, but Islampur is filled with Muslims. You can spend the night here and go home in the morning.

What about you?

I'd better go. The boatman's voice cracked in anxiety and apprehension. I can't stay. It's been eight days since I left home. Allah alone knows what state they're in. I'll just have to sneak into the lane somehow. Even if I don't get a boat I can swim across the river.

What are you saying, mian? The millworker clutches the boatman's shirt anxiously. How can you go this way? His voice quavers.

Don't try to hold me back, bhai, I have to go. Tomorrow's Eid, don't you see? My family must have been looking out for the Eid moon tonight. My children expect to dress in new clothes tomorrow, to climb into my lap. My wife is weeping her heart out. I can't stay, bhai, I can't, you cannot imagine how I'm feeling. The boatman's voice is choked with tears. The millworker feels his heart breaking. He loosens his grip on his companion's shirt.

What if they catch you? His voice carries a mixture of dread and compassion.

Don't be afraid, they won't be able to catch me. But you must stay here, bhai, don't leave this place. I won't forget this night. We'll meet again, if fate decrees it. *Aadaab.*

I won't forget either, mian. *Aadaab.*

The boatman steals away.

The millworker remains standing, his mind clouded by anxiety. His heart refuses to slow down. He stays vigilant – please god, don't let the boatman come to any danger.

The moments pass with bated breath. It's been a long time, the boatman must have got away by now. How eagerly his children must be waiting for him to bring them new clothes, how happy they will be to see him! A father's heart, after all, poor fellow. The millworker sighs. Miansahib's wife will throw herself into his arms with love and tears.

You're back from the dead?

A smile appears on the millworker's lips. And what will the boatman do then? The boatman will . . .

Halt!

The millworker's heart leaps into his mouth. Some people in boots are running about. They're shouting.

He's escaping!

The millworker leans out to see the police officer leap into the street from the veranda with his gun. Shattering the silence, his firearm roars. Once, twice.

Two bangs. Two streaks of blue. The millworker bites his nails in anxiety. The policeman vaults on to his horse and gallops into the lane down which the boatman tried to escape. He can hear the death rattle of the man he has shot.

An image floats up in front of the stupefied millworker's eyes. The blood flowing from the boatman's body is soaking his children's and wife's clothes. The boatman is saying, I couldn't do it, bhai. My wife and children will be swept away by tears on the day of the festival. The enemy did not let me go to them.

MAHASWETA DEVI

Draupadi

I

Name Dopdi Mejhen, age twenty-seven, husband Dulna Majhi (deceased), domicile Cherakhan, Bankrahjarh, information whether dead or alive and/or assistance in arrest, 100 rupees ... an exchange between two medallioned *uniforms*.

FIRST MEDALLION. What's this, a tribal called Dopdi? The list of names I brought has nothing like it! How can anyone have an unlisted name?

SECOND MEDALLION. Draupadi Mejhen. Born the year her mother threshed rice at Surja Sahu (killed)'s at Bakuli. Surja Sahu's wife gave her the name.

FIRST. These officers like nothing better than to write as much as they can in English. What's all this stuff about her?

SECOND. *Most notorious* female. *Long wanted in many ...*

Dossier: Dulna and Dopdi worked at harvests, *rotating* between Birbhum, Burdwan, Murshidabad and Bankura.

In 1971, in the famous *Operation* Bakuli, when three villages were *cordoned* off and *machine-gunned*, they too lay on the ground, faking dead. In fact, they were the *main* culprits. Murdering Surja Sahu and his son, occupying *upper-caste* wells and tube wells during the *drought*, not *surrendering* those three young men to the police. In all this they were the chief instigators. In the morning, at the time of the body count, the couple could not be found. The *blood sugar* level of Captain Arjan Singh, the *architect* of Bakuli, rose at once and proved yet again that diabetes can be a result of anxiety and depression. Diabetes has twelve husbands – among them *anxiety*.

Dulna and Dopdi went underground for a long time in a *Neander-thal* darkness. The special forces, attempting to pierce that dark by an armed search, compelled quite a few Santhals in the various districts of West Bengal to meet their Maker against their will. By the Indian Constitution, all human beings, regardless of caste or creed, are sacred. Still, accidents like this do happen. Two sorts of reasons:

(1) The underground couple's skill in self-concealment; (2) not merely the Santhals but all tribals of the Austroasiatic Munda tribes appear the same to the special forces.

In fact, all around the ill-famed forest of Jharkhani, which is *under* the jurisdiction of the police station at Bankrajharh (in this India of ours, even a worm is under a certain police station), even in the south-east and south-west corners, one comes across hair-raising details in the eyewitness records put together on the people who are suspected of attacking police stations, stealing guns (since the snatchers are not invariably well educated, they sometimes say 'give up your *chambers*' rather than 'give up your gun'), killing grain brokers, landlords, moneylenders, law officers and bureaucrats. A black-skinned couple ululated like police *sirens* before the episode. They sang jubilantly in a savage tongue, incomprehensible even to the Santhals. Such as:

Samaray hijulenako mar goekope

and

Hendre rambra keche keche pundi rambra keche keche

This proves conclusively that they are the cause of Captain Arjan Singh's diabetes.

Government procedure being as incomprehensible as the Male principle in Samkhya philosophy or Antonioni's early films, it was Arjan Singh who was sent once again on *Operation Forest* Jharkhani. Learning from intelligence that the above-mentioned ululating and dancing couple were the escaped corpses, Arjan Singh fell for a bit into a *zombie*-like state and finally acquired so irrational a dread of black-skinned people that whenever he saw a black person in a ball-bag, he swooned, saying 'They're killing me', and drank and passed a lot of water. Neither uniform nor scriptures could relieve that depression. At long last, under the shadow of a *premature* and *forced retirement*, it was possible to present him at the desk of Mr Senanayak, the elderly Bengali *specialist* in combat and extreme-left politics.

Senanayak knows the activities and capacities of the opposition better than they themselves do. First, therefore, he presents an encomium on the military genius of the Sikhs. Then he explains further: is it only the opposition that should find power at the end of the barrel of a gun? Arjan Singh's power also explodes out of the *male organ* of a gun. Without a gun even the 'five Ks' come to nothing in this day and age. These speeches he delivers to all and sundry. As a result, the fighting forces regain their confidence in the *Army Handbook*. It is not a book for everyone. It says that the most despicable and repulsive style of fighting is guerrilla warfare with primitive weapons. Annihilation at sight of any and all practitioners of such warfare is the sacred duty of every soldier. Dopdi and Dulna belong to the *category* of such fighters, for they too kill by means of hatchet and scythe, bow and arrow, etc., in fact, their fighting power is greater than the gentlemen's. Not all gentlemen become experts in the explosion of *chambers*; they think the power will come out on its own if the gun is held. But since Dulna and Dopdi are illiterate, their kind have practised the use of weapons generation after generation.

I should mention here that, although the other side make little of him, Senanayak is not to be trifled with. Whatever his *practice*, in *theory* he respects the opposition. Respects them because they could be neither understood nor demolished if they were treated with the attitude, 'it's nothing but a bit of impertinent game-playing with guns'.

In order to destroy the enemy, become one. Thus he understood them by (*theoretically*) becoming one of them. He hopes to write on all this in the future. He has also decided that in his written work he will *demolish* the gentlemen and *highlight* the message of the harvest workers. These mental processes might seem complicated, but actually he is a simple man and is as pleased as his third great-uncle after a meal of turtle meat. In fact, he knows that, as in the old popular song, turn by turn the world will change. And in every world he must have the credentials to survive with honour. If necessary he will show the future to what extent he alone understands the matter in its proper perspective. He knows very well that what he is doing today the future will forget, but he also knows that if he can change colour from world to world, he can represent the particular world in question. Today he is getting rid of the young by means of '*apprehension and elimination*', but he knows people will soon forget the memory and lesson of blood. And at the same time, he, like Shakespeare, believes in delivering the world's *legacy* into youth's hands. He is Prospero as well.

At any rate, information is received that many young men and women, *batch by batch* and on jeeps, have attacked police station after police station, terrified and elated the region, and disappeared into the forest of Jharkhani. Since, after escaping from Bakuli, Dopdi and Dulna have worked at the house of virtually every landowner, they can efficiently inform the killers about their targets and announce proudly that they too are soldiers, *rank and file*. Finally the impenetrable forest of Jharkhani is surrounded by real soldiers, the *army* enter and split the battlefield. Soldiers in hiding guard the falls and springs that are the only source of drinking water; they are still guarding, still looking. On one such search, army informant Dukhiram Gharari saw a young Santhal man lying on his stomach on a flat stone, dipping his face to drink water. The soldiers shot him as he lay. As the .303 threw him off spreadeagled and brought a bloody foam to his mouth, he roared 'Ma-ho' and then went limp. They realized later that it was the redoubtable Dulna Majhi.

What does 'Ma-ho' mean? Is this a violent *slogan* in the tribal language? Even after much thought, the Department of Defence could not be sure. Two tribal-specialist types are flown in from Calcutta, and they sweat over the dictionaries put together by worthies such as Hoffman-Jeffer and Golden-Palmer. Finally the omniscient Senanayak summons Chamru, the water-carrier of the *camp*. He giggles when he sees the two specialists, scratches his ear with his bidi, and says, the Santhals of Maldah did say that when they began fighting at the time of King Gandhi! It's a battle cry. Who said 'Ma-ho' here? Did someone come from Maldah?

The problem is thus solved. Then, leaving Dulna's body on the stone, the soldiers climb the trees in green camouflage. They embrace the leafy boughs like replicas of the great god Pan and wait as the large red ants bite their private parts. To see if anyone comes to take away the body. This is the hunter's way, not the soldier's. But Senanayak knows that these brutes cannot be despatched by the approved method. So he asks his men to draw the prey with a corpse as bait. All will become clear, he says. I have almost deciphered Dopdi's song.

The soldiers get going at his command. But no one comes to claim Dulna's corpse. At night the soldiers shoot at a scuffle and, descending, discover that they have killed two hedgehogs copulating on dry leaves. Improvidently enough, the soldiers' jungle scout Dukhiram gets a knife in the neck before he can claim the reward for Dulna's capture. Bearing Dulna's corpse, the soldiers suffer shooting pains as the ants, interrupted in their feast, begin to bite them. When Senanayak hears that no one has come to take the corpse, he slaps his *anti-Fascist paperback* copy of *The Deputy* and shouts, '*What?*' immediately one of the tribal specialists runs in with a joy as naked and transparent as Archimedes' and says, 'Get up, *sir*! I have discovered the meaning of that 'hendre rambra' stuff. It's Mundari *language*.

Thus the search for Dopdi continues. In the forest *belt* of Jharkhani, the *Operation* continues – will continue. It is a carbuncle on the government's backside. Not to be cured by the tested ointment, not to burst with the appropriate herb. In the first phase the fugitives, ignorant of the forest's *topography*, are caught easily, and by the law of confrontation they are shot at the taxpayers' expense. By the law of confrontation, their eyeballs, intestines, stomachs, hearts, genitals and so on become the food of fox, vulture, hyena, wildcat, ant and worm, and the untouchables go off happily to sell their bare skeletons.

They do not allow themselves to be captured in open combat in the next phase. Now it seems that they have found a trustworthy *courier*. Ten to one it's Dopdi. Dopdi loved Dulna more than her blood. No doubt it is she who is saving the fugitives now. 'They' is also a *hypothesis*.

Why?

How many went *originally*?

The answer is silence. About that there are many tales, many books in press. Best not to believe everything.

How many killed in six years' confrontation?

The answer is silence.

Why after confrontations are the skeletons discovered with arms broken or severed? Could armless men have fought? Why do the collar bones shake, why are legs and ribs crushed?

Two kinds of answer. Silence. Hurt rebuke in the eyes. Shame on you! Why bring this up? What will be will be . . .

How many left in the forest? The answer is silence.

A *legion*? Is it *justifiable* to maintain a large battalion in that wild area at the taxpayers' expense?

Answer: *Objection*. 'Wild area' is incorrect. The battalion is provided with supervised nutrition, arrangements to worship according to religion, opportunity to listen to Bibidha Bharati and to see Sanjeev Kumar and the lord Krishna face to face in the movie *This is Life*. No. The area is not wild.

How many are left? The answer is silence.

How many are left? Is there anyone *at all*? The answer is long.

Item: *Well, action* still goes on. Moneylenders, landlords, grain brokers, anonymous brothel keepers, ex-informants are still terrified. The hungry and naked are still defiant and irrepressible. In some *pockets* the harvest workers are getting a *better wage*. Villages sympathetic to the fugitives are still silent and hostile. These events cause one to think . . .

Where in this picture does Dopdi Mejhen fit?

She must have connections with the fugitives. The cause for fear is elsewhere. The ones who remain have lived a long time in the primitive world of the forest. They keep company with the poor harvest workers and the tribals. They must have forgotten book learning. Perhaps they are *orienting* their book learning to the soil they live on and learning new combat and survival techniques. One can shoot and get rid of the ones whose only recourse is extrinsic book learning and sincere intrinsic enthusiasm. Those who are working practically will not be exterminated so easily.

Therefore *Operation* Jharkhani *Forest* cannot stop. Reason: the words of warning in the *Army Handbook*.

2

Catch Dopdi Mejhen. She will lead us to the others.

Dopdi was proceeding slowly, with some rice knotted into her belt. Mushai Tudu's wife had cooked her some. She does so occasionally. When the rice is cold, Dopdi knots it into her waistcloth and walks slowly. As she walked, she picked out and killed the lice in her hair. If she had some *kerosene*, she'd rub it into her scalp and get rid of her lice. Then she could wash her hair with baking soda. But the bastards put traps at every bend of the falls. If they smell *kerosene* in the water, they will follow the scent.

Dopdi!

She doesn't respond. She never responds when she hears her own name. She has seen in the panchayat office just today the notice for the reward in her name. Mushai Tudu's wife had said, what are you looking at? Who is Dopdi Mejhen? Money if you give her up!

How much?

Two . . . hundred!

Oh god!

Mushai's wife said outside the office: a lot of preparation this time. All new policemen.

Hm.

Don't come again.

Why?

Mushai's wife looked down. Tudu says that sahib has come again. If they catch you, the village, our huts . . .

They'll burn again.

Yes. And about Dukhiram.

The sahib knows?

Shomai and Budhna betrayed us. Where are they?

Ran away by train.

Dopdi thought of something. Then said, Go home. I don't know what will happen, if they catch me don't know me.

Can't you run away?

No. Tell me, how many times can I run away? What will they do if they catch me? They will *kounter* me. Let them.

Mushai's wife said, we have nowhere else to go.

Dopdi said softly, I won't tell anyone's name.

Dopdi knows, has learnt by hearing so often and so long, how one can come to terms with torture. If mind and body give way under torture, Dopdi will bite off her tongue. That boy did it. They *kountered* him. When they *kounter* you, your hands are tied behind you. All your bones are crushed, your sex is a terrible wound. *Killed by police in an encounter ... unknown male ... age twenty-two ...*

As she walked thinking these thoughts, Dopdi heard someone calling, Dopdi!

She didn't respond. She doesn't respond if called by her own name. Here her name is Upi Mejhen. But who calls? Spines of suspicion are always furled in her mind. Hearing 'Dopdi' they stiffen like a hedgehog's. Walking, she *unrolls the film* of known faces in her mind. Who? Not Shomra, Shomra is on the run. Shomai and Budhna are also on the run, for other reasons. Not Golok, he is in Bakuli. Is it someone from Bakuli? After Bakuli, her and Dulna's names were Upi Mejhen, Matang Majhi. Here no one but Mushai and his wife knows their real names. Among the young gentlemen, not all of the previous *batches* knew.

That was a troubled time. Dopdi is confused when she thinks about it. *Operation* Bakuli in Bakuli. Surja Sahu arranged with Biddi-babu to dig two tube wells and three wells within the compound of his two houses. No water anywhere, drought in Birbhum. Unlimited water at Surja Sahu's house, as clear as a crow's eye.

Get your water with *canal* tax, everything is burning.

What's my profit in increasing cultivation with tax money?

Everything's on fire.

Get out of here. I don't accept your panchayat non sense. Increase cultivation with water. You want half the paddy for sharecropping. Everyone is happy with free paddy. Then give me paddy at home, give me money, I've learnt my lesson trying to do you good.

What good did you do?

Have I not given water to the village?

You've given it to your kin Bhagunal.

Don't you get water?

No. The untouchables don't get water.

The quarrel began there. In the drought, human patience catches easily. Satish and Jugal from the village and that young gentleman, was Rana his name? Said a land owning moneylender won't give a thing, put him down.

Surja Sahu's house was surrounded at night. Surja Sahu had brought out his gun. Surja was tied up with cow rope. His whitish eyeballs turned and turned, he was incontinent again and again. Dulna had said, I'll have the first blow, brothers. My great-grandfather took a bit of paddy from him, and I still give him free labour to repay that debt.

Dopdi had said, his mouth watered when he looked at me. I'll put out his eyes.

Surja Sahu. Then a *telegraphic message* from Shiuri. *Special train. Army.* The *jeep* didn't come up to Bakuli. *March-march-march.* The *crunch-crunch-crunch* of gravel under hobnailed boots. *Cordon up.* Commands on the *mike.* Jugal Mandal, Satish Mandal, Rana *alias* Prabir *alias* Dipak, Dulna Majhi-Dopdi Mejhen *surrender surrender surrender. No surrender surrender. Mow-mow-mow down the village.* Putt-putt-putt-putt – *cordite* in the air – putt-putt – *round the clock* – putt-putt. *Flame thrower.* Bakuli is burning.

More men and women, children . . . fire . . . fire. Close canal approach. Over-over-over by nightfall. Dopdi and Dulna had crawled on their stomachs to safety.

They could not have reached Paltakuri after Bakuli. Bhupati and Tapa took them. Then it was decided that Dopdi and Dulna would work around the Jharkhani *belt.* Dulna had explained to Dopdi, Dear this is best! We won't get family and children this way. But who knows? Landowners and moneylenders and policemen might one day be wiped out!

Who called her from the back today?

Dopdi kept walking. Villages and fields, bush and rock – *Public Works Department* markers – sound of running steps at the back. Only one person running. Jharkhani forest still about two miles away. Now she thinks of nothing but entering the forest. She must let them know that the *police* have set up *notices* for her again. Must tell them that that bastard sahib has appeared again. Must change *hide-outs.* Also, the *plan* to do to Lakkhi Bera and Naran Bera what they did to Surja Sahu on account of the trouble over paying the field hands in Sandara must be cancelled. Shomai and Budhna knew everything. There was the *urgency* of great danger under Dopdi's ribs. Now she thought she had nothing to be ashamed of as a Santhal about Shomai and Budhna's treachery. Dopdi's blood was the pure unadulterated black blood of Champabhumi. From Champa to Bakuli the rise and set of a million moons. The blood could have been contaminated; Dopdi felt proud of her forefathers. They stood guard over their women's blood in black armour. Shomai and Budhna are half-breeds. The fruits of war. Contributions by the American soldiers stationed at Shiandange. Otherwise crow would eat crow's flesh before Santhal would betray Santhal.

Footsteps at her back. The steps keep a distance. Rice in her belt, tobacco leaves tucked at her waist. Arijit, Malini, Shamu, Mantu – none of them smokes or even drinks tea. Tobacco leaves and limestone powder. Best medicine for scorpion bite. Nothing must be given away.

Dopdi turned left. This way is the *camp*. Two miles. This is not the way to the forest. But Dopdi will not enter the forest with a cop at her back.

I swear by my life. By my life, Dulna, by my life. Nothing must be told.

The footsteps turn left. Dopdi touches her waist. In her palm the comfort of a half-moon. A baby scythe. The smiths at Jharkhani are fine artisans. Such an edge we'll put on it, Upi, 100 Dukhirams – thank god Dopdi is not a gentleman. Actually, perhaps they have understood scythe, hatchet and knife best. They do their work in silence. The lights of the *camp* at a distance. Why is Dopdi going this way? Stop a bit, it turns again. Huh! I can tell where I am if I wander all night with my eyes shut. I won't go in the forest, I won't lose him that way. I won't outrun him. You fucking jackal of a cop, deadly afraid of death, you can't run around in the forest. I'd run you out of breath, throw you in a ditch and finish you off.

Not a word must be said. Dopdi has seen the new *camp*, she has sat in the *bus station*, passed the time of day, smoked a bidi and found out how many *police convoys* had arrived, how many *radio vans*. Squash four, onions seven, peppers fifty, a straightforward account. This information cannot now be passed on. They will understand Dopdi Mejhen has been *kountered*. Then they'll run. Arijit's voice. If anyone is caught, the others must catch the *timing* and *change* their *hideout*. If *Comrade* Dopdi arrives late, we will not remain. There will be a sign of where we've gone. No *comrade* will let the others be destroyed for her own sake.

Arijit's voice. The gurgle of water. The direction of the next *hideout* will be indicated by the tip of the wooden arrowhead under the stone.

Dopdi likes and understands this. Dulna died, but, let me tell you, he didn't lose anyone else's life. Because this was not in our heads to begin with, one was *kountered* for the other's trouble. Now a much harsher rule, easy and clear. Dopdi returns – good; doesn't return – *bad*. *Change hideout*.

The clue will be such that the *opposition* won't see it, won't understand even if they do.

Footsteps at her back. Dopdi turns again. These three and a half miles of land and rocky ground are the best way to enter the forest. Dopdi has left that way behind. A little level ground ahead. Then rocks again. The *army* could not have struck *camp* on such rocky terrain. This area is quiet enough. It's like a maze, every hump looks like every other. That's fine. Dopdi will lead the cop to the burning 'ghat'. Patitpaban of Saranda had been sacrificed in the name of Kali of the Burning Ghats.

Apprehend!

A lump of rock stands up. Another. Yet another. The elder Senanayak was at once triumphant and despondent.

If you want to destroy the enemy, become one. He had done so. As long as six years ago he could anticipate their every move. He still can. Therefore he is elated. Since he has kept up with the literature, he has read *First Blood* and seen approval of his thought and work.

Dopdi couldn't trick him, he is unhappy about that. Two sorts of reasons. Six years ago he published an article about information storage in brain cells. He demonstrated in that piece that he supported this struggle from the point of view of the field hands. Dopdi is a field hand. *Veteran fighter. Search and destroy* Dopdi Mejhen is about to be *apprehended*. Will be *destroyed*. Regret.

Halt!

Dopdi stops short. The steps behind come round to the front. Under Dopdi's ribs the *canal* dam breaks. No hope. Surja Sahu's brother Rotoni Sahu. The two lumps of rock come forward. Shomai and Budhna. They had not escaped by train.

Arijit's voice. Just as you must know when you've won, you must also acknowledge defeat and start the activities of the next *stage*.

Now Dopdi spreads her arms, raises her face to the sky, turns towards the forest and ululates with the force of her entire being. Once, twice, three times. At the third burst the birds in the trees at the outskirts of the forest awake and flap their wings. The echo of the call travels far.

3

Draupadi Mejhen was *apprehended* at 6.57 p.m. It took an hour to get her to *camp*. Questioning took another hour exactly. No one touched her, and she was allowed to sit on a canvas camp stool. At 8.57 Senanayak's dinner hour approached, and saying, Make her. *Do the needful*, he disappeared.

Then a billion moons pass. A billion lunar years. Opening her eyes after a million light years, Draupadi, strangely enough, sees sky and moon. Slowly the bloodied nailheads shift from her brain. Trying to move, she feels her arms and legs still tied to four posts. Something sticky under her ass and waist. Her own blood. Only the gag has been removed. Incredible thirst. In case she says 'water' she catches her lower lip in her teeth. She senses that her vagina is bleeding. How many came to make her?

Shaming her, a tear trickles out of the corner of her eye. In the muddy moonlight she lowers her lightless eye, sees her breasts and understands that, indeed, she's made up right. Her breasts are bitten raw, the nipples torn. How many? Four-five-six-seven – then Draupadi had passed out.

She turns her eyes and sees something white. Her own cloth. Nothing else. Suddenly she hopes against hope. Perhaps they have abandoned her. For the foxes to devour. But she hears the scrape of feet. She turns her head, the guard leans on his bayonet and leers at her. Draupadi closes her eyes. She doesn't have to wait long. Again the process of making her begins. Goes on. The moon vomits a bit of light and goes to sleep. Only the dark remains. A compelled, spread-eagled, still body. Active *pistons* of flesh rise and fall, rise and fall over it.

Then morning comes.

Then Draupadi Mejhen is brought to the tent and thrown on the straw. Her piece of cloth is thrown over her body.

Then, after *breakfast*, after reading the newspaper and sending the radio message 'Draupadi Mejhen apprehended,' etc., Draupadi Mejhen is ordered to be brought in.

Suddenly there is trouble.

Draupadi sits up as soon as she hears 'Move!' and asks, where do you want me to go?

To the Burra sahib's tent.

Where is the tent?

Over there.

Draupadi fixes her red eyes on the tent. Says, come, I'll go.

The guard pushes the water pot forward.

Draupadi stands up. She pours the water down on the ground. Tears her piece of cloth with her teeth. Seeing such strange behaviour, the guard says, she's gone crazy, and runs for orders. He can lead the prisoner out but doesn't know what to do if the prisoner behaves incomprehensibly. So he goes to ask his superior.

The commotion is as if the alarm had sounded in a prison. Senanayak walks out surprised and sees Draupadi, naked, walking towards him in the bright sunlight with her head high. The nervous guards trail behind.

What is this? He is about to cry, but stops.

Draupadi stands before him, naked. Thighs and pubic hair matted with dry blood. Two breasts, two wounds.

What is this? He is about to bark.

Draupadi comes closer. Stands with her hand on her hip, laughs and says, the object of your search, Dopdi Mejhen. You asked them to make me up, don't you want to see how they made me?

Where are her clothes?

Won't put them on, *Sir.* Tearing them.

Draupadi's black body comes even closer. Draupadi shakes with an indomitable laughter that Senanayak simply cannot understand. Her ravaged lips bleed as she begins laughing. Draupadi wipes the blood on her palm and says in a voice that is as terrifying, sky-splitting and sharp as her ululation, what's the use of clothes? You can strip me, but how can you clothe me again? Are you a man?

She looks around and chooses the front of Senanayak's white bush shirt to spit a bloody gob at and says, there isn't a man here, so why should I be ashamed? I will not let you put my cloth on me. What more can you do? Come on, *kounter* me – come on, *kounter* me –?

Draupadi pushes Senanayak with her two mangled breasts, and for the first time Senanayak is afraid to stand before an unarmed *target*, terribly afraid.

(Translated by Gayatri Chakravorty Spivak)

Translator's Note: I am grateful to Soumya Chakravarti for his help in solving occasional problems of English synonyms and in archival research.

LOKENATH BHATTACHARYA

The Illness

Thank heavens Mrinmoyee hadn't seen him. What would have happened if she had? Or, who knew, maybe she had, but hadn't told him. No, she hadn't, she couldn't have – because if she had, her behaviour would have changed. But no, there was no change.

Thank heavens Mrinmoyee hadn't realized anything. No one had realized anything, no one had seen anything, no one had found out. Only he had seen – he, Sudhir, he alone had seen, he alone had realized. Or perhaps he hadn't either – it was his own doing, but he had not understood yet, perhaps he never would. For what was there to understand anyway, was it even conceivable? And that was what Sudhir was thinking. He couldn't believe that he . . . could have done something like this. And yet what was he to do but to believe it? Whatever had happened was his own doing – and what a horribly barbaric act it had been, perverted, unbelievable – now where could he escape to forget what he had done? Which pool of atonement could he dive into as punishment?

No one had seen him, it was true. But he had. How was he to face himself now? How was he to respect himself, to trust himself any more? And it wasn't exactly true that no one but he himself had seen everything. For there was the furniture in the room, the window was open, the parted curtains, the breeze slipping in through the gap, the light – all of them had seen, all of them were witnesses to that brutal moment. Come to think of it, he was not in fact alone in the room. Countless unseeing eyes had been staring at him in silent astonishment, boring into his back, his face, his hands . . . from all directions.

Khokon had seen him too, observing, understanding, sensing in a way that even Sudhir could not have sensed. Little Khokon, the three-month-old baby, darling Khokon, a slender band of gold around his wrist, lying on a rush mat on the floor, playing with his legs up in the air. He didn't know anything, didn't guess anything. He wasn't old enough to have guessed either. And even after what had happened, how was he to understand its significance? But in fact Sudhir had had no intention of doing anything, he was only in the grip of a lethal curiosity.

But then who had ever heard of such unnaturally dangerous curiosity? He could still see the whole thing unfolding in front of his eyes. Over the past few minutes he had seen it take place in his head many times. Each time he had jumped in fear. What would have happened had Mrinmoyee not come into the room at that moment?

'What's my darling doing?' he recalled Mrinmoyee saying as she entered. He didn't remember her reason for coming in, it was no time to wonder about this. It must have been something she had to do in the room, must have been a task of some kind. Or, you never knew, maybe there was no reason at all, perhaps she had come only to check on her son. Or was it to breastfeed him? Oh yes, that was what it was.

All Sudhir remembered was how he had leapt up on hearing his wife's voice. The kind of leap with which a tiger abandons its prey and hides in the bush on hearing a distant gunshot. But what kind of thinking was this about Khokon? How could Sudhir's own son, his dearest Khokon, his very heart, his long-cherished desire, be his prey? But he had indeed leapt up, not to hide in a bush, but to put a yard or two between himself and Khokon. He remembered a constant hammering in his heart.

'What's happened to Khokon today, he hasn't cried even once all morning. When did he become such a good boy?' That was what Mrinmoyee had said. Sudhir wasn't sure of her exact words, but she had said something to this effect. Later, when she had taken her son in her arms: 'Oh oh, why is my baby so pale? What's happened, my sunbeam?'

The boy cried out loudly at once, Sudhir remembered this too, as well as his own response.

'Why, nothing.'

Was he not mortified to say this?

It was true, nothing had actually happened. But it could have. And what *had* happened was not trivial. What had happened, and what had not but could have happened, what was about to happen, it could be said to have all but happened – both these things were so horrifying that it sent tingles of fear down his spine.

Suppose something had happened, what would the outcome have been? Would Mrinmoyee have reported him to the police? Yes, the very same Mrinmoyee, she would have reported him to the police. And why not? Who was more important to her, husband or son? Was her love for her husband stronger than a mother's heart? Then custody, a trial. The grotesque account of which would be published prominently in the newspapers. Readers would be silent, who had ever heard of such cruelty, of anything so macabre? Perhaps a lengthy trial would be unnecessary, it would be over in a day. Where was the scope for dispute over such a heinous act, a fact that could be proven quite easily? And why say it could be proven, it had already been proven, as soon as it took place, there would be no room for trivial arguments or doubts. And it wasn't as though Sudhir himself would have allowed such a possibility. Would he really have been able to stand in court and say, or have the inclination to say, 'No, I didn't do this, or, prove that I did it, send for your witnesses.' How would the prosecution find witnesses? Would the furniture be summoned in that case, the open window, the parted curtain, the breeze that had blown in, the light, all of them? So no, there would be no witnesses. And Mrinmoyee could not have claimed either that she had seen it with her own eyes, the whole thing would have been over before she had entered the room.

The only one who could have borne witness was Khokon. But he was a baby of three months – and besides, he would not even have been there any more. Grief welled up in Sudhir's breast.

No, he would not have lied in court. Why should he? What self-interest would he have? He had lost his wife's love, his child, his own child, whom he had with his own hands . . . ohh! And what would his mother-in-law have said, the same mother-in-law who had installed herself here in this house, in this congested, rented building in Calcutta, in this second-floor flat of three small rooms with the paint flaking off the walls? She was visiting, good for her, of course she would visit, it was her daughter's house, why shouldn't she? But what would she have said, that was the main thing? Would she not have screamed the place down, telling her daughter, 'I told you so many times, you didn't listen, I didn't like Sudhir from the beginning, I didn't care for his appearance or for the look in his eyes or the way he spoke or anything else, but you were so adamant, so insistent, you didn't listen, and now look at what you've brought on yourself?'

She would have struck her brow with her hand, or beat her head against the wall. Sudhir felt he could see it. Her dearest grandson Khokon, for whom she had bought a house in Madhupur only a month ago and named it Khokon House.

But then she would have done what she had to, that wasn't the main thing. Even if he had to go to jail or was hanged, that wasn't the main thing either. The main thing was that he would have lost Khokon – and this loss, especially the manner of this loss, would make any other punishment or remorse inconsequential.

Glancing at his watch, Sudhir discovered it was ten o'clock. He simply had to get going now, although he should have done it much earlier.

'What's this, you haven't bathed or eaten yet, don't you have to go to work today, or are you not planning to?' Mrinmoyee asked from the other room.

'Yes, I'll get ready now, I got really late today,' said Sudhir. Was that a quiet sigh, unseen by anyone?

In fact he had no wish to get ready, he seemed to be lacking the strength. As though his life had suddenly frozen at a point. The key was hanging from the trunk, which seemed to be open. Why wasn't it locked, especially considering the key was right there? And if it was locked, why leave the key hanging there? Maybe Mrinmoyee had forgotten. What if she had? They didn't exactly have gems and jewellery in there. And this was a matter of regret for Mrinmoyee's mother, whom Sudhir could also address as ma now, whom he had to address as ma. Because convention dictates that your wife's mother is your mother too, just as your mother is your wife's mother as well. So he had to address her as ma, which he did. It involved neither willingness nor unwillingness. Why should there have been unwillingness anyway? Mrinmoyee's mother had acted as she had seen fit, Sudhir didn't blame her for it. She had not been in favour of their marriage, she had in fact been staunchly opposed to it. Naturally. After all, what did Sudhir have then, and what did he have now, for that matter? The only thing he could count on was the 400-rupee job which he had then and had now too – it was just that his salary had risen by thirty rupees in these fifteen months. What was the difference between 400 and 430? Next to nothing. Mrinmoyee came from a well-established family, she was the only child of her rich, widowed mother. So Sudhir didn't blame his mother-in-law. She had tried in so many ways before the marriage, she had created such scenes. Not only had she tormented her daughter in various ways, she had also humiliated Sudhir greatly. 'A broken plank of wood, a roadside beggar, an unfeeling useless object, how dare you imagine I will let my daughter marry you,' etcetera etcetera. He recollected everything clearly – it felt like just the other day. That wasn't all, she had tried to harm Sudhir in as many ways as possible – so much so that he was on the verge of losing his treasured job. One of his mother-in-law's friends knew the top boss in Sudhir's office. Mrinmoyee's mother had made many false complaints to his employer, including one that said he had borrowed 1,500 rupees from her and not returned it. The same woman who was now his mother-in-law, his Mrinmoyee's mother. Yet she couldn't prevent the marriage. Anyway, why rake up the past? Everything had been sorted out, they had arrived at a compromise – Sudhir behaved as though there had never been any disagreement between them, so did his mother-in-law. Just as well, what harm could it do? And then Khokon had arrived, drawing the curtains on all hostilities like a god-given gift. Mrinmoyee's mother seemed to have been saved by her grandson, heaven was within reach. And why not? Such a bonny baby, and then a son in their family after a long time.

Oh yes, now he remembered why Mrinmoyee had unlocked the trunk in the morning. She had asked a tailor to make a set of new clothes for Khokon. They had been delivered, so she had meant to put them away. But thinking of Khokon made Sudhir feel someone was twisting his heart in a vice. As though a blood clot had struck him without warning somewhere inside his chest.

What had Sudhir done? Was he a man or a beast? And what kind of beast? Imagine taking his own son and . . . he couldn't think about it any more, there was a tangle of thoughts in his head. But he had never questioned himself before on whether he was human. No hidden immoral aberration, no mental perversion, no irrational outburst, he had never experienced any of this. Was he then in fact the basest of animals, more loathsome than a man-eater, who had simply not recognized himself all this while – and the intolerable moment of this cruel discovery had arrived only today. The passage of people outside remained unrestricted, the world was moving to its usual rhythm, a normal world. But he, Sudhir, Mrinmoyee's husband, Khokon's father, he had eventually ... absolutely not, how was he to acknowledge such a possibility as the truth?

No, he really would go mad if he kept brooding. It would be better to go to the office – it was true he was late, but he could offer an excuse. For instance, that his son had fallen ill and he had had to take him to the doctor. But bring up his son again? What harm had the child done for Sudhir to use him to meet his own repugnant objectives?

Still, Sudhir rose to his feet. He noticed his father's photograph on the wall was hanging crookedly again. Every time he straightened it, it resumed this position. It wasn't his fault, he had always tried to straighten the photograph, never failing to display his respect for his dead father. But what was this he was thinking? Had he taken a vow to prove himself guilty for whatever he did today?

In truth he had done nothing wrong, he hadn't done anything at all – he was a normal, balanced individual. What he probably needed was to give himself some respite from his thoughts. It was best to go to the office, if he could just immerse himself in work or conversation for even two or three hours, that would save him this time round. All his mental fatigue, physical exhaustion, this madness, all of it would vanish. Otherwise, you never knew, he really could become insane.

On his way to the bathroom, he suddenly made eye contact with his mother-in-law. When was it she had said she was going back? Next Saturday, probably. That was fine then, a matter of just a few days more.

He sat down to his meal after his bath. Casual exchanges with Mrinmoyee. No, she hadn't found out, she hadn't realized anything at all.

'Will you remember to get a nice ripe papaya if you find one?' Mrinmoyee said, fanning him as he ate.

'A papaya?'

'Ma needs some fruit every day. It's all so expensive locally, and you don't get it fresh either. I was thinking, maybe from New Market on your way back from work ...'

'Hmm.'

'And maybe you could get a couple of pairs of shorts for Khokon too.'

Again Sudhir's heart leapt into his mouth.

'What's he doing?' he said.

'Who?'

'Khokon.'

'Asleep. He's been very sweet all morning, the darling. Just that one time that he was wailing, I don't know why.'

Once again everything began to swirl in Sudhir's head. Jumping to his feet, he put on his shirt and looked at himself in the mirror as he buttoned it. Did he really look like a murderer or a potential murderer? This nose, this mouth, these eyes, all of them so familiar, he had seen this face so many times in the mirror that he could conjure up a detailed description even with his eyes closed. The tiny mole on the left half of the lower chin was as sharp as ever. Everything was familiar, and yet it all seemed unfamiliar. Who was this man named Sudhir really, whose long-familiar face was reflected in the mirror? Who actually lived behind the mask, did Sudhir know him at all?

What exactly had happened? In a flash he tried to recollect the incident. Khokon was lying on his mat when Sudhir entered. Khokon knew nothing – he was so little, what could he possibly know – and nor did Sudhir. Khokon didn't think of Sudhir as his father yet, he didn't even know what this father business was. But in his brief three months he had certainly come to know that he saw this man regularly, the man hugged and kissed him, the man loved him, he had nothing to fear from this man. So the sight of Sudhir had brought forth a faint expression of happiness on his face, he threw his right fist into the air and brought it down on the floor, lowered his legs a little. Sudhir had come to spend a few moments with his son, to give him a kiss or two – he was not aware of anything more. There was no one else in the room.

And then? Sudhir sat down next to Khokon, hugged and kissed him, and recited a rhyme, rotating his fists to match the words. Khokon gazed in puzzlement at the moving hands, occasionally flinging his legs and arms outwards in dance. His gestures indicated he was enjoying himself.

Sudhir kissed his son on the cheek with some intensity – he had an urge to bite the boy's cheek. Khokon was finding it hard to breathe, he gasped once or twice. Sudhir moved his own face away, and Khokon, now freed, flung his arms and legs upwards again.

And that was when Sudhir felt the impulse. Not for the first time, it had happened earlier too. And each time he had experimented with his precious child. But he himself hadn't gauged the extent of the impact this time.

Seeing that Khokon was finding it difficult to breathe, Sudhir was tempted to have some fun. Taking his mouth close to his son's nostrils, he blew into them. Khokon was startled. Sudhir blew again, a little harder this time – Khokon was even more startled. He blew yet again, and once more Khokon was startled. This was fun! As though he quite liked the sight of the little boy's face as he gasped for breath every now and then. Then Sudhir kept blowing, again and again, harder each time, even harder, even harder, even harder. He didn't give the baby a moment of respite. He had bent over the boy, taking his mouth close to his nostrils, and kept blowing into them for all he was worth. He was possessed by some sort of madness, it was a monstrous game now, he had taken leave of his senses. The earth seemed to be swaying, the sky fusing with the earth, the earth rising to become one with the sky, he wasn't going to stop till the game had reached its end. And the baby? He was on the verge of going, perhaps it would take just one more deep inhalation and then blowing the air out ... But at that precise moment, possibly at the moment before the final one, Mrinmoyee had entered.

Thankfully she had arrived at the right time. And thankfully, too, she had not come to know. Even if she had, that would not have caused as much harm as would have been the case had she not entered in the nick of time. A stormy sea was raging within Sudhir. He didn't know what he wanted to do – he didn't know what he could have done or what there might have been for him to do. He was itching to do something, if only he could have grabbed something nearby, he would have smashed it into pieces. There were in fact many things within reach – clothes, a mug, toothpaste. But he wasn't interested in any of this. He wanted to break something into smithereens. If he could have just wrapped his fingers around Khokon's throat, if he could have just choked him to death in a moment. And after that? Would he have felt terrible about it? Would he have had to pass the rest of his life in a state of extreme contrition?

But what was this he was thinking? Was he really going insane? He wanted a little light, the sky, some air, some space, he was choking for breath in this room, in this prison. Of course he would go to work, he was late already, would it matter if he was a little more late? Or he wouldn't go at all, tomorrow he'd say he was ill. And that wouldn't entirely be a lie. Even if it was, what of it? It wouldn't be the first lie he'd be telling in his life. Just a short while ago he'd told Mrinmoyee a huge lie, he had deceived her in the most low, sordid and despicable way. He did not have the courage then to tell his wife the truth. 'Yes, something has happened, a great deal, actually I was about to murder Khokon, I wanted to see what he looked like when dead.' No, he had not been able to tell her this.

And is there anyone who doesn't lie? How many people had he met who told nothing but the truth? Was he some great spiritual soul who could put his hand on his heart and claim never to have uttered a lie? If he did, he would only be telling one more lie. And besides, if he did tell them at work that he had been ill, it wouldn't be much of a lie. Because if this wasn't an illness, then what was? An illness didn't mean only a fever or an upset stomach.

He needed light, he needed the sky. The roof was on the third floor, Sudhir climbed up there. The other tenants' clothes were drying on lines, they lived on the first and ground floors. It was barely ten-thirty, but already the sun was scorching. There wasn't another soul on the roof. Sudhir came to a halt, his eyes blank and bewildered. The wind blew in a dry leaf shed by a tree somewhere and dropped it near his feet. He picked it up. On a whim he went up to the railing and tossed it towards the main road, watching as it fell, turning, swaying, drifting to the left and to the right, sometimes rising a little, then falling. In this way, at a slow, leisurely pace, it finally came to a rest on the pavement a few buildings away, in front of Tollygunge Shoe House. But nothing happened to it, the leaf remained as it was. But then what could happen, it didn't have a life that would end. It was nothing but a dry, fallen leaf. It had no weight to speak of, so there were no wounds. It only fell from the third floor, laughing and playing, to the pavement.

But what if it had been a flesh-and-blood human instead of a leaf? What if it had been Khokon? Should Sudhir jump and see for himself what would happen? He had read in the newspapers any number of times about what happens, he had heard people talk about it, but why not find out for himself? No, impossible, he was frightened.

'What's this, you haven't gone to work yet?'

Startled, Sudhir turned round to find Mrinmoyee behind him. She had come up to the roof with three or four wet saris to put them up to dry.

Sudhir had a momentary impulse to say, 'No, I'm not going to work today.' But the very next moment he thought, what if Mrinmoyee suspected something?

'Yes, I'll go now.'

Throwing him a questioning glance, Mrinmoyee said, 'What's the matter? What is it? Are you not feeling well? Why did you eat then?'

'Of course not, nothing's the matter. I was just being lazy, I got late.'

'Time you went. What will people say?'

'What can they say? Am I never allowed to be late?'

'You know best. It's your job, not mine.'

'All right, I'll leave now.'

He was about to go down the stairs when Mrinmoyee said from the back, 'Listen.' And then, after a pause, 'What's the matter? I feel you're hiding something from me.'

Oh hell! She had probably found out.

'What's all this?' said Sudhir. 'Nothing's the matter, I keep telling you.'

'You've been behaving strangely since morning, you haven't been talking.'

'For heaven's sake, what should I be talking about? I played with Khokon in the morning, then bathed and ate. You told me what to buy. Now I'm going to work. Just that I got a bit late today.'

'But you're never late. I don't think I've ever seen you dawdle deliberately. What did you come up to the roof for?'

'Now you're interrogating me. Am I not allowed up on the roof now and then?'

'Listen, have you fought with anyone at work?'

'Honestly, I haven't, nothing's the matter, it's just that I got late today for no good reason, that's all. Believe me. I'll get even more late if you start a full-fledged interrogation now.'

'All right, never mind.'

'I'll go now. Take care of Khokon.'

'I do every day.'

'Yes, like you do every day.'

Sudhir went on his way down the stairs. Really, why did he have to

bring up Khokon? He could have sowed the seeds of suspicion in Mrinmoyee's mind, unknowingly and yet deliberately. You never knew what
Mrinmoyee might be thinking now. She had probably found out – no,
surely not. Anyway, I'll be relieved to get to the office, Sudhir reflected, I
was on the brink of disaster, everything might have come out under the
onslaught of her interrogation.

One advantage of being late was that it would be easier to take the tram
now. He did in fact get on easily enough, and even found a seat in a couple
of minutes. Still the thought wouldn't leave him, he couldn't forget it despite his best efforts. His eyes were on the moving shops outside the
window, but he wasn't seeing them. Having your eyes open didn't mean
seeing, the mind had to participate, only then was it possible. And Sudhir's
mind was elsewhere today. How could he have done such a thing – and
that, too, to his own son? He, who was so fearful of death, who looked left
and right twenty times before crossing the road, who didn't let anyone go
close to the railing on the roof, who screamed when he saw children leaning out of the window, 'Get down, you'll fall, you'll smash your head.'
Mrinmoyee would laugh, 'Always overdoing things.'

Just the other day, they'd gone to inspect a house in Behala for renting.
It was very congested where they lived in Tollygunge, Behala was still
relatively unpopulated, so he'd thought of moving in case he found something cheap. Mrinmoyee was with him. The house was still under
construction, it was incomplete, there was no railing yet on the first-floor
balcony. He remembered holding Mrinmoyee back when she approached
the balcony. 'Don't go so close, you'll fall,' he had said. Mrinmoyee had
died laughing.

There were many more such incidents that he could recollect. The village
in which he had spent his childhood had a well, as wide as it was deep.
He would toss in pebbles and count the seconds till the splash. He would
never go too close, at most peering over the rim for a moment to gaze at
the darkness below. What if I fall in, he would fret.

Imagine the same Sudhir doing what he had today. But then he recollected another trivial incident too. Something that had happened often in
his childhood, and still did now. Why did these things happen, why did
Sudhir behave this way? This morning, for instance, this very morning,
before the incident with Khokon, when Sudhir was in the toilet, he had

found a cockroach trying to climb up the inner wall of the commode. Every time it tried, it slipped. Once, twice, three times, it tried over and over. Finally, after much effort, it did manage to clamber up over the edge. Most entertaining, Sudhir thought, the fellow has survived after all. He was quite pleased at the cockroach's success. But the very next moment he wondered, let's see if it can climb again. With this thought he used a mug of water to send it back into the pot. Again it tried several times before climbing back up again. What a strong survival instinct, mused Sudhir. There was no telling how long the game might have continued, but because he was getting late, or perhaps it was for some other reason, Sudhir pulled the flush as the cockroach was struggling to safety yet again. At once the rush of water sucked it back into the pot and the sewage pipe. Let's see you climb back now, Sudhir thought to himself.

But why were these horrifying thoughts crowding his mind? Was he really going insane? It seemed to him that all the ideas and principles of his life till now were changing, that he was about to discover himself in a horrifying form. His hands were still itching to do something, his chest seemed to be on fire.

They had arrived at Dalhousie Square. Sudhir got off the tram. The room he worked in was on the second floor too. When he climbed two flights of stairs and went in, he found the world inside unchanged and functioning in its usual way. He wasn't expecting novelty, but he would have liked to have seen some change, something unexpected, at least a new employee. But no, the desks were laid out in rows as before, with everyone working at them. It was like the long trestle tables lined up at a wedding for guests to eat at, and they were all seated, only the food was yet to arrive. Was he the food? Really, what were these wild ideas?

Pannalal-babu had his seat opposite Sudhir's. Raising his eyes from his file, he said, 'So late?'

'My little boy's had a fever since the morning, so I had to take him to the doctor,' Sudhir said without batting an eyelid.

'Yes, the flu is doing the rounds, my son has a fever too, don't even ask. Oh yes, the boss was looking for you.'

'Looking for me? Why?'

'No idea. Go meet him, let him know you're here.'

Sudhir was about to get out of his chair when he heard a woman's sharp scream. The sound seemed to shake the building to its foundations as it descended from above and went downwards. A moment, and then silence. What was it? Everyone exchanged glances. There was a crowd already at the window that looked out on the street below, everyone was peering to find out what had happened. There was an uproar in the office, with many employees racing down the stairs. Sudhir sat down again in a daze.

Ramdhan the bearer was the first to bring the news. Gasping for breath, he told everyone that Sulochona Sen had killed herself. One of the typists in the managing director's office. She had jumped from a second-floor window a few moments ago.

'How is that possible?' someone said. 'I saw her this morning, she smiled and chatted with us, even made a joke, what could have happened in just two hours for her to ...'

'Who knows what goes on in a woman's mind,' someone else said. 'No one commits suicide by choice, there can be so many reasons, financial, psychological, family. Did any of us know her personal life well enough to comment on it? We only exchanged a few words with her in passing.'

An expansive round of speculation began – why had Sulochona Sen killed herself? The room rang with diverse opinions. Someone said, 'This is what happens with unmarried women. There's an age after which women can't do without it. It's not like us men who can visit a whorehouse if we feel the need. But what will a woman from a decent family do? Let's say her father hasn't got her married, or perhaps her parents have died, and she can't find a man either, what is she supposed to do, tell me?'

'Yes, she must commit suicide,' someone else responded. 'For heaven's sake, you can think of nothing but sex.'

Sudhir stared blankly into space, deaf to all the commotion going on around him. All that had taken place since this morning appeared to have robbed him of the power of speech, of hearing, of thinking coherently. He seemed to return to his senses suddenly and shot upright in his chair. Jumping up, he strode off towards the staircase and ran down the stairs. From the staircase to the pavement, and then directly into the crowd.

So many people! Not a toehold to be found. All the windows in the buildings nearby were lined with faces. How many people lived in Calcutta, anyway? So many of them in each of these buildings, employees and work-ers all of them. Sudhir seemed possessed by a stubborn resolve, he was determined to push through the crowd. As he went forward, the others, assuming he was a member of the dead woman's family, made way for him. He went all the way to the front and looked at the woman lying on the ground. How strange, it was the same woman, but she would never move again! never talk again, never smile again, never go up and down the stairs again. Sudhir was very close to her now, looking at her covetously. Her head was split open, with blood and some other things oozing out. Her left eye had sprung out of its socket. Her name was Sulochona, and how her beautiful eyes justified her name today! Her sari had folded back on itself from the bottom and fallen on her breast, she was lying on the street with her naked thighs parted. You have no shame today, no shame, Sulochona.

And yet, how strange it was that her shoes were undamaged. The high-heeled shoes were still attached to her feet, intact. Bravo, what an accomplishment by these man-made objects!

So this was what happened to a living being, Sudhir reflected, unlike the leaf in the morning. He seemed to have found an apt answer to the question that had been tormenting him all day. His hands were no longer itching to do something, his chest no longer felt as though it was on fire. Sudhir did not know what the question was, nor what the apt answer was right now, he could not explain it. Not all truths can be analysed, not all truths can be known, some can only be received from time to time. Thank heavens Khokon had survived today – a sigh of relief rose from somewhere deep within Sudhir. Yes, he was cured, he would never play such a monstrous game with the boy again. Or would he? No, he wouldn't, he wouldn't, he wouldn't.

A number of policemen had gathered already; now they were joined by an ambulance that would pick up the corpse.

'Well, let's go?'

Startled, Sudhir turned to find Pannalal-babu behind him.

'Go where?' he asked.

'Home, of course.'

'What! It's barely twelve.'

'Yes, the office has been closed, haven't you heard? An employee has died like this, after all.'

The sun was merciless overhead. But still Sudhir didn't feel like taking a tram immediately. He was returning on foot. Suddenly it occurred to him: he hadn't murdered her, had he? Could he have pushed her off without even knowing what he was doing? What he wanted to do this morning, on the roof of his house, but could not because he was a coward – had he conducted the experiment with this woman? Even if he had not killed her directly, was he not at least partly responsible for her death?

What rot, what was this he had begun thinking again? Even if there was an invisible similarity between the woman's death and Sudhir's own grievances or thoughts today, it was nothing but a coincidence. Sulochona Sen had died, what could he have done about it, what was there for him to do about it? Sulochona Sen was dead, and he was reborn, felt Sudhir. The very next moment he thought, poor thing, she died today, she had to die this way. Suddenly he felt a surge of affection for Khokon, he felt great pity for the boy. He was dying to hug and kiss Khokon, oh, hug and kiss again?

No, it was impossible to walk any more, Sudhir felt. Might as well take a tram. Oh, mustn't forget to get a papaya for the mother-in-law from New Market, and shorts for the darling son.

SYED MUSTAFA SIRAJ

India

A small market had sprung up where the asphalt highway turned to the left. The village stood behind it, hidden from view by a dense bamboo grove. The village had no electricity, but the market did. There were three tea shops, two for sweetmeats, three for garments, one stationery store and two groceries. There was a godown too, and a husking machine, besides a brick kiln at the back. People came from nearby villages. There was always a hubbub here till about nine at night, when the market emptied out. Only some lights kept burning thereafter. The shadows of mongrels moved around the asphalt surface. Sometimes a truck passed in the direction of the distant town. Silence again. Even the hooting of the owl in the banyan tree standing at the bend in the highway seemed part of the silence.

It was winter then. A bone-chilling wind blew in constantly from the enormous field to the north of the market. Then the sky turned grey with clouds, and a light rain began. The cold in this part of Bengal was always extreme, and now the rain made it sharper. The gentry called it *poushey baadlaa*, while the working class referred to it as *daaur*. When the wind grew strong along with the rain, it was known as *faanpi*. The weather turned to *faanpi* this time. The paddy had not yet been harvested in the distant fields, and the untimely deluge could harm the crops greatly. This put the people in a bad mood. Congregating at one of the tea shops, the farmers waited for a day with sunshine and cursed the gods of their respective religions. Eventually a furious young cultivator declared at the top of his voice, 'There's no one up there looking after us, damn it, no one.'

Since there was no one up there, everyone could do as they pleased. Rising tempers led to arguments, taking things to the brink of a fight. No specific subject was needed – anything would do. No one knew how to pass their time at home during this unseasonal, inclement weather. Everyone gathered at the small fire of civilized life to warm their feet, which was the only comfort that was available. To dispel the boredom, discussions ranged around various themes, from film stars and popular singers to the prime minister, chief minister and legislators – or Shawra Bauri's daughter, who had got herself a lover from the city. Hot words were exchanged, and sales rose at the tea shop. It was harvest season, which meant all payments would be settled sooner or later, so the amount sold on credit kept increasing.

Suddenly an old woman appeared from nowhere. A doddering, hunch-backed beggar woman with a dreadful appearance. A headful of white hair, dressed in a torn, dirty sari, with an equally filthy blanket wrapped round herself. She had a short, stout stick, with the help of which she walked up the asphalt highway with an unbroken rhythm. Her wizened, withered face held clear signs of having lived a long time. Entering the shop in the midst of a heated argument, she asked for a cup of tea. The argument stopped when the participants saw her. They were astonished that she had survived a long walk through this terrible weather.

Drinking her tea with great enjoyment, the old woman looked around at everyone, though she didn't speak. 'Where did you come from, old woman?' someone asked.

She was bad-tempered. 'What business is it of yours?' she snapped back.

Everyone laughed. 'Listen to her, so fiery! A spirited horse out for a trot in the rain.'

She was furious now. 'Your father is a horse. Don't you dare say these things to me. What business is it of anyone's where I'm coming from?'

One of the cool-headed people said, 'They're asking where you live, old woman.'

'In your heads.'

Retrieving some money wrapped in a rag from beneath her blanket, she paid for her tea and stepped out on the road again.

'She's going to die,' people shouted, 'the old woman will die.'

'All of you can die, your entire families can die,' she said, wheeling round.

Everyone watched as she tottered off towards the banyan tree standing at the bend in the road. The spot was devoid of people, and the ground was covered in mud after the rain. The old woman sat down on a thick root in full view of everyone. The surface of the trunk behind the roots was pitted, she leant her back against it and spread her legs out in front. She was clearly an experienced woman, someone who lived amid trees.

Some people said, 'If only she had gone to the village instead. She's bound to die any time.' This led to speculation about the old woman. Everyone joined in animatedly.

There was an old saying in the village about weather like this.

Seven days on Saturday, five days on Tuesday, three days if it comes on a Wednesday. On all other days it won't last long, beyond a single day.

This time the rain had begun on a Tuesday, and while no one had calculated how long it took to clear, when it did the sky turned blue and the sun shone brightly. And the old woman was discovered lying on her back beneath the banyan tree with her back to the pitted trunk. Inert.

When she didn't move even after several hours, Joga the tea-seller said, 'Must be dead.'

'This means trouble,' said someone. 'Those animals will tear her body apart, the stench will be horrible.'

The crowd grew in ones and twos. Someone touched her forehead – it was ice-cold. Someone else checked her pulse and found it was not beating. Dead, therefore.

The chowkidaar in the village, the sole representative of the administration, was told. 'What's the use of informing the police station?' he said. 'A beggar has died in the *faanpi*, why do the police need to be involved? They're ten miles away, it will be midnight by the time they arrive. The body will start rotting. Who knows when she died, don't you see how swollen the body is?'

'What should we do then?'

'Throw her into the river. The currents will take care of it.'

The experienced chowkidaar's advice was heeded. The river was two miles away, on the other side of the large field. It was dry now. Some people picked up the corpse and left it on the riverbed. The old woman's body lay stiff on the hot sand in the bright sunshine.

After their return everyone trained their eyes on the horizon in anticipation of vultures.

*

A strange sight was seen that afternoon. A body was being carried across the field, dangling from a horizontally held bamboo pole by its arms and legs. The details became clear when it reached the market. The Muslims of the area had picked the old woman's corpse up from the riverbed. They were chanting in Arabic, and some of them had caps on.

Those who had dumped the body were Hindus. Both surprised and angry, they asked what was going on.

'She was Muslim.'

'Where's the proof?'

'Plenty of proof. Many people heard her say *Bismillah*.'

The local Islamic priest proffered evidence. 'She was dying when I passed this way to take the bus after the dawn prayer. I clearly heard her recite the *Kalima*. Who knew the hag was dying? I was on my way to the town for a court case, so I could not take a closer look. When I returned I heard she had been left on the riverbed. The lord forgive me, how can this be allowed while we're alive? So we have made arrangements to bury her in a grave.'

Bhattacharya, the local priest, had just got off the bus. Sizing up the situation, he said, 'Impossible! I went to the town on the same bus as the maulvi, does he think I'm deaf? I clearly heard the old woman chanting Hari's name.'

Several of the others supported his claim. Nakri the barber swore, 'I was at the spot yesterday to shave my customers, but I realized my place beneath the tree was taken. That was when I heard the old woman clearly recite our gods' names.'

'You heard wrong,' said Fazlu Sheikh. 'I distinctly heard her say *la ilaha illa*.'

Nibaran Bagdi was prone to anger; he used to be a highway robber earlier. 'Lies!' he shouted.

Karim Farazi was regular with saying the *Namaz* and considered himself a servant of the lord these days. A professional stick-fighter earlier, he was unwilling to cow down before Nibaran's aggression. 'Don't you dare!' he screamed back.

The dispute became more intense. There were arguments back and forth, raised voices, mounting tension. Then two groups of people began tugging at the body attached to the bamboo pole. Things grew heated in no time, the shops began to close their doors, and soon a large number of people were running up from the village, armed with lethal weapons.

The body was lying on the asphalt now. Two distinct groups had been formed on either side, both armed. They were hurling invectives at one another. 'My Muslim brothers!' the Muslim priest shouted at regular intervals. '*Jihad! Jihad! Nara e takbeer, Allah hu akbar.*'

Meanwhile Bhattacharya screamed, '*Jai Ma Kali!* Help us slay the infidels, O goddess! *Jai Ma Kali!*'

Roars and counter-roars rent the skies, while the blue-uniformed chowkidaar, hapless keeper of the law, stood in the middle with his stick upraised, trying to talk to both sides. Whenever either group surged forward he knocked on the ground threateningly with his stick, crying, 'Don't you dare!'

But there was no telling how long he would be able to keep the belligerent mobs apart. He began to knock on the ground madly with his stick, first on one side and then on the other. There was a fusillade of sounds.

And then a strange scene unfolded. The corpse began to move. The body was not only moving, but also trying to sit up. The armed groups on either side stared in disbelief. The chowkidaar gaped.

The old woman sat up. She looked to left and right, and saw that mobs had gathered on both sides. A sly grin appeared on her wizened, withered face.

Finally the chowkidaar spoke. 'So you aren't dead!'

'You can die, along with your entire family.'

'Are you a Hindu or a Muslim, old woman?'

Losing her temper, the old woman said, 'Are all you idiots blind? Can't you see for yourself? Can't you see what I am, you demons from hell, you vulture-eyed creatures? I'll gouge your eyes out – shove off from here, all of you.'

She continued tottering along the road. The crowd parted to make way for her. The further she went, the more indistinct she became in the late-afternoon sunlight.

MOTI NANDY

The Pearl

Chandan Mitra had not imagined his car would let him down like this.

They had travelled smoothly to Kharagpur after leaving Digha at dawn. Chandan had seen Bratati and the one-year-old Bablu off on the train to Jamshedpur. Bratati was going to spend a fortnight with her elder sister. They had spent a couple of days in Digha at a house owned by one of Chandan's fans.

It was an old Standard Herald, which Chandan had bought for 6,000 rupees four months ago. He hadn't got round to learning how to drive yet, though he meant to. So he had hired a driver. The 300 rupees he was spending pinched him, but he had a strange fear of having an accident if he drove.

Most of the things that an astrologer had forecast after reading his horoscope four years ago had come true. Foreign travel, fame, financial success, marriage, a job – practically all of them. He had been to Bangkok and Tehran to play in the Asian Games, and toured Hong Kong, Seoul, Nairobi, Singapore, Kabul, Colombo and Rangoon with the Indian team. He had been to Kuala Lumpur twice for the Merdeka Tournament. Chandan didn't quite grasp what fame and glory meant. All he had noticed was people staring at him, women whispering, cars stopping to offer him a lift, invitations to the homes of strangers and to the finals of football tournaments to give away the trophy and make a speech. He featured in newspaper headlines, with adjectives like 'fragrant' being added to his name (which meant sandalwood). Once he had heard someone say as he passed in a taxi, 'That's the son of god there.' His goal, the only one in the match, had given Juger Jatri the IFA Shield just a few days earlier. If all this implied fame and glory, then Chandan had fame and glory.

He had certainly been successful financially. Chandan had just about scraped through his school examinations, but his club had got him a job with a bank, where he currently earned almost 1,800 a month. The astrologer had asked him to wear an onyx and a topaz, which he did. That same year his fee had risen to between 40,000 and 45,000. He was now the owner of a flat, and he owned a pharmacy, though not under his own name, 50,000 rupees given out as loans that earned interest, and this car.

The astrologer had predicted a beautiful wife, and Bratati was indeed pretty. A film director fan of Chandan's had even chased her for some time to give her a role. Chandan wasn't in favour of her acting in the movies. Bratati loved him, and he her. She wished he would drive, as confident people did. But the astrologer had said there was a threat to his life after he turned thirty, it would be best if he wore a pearl. He had been twenty-seven then. Let me turn thirty first, he had decided, and had not bought the pearl then. He still hadn't.

His first thought on getting the car had been about the threat, his skin tingling in fear. The same Chandan Mitra who did not hesitate to take on the most violent of defenders in the penalty box was secretly afraid of an accident. Severed limbs, crushed ribs, a mangled torso – he felt miserable whenever this image of himself floated up in front of his eyes. He had instructed Tripit Singh, the driver, repeatedly before they drove to Digha – don't go over thirty miles an hour, don't race with other cars, don't overtake, make way for trucks and buses and lorries.

Saying all this had made him feel he really had aged. It was obvious that his playing days were ending. The club had spirited away Tanmay, Basab and Pradip ten days before the transfers began, but the officials had seen no need to make an effort to keep him out of reach of other clubs. His value had dropped 10,000 in a shot.

Looking at the broken-down car on Bombay Road, Chandan told himself he was getting old. The club was bound to discard him in a year or two. His earnings would drop. Did he really have to buy the car? Even ten years ago he had depended entirely on trams and buses. And before that, there were those days when he played local matches for money and often wondered where his next meal was coming from.

Tripit Singh had returned to Kharagpur with the faulty distributor box. Chandan had tried to flag down a truck headed for Kharagpur, but it had swept past him without stopping. A private car behind it had stopped. The man in the back seat had opened the door and said, 'Get in.'

Chandan had felt a mild sense of pride. But there was no one besides Tripit to witness the incident. Even last year he had been on the cover of two magazines. They were halfway through the Calcutta League, and his photograph had already appeared three times in the newspapers. Several million people knew what he looked like. Cars stopped only because of him, they still stopped for him. Bengalis really loved their football.

Tripit had gone to Kharagpur in his own car. Who knew when he would be back. Probably not for another couple of hours. Chandan stayed back to keep an eye on his own car. But, growing impatient after some time, he locked the doors and decided to take a walk.

The highway here was broad enough for six lorries. There was farmland on both sides – rice and jute. Searing heat had made way for rain two weeks ago. It had rained last night too. A farmer was ploughing the soil in the distance. Gazing at him for some time, Chandan felt the urge for a cup of tea.

Several narrow trails led off from Bombay Road into the villages. He walked up to the head of one such path. A handful of shops with thatched roofs, a walled factory next to them. Two single-storey buildings. The hint of a village behind the trees.

A blacksmith's shack, followed by one for cycle repairs, and then a tea shop. Two men were sitting outside it on a bamboo bench with suitcases and bags. Probably a bus stop. Chandan sat down next to them. The time on his watch was ten-thirty.

The shop was run down, and so was the woman running it. Chandan could tell that her sari had been red once upon a time, just as he could tell that her complexion had once been fair. Perhaps she used to look both graceful and youthful. Now her eyes held an irritated anger, and her face was pallid. A boy of about ten was breaking lumps of coal.

'Do you have any tea?' Chandan asked quite loudly.

'We do.'

There was bread and lozenges, besides biscuits and cake. Paan and cigarettes too. All of them cheap, looking like they had been languishing for a long time.

So this woman was the owner. How did such a shabbily maintained shop do any business? Maybe her husband worked somewhere. Looking around as these thoughts ran through his mind, Chandan found nothing in the natural beauty of Medinipur capable of attracting his attention, and returned his attention to the shop. His car was visible from this spot.

A framed photograph hung from one of the walls, which were made of bamboo. Glancing at it idly, Chandan tried to make out its subject. It was faded, and the glass covering it was grimy. Unable to see clearly, he went up to the photograph out of curiosity.

The woman turned to look at him as she made his tea. The boy, nearly naked, was blinking at him. The men on the bench were on their feet, the bus was probably approaching.

Chandan discovered that behind the dirty glass was a photograph of a football team. What he saw on rubbing the dust off with his fingertips was indeed a huge surprise – it was the 1947 team of the IFA, which had toured Burma and Singapore.

'Who put this photo here?'

Chandan's question was directed at the woman.

'His father.'

She jerked her head in the boy's direction. Her voice was as harsh as her expression.

The same photograph was also to be found hanging on the wall of the Juger Jatri tent. Four of the club's players were in the team. Chandan knew their names.

'Is he very fond of football?'

There was no answer. Instead of the woman, the boy spoke. 'My father is in that photograph.'

'Pot or glass?'

The woman was staring at him in annoyance.

'Pot.'

'Which one's your father?' Chandan asked the boy curiously.

He came forward and laid his finger on the face of one of the four seated figures.

Shivakrishnan.

Chandan gazed at him in astonishment and turned back to the photograph.

Yes, Shivakrishnan of Juger Jatri. The formidable inside-left. The most popular player of his time. Arriving in Calcutta as a young boy from a village in Hyderabad, he had played for Kalighat and Sporting Union and then for East Bengal for two years before joining Juger Jatri. Chandan was four when he retired. Shivakrishnan's name was certain to come up whenever the old-timers spoke of the past.

Apparently he was a master of the through pass. A calm, controlled player. Not particularly good at shooting or heading the ball, he had always played barefoot. The ball stuck to him like glue, he could dribble past three players effortlessly. 'There's no inside forward like Shiva in Calcutta football today. How many players can dribble past their opponents now? Remember how he feinted past KOCB's Henderson six times in a row?'

Everyone would nod in unison. The way Shiva held the ball was apparently a sight to behold. 'He ruined himself with drugs. Ganja, bhang, charas, everything possible. There wasn't as much money in the game then as there is now. Still, he squandered whatever he earned, twenty or twenty-five or whatever it was. But his passes!'

Everyone would nod again. Chandan had heard these stories about Shiva over and over. At first he would marvel at them, but later they began to irritate him. For the old-timers, everything good lay in the past. Apparently players would lay down their lives for their clubs, without even thinking of money. Integrity dripped off them like molten butter back then. 'The Juger Jatri that you see now, all this money, all these trophies, all of this began back in that time. They were the first to earn success for the club, to get it into the semi-finals and finals of Rovers Cup and Durand Cup. They were the ones who made Jatri popular, an all-India force.'

Everyone would nod. Chandan acknowledged all this. He had often advised youngsters in his speeches – respect your elders, don't forget the past. He himself touched the feet of veteran footballers with great respect whenever he saw them. And then, when he saw people looking at him admiringly, he felt himself growing a little taller.

'Is Shivakrishnan your father?'

There was clear disbelief in Chandan's eyes. The boy looked shyly at the woman.

'Yes,' she said, offering him the small clay pot of tea. Accepting it, Chandan said, 'And you are?'

'His wife.'

'He's the same Shivakrishnan who played for Juger Jatri.'

'No idea.'

'No idea!'

She frowned at Chandan's astonished echo.

'He played football, didn't he?'

'Perhaps. I don't know anything.'

'Where is he?'

'At home.'

'Is he doing something right now? I mean, is he busy? Can I meet him?'

'What can he be doing? I do all the work. He's in bed all the time.'

'Is something wrong with him?'

'Headaches, pain in the knee, asthma, cough and cold – does he know you? Can you have him admitted to a hospital?'

'I can try.'

Fixing her eyes on Chandan for a few seconds, Shivakrishnan's wife told her son, 'I can't leave the shop, take him to your father.'

As soon as Chandan started walking she reminded him from the back, 'Your payment?'

Paying up, he set off with the boy. The car breaking down seemed to be a blessing in disguise now. Everyone in Calcutta would be dumbfounded.

He had tracked down Shivakrishnan and spoken to him. Everyone had assumed he was dead.

The first people to gather around him when he recounted the story of meeting a living Shivakrishnan would be journalists from newspapers and magazines.

A small hut stood a short distance away. Just the one room. Pausing at the door, Chandan looked inside. An opening in the wall served as the window. A man seemed to be resting on a low cot. There was no other furniture in the room. A couple of aluminium plates and an upside-down mug on the floor. A clay pot, a pitcher of water and a few bottles. A tin trunk beneath the cot, along with a pair of old slippers. Clothes hanging on the wall. Some cans and a small mirror in a niche in the wall.

The man, that is to say Shivakrishnan – who was well known as Shiva on the football fields of Calcutta and of India just twenty-seven years ago – was lying on his side, dressed in nothing but a tattered lungi wrapped around the bottom half of his body.

He turned towards Chandan when his son tapped him on the back.

'I'm from Calcutta. My car broke down and I stopped at the shop for a cup of tea. When I saw you in the photograph I thought I'd meet you, I've heard so much about you.'

Shiva sat up on the cot. There was virtually no resemblance to the figure in the photograph. His hollow cheeks were covered with a grey stubble, his arms were like reeds, each of his ribs could be counted. Only the shape of his head identified him as someone who might be Shivakrishnan. It was disproportionately large in comparison to his body, the forehead extraordinarily wide. Yet his heading of the ball was supposed to have been terrible.

'You must have heard stories about me, you can't have seen me play. How old are you?'

His voice was faint. His Bangla pronunciation was flawless, by virtue of having spent forty years in the state.

'No, I didn't see you play. I wasn't born at the time of that photograph. Are you ill? Is it serious?'

'No, I'm not ill or anything. Footballers always have niggles. Half an hour with the ball on the field and I'll be fine.'

'Do you still play?'

Chandan didn't know whether to be astonished. At this age and in this state of health – what was he saying?

'Play? Where's the pitch? Where's the ball?' He smiled. 'Look at my health, look at my age. The thing is, I think footballers can get better only if they play, only if they move around with the ball. Don't keep standing, sit down.'

The boy had taken a rubber ball out from beneath the cot and was dribbling it around. Hearing his mother scream for him from a distance, he ran off.

'My wife is Bengali, her home is close by. She used to work in the same restaurant in Calcutta as me, that's when we met. She did a lot for me, still does.'

'Considering your condition, there's so much help available for ex-footballers these days, pensions, why don't you apply?'

His eyes didn't seem to convey a sense of grievance. Yet it was usually the old men who felt that way.

'The money would always be helpful.'

'Why did I play football then? I could have earned money some other way. I made no money from football.'

Chandan felt some discomfiture. This was true, what did these people play for? Was it for applause? What else could it be if not the pittance they earned?

'Do you play?'

Chandan was about to say, I'm considered a star at your club now. But something seemed to choke his voice. 'A bit of football,' was all he could say.

'I see.'

No illness, no financial difficulties, I'm fine – Chandan felt the aged ex-footballer was a bit of a humbug.

'Do you watch football?'

'I watched a game in Kharagpur five years ago, that was after a gap of sixteen years.'

Chandan had taken 150 rupees to play in an exhibition match in Kharagpur five years ago. Was it the same game?

'What did you think of the players you watched?'

Silence.

'The game has changed a lot since your time.'

'But what about skill, what about football sense, what about shooting?'

It was Chandan's turn to be silent now.

'I kept thinking of Rashid, of Somanna, of Mewa, of Appa.'

Chandan stole a glance at his watch. Nearly two hours had passed since the car had broken down, Tripit should be returning soon. He would start looking for Chandan. There was a game with Port tomorrow. An easy affair, but he should still get home quickly and rest. The past three days had been strenuous . . .

'But the goals they were missing . . .'

Suddenly Chandan had an urge to make this man suffer. He had often encountered such contempt. It was nothing but envy.

'Do you know how much footballers earn these days?'

'No, I cannot read the papers, I haven't even been to school.'

'Forty, fifty, even sixty thousand.'

'I once got two hundred rupees for scoring against Mohun Bagan. Bokai-babu gave it to me because he was happy. I wouldn't have scored if it hadn't been for the pass from Kamal. I gave him a hundred.'

'Many players have cars these days, some own houses, they've set up their own businesses, saved thousands of rupees.'

None of this seemed to register with him. He appeared to have gone back thirty-five or forty years in time to relive his goal. A smile had appeared on his face.

'My heading was supposed to be poor and yet I scored with a header. Lies were spread about me. I've scored many goals with headers.'

Getting off his cot, he handed the rubber ball to Chandan and then led him outside.

'Throw this at me, I'll show you how I scored. Throw it.'

Both disturbed and amused, Chandan tossed the ball lightly up in the air above Shivakrishnan's head. He was ready, standing slightly hunched, his fists balled.

The ball fell on his shoulder. He had missed it. Fetching it, Chandan threw it up lightly again, even higher this time.

Shivakrishnan was waiting, his face raised. As the ball dropped he jerked his head to head it to his left. It bounced on his chin.

Taken aback, Shivakrishnan stared at the ball, his eyes lowered.

'Again.'

Chandan tossed the ball up three more times. Shivakrishnan missed each time.

'Never mind.'

'No, I can do it, throw it once more.'

A car honked, twice. Must be Tripit.

'Let it be, you're not well.'

'Once more, just once.'

The old man seemed to be begging. Chandan felt a stab of pity.

'One last time.'

Shivakrishnan was waiting. His eyes were bulging, the veins in his shoulders and arms pulsating. There was bright sunshine. An enormous banyan tree with all its branches in the background. The fields behind the tree rolling away. Tender paddy shoots. A farmer was ploughing the land. A pond on the right. Another banyan tree. The whistle of a train in the distance. Amid all this, a former footballer, ailing, holding on obstinately to his desire to return to his salad days forty years ago. He wanted to demonstrate how to head the ball, for the last and final time in his life.

What if he missed this time too? The horn sounded impatiently in the distance.

If he missed again, the old man would be destroyed. Let it be. There was no point. Chandan dropped the ball on the ground.

'What's the matter?'

'I'm late, the driver is honking.'

'Just once, one last time.'

Chandan had started walking. Shivakrishnan followed him.

'How long can it take, just once . . . I'll show you whether I can head a ball or not. You can tell them in Calcutta, I saw Shiva head a ball . . . yes, Shiva at sixty . . . it won't even take a minute . . .'

Chandan speeded up. Unable to keep pace, the old man stopped.

He looked over his shoulder on reaching the highway. Against the backdrop of an enormous field and a gigantic tree, he saw a frail man standing on the edge of life.

An accident had been narrowly averted. Chandan decided to follow the astrologer's advice and order a pearl ring immediately.

PURNENDU PATTREA

Conversations

I

Why are you so late?
Were the roads crowded?
I was a little late too
All roads have cracks
Why so many people on the streets?
A funeral procession? Who's died?
No one we know, I hope.
Jogo left just the other day
He went off running, hasn't returned yet
Before and after him, Shankar and Bimal
Those whom we need run away
Towards the distant sea
Like dark-skinned swimmers into oblivion
More of them will go, we'll go too
Like local trains, death
Is quite frequent these days
What sort of death would you like?
Me? A cerebral stroke
Are you angry because I'm talking of death?
Let's drop the subject of dying then
And discuss living instead

Why is there a shadow on your mouth?
Were you in the darkness?

Why do I have sweat on my brow?
I was in the sun
You didn't wear your bindi today, Nandini
I didn't wear my kurta
Why is your hair dishevelled?
Were you in a storm?
Why is there blood in my hair?
Lightning struck
There's a cyclone every day these days
Trees fall, so do lamp posts
Even men, like birds torn apart,
Fall into pits
The storm thinks it's a bullet train
Gobble, eat, bite
Human meat in sight . . .
Are you angry because I'm talking of storms?
Let's drop the subject of dying then
And discuss living instead

Why are your eyes red?
Were you drenched in the rain?
Why are the veins in my arm blue?
They've been burnt by a fire
You said you'd give me a letter today
Have you brought it? Lovely, many thanks
But what's this? It's just an envelope
Where did the letter go?
Blown away in the storm?
All the words in my letters too
Have been washed away by the rain
These days even the water has learnt
All sorts of deception
The water wets some people's saris
The water robs some of their homes
Knocking busily on the door
The water had driven us out of our house once

Opening its jaws like a shark to swallow
Beds and mattresses and pots and pans
In the putrid currents we formed a kinship
With the fungus
And the moss
Are you angry because I'm talking of water?
Let's drop the subject of water then
And discuss living instead

Where were you in your dream last night?
Egypt? You went to Egypt?
So strange! Last night in my dreams
I was in Egypt too
Rows of skeletal mummies
Eyes like eyes of diamonds
Teeth like teeth of pearl
All the comforts of life, except life itself
Luminescent like glowing stars
Do you suppose they'll ever die?
You had asked the question of me
They are sculptures of death
I had said.
Your eyes turned into rivers
Moonlight cascaded on your mouth
You became a blue sky with pleasure
You said, I want to be a mummy
As you were dying
As you were being destroyed
As you were changing into a mummy
Are you angry because I'm talking of mummies?
Let's drop the subject of mummies then
And discuss living instead

2

What's the matter? Why the furrowed brow?
Has there been a burglary? Tell me all
In the white lotus morning sunshine
Why does evening gloom cast a pall?

Tell me everything that has happened
Have you lost your precious silver anklet?
Or the page you tore out with the address?
A secret letter? Your necklace and earring set?

What's that? The scent of honeyed memories
From a mad, rainy day? Is that true?
Didn't you take it from your breasts
And pour it into palms I cupped for you?
I put it in a locked room in my heart,
Although I light a lamp at dusk for it

3

Who's your friend? Is it a sigh?
Mine too
My emptiness can't be measured
Yours too?

The seasons pass along a distant road
They don't come to my door when I call
In vain I go out when the flute plays
The wind just laughs at me with scorn

You had a basket, not a garden?
Me too
I had a river, not a boat
You too?

The rain lashes your bed
A dust storm sweeps my room
In your room is my cloud
In my bed is your frost.

4

Name a flower, any flower
– Sorrow
Name a river, any river
– Agony
Name a tree, any tree
– Sighs
Name a star, any star
– Tears
I can tell your future now
– Tell me
You will be very happy, Nandini
Your feet will step on marble
Your body will rest in a bed of gold
Seven chambers in front of you
Seven chambers behind
You will bathe in waterfalls
Rinse your mouth in fountains
You will say, I want to dress up
Flower girls will thread garlands in the garden
Maids will make a paste of sandalwood
You will say, I want to sleep
At once the pakhwaz and the stringed tanpura will play in trees
At once a million dancers will appear beneath the moon

And so remain a long time on the Ferris wheel of happiness
Then
Boring a hole through a rib on your right
Digging a tunnel through a path reddened with blood
A snake
Its skin a woven pattern like silk
Its eyes vermilion like twilight over the river
Its smile the plaintive music at a wedding
Venom like beads of pearl in its fangs
Will coil around you
Like banyan roots
Whose embrace bursts through the soil
Slowly all your smiles will be the colour of jaundice
Slowly all your ornaments of gold will be tarnished
Slowly the raindrops, the raindrops will
Turn your satin bedspread white
– Are you the snake?
No
– Then who are you?
Memory
The one you left behind by the incense
When entering the bedroom on your wedding night

5

I am the tree you travel by
You are my roadside inn
Suddenly the cloud screamed – why? –
The lock's so big, I can't go in

You are my ocean front
I am your hair that flies
Suddenly the cloud screamed – why? –
It's all wrong, for these are lies

I am the lines that crease your palm
You're my fist which holds something
Suddenly the cloud screamed – why? -
You cannot go, this boat is leaking

6

You didn't come yesterday, today's gone by
It's cloudy now, it'll rain soon
Terrifying rain, Calcutta will drown
Are you still looking for your nail polish?
Were you dressed? Why didn't you come then?
Were your shoes torn? They weren't torn?
You didn't have any kohl? Why bother with it
I already know the doe in your eyes

You didn't come yesterday, today's gone by
It's twilight now, in a moment Calcutta will
Put on its dark burqa and drown in a deeper mist
Are you still looking for your safety pin?

7

Your letter arrived around four o'clock this afternoon
A million thanks for your reply, although it came none too soon
Are you shedding tears for me? Turn your heart to stone forever
Charulata is playing again, would you like to go together?

When shall we meet and where? You haven't even dropped a hint
Now that you've got fairy wings, you can fly out on the wind
Will you come to Sitangshu's cafe if it doesn't rain?
The songbird's fluttering, now it wants to peck the silver grain

8

– You're turning more horrible by the day
From now on I'll call you
Furnace
You know why, Nandini? You keep burning me
What you give me when I ask for pleasure
Is nothing but fire

– You're becoming worse by the day
From now on I too will call you
Executioner
You know why? You keep killing me
The regret of all that I cannot give you
Is nothing but the knife

9

Today I have a hundred names with which I'll
Call you
You're the first rain, a scent of jasmine, I'll
Wear you

Inside the deepest song today the ferry boat was
Sailing
Then you smiled, and from the sky a golden ring was
Melting

I'll call you a crochet needle from now on
All right?
I was a thread, you're knitting me in patterns
So tight

10

What did you do when you got back home yesterday?
– I wept. You?
I wrote
– Poetry? Show me.
I tore it to shreds as soon as I finished
– Why?
A cry of pain kept talking through my joy
A strange calmness hummed inside the cry of pain
And a storm whistled over the sea within the calm
Letters which should have been red when written
Were all turning ivory
Words meant to be swaying like white stalks
Seemed to be dry leaves flying everywhere
Nandini, I realized I do not have the language
In whose mirror love can see itself
– That doesn't mean you had to tear it up
Raucous laughter leapt out of the wind to say
Burn to ashes like the wick of a lamp a while longer
Burn to ashes.

11

You're smoking too much these days, Shubhankar
– I'll throw it away this moment
But what will I get instead?
So greedy. As if you've never had one before.
– I have.
But it's a mere morsel for my appetite
I can eat all of Calcutta in one bite
Slicing the sky like an omelette
Popping the stars like peanuts into my mouth
Crunching the mountains like wafers

And the river?
It's a glass of juice
Never mind. So valorous.
– Indeed
I'm a mighty explosion just like this to the world
Only near you am I an unweaned little boy
Only with you am I the crippled pavement beggar
A coin or two, or a slice of bread,
I cannot snatch anything more.
– Liar
– Why?
– Didn't you want to take my sari off entirely?
– Maybe.
Can't the beggar want to be a robber for a day?

12

– Did you find out
What the giant tiger was looking for
With its chin on your shoulder
Last evening?

– Oh, I know
It was looking for the source of its river of joy
And the final fare
For the crossing

– All night long
It dug through the rock in its own heart
To let harmful torrents
Flow

– My darling
I walk with you always
Through sun and shade
When you ache by the sea
I lay out a cooling mat of sand
Not near the heart and yet
My home is in your heart
Make no mistake

13

– It's you I'd like to live in forever
Some land and a house in you, one-storeyed for now
Why're you laughing? Tell me why you're laughing.

– I don't like ground floors at all
I must talk with the moon mornings and evenings
What use is a house that isn't high enough?

– Very well, so it shall be
The house will touch the moon
With spiral stairs like in mystery novels
Dream sequences framed in gold at every turn
A magic deer's head, with the horns intact
Why're you laughing? Tell me why you're laughing.

– A hunted-down deer on the wall? Unbearable.
The deer will be in the forest, the forest will be
Around our bed, a low hill
Beneath our bed, a waterfall
Slicing through its belly

– Very well, so it shall be
A waterfall slicing through the hill, on it a carpet from Kashmir
Chandeliers from Rajasthan on the ceiling, clouds on

Windows like upside-down colanders, dressed in breezy cotton
Kurtas
With chikan embroidery from Lucknow
Why're you laughing? Tell me why you're laughing.

– Why should the clouds wear kurtas every day?
Sometimes they will dress in silk saris or
Light prints from Khatau Mills
Hair piled high on the head, held by a diamond butterfly
And at once Raag Jayjayanti on the shehnai
And at once the roars of wild animals in every opening in the forest
The waterfall will be aroused to leap into the ravine
Bows and arrows for hunting, war drums and bugles
Why're you laughing? Tell me why you're laughing.

– You talk as though
Love is a terrifying battle between
Sworn enemies
I'm scared
Tell me a different story

14

– Look, like crickets we've kept talking
Till eternity
And we're still not done with anything
You were going to tell me the story of a weeping red rose
When will you?

– Let's go. It's far too hot here.

– Look, like dry bamboo leaves we're roamed
Till eternity
And still we haven't managed to touch each other

You were to have gifted a full moon to a black deer
When will you?

– Let's go. It's far too stormy here.

15

The melon is green outside
Red within
Can you tell me why this came to mind?
You can't?
Because I saw your green sari

16

Hello beautiful! Remember it's 3 June tomorrow?
What? You forgot? You're a very dangerous woman
How could you forget our first wedding anniversary?
No, madam, this isn't a joke or a prank
Did you think this is a game I'm playing,
The way the flippant wind messes with
The shaggy treetop's plaits just for fun?

I agree with what you say. Yes, sir.
We're not married and never will be
So what? In my head you're Parvati
Since the evening of 3 June. Right?

The third of June was when the cyclone hit us
The third of June was when the downpour began
The first blossom flung fragrance at the sky
A handkerchief around your hand and mine

We came close on the third of June
Your chariot wheels crushed my ribs
The jagged lightning of your smile set fire
To walls and doors and floors and beds and sheets
We became each other's on the third of June

Your moon rose in my sky on the third of June
My hair flew in your breeze on the third of June

17

Nandini, you are just a drop of water
Still I'm swept away by your flood
You too are a mild breeze, Shubhankar
Still you raise a storm in my blood

18

Hello, hello, when are you coming?
What clouds? There aren't any clouds
Hello, hello, but what if it rains?
Get drenched, hello, we'll just get drenched
Just the way the rain bathes the trees
And turns a blade of grass into a prince
Hello, hello, let the rain drench us
You shall be the smell of moist earth
I shall spread my branches on that soil
Can you hear me? Hello, hello, hello
Come out now, the rainbow's in the sky
Hello, the sun's coming out now
The sunshine holds a spear, hello, hello
When they hear the anklets on your feet
The clouds and darkness will go, hello

The clouds and darkness, hello, hello
The clouds, hello, hello, hello

19

There's a funny story I forgot to tell you.
It was Thursday. The sky flung down a cyclone.
On College Street, Amitava said as soon as we met,
Shubhankar, how are you, after the preliminaries,
The main question, are you still wrapped up in Nandini?
Everything you're writing makes me think
Nandini is your sky and you're a bird in flight.

Amitava, as you know, is dedicated to politics,
So I told him,
If you think of Nandini as a giant revolution
I am all its slogans rising skywards.

20

– Three poems in the *Illustrated Weekly*
But you didn't tell me
I met Madhumita at Elias, she told me
I was so upset I thought I'd stop talking to you
Must I hear of your poetry from someone in a crowd?
I wrote a letter to you in rage, but buried it
Beneath the quilt

– Cannon to left of them, cannon to right of them, volleyed and thundered
Such is my fate
It was from you my dry leaves got their first rainfall
You were the first to play the flute that was balm on my wound
And today again you are the first

To tell me of *Illustrated Weekly*
I haven't even set eyes on it yet
Now let the clouds of fury be dispersed
And your pleased countenance be revealed

21

– How bad are the power cuts in your area?
– Don't ask. They're killing us, day and night.
– What do you do then?
– I open the doors
Open the windows
Draw the curtains apart
The wind is also a swindler these days
As soon as it's dark it flees human company
– What do you do then?
I can't keep my clothes on any more
I take them all off
My glasses, my ribbons, my sari, my embarrassment, everything
– If I had the money, I'd pave a bank by the river and name it for you
Such is your turbulent kindness
You can easily take off all your sparks of fire for the darkness
But if Shubhankar even tilts like a cloud
Stop it!
If Shubhankar waves his foliage of hunger and thirst
Stop it!
If Shubhankar moves his sunburnt deer tongue
Stop it!
In my next life I'll be born as the darkness on every horizon

22

You had promised to come on 13 July
Accordingly I had set out in the sky

Millions of blue fireflies with busy lights
Accordingly I had informed the river
There'd better not be a shadow of clouds or trees
On the water. July 13 – you didn't come.
A fever? But you have a phone at home?
If I'd known, I'd have been a thermometer
The bird would touch the blueness, be fulfilled

23

– I thought of you many times yesterday
I wore the necklace that you gave me
Yesterday it was my birthday

– My necklace means more to you than me
You gave away your embraces to the sand
Not a scrap or morsel for the sea

– What could I do? Your phone was dead
I tried to call you so many times
No sign of life, just a corpse on its bed

– There was a wind, and in the wind a bird
There was a sky, and in the sky a moon
If you'd told them, they'd have sent word

– I did that too, I told them, my good sir,
They said we are dying of power cuts
We cannot move, we simply cannot stir

24

– Why do you look so frail nowadays, Shubhankar?
So dejected,

As though torrential rains, grey wings of clouds, the chatter of water
Have torn you apart
Like the ancient smell of a broken-down temple
Like the slimy moss on a pillar from the past
You were green once, now as bereft as grief
Are you trapped inside a prison?
Blackened bars, a wall of trees?
Or have you lost something, a personal possession?
Some birds only weep when the evening star sets
Has your gold ring been swept away in a ravine of water?
Where have you left behind your jasmine complexion
Your marvellous front cover?

– Nandini, you know very well I have no garden
What there was I shed with my childhood
Because you love flowers
Because you are the propitious celebration on a flower stalk
In search of flowers I have to seek out the roads
To distant places like the Indus River, the Hindukush Mountains, Harappa
Many dilapidated airports lie on the way
Bones of warships, graves for machine gun
Skeletons, crude machinery and charcoal and hay
There are many flags on those roads but no signs of life
The air is rent to shreds by the ragged breathing of incurable diseases
And many rocks too, rocks as large as highway robbers
Which make you bleed
On that journey spirit and desire, the arms and garments of bark
Are rusted blue

25

– Did a seagull swoop on your watch and steal it?
Did a giant fish swallow it like Shakuntala's ring?

Conversations

– Why?

– When were you supposed to be here? And when did you come?
I feel like I've been here for centuries, an upside-down idol in a ruined temple
Cups of tea, cigarettes, and repeat – waiter, coffee!
Checking my watch, and jumping at every footstep
It felt as though waiting till eternity is another name for love

– You're right, sir. What to do, the roads were swarming with people like flies
Every street was blocked by red processions and lorries
And then this blazing sun and searing wind, so horrible! Burnt to cinders
Is the sky ill with something?
Even in June the monsoon clouds have dry pitchers
I thought an entire century would pass
But the traffic on Lenin Sarani would never make it to Theatre Road
And then I didn't sleep all night, only wept
But do you suppose I can even cry in peace?
My sister sleeps by me, an aunt sleeps on the floor of our room

– Why the sudden tears?

– My father's got hold of one of your letters somehow
He's looking grim. Which means an explosion in a day or two
I will be thrust into a circle of restrictions

– It's best that the inevitable happens quickly
The morning papers say a storm is coming
With winds of eighty miles an hour
I realize, hereafter
I needs must don armour on my body
Do you remember? One winter evening next to you
On the Victoria Memorial lawns
Warming myself at the fire of your body
I spake thus, Nandini! Don't forget
Love is a bloody battlefield till we die

26

– Where's the reply to my letter?
If you haven't brought it today
I'll raise such a storm with my arms
Your clothes will fly off to distant farms
Breaking out of the jail of your hairdo
Your imprisoned tresses will attack your face
I'll be a cobra. Seven times I'll circle
The peak and base of your nakedness, my coils
Will break your bones. What do I care?

– I've never seen a man
As impatient and restless
I believe you're reading a lot
Of Rimbaud and Verlaine these days
Do you plan to singe my shoulders
With the heat of their flames?
Here's your letter, now calm down
Don't go breaking my bones any more
If you do, whose flower will you pick
Every day, good sir?

27

What brings you here? You seem
to have forgotten. I had as well.
Photos printed by shadowy memories
Were stuck on the trees.
You've lost weight. I have too?
It's possible. Sand has infiltrated
The depths of the currents.
The clock's ticking. The blue
Will slowly turn bluer.

But a few red flowers are still
Blooming. I don't know who
Makes them bloom. Is it your
Flash of light? Or the secret
Bleeding in my square cell?
Do you plan to keep standing?
Why don't you sit? The mat
Is spread out all over my body.

28

– Have you never loved anyone before me?
– Why ever not? So many.
Bhromor from *Krishnakanta's Will*
Kumu from Tagore's *Connections*
Kusum from *The Legends of Puppet Dances*
And from *The Unvanquished* . . .
– Don't joke. Tell me the truth.
– By the banks of Brindaban I loved the slim and slender Yamuna
Mountain girl Phultungri in Ghatsila
That shrew Torsa in the jungles of Jalpaiguri
And the empress, in her blue zari-embroidered burqa,
Her name was Chilika
– You're hiding behind a wall of nonsense again
– Not nonsense, the truth.
They're the ones who taught me to love
An endless afternoon chasing a dragonfly
My entire childhood in pursuit of a kingfisher
Cotton seeds popping
Two or three winters and springs gazing at them
This was how the water of love oozed
Through the canals and channels in my body
In this way, the heartbreaking compromise
Between resemblance and reality, between flesh and the scent of musk
As a boy I had an affair

With a love apple tree
Ever since then, whenever I see
The innocent transparency of that fruit
Dense in dangerous pink
I fall in love hopelessly
With the mountain if it's a mountain
With the river if it's a river
With the parrot if it's a parrot
With the woman if it's a woman

29

– You go away, but your face
Stays, drawn on the clouds. Like
A many-hued Baluchari sari flying
In the white veranda of the wind.
The song has ended but still
Its echoes are everywhere.
As though it's only you, and your
Statues that the museum, that Calcutta,
Deep in the pit of tram lines and ashes,
Is stuffed with
How do you do this
Nandini?

– It's easy magic. Want to learn?
Give me your handkerchief, let me
Blindfold you with the tightest
Knot. And then touch you with my
Wand. Come closer.

– I'm not so foolish, Nandini!
I have an inkling of how you
Make a pet bird out of a man
Revealing the waterfall but never

Unlocking the source with your key
You'll make a bed of satin
But offer a chair to sit on
Shelves packed with seeds and manure
For fertility laid out in the shop
But shuttered morning and evening
The playful water revels in sweeping away
The tree, let it be drowned to death
What does the water care?

– Lies! Lies! Shubhankar?
It was you who mistook the tree
For a cloud and wanted rain,
From the candle of limited lifespan
You constantly want a light
That's eternal,
You people weave with your imagination
In a mould of what we are not
Long laces of golden thread

– Nandini! Oh, it's because
This tyranny still exists that
I haven't yet sought the end
Of this decrepit and dead earth
Else I would have strung it up
From a roof beam long ago. And
The credit is all yours
You, meaning women, at whose touch
Cow dung burns to become fragrant incense

– Shut up now, shut up
Your tongue's got the better of you

– This too is joy. So long as
You're by me, I am a river

A sail on a boat, a stormy wind
When you're gone I'm a mountain
Or not even that, just brick or timber
A wooden desk, a bookcase
I am so bereft of words that
People assume I died long ago
Remember what you said a moment ago
Long laces of golden thread
That's what I weave then
So that everyone can see
The secret colony
Of their own heart

30

– You have ruined me, Shubhankar
I find everything hateful. Everything.
Smoke from wet coal and shortness of breath
Have swamped the horizon all around me
When it rains now I only hear
The ominous sound of the river flooding its banks
When the moon is full now I only see
The darkness rushing like a funeral procession in search of a corpse
I find everything hateful. Everything.
Earlier I could primp for hours before the mirror
Something like the pleasure of washing myself white like clothes
With powder and soap and perfume and kohl
When I look at my reflection now
My face fills with pimples like pepper grains, bitter and beleaguered
All dreams are now like grotesque chortling masks
Every bridge to cross the nightmare has been pulverized
I find everything hateful. Everything.

– Have you not ruined me too, Nandini?
Before, I was tiny, like a grain of pepper
It's you who's turned my tiny cage into a long terrace

31

– All the time you're by me, all the time we touch,
I'm a bird of cloud and water, beside itself
Which bird? Do you know?

– All the time you're by me, all the time we watch
I paint pictures in the dark with meteor sparks
What pictures? Do you know?

– All the time you talk, laughing, making the water flow
Plants sprout endlessly from seeds, forests are formed
Which plants? Do you know?

– All the time you're by me, earthquakes, the terror of joy,
I arrive at the place where it's spring round the year
Which land? Do you know?

32

I brought you a gift.
Can you name it?
A rainbow? Rubbish, as if it's within reach
Just because you want one
A mother lode of mica? A blue mountain peak?
Am I an industrialist like Birla or a Tata?
I've dredged my blood to bring you
A bowl of sandalwood

33

Don't you dare. Take your hand away.
Put the money back in your wallet.
I'll pay for everything today.
What's this, Shubhankar? Why this wave of madness?
This is why I get angry with you.
Sometimes you grow as stubborn as a finance minister
I beseeched you yesterday, let's go now, let's go
The sky is the colour of tar, let's go now
You sat like an ancient banyan tree on the grass
Calcutta sank, and you sank with it
And you let me sink as well
Why don't you listen to me sometimes?
Am I an election promise that's lost in the forgotten dark
As soon as you rest your back on the throne?
Like water in the tap
Like dates on the calendar
Like drought with the flood
I'm always with you. And will be.
Then why do you never listen to me, Shubhankar?

34

– Can you tell me how old it is?
– Who?
– The one with a head of green cedar hair
Whose tottering feet are always on the wrong, thorny path
All whose words are incoherent, coded and explosive like terrorists
The one who keeps dragging you by the hand to the garden
Where touching a flower invites a laughing bolt of lightning
Where the vines hide a treacherous pit of roses to plunge into
And a fierce current that can lure you away
Can you tell me how old it is?

– Three years
– Then do you remember, three years ago at this very spot
At five-thirty on an ashen evening just like this one
Behind a torn curtain the colour of a cockroach
It was born from the seed of our joint euphoria, yours and mine
Whom you named, in your first letter, an unbearable pleasure
Whom I named, in my first letter, a rebirth?

35

– You write poetry with your needle
They say you're very good at sewing

– Are you a spy? I have my secrets
Must you find out everything?

– Don't argue, my heart has a wound
Will you stitch it in a trice?

– I could, but it will cost a lot
Can you pay my asking price?

– I'll pay, of course, for flawless work
I'm not afraid, not one bit

– The waterfall that's in your heart . . .
You must let me bathe in it

36

If I'd known you'd be my ruination
Would I have set the dinghy adrift this way?
Would I?
If you'd said you'd go off to the sea

Would I have let the storms touch me?
Would I?
You were a brook dancing over gravel
Your anklet ringing. I cupped you in my hands
You let me
Now the currents are flooding both the shores
The high-masted ship has come to call you
Answer him

37

Love, that too is riddled with conspiracy,
Nandini! Do you ever think of this?
Like a plot, soaked in criminal intent
A young man comes up to a young woman
Learning how to embroider a handkerchief
As though this proximity is a social danger
As though they've found illegal weapons in Mallikbagan
As though they've learnt the hijack manual
And have loaded all their secret guns

If at every bird-hued dusk a young man
Laces fingers with his woman
It's as though lightning bolts will damage Calcutta
As though a jungle will spring up in Calcutta
As though snakes will devour Calcutta
All these whispers, everywhere this unending
Squeak of rats
Whenever a young man sits close to a woman

Nandini, do you remember?
That ancient bag of bones who walked up
Looking like a knowledgeable father-in-law
He asked, why all this canoodling with her?

Does she have the key to hidden treasures?
An airport hidden somewhere?
A press to print counterfeit notes?
An international ring of vice?
Then why like the needle and the thread
Are summer and winter together?

38

– Nandini! I am scared, so very scared
Some day I will get a fever, the kind that breaks a house
Like snowfall a cascade of fire will descend
Silently occupying this body's streets and harbours
Tearing through the barriers of the pillowcase
The cotton is now a cloud, a flying duck, a pigeon
In the same way my fever will take me to another galaxy
Nandini! I am scared, so very scared

– What joy you get from spouting nonsense, Shubhankar!
I really don't understand
For whom are you playing this game with a knife
Do you want to draw patterns with blood on my face?

– What knife? I tossed it into the forest
I did have a blade as long as a desolate afternoon
There were rivals then
The possibility of war and riots and robbery and arson
There's no opponent now but a terrible fear
No war, no cannon being fired, no diseases
No deadly infection from any virus except fear

– I have given everything I had, Shubhankar
Even stuffed your tiger claws with food
Made a canopy with the shade of the densest trees

Overhead, knitted to the precise measurement of the sky
Still you're so afraid?
Still afraid of what?

– Since childhood all I touched just broke
The way the storm shattered the glass chimney at school
The long verandas of the family home turned to shreds of paper
With tender hands I had planted a cheerful garden
Ants and worms and insects ate it up
There was a flag, like the one and only sun
Arguments and strife tore it to pieces
Was it wrong to touch the village river?
Was it wrong to touch the bridge over it?
Was I wrong to touch paper and the press?
Nandini!
What if I lose you like the garden, the flag, the bridge, the paper?

39

I play you
You're a seashell
Plants flower
Fruits become girls
The branches
Write letters
In green leaf envelopes
Declaring love
The entire forest gives up
Frocks for dresses
I cast you off
You're a boat of clouds
You know the blue island
Of red coral
You stop at the gates
Of the abode of gods

The moonlight lays out
A bed for you
Luna, aged,
Lights a chandelier
On earth's cracked cheeks
A full moon laughs

40

– Suppose you floated far away one day
And only the agitated waves remained for life
Like a gold-framed painting in my breast
What if they were covered in grime and smoke
And slowly became a happy home for worms?

– Suppose I floated far away one day
My tin of gold would fill up with each hour's
Deep shades, spring breezes, rainwater
Watercolours painted randomly
Would brighten, untarnished, in the amorous sun

– That means you really will go away?

– That means I will never go away

41

– So that our conversations aren't lost
I think the bark on trees has tattooed
The words in hieroglyphs on its body
The trees of the world know our deepest secrets
Even the things I've never told you
The trumpet notes and laments of my heart

– Gazing at the constellations, that's just what
I thought too. Rummaging through a hidden bureau
The stars have printed, from every letter that I
Wrote to you, even from every letter I didn't,
Droplets made of crystal and of tears.

SANKAR

The Priest's Manual

He was like a dry, stale eggplant at Koley Market on the pavement outside Sealdah Station. Harakinkar Bhattacharya's appearance instantly reminded one of a week-old aubergine. His skin was wrinkled outside, and even the flesh within had dried into coir. His thin, long nose was like an exclamation mark. It was obvious he used to be fair once – there were remnants of the complexion. He had large eyes, but they were dulled now, like a hundred-watt bulb giving off twenty-five-watt light.

A bare-bodied Harakinkar was sitting on the veranda in front of his house, using both his hands to grasp the Brahmin's sacred thread that he wore all the time and scratch his back with it. Spotting the postman, he said, 'Anything for Harakinkar Bhattacharya?'

'Nothing,' the peon said.

'Might be addressed to Harakinkar Dev Sharma.'

'Why wouldn't I give you your letter if there was one?'

'You people say that all the time but letters do get lost. You delivered my letter late the other day. It was a request to conduct the rituals after Ramesh Ghoshal's death. The rituals were done by the time the letter came. None of you will understand how this harms a Brahmin priest.'

Annoyed, the peon said, 'Complain to the postmaster general if you don't believe me.'

The argument would have continued, but Harakinkar's daughter Subrataa appeared in the distance. She worked at the government milk distribution centre every morning, and was on her way back home. Shooing away the peon, she told her father, 'You're working yourself up for no reason, baba.'

'It's not for no reason,' Harakinkar said, sounding helpless. 'What if

Sudarshan Roy's family decides not to do the Durga Puja this year? I don't see how that's possible, though. They've been doing it for such a long time. My grandfather was the priest for the rituals, then my father, and then me for all these years. They didn't stop even after the Partition. They brought the family idol from Jessore to Naktala. By god's grace they didn't lose their entire wealth. Why should they stop now? The letter must be lost.'

Subrataa was silent. Harakinkar said, 'I accept that something may have gone wrong with the first letter. But what about the postcard I wrote them?'

Now Subrataa's face fell. 'But the reply did come yesterday, baba.'

'Yesterday? And here I am wasting my time with the peon.' Harakinkar flew into a rage.

'You'd gone to the river for your bath,' Subrataa said.

Harakinkar looked sullen after reading the letter. The Roys had decided to stop the family Durga Puja. The next generation considered it a waste of money. Contorting his face, Harakinkar said, 'There'll be nothing left of our old faith.'

'Would you like some tea, baba?' said Subrataa. 'Shall I put the kettle on?'

'Just as well, I've been saved from embarrassment,' Harakinkar muttered to himself. 'Sudarshan Roy's eldest son has married outside his caste. Unthinkable in a Brahmin family. Best not to do the rituals there and invite misfortune.'

Subrataa brought him a cup of tea. Harakinkar continued speaking to himself, 'The old man of the family knew how to honour Brahmins. Have you seen the size of the gamchhas they used to give me? The ones I get from others won't even do as handkerchiefs, leave alone using them as towels. No wonder they call them ritual gamchhas.'

'Drink your tea, baba,' Harakinkar's daughter said.

'I doubt if I can make a living as a priest any more in this day and age. People consider us a nuisance. We extract money without doing any work, a polished version of beggars.'

'Nabarun Sporting Club is holding an elaborate Durga Puja this year, baba. Their secretary comes every morning for milk, he was talking about you today as well.'

'What's that?' Harakinkar screamed as though someone had planted a booted foot on his toes. 'You expect me to conduct a public Durga Puja at this age? Next thing you know someone will . . .' Harakinkar didn't utter the remaining words in his daughter's presence, '. . . ask me to do the rituals in a whorehouse.'

His daughter said, 'Priests compete with one another for the privilege of conducting the Nabarun Sporting Club Durga Puja.'

'There's competition for dead bodies in morgues too. It's these public Durga Pujas that are ruining our old faith. Nobody cares for priests in these places, the same priest does the job at three such Durga Pujas.'

Subrataa was silent. 'We're talking of goddess Mahamaya here. Ramchandra had to get her blessings to kill Ravan. The ten-armed goddess slayed the bovine demon and re-established the gods in heaven. If the rituals of worship are flawed, who's going to save me from her ire?'

His daughter didn't dare protest any more. Harakinkar said, 'I'll go to that shop, maybe I can sell some of the things I've been given for conducting rituals. The scoundrel specializes in daylight robbery. Just imagine, he refuses to pay more than two and a half rupees for those beautiful brass bowls or pure gunmetal plates. I would have got more if I could have held on to them a while longer. But I couldn't afford to.'

'Don't quarrel with the shopkeeper, baba,' said Subrataa. 'You know very well they're cheats.'

'Fate,' Harakinkar told himself. 'It's the goddess's will, or why would the old faith be threatened today? Why did we have to abandon our home to be forced to live in these slums in a foreign land?'

Harakinkar rose to his feet with the intention of going out. Suddenly someone was heard asking outside, 'Where does Subrataa Bhattacharya live?'

Subrataa opened the door and looked surprised. 'Oh, Subhra-di. What brings you here?'

'Am I not allowed to be here?' Subhra smiled.

Leading her to Harakinkar, Subrataa introduced her. 'Baba, Subhra Roy is a professor at the Women's College. She's the one who arranged for my fees to be waived.'

'I see.' Harakinkar joined his palms to greet her. His daughter had already laid out a mat for the guest to sit on. Subhra wasn't very old, many women her age were still college students. And besides, there was a grace to her appearance that made her look like she was eighteen or nineteen. Harakinkar compared her appearance to his daughter's. Despite the poverty-stricken conditions they lived in, Subrataa was much fairer, and several inches taller too. She was so well developed in spite of hardships – no one would believe she wasn't even seventeen yet.

'Please forgive us, we can't even offer you a chair,' a troubled Harakinkar told the well-dressed Subhra.

'What is it, Subhra-di?'

'Actually I'm here to meet your father. Since I live close by, the principal told me, why don't you go talk to him.'

'Talk about what?' Harakinkar asked.

'We have decided to have a Durga Puja in our college this year,' Subhra told him.

'A Durga Puja in a college, and in a women's college at that!' Harakinkar made no effort to hide his astonishment.

A pleasant smile spread across Subhra Roy's face. Subrataa had been observing how courteous she was. She had heard Subhra was from a very rich family, and yet how courteously the professor spoke! 'Everyone who hears is surprised,' Subhra said. 'It's our principal Subhadra Haldar's idea. She feels that the state of the country warrants the worship of the goddess Shakti by women.'

'I see,' said Harakinkar.

Subhra said, 'The so-called modern teachers among us didn't show much interest. But the principal wants our girls to know of religious rituals – let them learn what goes into conducting a Durga Puja. Reading Shelley, Byron and Keats will be of no benefit to the nation.'

'Has a Durga Puja ever been conducted in the college?' Harakinkar asked.

'Subhadra Haldar says there's no use fretting over what may or may not have been done earlier,' Subhra said. 'Since it's a good thing to do, why not go ahead? The goddess is not male, women can set a new tradition if they want to.'

'Durga Puja is almost at hand,' said Harakinkar.

'You're right, there's no time at all,' Subhra said. 'Some people were worried we wouldn't be able to pull it off so quickly. But Mrs Haldar said she was married at twenty-four hours' notice herself.'

Subrataa's apprehensions were proved correct at this point. Without any hesitation Harakinkar told Subhra to her face, 'I may be an impoverished Brahmin, but I abhor the public observance of Durga Puja. When there are a thousand people in charge all that ensues under the guise of rituals is song and dance and mirth and licentiousness. I will starve to death before I conduct such a Durga Puja.'

Subrataa had meant to placate her father, but after a look at his eyes she didn't have the courage.

Subhra, however, was not displeased at all. 'Mrs Haldar agrees with you wholeheartedly,' she said. 'She too wants the sanctity of the Durga Puja to be maintained, with the religiosity kept intact. Loudspeakers, light displays, decorations, processions – we will have none of these. Our idol too will be made in accordance with the holy texts.'

'You mean you do not want an ultra-modern figure with the face of a film star?' Harakinkar said.

Subrataa started at the mention of a film star, but neither of the other two noticed.

'Our principal wants the Durga Puja to be conducted on traditional lines,' said Subhra. 'Only then will our girls receive divine blessings. We have taken the entire responsibility, the women are doing all the work. We are collectively requesting you to conduct the rituals. Mrs Haldar has heard you speak somewhere. Perhaps you could meet her.'

Harakinkar tried to convince himself that a Durga Puja in a women's college couldn't be called a public affair. 'You have helped my daughter greatly,' he told Subhra, 'I don't know how to thank you. For three generations we have conducted the Durga Puja nowhere else besides the Roy family residence. I have never done the rituals for anyone else. Let us see how the goddess responds this time. I will go to the college today.'

Harakinkar got to his feet – it was time he went to the utensil shop. Before he left he told his daughter, 'Your teacher is visiting you at home, make her a cup of tea at least.'

Shubhra examined the miserable state of the room. 'The roof's cracked, does water drip from it?'

'Floods the room,' Subrataa answered.

'Why haven't you been going to college?'

'It's been quite some time since I went. Please don't tell anyone, Subhra-di, I'll lose the milk distribution centre job. They don't hire anyone but students.'

Subhra seemed to understand, given the appearance of the room and Subrataa's expression.

Subrataa was embarrassed. 'Don't be upset with baba, Shubha-di. He's absolutely rigid when it comes to religious rituals, he cannot tolerate any deviations. Which is why he is pained.'

'Pained at what?'

'He lashes out at those who engage him for priestly duties whenever he sees anything unscriptural. Why should they accept this? There's no lack of priests here. And besides, we're outsiders, we've drifted here after losing our home in Pakistan. Why will anyone engage him instead of local priests?'

Subhra listened in silence.

'I tell him, you have an education, why did you pick this hopeless profession? Baba says, it was the custom for at least one male in every generation to be a priest. Besides, it was an honourable profession when he was young.'

'What about your family?' Subhra asked.

'I have an elder brother who works in another city. My mother's dead. I look after the household now.'

'Why have you stopped going to college? Is your marriage being arranged?'

Subrataa smiled without answering.

'I have to go now, come to the college during the Durga Puja,' said Subhra, and left.

Subrataa could not say what Subhra had made of her smile. She sat there glumly. Marriage, indeed! Her brother worked in Dhanbad, he hadn't sent any money for two months now. Apparently he had got involved with a woman from another caste in the railway colony. Hats off to men, such an exemplary sense of responsibility! A railway clerk with a salary of 130 rupees a month in search of a romantic relationship.

Her father could sing the praises of the scriptures at the top of his voice, but money – money was the most important thing. Essential for survival.

Mr Chatterjee, the secretary of the Dalton Company Employees' Recreation Club, collected milk every morning at the distribution centre. 'You have a very sweet voice,' he had told her.

'Why do you say that?' Subrataa had asked in annoyance.

Not put out at all, he had said, 'You would shine in the acting line. Plenty of demand from employee associations and neighbourhood clubs these days. We have an emergency – Kamalini, who was acting in our play, has suddenly got typhoid. Meanwhile the date has been fixed and the theatre has been booked too, there's no going back now. Why don't you join us? You'll be paid, you might win a medal too. Once you're famous people will be lining up at your door.'

Subrataa had agreed and gone for rehearsals. After which she had performed on stage. No medal, but she had made sixty rupees, which had proved extremely useful. 'Any chance of getting a job in your company?' she had asked.

'They only hire white-skinned ladies. And why should you get a job? This profession can earn you ten times as much. And if you catch the eye of a film producer, your career will be made.'

It wasn't a bad idea. If she caught someone's eye there'd be no looking back. One of Mr Chatterjee's friends was an assistant cameraman at a studio. Subrataa had met him.

'You have sharp features, you will look wonderful on camera,' he had told her. 'You have all the qualities needed to be a heroine. Try to get hold of someone important in this field. You only have to do it once, to get a break. If fortune favours you, the same person will be begging and pleading with you for shooting dates afterwards.'

Maybe people would criticize her, but Subrataa didn't care. She would do as she pleased to secure her future. Since no one was going to give her money, why should she pay any heed to them? The fact was that her father was the only one she was concerned about, for he was rather innocent. Despite his knowledge of the holy texts and his deep learning, he couldn't get them two square meals a day. He would stop her without understanding her need. It was best not to tell him anything now. But when she had made a great deal of money she would make him a beautiful space in which to worship his gods and goddesses. He wouldn't have to go looking for work as a priest.

She had meant to tell Subhra, but she didn't get round to it. Just as well, perhaps. When Subrataa Bhattacharya was nationally famous, when her name was on everyone's lips . . . that would be the time she would reveal the story. When reporters approached her for the story of her life, she would also mention how large-hearted Subhra had been. She would not hide the fact that it was thanks to Subhra that she had not had to pay college fees.

Her glance fell on the clock on the shelf. She couldn't sit here wasting time any more, she had to go out.

No more hesitation. She had to go in search of opportunities.

Arrangements for the Durga Puja were in full flow at the Women's College.

Adjusting his shawl, Harakinkar said, 'If we do not collect all that is needed in the precise way laid down in the holy texts, it will bring misfortune not just upon you but also upon me. This is Durga Puja, after all.' He proceeded to reel off the names of the ingredients he would need to conduct the rituals.

The list would have been longer had Shubhra not interrupted him to say, 'Don't worry, we will arrange everything. Please give us the list.'

'You have probably never organized a Durga Puja,' Harakinkar said.

'I've been told there used to be a Durga Puja at home,' Subhra said shyly. 'But I was very young then. Please teach me.'

It had been a long time before Harakinkar had come across such pleasant behaviour. In this world of instant sensations, he had not expected to find a true devotee. 'Don't worry,' he said with great enthusiasm, 'I will show you everything. Our old faith survives today only because of our mothers. If the educated among them learn everything we have nothing to fear.'

Subhra said gently, 'Not knowing the rituals of my own religion is nothing to be proud of. The history of our civilization and society is embedded in them.'

'But does anyone understand?' said Harakinkar. 'I don't conduct public Durga Pujas, people call me a fanatical priest, some even say I'm mad. But I tell you, those events have nothing sacred about them. No one even bothers to ask whether all the ingredients necessary for the rituals have been procured. Make do with what you have, they say if something is missing. But can the priest decide this? Everything has been written down thousands of years before his ancestors were born.'

'We agree with you completely,' said Subhra. 'Our principal says, do it properly, or don't do it at all.'

Harakinkar began to dictate the requirements. Subhra used to be a swift writer as a student, but she had to concede defeat to the priest's speed. Harakinkar chuckled. 'No need, I'll write it down myself. Many people don't even care for a list, they just go to the shop where you get these things and buy anything at all. And the shopkeepers are not like they used to be, they're all cheats now who will hand you whatever they have.'

Subhra gazed at Harakinkar's handwriting. He told her, 'Be careful when getting these, they sell too many spurious things these days.'

'How are things progressing, Subhra?' asked Subhadra Haldar.

'Very well. The priest is a fine gentleman – a little bad-tempered but devoted to his work.'

'There's a dearth of dedicated priests these days,' the principal said. 'They're no different from cooks as far as most people are concerned.'

A festive air had descended on the college. The principal had also lowered her usual mask of gravity in keeping with the cheerful atmosphere. Professor of economics Shipra Mitra took advantage of this in the teachers' room to ask, 'Why do you say that, Mrs Haldar?'

'Because I know. Ours is a family of priests too, so to speak. But no one continued in the profession, because there's no money to be made. These days it's those without an education who become priests. But how will they read the sacred texts unless they're literate?'

Several of the professors agreed with the principal. Mrs Haldar said, 'Unfortunately, gold and dross cost the same in our times. We used to have a copy of Suren Bhattacharya's manual for priests at home when I was young. I remember him rueing that a culinarian and a cleric will earn the same amount today to conduct religious rituals. No wonder the best people are deserting the profession.'

'What does culinarian mean?' asked Romola, the secretary of the students' union and the leader of the volunteers.

'What do you teach nowadays, Subhra?' said Mrs Haldar. 'We used to learn the language, you people only make them read modern novels. How will students know what culinarian means?'

Romola was embarrassed, but the principal said, 'No need for embarrassment, it's better to be ignorant and ask than to feign knowledge. A culinarian is a cook – what they call a chef these days.'

Turning to the teachers, Subhadra Haldar said, 'Some of you may be unhappy with me for proposing to have a Durga Puja in the college. You may consider it a waste of time and money. But actually organizing a Durga Puja will teach our girls more about religion than two dozen textbooks can.'

Pausing, she continued, 'Durga Puja needs such strange things, I had no idea, although I come from a family of priests. We would learn so much about our country, about our social system, about the way we live – if only we involved ourselves. Take this business of the grand ritual ablution on the first day of Durga Puja. You've got the list, Subhra, will you read it out?'

Subhra began to read, but halted suddenly after reeling off eleven items, the last two of which were soil from outside a palace entrance and soil from a crossroads.

'What is it? Go on,' said Subhadra Haldar.

But Subhra couldn't continue. Her face reddened.

'What's the matter?' said Shipra Mitra, and leant towards the list for a look. She looked taken aback too. 'What's in there, Shipra-di?' two of the students asked in unison.

'Nothing, no need to worry about it,' Shipra Mitra said.

Unable to understand, the principal said, 'There's a great deal to do, we cannot waste time, read on.' Shipra said,

'Skip that one.'

This made everyone even more curious. Several other professors went up to Subhra for a look at the list. Their expressions changed at once.

'Is this true?' said one of them. 'I've been to so many Durga Pujas, never heard of something like this being necessary.'

'Must be necessary, or why would the priest ask for it?' said another one.

The students had no idea what was going on. 'What is it, what is necessary?'

The teachers exchanged glances. 'Nothing,' Subhra said uncomfortably, and continued reading after omitting the offensive item. But everyone seemed intent on finding out what was missing.

'What is it?' said Subhadra Haldar.

Subhra had no choice but to go up to the principal and show her the list. She looked astonished. She checked the number of students in the room – there were two. 'Find out if the fruit has been delivered,' she instructed them, 'we don't have much time.'

Realizing something was wrong, the students went out without a word.

'Hmmm, I didn't know,' the principal said.

'Most embarrassing,' said Shipra Mitra. 'We have all these young unmarried girls. Of all things in the world, imagine requiring soil from outside the entrance to a whorehouse.'

'What's it for?' one of the teachers asked.

'According to Harakinkar-babu's list it's needed for the grand ritual ablution on the first day,' said Subhra.

Everyone was too red with embarrassment to speak.

After some thought the principal said, 'I admit it's embarrassing, especially for an educational institution like ours. But what can we do about such ancient traditions?'

'Why not leave it out?' suggested one of the teachers.

'How can we do that? That will mean leaving out the entire rituals of the Durga Puja.'

Subhadra looked at the sociology professor, Tandra Roy. 'Can you throw some light on this? How did such an unholy thing become part of sacred rituals?'

Professor Roy had just completed her PhD. 'Might be worth looking up the *Encyclopaedia of Religion and Ethics*,' she said. 'But I think there could be two reasons.'

'What are they?' Subhra asked.

'It is believed in India that a man leaves all his virtues outside the door of a prostituted woman's house before entering,' said Tandra Roy. 'Maybe the soil is specially enriched for this reason.'

No one had anything to say. All of them, including Shipra Mitra, were staring at Tandra Roy. She said, 'Another possibility is that Hindu sages desired the cooperation of all, high or low, for Durga Puja. The place of worship was to be made sacred by everyone's presence.'

'Interesting,' said the principal. 'But it's best not to discuss this in the presence of the students. Please carry on with your respective tasks.'

Harakinkar was busy with his evening prayers, but several thoughts were running through his head. His son had not turned out as he would have liked, quite the opposite, in fact. How could he forget his responsibilities and share his bed in Dhanbad with a low-caste Shudra woman? Why had this happened? He had not neglected to perform any of the necessary rituals before the boy was born – nor afterwards. God alone could tell why his son had gone astray. He would disclose his unhappiness to the goddess during the Durga Puja rituals this time.

Someone was knocking on the door. Who on earth was disturbing him now? His home was turning into a marketplace. Who was it? His daughter seemed to be greeting the visitor warmly. 'Oh, come in Shobhon-babu, it's been so long. To what do I owe this honour?'

The man was saying something about acting. 'Don't worry,' he was telling Subrataa, 'I will make sure you get a good role.'

'You've been saying that forever, Shobhon-babu. I can't take this amateur theatre any more. The shows are all right, but I cannot do these long rehearsals. Earlier a couple of days of rehearsals were all that was needed, now the gentlemen want two weeks. They won't even pay the taxi fare.'

Their voices floated into Harakinkar's hearing, and he had an urge to charge at them with a stick. But he felt paralysed, unable to rise to his feet.

Harakinkar heard his daughter say she was desperate to get into films. 'Start with supporting roles,' the man was telling her, 'you can move on to bigger ones.'

'Impossible, Shobhon-babu,' Subrataa said. 'You've been in this business for a long time, a heroine is a heroine from day one. A supporting-role actress remains a supporting-role actress till eternity.'

Was Harakinkar's daughter trying to develop an intimacy with the visitor? 'No Shobhon-babu,' she was saying, 'your contract is to supply extras, please go ahead with that, but find me a good producer. If I get a chance I'll show all of you that your favourite actresses are nothing in comparison ...'

Shobhon's voice dropped. He was whispering to Subrataa. What had this house turned into? Was the head of the family dead? But Harakinkar's paralysis appeared to have become worse – he didn't have the strength to move a finger.

The rent was due, he recalled. The landlord had sent a legal notice asking them to leave. The house was to be demolished. Harakinkar was looking for another place, but everyone was asking for higher rent and three months' advance payment. They owed seven months of rent here. Money was essential – a lot of it, it might help them survive. Money had become a poison that had percolated into the lifeblood of the nation – it was this poison that had numbed his nerves into a state of paralysis.

They were whispering. Harakinkar began to mumble the holiest of all incantations for Brahmins.

It seemed to give him strength. He got to his feet and went to the door, where he heard his daughter say, 'Very well, I'll do that. Don't worry.'

Harakinkar was trying to put the conversation out of his mind. His eyes and ears seemed to have stopped working because of the poison. He was an omnivorous creature with a huge belly, living permanently in his bed.

Subrataa turned to her father. 'Are you going out?' he asked her.

'Yes, I have some things to do.'

Harakinkar was silent. 'I'll find out about a house too,' his daughter said.

Still he didn't speak. 'What do you worry about so much, baba?' Subrataa said. 'Everything will be all right.'

Harakinkar went directly to the shop where he would have to buy everything needed for the Durga Puja. Subhra had passed on the responsibility to him eventually. The strangest things in the world were available at these shops. Harakinkar began checking the items on his list. 'Everything is genuine, I hope. Or are spurious things being foisted on Durga Puja arrangements these days?'

'Why do you ask?' asked the irate shopkeeper.

'Why don't the rituals lead to results nowadays? Maybe it's the impurities.'

The shopkeeper looked sullen. 'Did you have to say this in the middle of the evening?'

Tallying the items, Harakinkar said, 'Where's the soil from outside the entrance to a whorehouse?'

'Don't have it.'

'You don't stock it?'

'What we have is spurious. It's nothing but ordinary soil.'

'No need then.' Harakinkar loaded everything into a large basket and got a porter to take it to the college. Everyone was busy there, the Durga Puja rituals would begin the next day. The drummers would arrive any moment, their drumbeats signalling the start of the festivities.

Harakinkar gazed at the girls. Were they going to perform the rituals to the goddess Mahashakti? Let them, why shouldn't they, he answered himself.

'Did you get everything?' Subhra asked.

'All but one, I'll get it now,' Harakinkar answered.

He was out on the street again, in search of something. Where was it? There had to be a neighbourhood nearby. As a child he used to know the one in his village. A few earthen huts at one end. An aged woman named Amodini Dasi had given up the profession and begun selling milk. Harakinkar had been to her house too.

But where was the neighbourhood here? He had never thought to find out. It would probably be unseemly to ask the policeman at the end of the road. The papers had said recently that prostitution had become illegal. Where would the soil for the Durga Puja come from if the profession was indeed abolished?

But it hadn't gone beyond the newspapers – introducing a law had changed nothing, business was still booming. Speculating about the distant future was pointless.

It might be best to ask at one of those roadside shanties selling tea. He went up and asked, at which they chortled. 'At this age! With one foot in the grave!'

'Who asked you to be his guardian,' said someone. 'He's asking, show him the way.'

'Of course,' said the shopkeeper. 'Many people come and ask. Not at this hour though, a little later.'

After looking Harakinkar up and down once more, he said, smiling covertly, 'Is this a new desire? Go down the road on the left. Turn right after five minutes or so. There's a cinema hall there. The lanes behind the building are where you'll find what you're looking for.'

Harakinkar walked away without wasting time. He had to ask once more at another shop near the cinema hall. They grinned too, and said, 'Want something to drink, sir? We have good stuff.'

Clenching his teeth, Harakinkar entered the lane. Some dressed-up women were standing outside the entrances to the houses. Harakinkar came to a stop abruptly. The women got a clear view of him in the gaslight. They didn't normally get such orthodox Brahmin customers draped in shawls with sacred words on them. 'Would you like to come in?' they invited him courteously.

Harakinkar glanced at their doors. There was something written in red vermilion – 'May Goddess Durga Help Us'. What was all this?

Walking on, Harakinkar discovered a door on which it said 'Residential Building'. His body was revolting. He would have to collect the soil quickly and go back.

This spot seemed a little darker than usual. The goddess's name was written on the door. The women of this building were not lined up outside. Maybe they were still dressing, or perhaps they did not need to go out on the streets. This soil would do. Harakinkar squatted to collect the earth, and moments later a woman's voice rang out. 'Oh god, what's that man doing there?'

Two or three young women rushed out and gripped Harakinkar's arms. 'And what do you think you're doing?'

'Nothing, nothing at all,' a flustered Harakinkar replied.

'Nothing at all. Look at him, pretending to be innocent.'

'It's the truth,' Harakinkar said in a stricken voice.

'Check what he's got in his hand,' said one of them, and another one prised open his clenched fist. 'What's the old man doing with all this dirt?'

One of the women had run out with her toilette incomplete. Smelling of cheap talcum powder and cream, she trembled in fear. 'Must be black magic, who knows what spell he's put on us.'

'Of course not, I'm a priest, why should I do black magic?' Harakinkar said apprehensively.

A portly man had appeared from somewhere at the sound of the women's voices. 'See for yourself, Ghetu-babu, this man was gathering soil here. Who knows what black magic he's up to.'

Ghetu grabbed both ends of Harakinkar's shawl, shouted an expletive, and said, 'I'll teach you a lesson.'

'Believe me, I am here only to collect soil for Durga Puja.'

Ghetu suddenly slapped Harakinkar's hand. The earth fell to the ground. One of the women said, 'Why ours in particular among all these houses? We're just about making a living, but they won't let us do that either.'

'Get out, you bastard,' Ghetu said, 'and don't ever come back here, or I'll kill you.'

Harakinkar was sweating, his body was trembling in agitation. What had he got himself into, trying to collect his soil? What harm would it have done them if he had taken a little?

He felt his body recoiling in revulsion. As though a group of rats from a drain had walked over him. He would have to cleanse himself with a bath, purify himself in the Ganges.

But what would he use for the grand ablution? How was he to collect the soil? But was he mad? Why was he worrying about this? All these Durga Pujas everywhere were being conducted with impure ingredients. One more would join their numbers.

Should he take a rickshaw? People would think he was drunk. Harakinkar kept walking.

He was nearly home. A car braked to a stop, almost hitting him.

An elegantly dressed man got out. He had a prominent paunch and a gold chain round his neck. 'Do you know where Miss Subrataa lives? She acts in plays for clubs.'

Harakinkar looked at him in annoyance. 'You cannot meet Miss Subrataa at home at this hour.'

Clearly inebriated, the man began to giggle.

'Oh really? Is she a nun?'

'Just listen to what I'm telling you. Subrataa does not meet people at this time of the night.'

'My heart bleeds for her. Should I spill the beans? But who the hell are you?'

'Mind your tongue.'

'Better get out while you can, or they'll find your body lying here.'

'Decent people live here, if you try anything funny they will ...'

Harakinkar would have slapped the man if he had the strength.

'Oh my god! I must ask Subrataa when she started living in a neighbourhood of decent people.'

Harakinkar could contain himself no longer. He tried to grab the stranger's collar – but how was he to contend with this man? The stranger pushed Harakinkar so hard that he went sprawling. 'Damn it, I thought I was the only drunk around here, but you're drunk too.'

He might have tried to plant his foot on Harakinkar's chest now. Meanwhile Harakinkar was rolling on the ground with the intention of grabbing his leg and sending him crashing to the ground. Something terrible might have happened, but the commotion brought Subrataa to the front door, where she halted abruptly.

'Here you are, Miss Subrataa. You said not to visit you at home, but I found myself free after you left. I was longing to see you again.'

Clambering up to his feet, Harakinkar said, panting, 'Go inside. A drunkard has turned up from somewhere. He's found out your name somehow. I'm going to teach him a lesson.'

But why was Subrataa still standing there?

'I made the big mistake of asking this fossil where your house is. Get ready, I've brought my car.'

Subrataa was rooted to the spot. Softly she said, 'Please leave, I won't go anywhere now.'

'Why not? You were at the hotel, they took your test in the dark room, you didn't object then. And now you're a changed person. Don't want to act in my film after all?'

'What's that you said?' Harakinkar charged at the man.

'Exactly what I said, sir.' The stranger laughed, baring his teeth.

'Leave at once,' Subrataa shouted. 'Or else I'll call everyone. I don't want to act in your film.' She was shaking uncontrollably.

The man realized he had made a mistake. 'All right, I'll go,' he said, and then added for Harakinkar's benefit, 'Probably has an appointment with someone else.'

Harakinkar shut the door. He was covered in perspiration. Subrataa was panting and weeping, weeping and panting. Harakinkar looked at her. 'Baba,' she said.

Her father was silent.

Still crying, Subrataa said, 'He was supposed to sign a contract with me tomorrow for his film. Just this once, we have to demean ourselves, when starting out. Then we make a name for ourselves – everything becomes all right after that.'

Harakinkar had turned to stone.

'Baba,' said Subrataa.

He did not reply.

It was very late at night, they had gone to bed. Subrataa woke up suddenly. Was the front door open? Yes, indeed it was. Reaching out, she found her father's bed unoccupied. Her heart leapt into her mouth.

Subrataa jumped to her feet in fear. 'Baba, where are you, baba?'

He was outside the door. 'Baba, why are you still up? Don't you have to do the Durga Puja at the college early tomorrow?'

Harakinkar was squatting outside the door, busy with something. He looked at his daughter. His eyes were blazing in the darkness.

'What are you collecting, baba?'

Now Harakinkar's eyes did seem to be giving off flames. 'Soil,' he said, clenching his teeth.

Subrataa was frightened by her father's appearance. Still she went up to him, wrapping her hand round his arm affectionately. 'What do you need soil for, baba?'

He was silent at first. As he gazed at her, his lips began to quiver. 'I'll need it for the Durga Puja,' said the priest, and sobbed in the darkness.

SUNIL GANGOPADHYAY

A Cup of Tea at the Taj Mahal

'Ram Ram Ustadji! Let's have some good news!'

Ustadji was dressed in some sort of patchwork robe, with a band around his head. A week-old stubble adorned his cheeks. He was probably about fifty. No one knew where his home was or whether he had a family. If asked, his answer was a gentle smile.

He turned up every now and then. Perching on a charpoy, he would swap stories with the villagers, giving them advice when they needed it. He stayed at someone's house for a couple of days, ate whatever he was given – sattu or roti and bhindi – with great relish, and then disappeared again.

During the drought last year, the contractor for the village had proved shameless and hard-hearted. Was he right to stop work on the dam in that period? No harvest, no money . . . how were people to survive without government wages? Ustadji had arrived in the nick of time to teach the damned contractor a lesson. They had clustered around him under a palm tree, not allowing him a morsel of food or a drop of water for twenty-four hours.

The day or two that Ustadji spent in the village made everyone happy. Hard labour was a way of life; fate dictated that they would toil until their last breath in order to survive. No one remembered the pleasures of life amid all this hard work. But Ustadji reminded them. Clapping them on the back he would say, 'There'll always be work, that doesn't mean you should forget to smile. Look at the animals in the forest and the birds in the sky, they sing and dance, too.'

Ustadji gathered all the villagers around him every evening for an impromptu soirée. He led the singing himself. He wasn't particularly tuneful, but he could make a powerful noise, covering his ear with one hand while extending the other arm. It was this singing that had earned him the title of Ustadji to signify his prowess as a classical musician.

The pocket of his robe held a newspaper. Ustadji was well read; he kept track of the world beyond this village. He had even said one day, pointing at the sky, 'Up there, so high that you can't even see that far, people are getting ready to fight.' No one could tell whether Ustadji made up stories just for fun.

Three or four people gathered now, drawn by Ustadji's voice. They squatted on the ground around old Ramkhelaon's cot. Greeting him, they said, 'Tell us, Ustadji, what good news does your newspaper have for us?'

Sitting down on the corner of the cot, Ustadji said, 'Nothing. They don't write about poor people like you and me in the papers. Only about important businessmen and ministers. What use is all that to you?'

With a gap-toothed smile, old Ramkhelaon said, 'What could the newspapers possibly write about poor people's lives, Ustadji? We don't want to hear about poor people either. Tell us stories about businessmen and ministers.'

A woman named Phulsaria said, 'Last time you told us a beautiful story about a village named Africa, tell us another one like that.'

Her husband Dhania asked, 'Ustadji, isn't it true that Indiraji's son Rajivji is the leader now? How many sons does Rajivji have? How old are they? Suppose, god forbid, Rajivji is killed suddenly . . .'

Some of the listeners started laughing. Others widened their eyes in dismay – this was not a laughing matter at all; they wished to hear Ustadji's views on the subject.

There was no work today. The skies were scratchy and dry, so sowing had not yet begun; they were just waiting for rain. The idle hours drifted by.

In the course of conversations on various subjects, Ustadji suddenly said, 'Can someone get me a cup of tea?'

The audience exchanged glances, expressing their mortification in silence. How shameful that he had to ask . . . a mere cup of tea . . . but how to arrange it for him? They were not in the habit of making tea at home.

Ustadji understood the situation from their expressions. His visits to the city had turned him into a tea addict. Raising his hand, he said, 'Never mind. No need for tea. Someone get me a glass of water. Then I will tell you the tale of the businessman.'

A young man rose to say, 'A Sikh has a restaurant at Pakki, I'll fetch some tea. Someone give me a bowl to bring it in.'

Pakki was the highway. It was two and a half miles away. The young man would run all the way there and back.

Dhania said, 'Bringing the tea from so far away might warm you up, but the tea will turn cold. Cold tea is like cat piss.'

He contorted his face, as though he really had tasted cat piss at some time. Everyone laughed.

Phulsaria retorted brusquely, 'Do you think we can't heat the tea? Go get it quickly.'

Ramkhelaon said, 'Take a big bowl. Brings lots.'

Ustadji raised his hand, pointed it at Ramkhelaon and said, 'Wait.' Then he was silent. He didn't say anything for a few minutes. The lines of a plan snaked across his forehead.

A little later he rose from the cot to say, 'Why should you go alone? Let's all of us go. What's the point of sitting here? There are so many cars on the highway . . . some of those trucks travel a thousand miles, two thousand miles, even watching them is a pleasure. Yes or no?'

Many of the listeners stood up in unison, cheering, 'Let's go!'

About thirty-five people joined the group. A few more who had heard came running.

Ramkhelaon said, 'Where are we going with this greedy gang? Who'll pay for everyone's tea?'

Raising his hand, Ustadji said, 'Let everyone come, we'll find a way.'

Phulsaria said, 'When Ustadji has asked us to go, why are you arguing? Don't his words carry any weight?'

A sudden procession. An unexpected picnic in the midst of an idle existence. On reaching the highway it was clear that there were two distant lands in two different directions. One of these was the capital of the country. It was only twenty-five or thirty miles away in terms of distance, but in fact was much further in every other sense.

They found the Sardar's tea shop after walking another half a mile to the right. But it was closed. The shop looked as though it had done no business in quite some time.

Slapping himself on the forehead in annoyance, Dhania said, 'Hai Ram! How could I not have remembered? There's been some trouble in Amritsar . . . the Sardars are furious, many of them have disappeared. This Sardar has not been seen since Indiraji's death.'

One or two among the others said, 'That's right. This shop's been shut for a long time.'

Everyone looked upset. The picnic was a failure. Ustadji had wanted to treat everyone to a cup of tea today.

Ustadji said, 'No problem. So what if this one's closed? There are others. Let's go on.'

Ramkhelaon said, 'Where do you want to go, Ustadji? The further we go, the closer we'll be to town. Things are more expensive there. Besides, we're not in our kurtas, nor have we put our shoes on; they won't let us in.'

Several of the others had come to a halt too. They had all had the same thought. You could still have a cup of tea at a roadside tea shop, but would a proper restaurant let them in?

Ustadji said, 'Is the tea for the kurta and the shoes or the people?'

A fleeting smile appeared on his face. As though a mischievous idea had occurred to him.

Taking the newspaper out of his pocket, he rolled it up and kissed it twice. Then he said, 'Come with me, I'll treat you to tea at the Taj Mahal today.'

Sometimes Ustadji said things they simply couldn't comprehend. 'What on earth is the Taj Mahal?' The villagers exchanged glances.

Dhania had the air of someone who knew it all. He said, 'The Taj Mahal is a very big house of the emperors. I've seen a photograph. On a calendar in the contractor's house.'

Ustadji said, 'Right! Have you people heard of Emperor Akbar? You haven't? Emperor Akbar's grandson made a gigantic palace for his wife. As white as the sun. Magnificent!'

Someone quipped, 'Why should we go there? Has the emperor invited us?'

Dhania said, 'Oh the era of the emperors and empresses is over. They're not alive any more. Didn't you know?'

Someone said, 'Then ministers are probably living there with their wives now.'

Ustadji said, 'Oh no, the building belongs to the public now. Even ordinary people like you and me can pay a visit.'

Most of them were still doubtful. How far was it? How much would it cost to have a cup of tea there? When would they return?

A smile flashed across Ustadji's face. Whipping out a 100-rupee note, he started twirling it in front of his nose.

Amazing! A 100-rupee note in the pocket of Ustadji's patchwork robe? Did he know magic?

'What's this you're showing us, Ustadji? Where did you get that?'

'What do you people take me for? A complete good-for-nothing? I got this as a reward for singing.'

The atmosphere had lightened again. Several people began to laugh. It was impossible to believe that someone had paid Ustadji to sing. But the 100-rupee note was real. It hadn't vanished into thin air yet.

Dhania said, 'Are you planning to spend that on us, Ustadji?'

'I don't save money. I got it unexpectedly. I'm ready to blow it in a day.'

'I have an idea. Why waste so much money on tea? It's better to spend it at the temple.'

'Impossible! I only worship my stomach, nothing else.'

'Listen to me. Sacrifice a goat or a lamb to the gods. Then we'll eat it.'

'Do you think you can get a goat or a lamb for a hundred rupees? Might get a couple of rats.'

Phulsaria said, 'My man always talks nonsense. Forget about mutton or lamb. If we live long enough we'll always have a chance to have meat. Hawa Mahal or whatever mahal Ustadji spoke of . . . that's where I want my tea.'

Many of the others agreed. There was no hurry to return home, so the rural brigade marched on. Towards the capital.

A little later they saw a man on the road beating on a pair of hand-held drums. With him were a mangy, skinny bear and two monkeys. Going up to the man and putting his hand on his shoulder, Ustadji asked, 'Where to, my friend?'

It was obvious that he knew Ustadji. He replied, 'Do you suppose I plan beforehand? I go whichever way fancy takes me. Where are you off to with this group?'

Ustadji said, 'We're going for a cup of tea. Come with us. I'm glad we ran across you.'

The bear owner said, 'So many people are going just for a cup of tea?'

'Come and see. I'll treat you to a superb cup of tea. You've never had such tea before.'

Someone shouted, 'We're going to the Taj Mahal to have tea.'

The man stopped abruptly. Shaking Ustadji's hand off his shoulder, he looked him in the eye. He was a worldly man who was not fooled easily by words.

He asked, 'What did that man say about the Taj Mahal? Where is it that you're going for your tea?'

With a smile, Ustadji said, 'The Taj Mahal.'

The man said, 'Do you consider me an idiot? Do you think I don't know the Taj Mahal? I know all these places. The Taj Mahal is far away. This road leads to the capital.'

Ustadji said, 'Why not come with us, my friend? You said you don't plan ahead. What if you do go to the capital?'

'But are you planning to walk all the way? Forget human beings, even my bear and monkeys will be exhausted.'

'Then we'd better make some arrangements.'

Three trucks had come up behind them. Ustadji took up a position in the middle of the road, his arms spread out. So did several others, following him.

Trucks didn't stop for one or two people on these roads, they simply ran over them. But nearly forty men and women had gathered here. The three trucks stopped with a screech of brakes.

All three were carrying full loads of goats. The truck drivers got out, wondering which party it was that was asking for contributions.

Phulsaria asked, 'Where are they going with all these goats, Ustadji?'

Ustadji said, 'To the capital. People there have enormous appetites. That's why they scour the villages for goats and chicken, and cows and fish and milk and take them all. They even take women.'

'Do they eat women too?'

'Ha ha ha. Don't worry, Phulsaria, with all of us here nobody can eat you.'

Stepping up to the truck drivers, Ustadji put his palms together respectfully and said, 'Bhaisaab, will you do us the favour of taking us to the capital?'

The drivers were actually quite pleased at this outlandish request. If these bastards had chosen to block the road, there would have been no way to proceed. At least twenty-four hours would pass before the police arrived to clear the road, which meant the loss of a lot of money. Besides, they hadn't asked for contributions either.

Still, they displayed some reluctance at first, citing lack of space. Then they dropped hints about payment. Ustadji said his people would hold the goats in their laps so that there was enough room for everyone. There was no question of payment, but he would treat the drivers to a cup of tea once they arrived at the capital.

Although the drivers agreed eventually, problems arose with the bear and the monkeys. Ustadji said, 'Have you seen the poor bear? Each of your goats is larger. None of them will be scared of him. Come along now, let's not waste any more time.'

Phulsaria and some of the other women were very pleased. This was great excitement in their humdrum existence. Who else but Ustadji could have had such a brainwave? No one knew where they were going. Who cared!

One or two of them burst into song. The rest clapped along. Such fun, such joy! What a magic trick you played with this business of a cup of tea, Ustadji! The day was transformed.

When they saw the line of the capital's buildings in the distance, they seemed to choke. They were like palaces from heaven! Even the sky appeared to hang lower here.

A few of the people in the group had, of course, been to the capital before to work as day labourers. But that had been a different kind of visit. Today, they seemed to be on their way to conquer the capital.

Phulsaria asked, 'Ustadji, the Taj Mahal is the biggest building, isn't it? But we won't be able to see it from such a great distance.'

'You will, you will. You'll see it when the time comes. Your eyes will pop, Phulsaria.'

The truck drivers let them out at the edge of the capital. They weren't allowed to go any further. They refused Ustadji's invitation to tea.

Ustadji's group walked through the dream city. My god, so many different kinds of cars and so many policemen! If only Ustadji had told them earlier, they would have dressed in their best clothes. Phulsaria had a pink sari in a flowery print. Instead of that one, she had come in an ordinary yellow sari. And torn, at that. So annoying!

Ustadji stopped every now and then to ask passers-by a question. He was very brave; he didn't hesitate to talk even to policemen. They lost count of the number of streets they passed through. After a lot of walking, Ustadji stopped in front of a large building. 'Stop. This is the Taj Mahal.'

Most of them were disappointed. They had expected something quite extraordinary – it was a matter of emperors and empresses, after all. Where was the palace they had hoped to see? True, this building was big, but they had seen several such structures on their way. Buildings even bigger than this one, in fact. And it certainly wasn't as white as the sun.

Dhania said, 'This is it?'

The bear owner said, 'Why are you playing the fool with us, Ustadji? How can this be your Taj Mahal? This is a hotel.'

Ustadji said, 'Of course it's a hotel. Where will you get tea except at a hotel?'

'Why didn't you say so earlier?'

'My companions would have been frightened in that case. But I didn't lie. This hotel really is called the Taj Mahal. Ask the doorman if you don't believe me.'

Many of them were intimidated by the prospect of visiting a hotel. They weren't bold enough to enter this kind of place. True, Ustadji had flourished a 100-rupee note – not a small sum, but not large either. It wouldn't even pay for a buffalo or a goat. Was tea available at 100 rupees in a hotel as grand as this, one meant for important people? Even if it was, would they be allowed in?

The head watchman of the hotel looked like a king or an emperor of yore. An enormous moustache beneath his nose; a perfect unwrinkled turban on his head; silk clothes. In his hand a small baton; although the head was capped with brass, it sparkled like gold. At the sight of all these barefoot beggars in filthy, tattered clothes, he roared, 'Get out! Get out of here!'

Most of them quailed at this stentorian yell. They tried to hide behind one another, each of them wanted to go to the back.

But Ustadji strode forward, right up to the head watchman. Without any hesitation, he placed his hand on the watchman's silk-covered chest and said with a charming smile, 'We are customers, you see, customers. We will pay and we will eat and drink. How can you turn us away?'

Still the watchman said, 'Go away. Clear the gate.'

Ustadji said, 'How can you turn customers away? Call the owner. We'll talk to him.'

There was panic within the hotel. The steward, the junior manager and the senior manager were fearfully discussing what kind of onslaught this might be. How could this intrusion be averted? The hotel had its own security guards, but still the police were summoned over the phone. There were many foreign ladies and gentlemen, several rich men and business barons at the hotel, their security had to be ensured. For what crime had the hotel been besieged by a bunch of hooligans from the villages?

From the first-floor balcony, the junior manager instructed the guard and the police in English, 'Remove them! Clear the gates!'

Ustadji said loudly, 'What are you saying, manager sahib? Why are you barking in English? Did an Englishman give birth to you? Your skin's the same colour as mine.'

The junior manager responded with an English accent, 'Go away! Don't make a scene. Else the police will throw you out.'

Ustadji said, 'What's this strange thing you're saying, Manager sahib? You're chasing customers away? I have read the Constitution – nowhere does it say you must have shoes on to enter a hotel. We'll pay, we'll eat, simple.'

'You can't eat here, go to some other hotel.'

'Why not? Do you tell all your customers to show their money first? It doesn't say so anywhere in the Constitution.'

The junior manager disappeared quickly to telephone a more important police station.

Carloads of policemen arrived in an instant. And their fierce-looking bosses.

The village people were distraught with fear at the sight of such a police force. They were wailing, 'What have you done, Ustadji? We came all this way because we trusted you. Are you going to have us beaten up under the pretence of giving us a cup of tea? Who will plough our land if the police arrest us? How will the children survive?'

Taking the hand drum from the bear owner, Ustadji played it a couple of times before raising his hand to say, 'Listen to me, brothers and sisters, a man must die if he cannot keep his word. I promised to treat you to a cup of tea at the Taj Mahal hotel. You have never had a better cup of tea in your life. Let the cowards retreat. Those who trust me should stay by my side.'

A murmur rose and then subsided. Not a single person retreated. No one wanted to be labelled a coward. Ustadji was their well-wisher, he wouldn't wilfully get them into trouble. This was an exhilarating business, like picketing the contractor.

One of the senior police officers came forward to ask Ustadji, 'Are you their leader? Come this way, we need to talk.'

Ustadji said, 'What do I have to talk about with a small-time inspector like you? Call the commissioner, or else call the prime minister. I can only talk to someone who has read the Constitution.'

The police officer was livid at this insignificant person's arrogance. If this had happened elsewhere, he could have thrashed them within an inch of their lives. A few deaths wouldn't have done any harm either. But this was the capital, with hundreds of foreign embassies, thousands of journalists – one never knew how things might get out of hand. The home minister would suspend him at once.

The police officers held another meeting with the hotel managers. There was only one way to get rid of this trouble. The beggars were ruining the beauty of the garden; the sooner they could be sent away the better.

Standing in the balcony, the senior manager said, 'Very well, since all of you are here for a cup of tea, the hotel management will treat you to a cup of tea as a goodwill gesture. Free of cost. Go stand outside the gate, the tea is being sent.'

Smiles appeared on the villagers' faces. Ustadji had won. They really would get their cup of tea.

Stopping them with an upraised hand, Ustadji told the manager con-temptuously, 'Rubbish! Are we such beggars that you expect us to have our tea on the road? We are free citizens! We're here to pay for our tea. We will sit inside in chairs and relax with our elbows on the tables. We won't leave before that.'

Addressing his followers, he said, 'Come along, let's go inside.' Everyone rushed inside under Ustadji's leadership.

Inside, white-skinned foreign ladies and gentlemen from different countries and brown-skinned Indian foreigners in perfect Western clothes sat at the tables. They jumped out of their skin, a lot of shoving and jostling ensued. The village people occupied all the tables and chairs.

Ustadji said, 'Give me a bidi, Dhania. Now that you've seen for yourself . . .'

Everyone said, 'Long live Ustadji!'

A steward with a black bow came up to Ustadji to tell him in a cold, formal tone, 'Look, since you want a cup of tea, we'll bring you some tea. But you're not allowed to enter a hotel with a bear and two monkeys. Please leave them outside.'

Whipping out the newspaper from the pocket of his robe, Ustadji spread out the front page under the steward's nose. 'What is this a photograph of? Take a good look. Don't you recognize it?'

The front page had a photograph of a bear.

Rising, Ustadji announced, 'Listen to me, brothers and sisters, this bear whose photograph you see here is owned by the hotel. Yes, I'm telling you the truth. The newspaper has it all. This hotel has sent this bear to the land of the French. The bear will perform in different hotels there. I don't lie, I always tell the truth; it's all in this newspaper. If this hotel can send a bear to other hotels, why can't we bring our own bear in here? Of course we can.'

Everyone laughed loudly to convey their support to Ustadji. If a bear could enter foreign hotels, why not an Indian one?

The police officers were trying to contact the home minister on the phone. But he had vanished. No one could give instructions on what weapon to use – sticks, tear gas or guns. It was better to give them a cup of tea instead.

Each of the tables held expensive ashtrays and vases. These buggers were bound to steal them. On the manager's instructions, the bearers arrived to take them away.

Ustadji grabbed one of them by his hand, saying, 'Hey, servant! Have you become a different person just because you're the servant of rich people? Didn't your forefathers till the land? Don't you recognize us?

Where does it say in the Constitution that you can stub out a cigarette in an ashtray, but not a bidi? Put them back!'

Summoning the steward with a snap of his fingers, he said, 'Bring that piece of paper, the one on which all the dishes and prices are written.'

Menu cards lay on every table; one of them was handed over to Ustadji. Pretending to read it carefully, he muttered, 'Bloody thieves! A hundred and fifty rupees for one grilled chicken! Twenty-five rupees for a plate of peanuts! Thieves! Traitors! No, all we'll have is tea. Bring forty cups of tea.'

Two or three foreigners had summoned the courage to peep at them through the doors. They held cameras. Calling out to them, Ustadji said, 'Come along, take pictures.'

Making a scrawny, emaciated man named Dukhiram pose, he said, 'Take his picture. Rajivji has gone to France and Africa to attend celebrations. He's taken statues from the museums to display India to foreigners. That's ancient India. Look at this Dukhiram. This is modern India.'

The police arrived to shepherd the foreigners away. They were not allowed to take photographs wherever they liked. Besides, there was no telling when violence might erupt. These people were laughing and joking and slapping the tables in glee. Why were they taking so much time to bring them their tea?

The tea arrived in large teapots. When the bearer was about to pour the tea into the cups, Ustadji said, 'Stop! Go away!'

Then, looking at Phulsaria, he said, 'You are the empress of the Taj Mahal today, Phulsaria Devi. You must pour the tea for everyone.'

When everyone had got their tea, they began slurping it noisily. Some of them said, 'Ah! I love this! What a lovely flavour! I have never had such tea in my life. Hats off, Ustadji!'

Only Phulsaria had tears in her eyes.

Ustadji asked her, 'What is it, Phulsaria? Why do you weep? What are you unhappy about?'

Phulsaria said hoarsely, 'I'm so happy, Ustadji. I am an ordinary woman. No one has ever given me such respect.'

'The tea was more aromatic and sweet because you poured it yourself. Am I right?'

'You're right,' everyone said.

The bear owner said, 'All of you have had your tea, but my bear and monkeys got nothing.'

That's true, that's true, big mistake. Everyone poured a little of their tea into their saucers. This tea was collected and given to the bear and the monkeys.

The listless bear's eyes began to sparkle as he drank his tea. He had never tasted anything so delicious, he seemed rejuvenated.

Clapping his hands, Ustadji said, 'Dance, bear, dance! Dance, Munna, dance!' Everyone surrounded the bear, clapping.

NABANEETA DEV SEN

The Miracle

Editor's note: The 'cross connection' was a phenomenon in Calcutta's telephone network in the 1970s and 1980s in particular. The telephones of two or more people would get inadvertently connected to one another, making it impossible for any of them to make or receive regular calls. They could only speak to one another till the crossed wires were uncrossed, which often took hours.

It's ten o'clock by the time I get back. I have to make a couple of phone calls before doing anything else. One to Khokon's house, to inform his grandparents he won't be back tonight. Both Bapi and Khokon will spend the night in the hospital. Bachchu has had to be hospitalized. He's not in good shape, can't recognize anyone, his body's going into rigor. The doctor wasn't confident about letting him stay at home. After much effort, with the help of my brother-in-law's connections, we've just got back after having him admitted to a hospital. Bachchu goes to college with Bapi and Khokon, he stays in a hostel. Bapi brought him over when his fever rose, but he can't be kept at home, the doctor is worried. The general ward at the hospital isn't reassuring either, he's trying to get a bed in the intensive care unit. After ringing Khokon's grandfather I'll have to telephone Uncle Bhoktibroto. He's a well-known doctor, surely he'll be able to help. Apparently there's a problem with Bachchu's heart, and his blood pressure has dropped alarmingly. He's a friend of Bapi's, how old can he possibly be? Nineteen or twenty. There was no pulse when he was being taken away in an ambulance. His local guardian is his brother-in-law, but that's only on paper, he lives in a suburb of Calcutta and is on tour twenty-five days a month. His wife, Bachchu's sister, is not very sophisticated, she's been crying ever since she was informed. Her husband is on tour right now, which means the entire responsibility lies with Bachchu's friends. But they're young too. Let's see, I'll probably have to get hold of Uncle Bhokti. It's best to try to contact him after ten at night. I'm no expert in these matters, but because I have a job I get to know about many things, that's about all. My husband's office had to pick just this time to send him off to Durgapur for five days – what am I supposed to do now? Khokon's parents are in Delhi right now, which leaves only his aged grandparents. I try to ring them – they must be extremely worried. I simply have to inform them that Khokon won't be back tonight.

As soon as I try to dial it becomes obvious the line is congested – a male voice says, 'Four eight six eight zero two three?' I say, 'No, wrong number, please disconnect.' I put the receiver back on the cradle and start dialling again. 'Four eight six eight, sorry, four six eight six zero two three?'

I fly into a rage at this indecisive approach to life and phone numbers while I'm bursting with unbearable anxiety. 'Can you make up your mind first?' I ask. 'Choose the correct number, which one do you actually want?' And at once it occurs to me he mentioned seven digits, but phone numbers don't have seven digits. 'Seven-figure phone number, is he mad?' I mutter to myself. Now a deep third voice booms through the phone, 'Cut the line madam, he's not mad, it's a Tamil tippler on the rampage.'

'What?'

'I said it's one of those Tamil tipplers. Do you think they're in their right minds? He's been going on for twenty minutes. A different number each time. You only just got here.'

After the recent communal incidents in Assam I have turned deeply pan-Indian now. A creature inspired by generous nationalism. I am fearful, for in my heart I have realized that parochialism is a grave sin. I get down to the task – this Tamilian-hater must be put in his place.

'I see, and Bengali drunkards are always in their senses. They are a superior species compared to Tamil tipplers.'

'That's not what I'm saying. All drunkards are abominable, all of them are public nuisances. Whether they're Bengali or Tamil. But Tamil tipplers are the worst.'

His grave conviction makes me even more furious.

'Why?' I demand to know why.

'Because on the one hand they won't eat meat, but on the other they will drink – how will the body cope? You can't mix strong drinks with ascetic vegetarian food, don't you see? Why do you suppose the term "meat and drink" exists? To tolerate alcohol you need meat, you need protein – you have to have a strong body.'

Oh no, now he's citing logical inconsistency between being ascetic as well as regal at the same time. But since the theme smells of parochialism, any logic is flawed logic. Absurd or sound, no manner of parochialism can be supported. So I start looking for examples of powerful vegetarians from history. Dinosaurs? Buddhist monarchs? Hitler!

'But what about Hitler, he was a vegetarian and powerful too?'

'No, he was a tyrant. Being powerful is a different thing altogether. And besides, he wasn't from Madras, was he?'

'Why do you hate Tamilians so much?'

'Who says I do? They make the best tenants. They make the best bosses. And you can tell from the elections that India's future lies in Tamil hands, all the unsweetened curd they eat lets them identify crucial political points with a cool head. Is it any wonder our president and our foreign minister and our finance minister are all Tamil?'

'But they're not, two of them are from Andhra.'

'Same thing. Dravidian culture. Other side of the Vindhyas. They don't have to be from Madras, they only have to be south Indians. Take the idli. We call it Tamil food, but do they eat it only in Madras? Or all over south India?'

'Hello six eight four eight ... sorry ... three eight four eight six zero two?' The question comes in a hesitant voice. The speaker gets an earful instantly.

'How dare you disturb us again? Put the receiver down. Go to bed. Sleep. These are wrong numbers, do you understand? No seven-digit phone numbers in Calcutta. Please disconnect. What is all this?'

'Yokay, yokay, sorry to disturb you, sir, good evening to you yall.' We hear a receiver being put down courteously.

Proudly I declare, 'Did you see how polite he was? Dravidian culture is far superior to the Bengali one.'

'Won't last more than a minute. He'll be back any moment. Drunkards and culture! Hmmph!'

Suddenly I remember I haven't rung Khokon's grandfather. What's all this, am I drunk too? I say in desperation, 'Can you put the phone down too please? I have to make a very important call, it's getting late.'

'Mine's very important too, you should be the one to put the phone down. I was here well before you.'

'Please! Won't take me more than a minute.'

'A woman will be done with a phone call in a minute? Don't make me laugh.'

'It's not that kind of a call. A boy's been admitted to hospital, I have to inform someone about it, it really is very urgent, believe me.' My voice is choking.

'All right, all right, I get it.'

I hear the loud crack of a receiver being returned to its cradle. Oh, what a nice man! Ah, the dial tone. I dial Khokon's grandparents' number carefully.

'Hello?'

The same booming voice.

'Oh god, why did *you* answer the call?'

'Why? Because my phone rang.'

'Oh no, disconnect, please, if you don't . . .'

'All right, all right, it's not as though I'm deliberately coming in your way. What have I got myself into? Go on, make your call.'

I hear the sound of the receiver being slammed down. The dial tone again. I dial Khokon's grandparents' number. After two rings –

'Hello?'

'Four two two two three two?'

'Not got through yet?'

'What! Don't tell me it's you again, for heaven's sake . . .'

'The lines are snarled. Doubt if you'll get through today . . .'

'None of your business. Put the phone down.'

Not a word in response, just the cracking sound of the receiver being replaced. Dial tone. I dial the number . . .

'Hello?' A distant voice this time.

'Hello, is this Khokon's grandfather? Good evening, it's Bapi's sister-in-law. You know who I am, don't you?'

'Good evening, of course I know who you are. Don't be angry madam, I . . . inadvertently . . .'

'What! You again? You're still on the line?'

'Not at all. The phone rang, I answered. No need to say more, I'm disconnecting.'

'Listen, don't answer the next time it rings.'

'How can I do that? I'm a receptionist, answering the phone is my job.'

'I'm very keen to know which company it is where the receptionist works at a quarter past ten at night.'

'None. All companies are graveyards after five p.m.'

'Well then?'

'I work for a hotel. I've been working here for twenty-eight years. Night duty. Bed of roses from ten to six. Or bed of thorns, take your pick.'

'I see. Do me a favour and don't answer the phone for some time. Allow me to pass on the news, it's very urgent.'

'Let's say I don't. It's still ringing here, the call's not going to Khokon's grandfather. The lines are snarled. What's this news you have to pass on?'

'Don't ask, a boy has had to be taken to hospital . . .'

'And admitted there. You've said that already. What was it? A bus?'

'No, high fever, delirium. Suspected encephalitis.'

'And Khokon's grandfather has to be informed? That you've had him admitted to hospital?'

'No, not Khokon, heaven forbid. Bachchu. But Khokon won't be back tonight, Bachchu's friends will be at the hospital all night, he's one of them. If I don't inform his grandparents they'll be so anxious, old people after all.'

'I see, Bachchu. But you won't be able to ring them today. Isn't there anyone who can go to their place and inform them?'

'No one. My husband's in Durgapur on work, his brother is at the hospital. There's just my sister-in-law and me at home.'

'I see.'

A moment of deep silence. Then . . .

'Where does Khokon live?'

'Jodhpur Park. Other end of town.'

'Give me the address. Let me try to inform them.'

'You'll inform them? Where are you now?'

'Sealdah. This hotel is near Sealdah Station.'

'Are you mad? Sealdah is nowhere near Jodhpur Park. And at this hour . . .'

'It's not very late, just twenty past ten. The buses are still running. I can pay one of these hotel boys to go and give them the news . . . Give me the address.'

'Don't be mad. Let me try to ring them from the neighbours' place. I have to make a couple of other calls too.'

'So you don't think you can rely on me.'

'It's not that. Many thanks for your kind offer. Honestly. Let me see, if I absolutely can't do it myself, I might . . .'

The neighbours across the road are very nice people. They are about to go to bed, thank goodness I haven't delayed things more. Fortunately I get through immediately. Khokon's grandparents have been really anxious. That's one of my tasks taken care of. Uncle Bhoktibroto next. I get him on the first try too. Hearing me out, he says, 'Wait, let me try to get hold of Dasgupta, else I'll have to contact Mandal. I'll ring you in a bit to let you know.' I waltz back home, and realize as soon as I'm back – what does he mean 'I'll ring you to let you know'? The phone isn't working. The lines are snarled. Locked in holy matrimony with the hotel in Sealdah. Meanwhile it's lights out at the neighbours' across the road. I can't possibly disturb them again, they're aged people. Auntie isn't well. What to do now?

Our phone is giving off a series of ghostly sounds – half-formed rings like the cries and laughter of a baby at play . . . ri ri ring . . . crririring . . . on and on it goes. Suddenly I notice it's ringing three times. How strange, why not the usual six to indicate that a six-digit number is being dialled? My younger sister-in-law Rinku has just started college, she's a wizard at maths, her mind works at the speed of lightning. 'Must be that man dialling one nine nine for assistance – try answering.'

As soon as I do, 'Hello, trunk booking?'

'No sir.'

'Well then? Is this one nine nine?'

'No sir. Don't you know who I am? It's Bapi's sister-in-law.'

'Oho, and I'm the receptionist . . .'

'I know.'

'Did you manage to let them know in Jodhpur Park?'

'Yes, it's done. Used the neighbours' phone. Thank you.'

'Thank goodness. Please disconnect now.'

'Where are you booking a trunk call to at this hour of the night?'

'Don't ask. Work. Booking a call to Delhi.'

'My goodness, Delhi. Then I can't reciprocate your courteous offer. Sorry.'

'Meaning?'

'Remember you wanted to deliver my message to Jodhpur Park? I'm not able to go to Delhi to deliver yours in return, that's all.'

'Of course not, how can you do that?' he replies gravely. 'That's impossible. You'd better disconnect instead. That's good enough. Don't answer even if you hear the phone ring.'

'How can I do that? I'm expecting a call from a doctor. I'll answer if I hear six rings but not if I hear three. You can keep trying meanwhile.'

I put the phone down. The ting-ting-ting, crring-crring-crring goes on. As though the phone is spending the night with the question 'Do I wake or sleep?' We cannot sleep either. Rinku and I lie awake in bed next to the delirious phone, just in case the call does come. Suddenly Rinku has a brainwave.

'I have an idea. Every time Uncle Bhokti rings us the call will go to the man in Sealdah. All the calls meant for us must be going to their phone. And theirs to our phone. Why not ask him to take a message instead of saying wrong number?'

'Not a bad idea. But how will you execute it? How will we get hold of the man?'

'Why, just dial the trunk booking number. See, three rings? I'm sure he'll answer. The phones have tied the knot after all.'

Pride in my sister-in-law's intelligence makes my chest swell to the dimensions of Cassius Clay's. I look up the trunk booking number and dial it.

'Hello?'

'Hello, trunk booking?' The same deep voice.

'No sir, it's me, you know, Bapi's sister-in-law ...'

'Thought as much. Whom are you ringing now?'

'You, actually.'

'What!' A clear touch of fear in his voice.

'I mean there's been no call from the doctor, so I wanted to tell you something ...'

'Oh. I see.' His relief is palpable. 'What is it?'

'In case you get a call meant for three five four six zero three ...'

'Yes, I did. Someone rang two or three times for that number ...'

'That's him! That's Uncle Bhokti, he's supposed to let us know whether they've managed to admit Bachchu to intensive care. That's the call I'm waiting for.'

'But the lines are snarled. The call won't go to you.'

'Which is where the problem lies. So I was thinking of requesting you ...'

'Tell me.'

'Please don't disconnect the phone the next time you get a call meant for three five four six zero three.'

'But that's not our number.'

'I know. But it's ours, isn't it? If the call comes again, will you be kind enough to take a message? Dr Bhoktibroto Bhattacharya, director of health services, will call.'

'Oh really? How fortunate.'

'He's part of our family.' Pride drips from my voice.

'Very nice, very nice.'

'If he asks for Bulti ...'

'Is your name Bulti?'

'A nickname, you know. For Bula ...'

'My nephew's name is Bulu. He's studying for his B. Com.'

'Really? What fun. Bulu and Bula are practically the same. So as I was saying, if Uncle Bhoktibroto calls ...'

'But why will he leave a message with me? What is my *locus standi*? Who am I?'

'*Locus standi?* Never mind all that, you could say something like this. Are you Dr B. B. Bhattacharya? Director of health services? Bulti's telephone line is snarked with this one, she asked me to take a message. How is Bachchu now? Has he been admitted to intensive care?'

'How-is-Bach-chu-is-he-in-hold on, please in-ten-sive- ...'

'What's all this, what are you doing?'

'Taking down your message, madam. Ca-re. That's it. This is the receptionist's job after all. This is what I do all the time. Taking messages and passing on messages. Booking calls and connecting people. Hello and hold on.'

'Oho sorry, your Delhi booking . . .'

'That's assuming they answer my call at trunk booking. Snoring their heads off.'

'How will they answer? It's ringing at our house. They have no idea you're trying to ring them.'

'Oh. That's true. It's horrible, horrible. We've earned the wrath of an apocalyptic god, madam . . . everything is falling to ruins. This entire city of Calcutta is breaking down everywhere. The roads are as bad as the trams and buses, the supply of oil and sugar is as abysmal as of kerosene. Our hospitals and our electric supply are in a shambles, there's no water in the pipes but there's garbage in the streets, I hear even the Ganga is dying. Can you imagine! It's because of all our sins, you know. An entire race has to be full of sin for such a thing to happen to them. This is where a civilization stands before it is wiped out.'

A temporary silence. Then I say, 'How right you are. Life in Calcutta is truly becoming unbearable. Umm . . . all right, may I tell you once more? In case someone calls three five four six zero three . . .'

'I'll take a message. Three . . . five . . . four . . . six . . . zero . . . three . . . Yes, you can rely on me.'

'My uncle's name is Bhoktibroto Bhattacharya, director of health services . . .'

'Uncle . . . Bhok-ti-bro-to . . . right? All right. Let him ring, I'll take a message. I'm right here. But how will I inform you?'

'Why, just dial one nine nine? Or trunk booking? Or fire or ambulance? Any of them. No matter whose number you dial the call will come to our phone.'

'That's true. Horrible, horrible. The whole system is breaking down madam. If there's an emergency now . . .'

'What do you mean if? Mine *is* an emergency . . .'

'That's true. What a thing to happen! These bastards . . . sorry . . .'

'Anyway, no use thinking about it. Good night . . .'

'Good night, madam, not that it's good night for me, more like good afternoon. Since my working day is ten p.m. to six a.m.'

'It must be so hard for you.'

'Not really, I've got used to it. You should go to bed, I'll let you know if there's any news.'

I doze off for an hour, and then the phone starts triple-ringing again. Like an indistinct signal. My heart does a high jump.

'Hello.'

'Hello.'

'Is that you? Did you get through to Delhi?'

'Delhi? No luck, still trying. Do your work, think not of the outcome. Yours has come, though.'

'It has? Uncle Bhoktibroto ...'

'Yes. The patient is well. He's been admitted to intensive care. Dr Dasgupta has paid a visit already. He has said the patient is young and in good health, he's fighting well, responding to medicines already ...'

'I don't know how to thank you ...'

'Listen to the entire message before you trot out your homilies. Dr Bhattacharya thinks chances of survival are quite high, but still he says the patient's family should be informed. They think the symptoms point to meningitis, the pathological tests haven't been done yet though, but the neck is rigid, and he's delirious ... the doctor has asked for the patient's parents to be informed at once.'

'But they're in Guwahati.'

'Make a trunk call. Do they have a phone?'

'I don't know. I have their address though.'

'In any case what use is a phone? It'll be like Delhi. Given the state of phones. Send a telegram.'

'A telegram? Go out at this hour of the night? It's two a.m., I can send it in the morning.'

'It'll go faster at night. Don't delay. Come on, give me the address. And the message. I'll send the telegram.'

'Why should you at this hour ... you're on duty ...'

'Why should I go myself? What are all these hotel boys here for? The form is right here, and the telegram office is next door, open all night. Quick, give me the address and the message, what do you want to tell them? But give me their name and address first, let me get the form out, just a minute. Yes, I'm ready now. Tell me ... Well? Tell me?'

'Should I?'

'Of course, am I supposed to guess? What's the father's name?'

'Satyen Barua.'

'Where does he live?'

'Professors Quarter No. five, Gauhati University, Gauhati.'

'Barua? Assamese? Why is he here then?'

'Studies at the Engineering College.'

'Bengalis aren't evil when it comes to education? Hmmph! It's all politics.'

'Yes, the common people are just puppets in the hands of politicians.'

'Now tell me what you want to say. I've taken the address down. I'll make it an urgent telegram, or it won't reach them. There's mayhem in Assam. Even with an urgent telegram there's no guarantee. Going from Calcutta, after all.'

'Yes, please make it urgent. Of course. Needless to say.'

'What's the boy's name again?'

'Bachchu.'

'Then say, Bachchu seriously ill stop hospitalized stop come immediately stop. What name below?'

'Make it Bapi. My brother-in-law has been on holiday to their house in Gauhati. They know who he is.'

'Now listen once more, listen carefully. Urgent telegram. Satyen Barua, Professors Quarter No. five, Gauhati University, Gauhati Bachchu seriously ill stop hospitalized stop come immediately stop Bapi. Right?'

'Excellent. But I can't give you the money right now, what about that?'

'Later. It isn't very expensive. Ten rupees at most. Less, probably. Now we have to add the sender's name and address. What should I write? Sender's name and address.'

'But the money . . .'

'Later, no need to worry. Give me the name and address first. You can send the money through your brother-in-law later. Now tell me what I should put down as the name and address. Of course, the phone number will work too. Bapi, care of . . . what?'

'Care of N. K. Dutta, three five four six zero three.'

'N . . . K . . . Dut-ta . . . three . . . five . . . four . . . six . . . zero . . . three . . .'

'Now tell me yours.'

'Yes. Got paper and pencil?'

'Yes.'

'All right. Write down – G. P. Chandar, Gyan Prakash Chandar, three five four two eight one.'

'That's it? G. P. Chandar, three . . . five . . . yes, got it. Now the address, please.'

'Address? My workplace is my address. I spend the daytime in a boarding house, the office at night. You won't get it. No need to, either. Take it down, Hotel Srinibash . . .'

'Hotel Srinibash . . .'

'It's on Harrison Road, opposite Sealdah Station, a three-storey building. They've just put in pink tiles, inside and outside. Your brother-in-law will find it easily. Now it's time you went to bed, you've been awake with anxiety all this while. I will have your telegram sent at once.'

'I will definitely send the money through Bapi tomorrow . . . the hospital's nearby . . .'

'All in good time. Let the boy get better by god's grace. He's far away from home . . .'

'I don't know what to tell you . . . running into someone like you . . . in this day and age . . .'

G. P. Chandar laughs softly in his deep voice. For the first time.

'This is nothing, one human being will always do this for another.'

'What do you mean it's nothing? Who helps this way? No one. They don't even shift in their seats to make room for someone else.'

'They do, they do. I've spent so many years in this hotel my hair's turned white. I've seen any number of people. I've seen the good as much as the bad. People always do this for one another. Aren't you doing it? For your brother-in-law's friend? Now let it be, please get some sleep.'

'Do you think I'll be able to sleep? What if there's some news from the hospital?'

'You can wake up if there is. If there's any news it will come here, I'll answer the call. Go to bed.'

'Thank you, Mr Chandar . . . I don't know how to . . .'

'No need to, Madam Bulti, just don't forget three five four two eight one, don't hesitate to ring if you need anything. You're like my daughter, just ring me. Once the lines are unsnarled this direct service won't exist any more.'

Bapi is looking incredibly worked up when he returns home in the morning. His face is red with excitement.

'How's Bachchu?'

'Much better. His blood pressure has stabilized. But something strange happened, this is what you probably call a miracle, around six or six-thirty this morning an ageing man in a dhoti and shirt, white-haired. He was looking for Bachchu Barua's friends, asked for Bapi and Khokon by name. Then he handed me a slip ... look, I've got goose pimples ... he gave me the slip and said, a telegram has been sent to Barua, here's the receipt. Give it to your sister-in-law. We were ... stunned. Spellbound. He disappeared before we could recover from our dazed state. Vanished into thin air. We never saw him after that. Who was he? How did he know about Bachchu? About us? About you? Who told him? Who sent the telegram? Just think about it ... What are you laughing at? Just look at this slip of paper, the telegram's actually been sent off. But who was he? Nobody knows him ... I really have goose pimples, see.'

Bapi clenches his fist and holds his muscular arm out with the sleeve rolled up. The hair on his arm is indeed standing on end. I stop laughing.

There's a phone call. It's Khokon. So the line is unsnarled. Khokon is all worked up too.

'Have you heard? Bapi must have told you everything. What a strange experience! Even thinking of it gives me the chills, there really are more things on heaven and earth. When I told my grandfather he said there's nothing more to worry about, your friend will survive. I'm not taking it so far, but it really is miraculous. This is what they call a twentieth-century miracle, don't you think? Have you seen the receipt? It's real. Can you believe it? That something like this can happen ...' Khokon's voice chokes in excitement.

Thank goodness Rinku's left for college already. I must warn her as soon as she comes back. The boys must never find out about G. P. Chandar.

They're so very deprived, they never get a whiff of this thing called faith. The poor things don't get the opportunity. Now that they've had a taste, let it stay with them forever. It's true, Mr G. P. Chandar is indeed a miracle.

I put the slip away carefully. Looks like I'll have to go myself to Hotel Srinibash with the pink tiles, opposite Sealdah Station, to return the money.

RAMANATH RAY

A Prayer to a Millionaire

My boss is a millionaire. He sent for me one day. My heart shrank in fear. I showed up, trembling. He was smoking his pipe. He lowered it when he saw me. 'I'm pleased with your work,' he said.

I wanted to jump for joy. But since this was no place to jump, I restrained myself. I had to hear the millionaire out.

'Ask for a boon,' he said.

I was startled. I couldn't believe my ears. My heart began to pound. 'A boon,' I said.

'Yes.'

'Any boon?'

'Yes.'

'Suppose I ask to be made the managing director?'

'You will be.'

'Suppose I want to be the prime minister?'

'You will be.'

'In that case . . . I . . . need to think a little.'

'Very well. I'm giving you a day. Will you be able to tell me by tomorrow?'

'Of course,' I said with great enthusiasm. 'I'll tell you tomorrow as soon as I get into the office.'

I left the millionaire's room. I wanted to whistle with joy. I wanted to whirl about in happiness. To dance across the floor. But I looked at everyone around me and remained poker-faced. I was going to be someone important soon. I shouldn't be doing anything that would make them think I was mad. In fact, I would have to behave as normally as everyone else. I would have to pretend nothing had happened. So I returned sedately to my chair. As soon as I sat down I realized everyone knew that the millionaire had sent for me. There had been plenty of speculation in my absence.

'What's going on, why did he send for you suddenly?' asked someone.

'To have cake,' another one answered on my behalf.

'You could have got some for us,' said a third.

I didn't respond to any of them. I tried to immerse myself in work.

But I couldn't concentrate. I had just the one thought in my head. What boon should I ask for tomorrow? What boon? I would ask to be made whatever I wanted to be. But what did I want to be? My first wish was to be the managing director of this company. And then it occurred to me, if I could be anything at all, why limit myself to managing director? I would be the prime minister of India. And once I was the prime minister ...'

Our working hours were till five. It was only three now. I would have to sit here for two hours more. Given my state of mind, this was extremely annoying. I turned restless. I wanted to leave. I wondered what to do. I decided to meet the head clerk. And tell him I had a stomach ache. That I couldn't work any more today. He was bound to let me go once he had heard this.

I rose from my chair and went to the head clerk's cabin. His personal bearer was seated outside on a stool. 'Is the head clerk in?' I asked.

'No,' said the bearer.

'Where has he gone?'

'He didn't tell me.'

'When will he be back?'

'He didn't tell me that either.'

I was irked with the head clerk. 'You are a strange man,' I said to him in my head. 'Why can't you tell everyone where you're going and when you will be back. Just you wait, I'll show you when I'm prime minister.'

I didn't feel like returning to my desk. So I wandered about a bit and went back to check whether the head clerk had returned. He had not. I was angrier with him now. 'Just you wait till I become the prime minister,' I said in my head. 'My first task will be to suspend you. Let's see who can save you then.'

I wandered around a little more and went back to check. The head clerk was not back yet. This time I was positively annoyed. 'The man is never there when you need him. And yet it's a heinous crime not to be there when he needs you. The first thing I'll do as prime minister is to sack him.'

I didn't want to be in the office a moment longer. I would leave, I decided. Damn the consequences! What consequences could there be anyway? I was about to become the prime minister. It did not behove me to worry about what head clerks might think of me.

I left the office at four-thirty. At once I felt the urge to tell someone about what had happened. Tell whom? I recalled a couple of friends. I recalled a couple of girlfriends. I recalled a couple of relatives. I had the urge to collect all of them around me and say, 'Do you know I'm about to become the prime minister?' But the very next moment it occurred to me that none of them might believe me. That they would consider it a joke and burst into laughter. Or that I had gone mad. What to do then? Whom should I tell? Pondering over this, I decided it would be best to go home right away. And tell them everything. They would also consider me mad. Let them. There was no harm in being considered mad by one's family.

It was almost evening by the time I got back home. My mother was in her room, chatting with the next-door neighbour. My sister was in her room, listening to the radio. I considered putting my arms round my mother and telling her, 'Ma, I'm going to be the prime minister soon. None of you will have any worries after this.' But I couldn't say it, because of the neighbour's presence. 'I'm hungry, ma,' I said instead, 'give me something to eat.'

'Want some muri?' she asked.

'All right,' I said. You couldn't get anything simpler than muri.

'Get him some muri,' my mother told my sister.

Abandoning the radio, my sister got me some muri. She looked annoyed. 'You're a pain,' she told me.

'Why do you say that?'

'Can't you eat at a restaurant?'

'I will from now on.'

'I've been hearing that forever.'

'You'll never hear it again.'

'I'll be relieved not to.'

She went back to her radio.

I finished my muri and relaxed in my room with the newspaper. But

I couldn't concentrate on it. I was dying to tell everyone what had happened.

My elder brother returned home at seven. He has an important job. He marched into his room. My sister's radio fell silent at once. The neighbour left.

Both my mother and sister went into my brother's room.

'Something nice for a snack?' asked ma.

'All right,' said my brother.

'Something delicious to go with it?' asked my sister.

'Anything you like,' my brother said.

Both of them went into the kitchen.

My sister-in-law arrived a little later. She had a paper box in her hand. She worked in a school.

Handing the box to my sister, she said, 'I looked everywhere to get this sari for you. See if you like it.'

Taking the sari out of the box, my sister said, 'It's beautiful.'

'You'll look lovely in it,' said my mother. 'Your sister-in-law has such good taste.'

Then my sister showed her new sari to my brother. She didn't show it to me. Unable to contain myself, I said, 'How come you didn't show it to me?'

'Do you understand anything about saris?' my sister said.

'You could still have shown it to me,' I told her.

'Couldn't care less,' she said, and went back to the kitchen.

'Couldn't care less!' I said. 'Do you know that ...'

But I couldn't say it. I knew that my mother would wish she had given me something nice for a snack instead of muri. 'I was wrong not to show him the sari,' my sister would reflect. My sister-in-law would tell herself she should have got me a gift too. 'We hardly talk to him,' my brother would muse. 'This isn't right.' Everyone would change in a moment. There would be a stampede in an effort to please me. My mother would say, 'The boy's lost a lot of weight, I must pay more attention to his food.' My sister would offer me a cup of tea frequently. My sister-in-law would say there wasn't another human as nice as me. 'The boy has talent,' my brother would say.

The nice snacks were prepared. My sister entered my brother's room with two full plates of snacks. 'Want some?' she asked me when she came out.

'No, I had a muri a little while ago,' I said.

'Have some anyway,' my mother said.

'No.'

My brother and sister-in-law settled down to watch TV after they had eaten. The TV was in my brother's room. My mother went in there to watch TV. So did my sister. So did I. I decided to tell everyone what had happened while we were watching TV.

Everyone's eyes were on the TV. My mother asked my brother as she watched TV, 'Did you meet him?'

'I did,' said my brother, his eyes on the TV.

'What did he say?'

'The groom's father wants a car.'

'What!'

'Yes.'

There was no conversation after this. My mother was silent. My brother was silent. A little later my mother asked my sister-in-law, 'Weren't you talking of someone?'

'Yes.'

'Did you find out more?'

'I did. Won't work.'

'Why not?'

'They don't have many demands, except one. A three-roomed flat for their son-in-law.'

'How strange!'

My brother looked at my sister-in-law and said, 'We're the ones who've been cheated. No car, no flat, not even gold jewellery.'

'What you and your family have got is much more valuable,' my sister-in-law said.

'How do you mean?'

'A working wife. You and your family are much more canny than these people.'

At once the atmosphere in the room became tense. Because the statement was directed at our late father. He was the one who had arranged this marriage.

Perhaps to lighten the mood, my mother returned to her original theme. 'You know so many people,' she told me, 'can you ask them?'

'No need to discuss this,' said my sister.

'Go away if you don't like it,' said my mother angrily.

But my sister didn't go away. She stayed there.

'I'll ask,' I said, 'but it won't be necessary.'

My mother was surprised. 'Why not?'

Should I tell them now? No, not now. The atmosphere was still tense. Let it ease up. No one had liked what my sister-in-law had said. Naturally. But it was not untrue.

'Why not?' my mother asked again.

'I'll tell you later.'

My mother was silent. I was silent. Everyone was silent. All eyes were on the TV.

My mother rose to her feet at a quarter to ten. 'Time to eat,' she said for everyone's benefit.

My brother switched the TV off. We sat down round the dining table. We began eating. After a few minutes I said, 'Something happened today.'

Everyone looked at me. But only mother said, 'What?'

'My millionaire boss sent for me today,' I said.

'Why?' asked my brother.

'Why do you suppose?' my sister said. 'Does no work in the office. Gave him an earful.'

'Didn't give him an earful,' said my sister-in-law. 'His expression would have been different.'

'Stop, all of you,' my mother said. 'Let him tell us.'

'The millionaire said, I'm pleased with your work,' I said. 'Ask for a boon. I couldn't ask him on the spot. I'll ask tomorrow.'

'What will you ask for?' my sister said.

'I've decided to tell him I want to be the prime minister.'

Everyone laughed.

'Are you drinking these days?' my brother said.

'Time to get him married,' my sister-in-law said.

'He's always been a daydreamer,' my sister said.

'He's had a screw loose since childhood,' my mother said.

I didn't protest at any of this. I endured all they said in silence. For

I hadn't become the prime minister yet. I would answer them when I did. 'Remember all the taunts?' I would say. 'And now?' But until I became the prime minister I would have to bottle up my rage. There was no choice. But there was something I couldn't understand. What was so unbelievable about this? A millionaire could always be pleased with an employee. And if they were pleased they could always offer a boon. And the person being offered the boon could always ask to be made the prime minister. Therefore there was no obstacle to my becoming the prime minister.

I didn't look at anyone. I kept my head lowered and finished eating. Then I washed my hands and rinsed my mouth.

'Don't forget us when you become the prime minister,' said my sister. 'Make me your secretary at least.'

'I want to be a governor, mind you,' said my sister-in-law.

'Then I'll be the president,' said my brother.

'I don't want a post,' said my mother, 'just take me on a pilgrimage.'

Looking at all of them, I said, 'All your wishes will be fulfilled. I promise.'

I didn't stay there. I went into my room. Shutting the door, I smoked a cigarette and then went to bed. This was not the time to think of my family. It was more important to think of things to do once I became the prime minister. Far more essential.

I tried to formulate a twenty-two-point plan of action. Its salient features would be as follows:

1. The majority of Indians were poor. Millions would have to be spent on schemes to improve their lot. At the same time, frequent speeches on TV and at public gatherings would be required.

2. Indians were as uneducated as they were poor. To rid the country of such ignorance every house must have a TV set. This would not only spread education but also be a shot in the arm for the TV industry.

3. It was most unfortunate that India had not won even a bronze medal at the 1984 Olympic Games. Therefore training centres for sports would have to be established in every state at a cost of millions. We had to win at least a couple of bronze medals in the next Olympics.

4. The pressure of population was increasing by the day. This population . . .

The door opened. My mother came in. 'Are you asleep?' she said.

'No,' I said from my bed.

'I have to tell you something.'

'What?'

'Is your millionaire boss giving you only a single boon?'

'Yes.'

'Then there's nothing I can tell you.'

'Tell me anyway.'

'If possible, ask for a suitable boy for your sister. She must get married soon.'

'Don't worry about it. Boys will queue up to marry her once I become the prime minister.'

'I don't have these absurd dreams. See if you can do what I asked for.'

She left. My sister came in a little later. 'Are you asleep?'

'No.'

'Was ma here?'

'Yes.'

'What did she tell you?'

'Why should I tell you?'

'Please tell me.'

After a pause, I said, 'She came to tell me not to ask my millionaire boss to make me the prime minister. Instead I should say, O lord, be good enough to find a suitable boy for my sister.'

My sister flew into a rage. 'You're such a . . .'

'Why am I such a . . .'

'You don't have to ask for a boy for me.'

'Then what should I ask for? What boon should I demand?'

'Can you ask for a boon on my behalf?'

'What boon?'

'A good job for me.'

'A job. Tchah!'

'Why tchah?'

'I thought you'd want to be the busiest heroine in Hindi films.'

'You're so crass.'

'What took you so long to find out?'

'Anyway, can you ask for this boon? Or will you selfishly ask for some-thing for yourself?'

'I'll think about it.'

She left. Now it was my brother's or my sister-in-law's turn. Which of them would come first? It turned out to be my sister-in-law. 'Are you asleep?' she asked.

'No.'

'I've come to ask you for something.'

'What?'

'First tell me if you'll do it.'

'First tell me what it is.'

'I'm saying stop this madness of wanting to be the prime minister.'

'Let's say I do. And then?'

'The headmistress at my school is retiring next month. I want the post. Can you ask your millionaire for this boon?'

'I'll try.'

'Trying isn't enough. You must. I'll go now, you can sleep. By the way, don't tell your brother, all right?'

'All right.'

She left. My brother came in a little later. The same question. 'Are you asleep?'

'No. Can't sleep.'

'How will you sleep? Stop this madness.'

'What madness?'

'You don't think it's madness? Is it so very easy to become the prime minister?'

'People seem to find it easy.'

'That's for others. You can never become the prime minister.'

'Let's see what happens.'

'What will you see? Better to ask for something that's possible.'

'Like what?'

'Ask your millionaire boss for a large plot of land for me in Salt Lake.'

'All right, I'll see.'

He left. I was quite tired now. I couldn't work on the twenty-two-point plan of action any more. I tried to sleep. But I couldn't. Thoughts of becoming the prime minister kept swirling in my head. I kept seeing images of my photographs in the newspapers, of my speeches and interviews being published, of travelling across the country and abroad, making one deal after another, signing documents constantly.

My family was making no effort to understand. They did not realize that since my millionaire boss was willing to grant me a boon, I had no reason to ask for such useless things. I wanted to be the prime minister. That was the boon I would ask for. And if I became the prime minister my sister would not only get a suitable boy but also a job, and my sister-in-law would get the headmistress's position. My brother would get his plot of land in Salt Lake. Everything would materialize in an instant. But they couldn't believe that I could actually become the prime minister. Or perhaps they didn't want me to be the prime minister. They wanted me to remain as I was, while their lives improved. Fantastic. I became angry and decided not to do anything for any of them when I became the prime minister.

My mother drew me aside before I left for the office the next morning, saying, 'You haven't forgotten, have you?'

My sister also drew me aside to ask, 'You haven't forgotten, have you?'

My brother drew me aside to ask the same thing. My sister-in-law also drew me aside to ask the same thing.

I didn't want to disappoint any of them. 'I haven't forgotten,' I told each of them. I was about to become the prime minister. There was no point hurting anyone now.

Today I did not take the tram or the bus. It did not behove me. I took a taxi to the office. There I immersed myself in work. I decided to work for an hour and then meet the millionaire to ask for my boon. What would he think if I went to him at once?

But he sent for me a few minutes later. I pranced into his cabin with joy. He was smoking his pipe as usual. When he saw me he said, 'What time did you leave the office yesterday?'

I wasn't prepared for this question. Gulping, I said, 'Four-thirty.'

'What are our office hours?'

'Nine to five.'

'Why did you leave half an hour early?'

'I was wrong to do it.'

'I don't need people like you in this company. You may leave now.'

It was like the sky falling on my head. What was I to do now? Everything was turning topsy-turvy. I stood there like a fool.

'What is it?' The millionaire shouted at me. 'Why are you still standing there?'

Suddenly I remembered the millionaire had wanted to give me a boon. If I didn't ask for it now, then when? Almost in tears, I said, 'You had wanted to give me a boon yesterday.'

'I know. What boon do you want? Do you want to become the managing director of this company?'

'No.'

'The prime minister?'

'No.'

'Well then?'

'That you forgive me.'

'So be it,' the millionaire said with a smile.

AKHTARUZZAMAN ELIAS

The Raincoat

It's been raining since dawn. Ah, the pitter-patter drizzle of the rain! God willing, it will go on for three days, since it's seven for Saturn and three for Mars, and day to day for the rest. That's the general statement. There are specific classifications as well. For example: if it starts at dawn on Tuesday, for three days the clouds will stay. Or: if it rains on Wednesday morn, by afternoon the clouds are gone. Thursday, Friday, none of the days has been left out – but right now, he's forgotten them. Whatever he does remember is enough to keep him curled up under the covers, catching a few more winks. At least there'll be none of that ratatatat for three days – surely the guns and ammo will rest a bit during the rain? Just a few days of worry-free relaxation.

But does that actually happen? One wonders . . . On this very excellent rainy morning, the loud banging on the door tears asunder late autumn's wintry curtain. Ruins everything. Military! Military in his house! Oh god! *Allahumma . . . anta subhanaka inni kuntu minazzhalimin.* Reciting the prayer, Nurul Huda goes towards the door. He's memorized so many prayers over these last few months, the six Kalmas – ready on his lips every time he leaves the house – who knows when or where the military will show up – still, something always goes wrong: the prayer seems correct, but he's forgotten to put on his cap.

As soon as he opens the door – unfastening two latches and the deadbolt, and lifting the wooden bar – the principal's assistant, Ishaq, walks in, accompanied by a blast of wind and rain. Praise Allah! Not military! He wants to grab the man and kiss him! But Ishaq, in his thin voice, says gravely, 'Sir sends his salaams.' Then he sucks the soft breath of his words into the stubble on his hollow cheeks and lets out a command: 'You've been summoned. You must go now.'

'What's happened?'

'There's no time to discuss details – someone set off an explosion next to the college wall last night.'

'Meaning?'

'Some miscreants destroyed the electric transformer. Then, on their way out, they threw a grenade at the principal's house, destroyed the gate.'

What a terrifying situation! The transformer is next to the front wall of the college. Beyond the wall there is a garden, then a tennis lawn. The college building comes after. Past that huge structure are the football and cricket fields. Beyond the field, to the left, is the principal's residence. The military camp lies alongside – the college gym is now the camp. Setting off a bomb at the principal's gate is like attacking the military camp. How did they get so far in, after setting off an explosion at the front wall, he wants to know. 'How?'

How would the messenger know? 'You tell me.'

'Meaning?' How would he know? Did the messenger think he was one of the miscreants? His head drops involuntarily and the words roll out of his mouth like water, 'Ishaq Miah, have a seat. Have some tea. I'll only need five or six minutes.'

'No.' Refusing the hospitality, Ishaq says, 'I need to go to Abdus Sattar Mridha's house. You come quickly. A colonel has already arrived. All professors have been told to come immediately.'

Ishaq walks out, leaving both the college and Nurul in the hands of the military led by the colonel. He gets into a tuk-tuk waiting on the road with its engine rumbling, and roars off towards the home of the geography professor. You could say Ishaq himself is like a military colonel these days. But perhaps the appearance of an actual colonel at the college this morning has demoted him to the rank of lieutenant-colonel, maybe even lower; but it's hard to push him below captain. From the onset of the military uprising, everyone at the college has been wary of him. Since early April he's stopped speaking Bengali. One of his grandfather's brother-in-law's uncles or somebody was the valet of someone in Delhi. On those grounds, he now speaks Urdu day and night. The principal is a short, pudgy man. Having to try and speak to his flunkey in this new language makes his blood boil. 'Ishaq Miah, there is much trouble in the country. Tell the professors and everyone else to be careful.

Tell them to not spread rumours. It is necessary to help the military people now.'

'*Zaroor.*' Ishaq nods, his small head a wet tip fitted on to a matchstick-thin body, and repeats thrice, '*Zaroor! Zaroor! Zaroor!*' As this '*zaroor*' – uttered by Ishaq several days ago – rings in his ears, reinvigorated by the rain, the word itself seems to explode with a boom. Has it started again, in this rain? No, no, that is just thunder. It seems to be getting worse. No, he must start off. God speed.

'Must you go? Getting drenched in this unseasonal rain might trigger your asthma . . .' Will it do for him to listen to these loving words from his wife? Will she share his humiliation at the principal's rebuke? On top of everything, there is a colonel at the college. God knows what's in store for Nurul today! If they make him face the firing squad, can he beg the colonel to order them to shoot him in the head? Won't the principal do at least this much lobbying on his behalf? He's been praying day and night for Pakistan. Always crying to god, yet finding time to swear at his colleagues. Around mid-April, he humbly stated to the senior military officers that, if Pakistan was to be saved, the Shaheed Minars in all the schools and colleges would have to be removed. These unauthorized constructions were comparable to Hindu Shiva Lingas, they were like thorns in the body of Pakistan. In order to heal Pakistan's pure and clean body, these thorns had to be pulled out. Well, the military listened to Dr Afaz Ahmed's advice. Whichever town or village they went to, the first thing they aimed their cannon at were the Shaheed Minars. Not a single undamaged Shaheed Minar exists in any college in the country. The principal gave them such important advice, won't they entertain his minor request when shooting an insignificant lecturer – to avoid all the other silly areas of the body and aim for the head? And he's provided such wonderful service to the principal, won't he do this little bit for his colleague . . . er . . . subordinate?

'Come back quickly,' he hears his wife say from the kitchen as he is pulling on his trousers. 'There were sounds of gunfire near Mirpur Bridge before it started raining. Who knows what may happen?'

What's the point of saying these things? The radio and television are regularly stating: situation normal! The enemy is completely under control. All miscreants have been eliminated. The president is determined to bring democracy back to the nation. His speeches can be heard every few days: 'Our ultimate objective remains unchanged, which is to hand over power to the elected representatives of the people. Everything is getting back to normal.' The governor is Bengali – that is, East Pakistani. The ministers are East Pakistani. Everything is normal. Why does his wife still say these unnecessary things? Uff! It's becoming impossible to deal with Asma! Two nights ago, tossing and turning in bed, she said, 'I can't fall asleep unless I hear some gunshots at night.' God knows what trouble she will bring down on their house.

'The umbrella isn't enough for this rain, dear.' He hears another round of affectionate chatter from his wife. 'You might as well take Mintu's raincoat.'

Lord! Mintu again! He has to be extra vigilant because of that brother of hers. Mintu left home – yes, their two-room flat in Moghbazar – in June, on the 23rd. They shifted to a new place on 1 July. Who knows, what if someone there suspected something? Three days after Mintu left, the round-faced lady from the neighbouring flat asked his wife, 'Bhabi, we don't see your brother around any more.' He started looking for a new place as soon as he learnt of this. This was the fourth time they had changed houses since the military came. One day, after they shifted to their current house, the gentleman downstairs said, 'I decided my brother shouldn't stay in Dhaka any longer. So much trouble everywhere, I sent him home.' His heart was palpitating when he heard this – what if the man asked about his own brother-in-law? He had come here to be safe. It was a long way from the college, far from their friends and relatives. Almost outside the city. A completely new area, with a view of swamps and rice paddies through the eastern window. But what a disaster it has turned out to be! Hooligans with guns come to this area by boat! People around here see nothing but boats – boats stacked with weapons. If his wife keeps bringing up Mintu on top of all this, the weapons will literally enter their home. He and his wife both know very well where Mintu has gone. But look at what his wife is telling the children, just to establish her pride in her brother. Even they say, 'Uncle Mintu has gone to kill the Khan Sena.' Can anyone tell which revelation will bring trouble, and of what kind? If Asma is so brave, why hasn't she joined her brother? He can't say it, but the words quiver on his tongue all the same: 'Forget about Mintu,

Asma. Forget him. We have no one. No one. Mr Kissinger has said, this is Pakistan's internal affair. They are massacring people, putting houses, markets, entire villages to the torch – it is no one's headache. It's all internal affairs.' No, it's not good even to allow such thoughts into your head. The owner of a welding workshop lives in the flat below. His father-in-law seems to be some sort of a boss-type pro-Pakistani traitor. Every two or three days he sends refrigerators, tape recorders, expensive sofa sets, fans, beds and other furniture to his daughter's house. Once he even sent an idol of a Hindu deity – it might actually have been made of gold, who knows? Truck after truck, goods come and then goods leave. Where does the traitor get all these? If the man figures out that the brother-in-law of the professor living upstairs is a miscreant who left this very person's house with an oath to kill the military, then the guns will be firing inside this house, in this room. Those gunshots will lull Asma to sleep forever. It's important to be alert when talking around here.

'Let's see if it fits you,' Asma says, putting the raincoat on him. 'Mintu is so tall. Will it fit you?' There she goes again, comparing Mintu's height to his. Is it right to go overboard like this about her brother?

'Excellent, it goes all the way down to your ankles. Even your legs will stay dry.' Asma is not finished. She brings the cap that came with the raincoat and puts it on his head. That Mintu! What great feat has this brother-in-law of his achieved this time? No, this time his accomplishment is different. 'He left the raincoat hanging inside the closet, and the cap on top of the wardrobe. I saw it lying there when I went to get the Quran Sharif.'

Mintu didn't leave anything else behind, did he? He checks the top of the wardrobe himself. The military found three Chinese rifles under the bed in a house in Moghbazar. Strangely, the resident of the house, an innocent doctor, knew nothing about them. It's good to check everywhere in the house on a daily basis.

'Abba's become Uncle Mintu. Abba's become Uncle Mintu!' He is alarmed to hear his daughter chanting in a voice still heavy with sleep. Is Mintu here with weapons? That means the military are following right behind. That means . . . no, the door is still locked and barred. His two-and-a-half-year-old daughter claps, still in bed, 'Abba is Uncle Mintu! Abba is Uncle Mintu!'

Does he look like Mintu? Will the military then mistake him for Mintu? In between all of this, his five-year-old son examines him solemnly and declares, 'Abba does look like Uncle Mintu. That means Abba's a freedom fighter, right?'

This is worrying. Standing in front of the dressing table, gazing at his own reflection, he is surprised by his new look. The raincoat is not quite khaki, but not olive either. The earthy tone seems a little burnt, but hasn't lost its lustre. He looks a bit like someone from the military. It's not safe to look like he's from the military. If the military deem the wearing of the raincoat impersonation of the military they'll arrest him and send him straight to the cantonment. No! He's getting frightened for no reason. Why would it be a crime to wear a raincoat in the rain? Do the military not have common sense? The principal, Dr Afaz Ahmed, has got it right: 'Listen, when the military arrest someone it's not for no reason. Whoever they catch is involved in subversive activities.' But he stays a hundred feet away from such things. His brother-in-law crossed the border and then came back into the country and killed a bunch of soldiers; how is he responsible? The military set fire to markets and slums in Dhaka city every day, kill people regularly, abduct women – has he ever said anything about it?

The military camp is set up beside the principal's residence, next to the college wall. All classes have been cancelled. Students don't come. Teachers still have to clock in, but many went into hiding long ago. He goes to work punctually every day. His colleagues are always whispering in the staffroom – about bridges that were blown up, about the seven corpses of soldiers shot by the young men, about which college students have gone to the battlefront – he never participates in any of those discussions. He leaves whenever such conversations begin, and goes to the principal's office. There he listens to Dr Afaz Ahmed make predictions in his raspy voice about the immediate and inevitable fall of India and the miscreants. No one goes near his office these days. The principal has recently started sweet-talking the Urdu professor, Akbar Sajid. But Sajid doesn't pay much attention to the principal. Instead he asks sometimes, '*Apka tabiyat bhalo haye?*', taunting the principal's poor Urdu with this contrived question in the language. Either because Dr Afaz Ahmed is anxious about safeguarding the undividedness of Pakistan, or because he cannot put together

enough correct Urdu words to come up with a response, he remains quiet.
Then, thinking Sajid might get upset if he doesn't answer, he laughs and
says, '*Ji haan*. At your mercy.' Sajid laughs, 'My mercy? Who am I to show
mercy? Say, at the General Sahib's mercy.' Running out of Urdu responses
to take the conversation any further, the principal goes quiet at this point.
The man is in two minds about the Urdu professor. It's getting harder
every day to differentiate between his jokes and his compliments. In fact,
one day, listening to the principal (who is overawed by the skills of the
military) analyse the war, Sajid said, 'Sir, you should do a PhD on military
science. A doctor in Mohammadpur has recently started practising hom-
eopathy, but he hasn't given up allopathy either. So the people of the area
are calling him double doctor. You should become a double doctor.' Then
he started laughing, and Dr Afaz Ahmed, with his single doctorate, had
no choice but to 'heh heh' along. The Urdu professor's colleagues were in
trouble. In these difficult times, they couldn't figure out which joke it was
safe to laugh at.

His feet have been tingling ever since he put on the raincoat Mintu
had thrown away (or left behind); he can't stand still a moment longer.
The principal had sent for him quite some time earlier!

There aren't any rickshaws on the road. He can't worry about that now.
He won't have any trouble walking to the bus stop, since he's wearing the
raincoat. The rain falls ceaselessly on the coat. But how wonderful it is –
not a single drop touches his body. He sticks his tongue out to catch stray
drops of water dripping from the rim of his cap. Not exactly devoid of any
taste. Has the spirit of the cap entered the water? Does he look like one
of the military? Punjab Artillery, or Baluch Regiment, or the commando
force, or paramilitary or military police – each of their clans has a different
name, a different appearance. Does he, in his raincoat, look like a member
of some new division? He walks briskly. There's a chill in the rains of late
autumn. But how wonderfully warm it is within the raincoat! Good thing
Mintu left it behind. Who knows when the rascal might come back for
it. Ah! Who knows where or next to which river the young man is lying
in ambush during this torrential downpour? Maybe a Pakistani Army pla-
toon has set a village ablaze somewhere, killed a couple of hundred people,
tossed away the corpses, and is carrying off the living young women in
their jeeps – no doubt Mintu's gun is aimed at these military men. Surely

he'll be able to kill them all and rescue the women. The sight of the military lorry on the main road makes him snap back to reality. He pours allegiance into his gaze and stares at the lorry in order to conceal all his thoughts about Mintu. No, man! It's better not to make eye contact with them. The lorry goes off towards the north, so he's forced to look south. But is it so easy to erase the sound of the lorry on the wet street? Asma heard gunfire coming from the direction of Mirpur Bridge last night. Was the lorry heading there? Who knows what will happen, or where. And Asma hears gunfire every night anyway. It's all speculation. The principal had once said, 'Listening to rumours and spreading them are equally bad. You know the saying – those who commit injustice and those who tolerate it . . .' Either because it was written by a Hindu or because he had forgotten the rest, the principal stopped at that point. And then continued in Urdu, 'Sajid sahib, all rumour is rumour, without sense.' Sajid responded immediately in rhyme, 'Whatever was rumour has today become violence.' Choking in reverence, the principal rattled on, 'Is that Iqbal? Wait, let me write it down.' Akbar Sajid stopped him, 'The lord forgive me, why should it be Iqbal? The words you used are in Bengali, in Urdu, it would be . . .' The principal cut him short. 'Yes, that's better. You recite the lines, I will write them down.' In order to maintain the rhythm, Sajid did not use the Urdu synonym for rumour. He recited the next line, *'Army ke armaan puray ho chukay haye.'*

'Meaning?'

'Meaning, the army's wishes are fulfilled.' Sajid crafted more lines, reciting the entire poem and gesturing with his hands and feet:

> Whatever was rumour has today become violence
> The army's wishes are fulfilled
> One Allah, one Rasul, one Pakistan as well
> Those who don't believe in this are traitors
> Destroy those traitors wherever they may be found
> The Pakistani Army will never be held back.

Entering the staffroom, Sajid said, 'The principal will be punished if he recites this to a major or colonel. Are you making fun of us, the military will say.' His colleagues were quiet. No one wanted to talk about these things in front of Sajid nowadays. Even his friend, the history professor, Ali Kabir, avoided him. As for the principal, he repeatedly recited the Urdu poem, written down in Bengali script, in his office in the presence of his personal assistant, Ishaq. Within a few days he started thinking of it as his own composition. His eyes closed in reverence and joy as he recited the lines.

The waves of rain beat against the raincoat to the rhythm of the poem, and suddenly it occurs to him that perhaps the principal is reciting it to the colonel right now. What if the colonel wants to know the Urdu word for 'rumour' and loses his temper when he gets no answer? The Urdu professor, Akbar Sajid, makes a lot of jokes about the army's proficiency. The geography professor, Abdus Sattar Mridha, once said in a whisper, 'I'm sure this man is using his mother tongue as a shield in order to work for the miscreants.' Then, one day, the English professor, Khandker, cautioned everyone, 'None of you must agree with what he says. He actually says those things to find out where you stand. He's definitely an agent for the military.' But for a few days now Akbar Sajid has been kind of quiet. Everyone starts to fidget when he's in the staffroom, and he doesn't like going into the principal's office any more either.

He himself has been staying away from Sajid. What's the point? But, standing in the rain, dry on account of the raincoat, his heart yearns to discuss some things with Akbar Sajid in secret. What can this mean?

No, such wishes are folly. He must stay as far away as possible from thoughts of making jokes about the army, in Bangla or Urdu. He has to look northwards for the bus once he reaches the bus stop. The military lorry is nowhere to be seen, but there is no sign of his bus either. He is the only living creature at the bus stop. The keeper of the small cigarette kiosk on the side of the road has raised his shutters and is looking northwards as well. Has there been some trouble up there? The shopkeeper is a bit of a chatterbox. Seeing him at the bus stop, he begins muttering, 'Haven't you heard what happened yesterday? They came in two boatloads by way of the Mirpur swamp. Blew up a jeep, at least five Khan Sena killed. BBC said more than half the area in Rangpur-Dinajpur has been freed. Did you listen to *Chorompotro* yesterday?' He doesn't want to linger near the shopkeeper. What if he too is arrested for listening to these rumours? Whatever was rumour has today become violence. The principal says rumours are the bane of Bengalis. They hold a very strong attraction; they are irresistible. But right here, right now, perhaps on account of the cover of rain or maybe from the relief of being protected by the raincoat, he moves closer to the shopkeeper. Hoping for some gossip, he asks, 'How long has the bus been due?'

'Forget the bus! Where will the bus come from?' The shopkeeper hurriedly lowers the shutters and disappears inside the kiosk. He wonders whether there's been an attack on the bus depot. Did the sound of gunfire Asma heard come from the bus depot? Did the military lorry go that way? There is a slum behind the depot, did the military set it on fire? It wasn't too far away, he could always go there and find out. The rain was also abating. Should he go? He doesn't get a chance – spreading a reddish glow in the drizzle, the red bus arrives.

The bus is fairly empty. No, not the falsely advertised 'empty bus' that conductors are always yelling about. More than half the seats are actually vacant. The water from his raincoat drips on the wet floor when he gets in.

He expects to hear insulting words because of this, at least a few jibes. But no one says anything.

So many empty seats on the bus! Spoilt for choice – he cannot exactly remember the phrase, but there's a faint smile on his lips. Is the reason for the silent but definite smile the fact that even though the water from his raincoat is flooding the bus, no one is making a sound? Is everyone intimidated by his outfit?

With the roads empty, the bus speeds along. But he can't decide on a seat. Swaying, he looks towards one seat, doesn't like it, and goes towards another. Suddenly two passengers from the back jump up, call out, 'Stop, stop,' and try to leap out of the moving bus at great risk. He looks at them and realizes they are fleeing because of him. Those two men must be criminals. One is a thief and the other a pickpocket. Or maybe they are both thieves, or both pickpockets. The one who seems to be the leader of the two looks back at him as they jump off the bus. His eyes are full of fear, nothing but fear.

As he plops down on to his chosen seat, the foam in the cushion hisses, making three passengers sitting in front turn round to look. Hmmph! He identifies these three as thieves or pickpockets as well. Might even be robbers. Or perhaps when the military set a slum on fire and leave, these three rush there to loot the place. Or maybe if the military do the looting themselves, they go over to pick up the leftovers. All three get to their feet well before the next bus stop and get off in a hurry as soon as the bus comes to a halt. Not one of the three criminals looks back at him, which means they are so frightened of him that they're going out of their way to avoid eye contact.

Excellent! Mintu's raincoat is coming to good use. All the thieves and pickpockets are fleeing from him. The decent folks can stay. He'll be in respectable company all the way to the college.

At the Asad Gate bus stop, a number of people are waiting in the drizzle. Those with their own umbrellas are standing under them. To protect themselves from the rain, many of those without umbrellas are twisting their bodies so as to keep at least some part of their heads under someone else's umbrella. When the bus stops, he notices that nine passengers get on, one after the other. He scrutinizes all of them thoroughly. On seeing him, three of the nine say, 'Hold it', one says, 'Stop,' and all four get off of the bus hastily. It seems the last one is just a petty thief, most likely a small-time criminal. And the first three follow the military everywhere. If they see a pretty girl they inform the military, or they take guns from the military and go around the neighbourhoods shouting, 'Long live Pakistan, long live Pakistan *zindabad*', abducting the pretty girls and delivering them to the military camps. Misguided, all of them, misguided pro-Pakistan traitors.

It's nice to be travelling on the criminal-free bus again. Droplets of rain fly past in the cool breeze outside the window. He feels extra-good on seeing a transparent layer of water on the trees, the people, the shops and houses. But his enjoyment is ripped away when the bus brakes suddenly. He is forced to look to his left, and notices the roof of the mosque under construction. A cool gust of wind from the door hits his face and enters his chest through his nose, where it makes an impact: on the morning after the night of the crackdown, the muezzin was shot down by the military from the roof of this mosque. The blast of cool air warms up so much inside the raincoat that it feels like a fire is burning within. They used to live on the third floor of the house opposite the mosque at the time. All night long the roar of the tanks, the barking of the machine guns, and the moaning of people had not let any of them sleep. He lay under the bed with his children and their mother. In the morning, when the military took a break from killing people, the children fell asleep and he went to their closed window, lifted the curtain an inch and looked down at the street. Across the road, the muezzin was standing on the roof about to chant the azan. He says his prayers regularly only on Fridays, but that morning he really wanted to hear the azan. He didn't move from the window, because he wanted to hear the muezzin call out the entire invitation to pray. The electricity was out in the entire area, and the loudspeaker of the mosque was not working. '*Allahu Akbar,*' cried out the muezzin in his booming voice, with as much volume as he could muster. He didn't get a chance to proclaim Allah's greatness a second time; he fell to the street before that, making a completely different sound. It wasn't raining that morning. Are the military planning to re-enact the same scene on this rainy morning? It isn't time for prayers right now, so what will they do about the azan? They must have issued a new decree which says any time of day can be considered suitable for the namaaz.

The military are stopping all manner of vehicles now, making the passengers get off and stand in a line on the edge of the road. Another group has its guns aimed at this row of people. A different group is searching through their clothes and the concealed places on their bodies. Those among them singled out by the military are being pushed towards a lorry waiting at the back. A tall, very fair military man gets on the bus.

There is no sound inside the bus now. The thumping within the passengers' chests gets louder in the silence, the sound thumps inside his head. The sounds rub against one other beneath the rimmed cap to light a fire whose flames emerge from his eyes. But the throbbing inside his head and chest is back under control as he shifts in his seat and, ignoring everything, looks directly at the military man's face. The man's eyes narrow and the pupils of his narrowed eyes pierce his face like darts. He, too, calms his dull but fiery eyes and casts them lightly over the military man's sharp nose, needle-like eyes and reddish skin around and under the eyes, nose and moustache. It works. The military man's sharp gaze moves away from his face and falls to his raincoat. He seems to be counting the drops of water on the garment. Do the drops seem a little reddish from the heat within? They are here to kill people in this land of water, so why do these water drops appear to have stunned the military man? Does he see signs of blood in them? The man abruptly finishes counting the drops and says, 'Move on.' The ignition is switched on, the bus leaps a couple of yards forward and, boosted by the sighs of relief from the passengers, speeds past the gates of Dhaka College. When it reaches New Market he gets to his feet and orders, 'Stop, I have to get off.' As the bus slows a little, he lets the water gathered by his raincoat drip. Stepping off the now criminal-free bus, he looks at his fellow passengers. His lips curve, revealing his front teeth. He thinks those who have seen this gesture will have correctly identified it as a smile.

Inside the principal's office, an imperious military officer is sitting in the principal's throne-like chair. It can be presumed from his authoritative face that he is a colonel or major or brigadier or major-general. The principal's face goes from black to purple on spotting him. Dr Afaz Ahmed, MSc, PhD, points at him and says, 'This is Professor Nurul Huda.'

Then Dr Afaz Ahmed, MSc, PhD, cannot help but correct his own mistake: 'Sorry, he is not a professor. A lecturer in chemistry.'

'Shut up.'

The principal stops.

Before putting him and Abdus Sattar Mridha in the military jeep, the imperious colonel or brigadier tells the principal sternly that it is a great crime to make up poems to poke fun at the military. He's being let off this time, but he will be kept under close watch. The principal doesn't benefit from using the Urdu professor, Akbar Sajid, as an excuse. Nurul becomes worried. If Sajid sahib doesn't flee, then only god and the military know what lies in store for him.

They are both blindfolded, and the jeep twists and turns. They are tossed into a very high-ceilinged room. When his blindfold is removed, he does not see Abdus Sattar Mridha. The place is unfamiliar. He has no idea how long he stays sitting. Someone from the military comes and takes a chair in front of him, asking him a lot of questions in English. He responds. When the man leaves, he is taken to another room where yet another man comes and questions him. He responds. The questions are fairly similar and his responses don't change. For example, several metal cabinets were bought recently at their college. Who transported them?

He answers, 'Right. Three for the office, two each for the Botany,

History and Geography departments and one for English, a total of ten cabinets were brought into the college.'

There is no need for him to talk so much. The cabinets were brought in on wheelbarrows. Surely he knows the people who man the wheelbarrows quite well.

How will he know them? Nurul Huda says. They are labourers, he is a lecturer.

Then why had he talked to them so much?

He had been checking the cabinets on the principal's orders – the thickness of the steel, the number and shape of doors, the quality of locks and paint, etc. His responsibility was to . . .

The military man says in a calm voice, as if relaying information, that miscreants had entered the college disguised as labourers. Who knows this better than him? They were caught today and gave Nurul Huda's name. He has regular contact with them, he is an active member of their gang.

'My name? Did they really? They gave my name?' The military man is not annoyed by Nurul Huda's sudden shouts; instead they encourage him. He repeats, 'The labourers were miscreants in disguise. They named Nurul Huda among all the teachers.'

Nurul Huda stares in disbelief. Do they know him? One of the labourers had been standing close to him when setting up the cabinet in the Chemistry department. That was in the middle of the rainy season, and it had rained a lot in Dhaka this time. He had said something about the endless rain, at which the labourer had muttered, 'The rainy season is the most fitting.' He had said it twice. What did that mean? Someone in the staffroom had whispered earlier once or twice, 'The bastards don't know the rains of Bengal. Russia had General Winter, we have General Monsoon.' Was this what the disguised young man had meant? Was that how much they trusted him? Nurul Huda looks around, encouraged. His silence convinces the military man further.

After some time – how much time, he does not know – the military man asks him the same question and, getting no response, punches him hard in the face twice. The first punch causes him to list sideways, the second sends him to the floor. Picking him up, the military man says surely he knows quite well where their hideout is located.

Yes, he responds.

They assure him that he will be released with full courtesy as soon as he tells them the address, and feed him bread and milk. The military men leave, giving him time to think it over. Sometime later – how much time, he does not know – the military men return and say once more, surely he knows the miscreants' address. Again he responds, yes. But getting no reply to their next question, they take him into another room. His short body is suspended from a metal ring on the ceiling. The whip cracks again and again on his buttocks. But because the strokes are continuous, after a while they seem a mere nuisance to Nurul Huda. Like the rain falling on Mintu's raincoat. They have removed his raincoat, who knows where they have put it. But its warmth remains on his body. The whip lashes his raincoat-like skin like rain, and he repeats endlessly that he knows the miscreants' address. Not just the address of his brother-in-law – knowing which is no great achievement – but also the hideout of the disguised labourers. They know him too, and repose great trust in him. Nurul Huda's suspended body trembles so violently from the allegation of his entente with them and the excitement of maintaining this alliance that he cannot bring himself to focus on the strokes of the whip.

(Translated by Pushpita Alam)

SELINA HOSSAIN

The Blue Lotus of Death

Hamid's wife had been in hospital for two days.

She was in the gynaecological ward of the Medical College Hospital. No sign of labour, although the pain kept coming at regular intervals. But not very intense.

When he asked the nurse she said, 'The doctor says he'll wait one day more. After that he'll operate on her.'

An operation.

His hand stole to his pocket as he heard the word. He had been out of a job for the past two months. The garment factory had shut down. The money he had borrowed from his brother couldn't even pay for his wife's treatment, let alone surgery. He gulped.

Hamid went to the open expanse of land behind the gynaecological ward and lit a cigarette. Even if he was starving, he couldn't do without a smoke. He saved carefully for his cigarettes instead of buying food. This was a safe area to smoke out of sight. Or so he thought.

For this was where the corpses of newborn babies piled up. A small number of such bodies were deposited here every day. They were all stillborn. Their eyes were closed. They were all unclaimed human offspring. They gave off a stench if there was a delay in transferring them to the morgue. Sometimes the smell mingled with the cigarette smoke in Hamid's breath. It percolated into his body, all the way to the heart. No, it did not make him want to spit. Before the world could break down in front of his eyes, he could see the rotting corpses in the faces of the people in this city. When he flung his cigarette butt into the distance, it was with the wish that everything would go up in flames.

He had noticed during the two days he had spent standing or sitting here that the newborn babies' corpses would be taken to the morgue at some point. And from there to some graveyard or the other in a van belonging to the Anjuman Mufidul Islam.

Hamid lit another cigarette. His head was in a whirl. Thank goodness there was an organization like the Anjuman Mufidul Islam. But how could people let their own children become unidentified corpses? Hamid's hand stole to his pocket again. There were many things people couldn't do when they were penniless, he consoled himself.

It wasn't right to question a man about his earning ability. Hamid stared at the pile of dead newborn babies with great concentration. They looked like a heap of garbage from a distance. Just like the mounds of rubbish scattered all over the city. The forms became discernible as bodies only when he went nearer. The shape of the arms and legs and head and feet and chest and back was exactly that of a baby's. Their parents abandoned them here when they were stillborn. Very few of them were laid lovingly in their graves by their fathers and mothers.

The grave was a cruel place.

Or was it a place of peace?

Hamid could not make up his mind. This was what he was like. It took him a long time to take a decision. The vacillation killed him.

Hamid entered the ward with the nurse's permission to see Feroza. When he stood by her bed, it suddenly seemed to him that her eyes were flickering like lamps about to go out. He shook her arm.

'Is that you?'

'How are you now?'

'I don't know.'

'Is the baby moving?'

'I can't tell.'

'Doesn't he kick?'

'Who knows?'

'Have you eaten?'

'Yes. You?'

'No. I'm saving money.'

'You haven't smoked?'

'I have.'

'How much did you save then?' Feroza turned her face away.

'Are you angry?'

'No. How long will you wait in the corridor? Go home.'

'I wait so I can hear the baby cry. I want to hear his first cry.'

'You won't be able to. I will.'

'All right. I'll wait near the dead babies till I can hear it too.'

Dead babies! Feroza's head slumped on her pillow. The nurse asked him to leave. Hamid went out.

He was starving. The last meal he had had was breakfast at his brother's house. He hadn't eaten anything since ten. Going outside, he pumped up some water with the tube well and drank it. The Anjuman Mufidul Islam van was parked outside the morgue. It had come to collect an unclaimed corpse. Those who had family in distant villages were all unclaimed for some reason. All of them were victims of accidents or murders or suicides or abduction. Oh, there were so many ways to die. Only those who died in their mothers' wombs never came to know any of this. What difference did it make whether they were claimed or unclaimed!

Hamid was rooted to the spot.

The Anjuman Mufidul Islam workers were cutting up some fabric to make a shroud for the corpse before taking it to the graveyard.

Hamid walked away, taking up a position beneath a tree in the distance. He had neither cigarettes nor matches. He began to lose his temper. Stamping on the ground, he said, 'This world is nothing but trouble. Fuck it. I'll just walk away from everything.'

He decided to spend the night beneath the tree. But before that he wanted to buy a small loaf for himself. A gigantic rage against the universe exploded in his head once again. Finally, he came to the conclusion that there was nothing wrong with leaving stillborn babies as unclaimed corpses. They had died already – what did it matter whether they were claimed or not? Hah! Hamid sank his teeth into his loaf of bread. He himself was an unclaimed man. He had no claim on life.

Hamid returned to his brother's house late at night, mumbling in response to his sister-in-law's blazing eyes, 'I ate already.'

'Where did you eat?'

'At a restaurant.'

'How is your wife?'

'Her eyes looked odd this evening.'

'What do you mean? What are you saying?'

Hamid began to stammer at her harangue. 'Nothing, it just felt that way. When she looked at me it didn't seem she could see me.'

'Did you inform the doctor?'

'No. What's the use ... ?'

'You're a very peculiar man. You must go to the hospital first thing in the morning. I will go in the evening.'

'You'll go?'

'Yes, why not?'

'I'm just saying that you weren't pleased about our staying at your house.'

'I certainly wasn't. Who needs all this trouble?'

'Oh, yes, that's right. I can't stand trouble either. I'm requesting you not to take the trouble of going to the hospital. There's no need. I can do it on my own.'

'I see. Very well then.'

Hamid went to bed without bothering to undress. He would leave in the same clothes in the morning. Why waste time? Hamid saw no possibility of rethinking his life. What new trajectory could he consider in a city where stillborn babies lay in a heap and were turned into unclaimed corpses?

He realized he would be able to sleep peacefully tonight. It turned out exactly as he had imagined. He passed the entire night in deep slumber. When he awoke, it occurred to him to ask his sister-in-law for breakfast. How else would he stay on his feet all day in the hospital? And what if the doctor said he wanted to operate on Hamid's wife?

Still in bed, his eyes heavy with sleep, Hamid burst into laughter all by himself. It would be a hilarious day. If the doctor suggested an operation, he would play hide-and-seek with everyone in the hospital. No one would be able to find him. Over the past two days he had spotted several places he could hide in. There were escape routes too.

At breakfast his elder brother asked, 'What did the doctor say?'

'She might need an operation.'

'An operation?'

Hamid's brother looked terrified. After locking eyes with him for a moment, Hamid lowered his gaze to his food.

'What will happen now? We don't have that kind of money. What will you do?'

'I'll play hide-and-seek.' Hamid looked squarely at his brother.

'What do you mean? What are you saying?'

'I should go to the hospital now, Bhaijan.'

Hamid left for the hospital without allowing himself to be distracted by anything. His brother kept calling after him, but he didn't respond. He told himself it was a mistake to claim unclaimed people. Hamid walked along the pavement. It was too early in the morning to be crowded. He was able to make quick progress without colliding with others. When he reached the hospital, he realized that he was not out of breath yet. He wasn't tired. He was in a pleasant frame of mind as he entered. He had no trouble getting to the corridor of the gynaecological ward.

The first person he ran into was a junior nurse.

'Oh, you're here.'

'You know who I am, don't you?'

'Of course I do.'

'Then why are you staring at me like that? Didn't I treat you to paan? You asked me whether I wanted a son or a daughter. Have you forgotten?'

The nurse could not speak. Her voice was choked. The man seemed so different today. But he would turn into a ghost soon.

'Why aren't you talking?'

'I have a headache. Your chatter isn't allowing me to think clearly.'

'Listen, if the doctor says an operation is needed, I'm going to play hide-and-seek with you.'

'Your wife won't need an operation. She's delivered her child.'

'Really? Let me go find out.' He wheeled round. 'What is it, a boy or a girl?'

The junior nurse walked away without answering.

'Phew!' Hamid exhaled noisily. He met the nurse at the entrance to the ward. She frowned at Hamid.

'When did you get here?'

'A few minutes ago. Am I a father now?'

'Come with me.'

'Where are we going?'

'To the doctor.'

'Let's go. Sounds like good news. My wife has given birth without an operation. Hah!'

Sitting across the desk from the doctor, Hamid began to perspire.

The doctor looked grim. He was busy with his own work, making Hamid wait. When he was done, he looked at Hamid and said, 'You saw your wife was not in a fit state for delivery. There was very little labour pain.'

Hamid continued to perspire.

'Your wife delivered a dead child early this morning.'

Dead! Hamid shifted in his seat, taken aback by the suddenness of it all. 'Has the child been kept with the other dead babies?' he blurted out.

'Yes, that's right,' said the nurse.

'I see. So it's an unclaimed baby now.'

'A couple of hours after giving birth, your wife died as well. We tried our best to save her.'

'I see. Very well.'

Hamid kept perspiring. He could not say anything more. He sat there in silence.

The doctor continued, 'We'll give you a death certificate in accordance with the rules of the hospital. You'd better make arrangements to take the corpse away.'

'I don't need a death certificate.' Hamid rose to his feet, still talking.

'Just a minute. I'm not done. You cannot take the corpse away without a death certificate.'

Hamid stood there without a word.

The doctor said, 'Isn't there someone from your wife's family who can accept the body?'

'There is,' said Hamid in a detached voice.

'Tell us who it is. We'll get in touch.'

'Anjuman Mufidul Islam,' said Hamid, even more dispassionately.

'What!'

Hamid left, ignoring the astonishment in the doctor's voice. He walked down the long corridor without a backward glance. He realized his mind had cleared now – Feroza used to be his wife. But so what? Once she was dead, she was nothing but a corpse. What did words like wife or husband matter now? Let hers be an unclaimed corpse. Considering he couldn't even afford to have her buried, what difference did it make whether he accepted or refused her body? There was no one who could do anything for Feroza. Her family was in the village. They wouldn't be able to make it even if they were informed. She would be taken to the morgue if no one claimed her body. The newborn baby's corpse would go to the morgue too. They would wait three days. If no one turned up by then, they would inform the Anjuman Mufidul Islam. They would drape the corpses in shrouds and take them to the cemetery. The City Corporation would arrange for poles and mats for the graves. The clerk at the cemetery would organize the burial.

Hamid had learnt all this during the two days he had spent at the hospital waiting for his child. His full name was Amdul Hamid Mian. Village: Halta. Union: Douatalla. Sub-district: Bamna. District: Barguna. He had worked at a garment factory in Dhaka. His hand stole to his pocket as he walked the length of the corridor and reached the gate. He told himself that everything would be taken care of. The only difference was that it was an unclaimed corpse that would be buried. No one would cry loudly. This was nothing to worry about. What was the point of crying when your pocket was empty? Why did the corpse have to be identified, for that matter?

Hamid went out of the hospital and stood on the road. He was agonized by the fact that he had arrived at a decision all by himself.

Finally, tears sprang to his eyes.

Once upon a time they had declared their love for each other. Sharing leftover rice from a plate, they had decided to join a garment factory in Dhaka. That was all that life was.

After Feroza became pregnant, she had said one day, laughing, 'If it's a boy, it's yours. If it's a girl, it's mine.'

He had interrupted her. 'No. If it's a girl, it's mine.'

Hamid stopped abruptly. He had not found out whether the stillborn child was a boy or a girl. Should he go back? No, he decided the very next moment. What difference did it make whether the corpse was a boy's or a girl's?

He walked all the way to New Market.

His heart was in turmoil. Everything was crumbling. He paused for a moment, and then, struck by the idea of walking past Nilkhet towards Katabon, he stepped on the road abruptly without checking if it was safe. A minibus knocked him down. He never recovered consciousness.

He was kept in a morgue for three days.

No one came looking for him. Then his corpse was loaded on the Anjuman Mufidul Islam van. He was to be taken to the Jurain graveyard. As the driver turned on the ignition, Ramen, who disposed of dead bodies, came racing out of the morgue. He began to cry, banging on the sides of the van.

'Why are you crying, Ramen?' asked one of the Anjuman Mufidul Islam workers.

'He was alone in the morgue. No one came looking for him. I'm mourning for him. I have never made a friend during my time here disposing of corpses. I am mourning for him.'

'Cry, then. Take your time and cry. We take away so many corpses, but we've never seen anyone cry like you. This unclaimed corpse is very fortunate.'

Ramen could not staunch his tears even after the van had left. He said, 'I used to enjoy talking to you from my heart, my friend.'

Hamid had told him that he loved walking in the Baldah Botanical Gardens. That when he had seen the blue lotus in the lake there, he had felt that this was what the colour of life should be like.

'I thought of you as my friend when you told me of the blue lotus, my friend. Be well, my friend.'

Ramen forgot to wipe away his tears.

HUMAYUN AHMED

The Game

Babu Nalini Ranjan, 'third sir' at the Khairunnesa Girls' High School, suddenly learnt to play chess one afternoon. He couldn't stand the game. Two people staring at a board for hours in the most annoying fashion – why? Still he was forced to learn. Jalal sahib, the geography teacher, was an old friend of his. He could not turn Jalal sahib down. During the lunch break he learnt how the pawn was supposed to move, how the knight jumped two and a half squares, how the bishop stood diagonally, his staff raised. 'It's a cerebral game,' said Jalal sahib seriously. 'Exercises the brain.'

Nalini-babu could not quite understand how it exercised the brain, but he defeated Jalal sahib in their very first game. Smiling wanly, Jalal sahib said, 'I took it too casually. Another round?'

There was no time. English composition in the fourth period. Nalini-babu rose to his feet. But he couldn't teach very well that day. The game of chess began to haunt him subtly. This had never happened before.

They played two games after classes. With a wooden smile Jalal sahib said, 'I see I have to work on my defence seriously with you.'

Jalal sahib worked on his defence seriously in the third round. The hour for his prayers went by. The game went on till the evening. Unable to lock the office up for the day, Bachhu-mian, the bearer, paced up and down the veranda with an irked expression. Jalal sahib sighed after the game. 'You seem despondent,' said Nalini-babu.

'One more,' requested Jalal sahib. 'The last one. You won't win this time – I'll play an ultra-defensive game.'

'Not today. I have to go to the coaching centre.'

'Come on, it won't take long.'

The final game ended in a draw. Jalal sahib emitted quick breaths. 'Let's go,' said Nalini-babu.

'Another round.'

'No more, it's late.'

'Just sit down and play, it's not very late.'

Nalini-babu sat down again. His triumphal march began. The people of Niyamatpur came to know in a very short time that an unbelievably good chess player lived in their town. No one could defeat him. His fame remained undiminished for fifteen years.

Fifteen years was a long time. He lost two teeth in this period, and developed a cataract in his left eye. And on a rainy July afternoon he retired as assistant headmaster. His farewell citation read:

'Babu Nalini Ranjan is an uncrowned king of the world of chess. He has created history by defeating Bangladesh's chess champion Janab Asad Khan three times in a row.'

It was true. Asad Khan's sister-in-law lived in Niyamatpur. He had visited her at some ill-fated hour, agreeing to a game of chess with Nalini-babu out of sheer curiosity. He had assumed that it was just another case of a small town where everyone extolled the skills of an average player. Even when the game began he did not realize his mistake. He saw that the short, thin man knew nothing about chess openings. For obvious reasons, he didn't even know as much as those who had read a book or two on the subject. As a result of which Asad Khan captured the pawn in front of Nalini-babu's king on his fifth move, smiling contemptuously. But the smile began to hurt his lips when he saw his bony opponent suddenly pouncing with both his knights. Asad Khan was astonished, but the people of Niyamatpur behaved as though there was nothing unusual about losing to Nalini-babu.

All Asad Khan's joy at visiting his sister-in-law paled that year. A fortnightly magazine published in Netrokona said, 'The veteran chess player Babu Nalini Ranjan of Niyamatpur, a teacher at Khairunnesa Girls' High School, has defeated the national chess champion of Bangladesh resoundingly. It is worth mentioning that this record-breaking chess player has lost to no one in the past ten years . . .'

It was unbelievable but true. Nalini-babu had won every single time. People used to travel long distances to play with him. On one occasion, the secretary of the national chess federation arrived with a foreigner. Niyamatpur had never been witness to a more momentous event. Even those who knew nothing about chess thronged the venue. A holiday was declared at Khairunnesa Girls' High School after the lunch break. Twice the federation secretary warned Nalini-babu, 'Play a very cautious game. The person I've brought is from Belgium. A highly rated player.'

'I always play a cautious game.'

'No need to hurry your moves, all right?'

Nalini-babu nodded. He had understood.

'It's best to play the Giuoco Piano defence with him. You know it, don't you?'

'No, sir, I don't.'

The secretary's brow was furrowed. The furrow deepened when he saw Nalini-babu responding to P-K4 with R4.

'What are you doing? Are you experimenting against him? What sort of move is this?'

The foreigner also said something, in English. Babu Nalini Ranjan was a teacher of English, but he could not decipher a word. His face falling, the secretary said, 'I thought I was going to put an untrained talent on display, but it looks like I'm going to be humiliated.'

They played three games. One was drawn, Nalini-babu won the other two. The secretary's astonishment was boundless.

'Why don't you play in Dhaka?'

'I have to teach at the coaching centre. And besides, I don't keep well. Asthma.'

'No, you must come.'

'I am a poor man. No money.'

'How can you be poor?'

The secretary embraced Nalini-babu.

At Babu Nalini Ranjan's farewell on the rainy July afternoon, therefore, the subject of chess cropped up repeatedly. And at the end, Suruj-mian – president of the meeting, secretary of the school committee and chairman of the municipality – announced in a most mysterious manner that he had made arrangements for a fitting display of honour for Babu Nalini Ranjan, the pride of Niyamatpur, unbeaten at chess. He was giving the school fund a cheque for 15,000 rupees. Anyone who defeated Nalini-babu would get this money. And if no one could, the school fund would get the money after Nalini-babu's death.

There was tumultuous applause. The headmaster had to hold the cheque up high to show it to everyone. No one had imagined such a dramatic move from Suruj-mian.

On an October evening Nalini-babu had a severe attack of asthma. The air seemed very thin. He strained to fill his lungs. A pulse in his throat throbbed repeatedly. But despite the state he was in, he sat down to play the final game of chess in his life. He would play it to lose. Today he would succumb to his old friend Jalal sahib, who would win 15,000 rupees. The money would be used for Nalini-babu's treatment. Warm clothes would be bought for winter, for he suffered terribly in the cold. Jalal sahib had persuaded Nalini-babu after a great deal of effort. One defeat would make no difference.

The game was being played in the school hall. Jalal sahib was playing the challenge game. Many spectators had gathered out of curiosity. Nalini-babu's position worsened. A careless move lost him a bishop. Soon afterwards, one of his rooks was pinned. A murmur rose among the spectators. Nalini-babu saw tears in Jalal sahib's eyes. The undefeated chess champion of fifteen years was about to lose. Jalal sahib's face was unnaturally pale. His hand shook as he moved his pieces.

Sobahan sahib, the homoeopath, said in surprise, 'Nalini-babu is in deep trouble.'

'It's all Nalini's pretence,' said Jalal sahib hoarsely. 'He will fix it at once, just watch.'

'Are you weeping, Jalal?' asked Nalini-babu softly.

'Of course not. There's something in my eye.'

Jalal sahib began to rub his eye to get rid of the invisible object.

Was that a faint smile on Nalini-babu's lips? He challenged the king with a check from his knight. The king moved one square. A second check with the pawn. The king moved yet another square. Nalini-babu brought his black bishop out of a seemingly invisible city. An astonished Sobahan sahib said, 'My goodness!'

'Check,' said Nalini-babu, pushing the bishop in front of the pawn.'

Despite his best efforts, he was unable to lose the final game of his life. Deep in penury, the pride of Niyamatpur died virtually without medical treatment on 12 November 1975. Tuesday. Khairunnesa Girls' High School was closed for two days to mark the occasion.

NABARUN BHATTACHARYA

The Gift of Death

Some people's lives are so dreary that in the process of putting up with the tedium they don't even realize it when they die. When you think about it, they seem to be under a cloud of doubt even after death. In that respect, few people are born as lucky as me. Whenever I get fed up with things, something inevitably happens to revive my spirits. But you can't tell too many people about this. Friends and relations all assume I'm grinding out an existence just like them. Hand-to-mouth. Brainless sheep, the whole lot. But then it's best for them to think this way. Else they'll be jealous. They'll look at me strangely. I don't know how to cope with envy. I'm afraid of the evil eye too. Good and evil – that's what makes the world go round.

The first thing I have going for me is how remarkable it is that I come into contact with lunatics at regular intervals. Chance or fate, it just happens anyway. An example or two will help me explain without harming the business venture I'm going to talk about. But it's best not to tell the psychiatrist my wife took me to. Suppose she changes my pills?

Just the other day this man – gaunt, half dead, looks like one of those people who can fly – got hold of me. Had two terrific schemes, he said. He'd sent the details to every world leader. Two of them had replied so far. Both Thatcher and Gorbachev had praised his ideas. He'd be talking to both of them soon.

He was flying out next month. I sat down to hear of his schemes.

The first one was to build a projection jutting out from the balcony of every flat in all the high-rise buildings coming up these days. Something like a diving board at a swimming pool. He would make a couple of prototypes to begin with. Once the government had approved enthusiastically, it would be added automatically to building plans, without having to be appended later.

Apparently it was essential for people to have such high spots nowadays to stand or sit on. Without railings, not very wide. It was meant for those who wanted to be by themselves. People were chased by thousands of things these days. He was being chased by the chief minister, by scientists, by the prime minister. The police commissioner too. Also by the Special Branch, the Criminal Investigations Department and the Research & Analysis Wing. That was when the plan struck him. A slice of space – but outside the building. Speaking for myself, the idea appealed to me too. Entirely possible. But because I lived in a single-storey house inherited from my father, I didn't give it too much thought. His second scheme was not exactly a plan – it was more of an adventurous proposal or proposition, though it was closely connected to the first one. He would stand as well as walk on the wings of an aircraft in mid-air. He wanted to demonstrate this practically. Today's youth would regain their courage if they saw him. The youth needed dreams, for the alternatives were drugs, cinema and HIV. He wanted to perform this feat on an Indian Air Force plane. He had written it all down in detail. There were diagrams too. All of it gathered in a thin plastic folder. He kept these documents in a file tied up with string. He wanted to know if I could help him with the second idea. Whether I knew an air marshal, for instance. When I said I wouldn't be able to help him, he requested that I at least pay for a cup of tea and a cigarette. I did.

I have met several such insane people, in various shapes and sizes, and with varying behaviours. I have seen people who have gone mad with sudden grief. I've encountered not a few suicides too. Some people develop a half-mad detachment before killing themselves. I've come across such people too. But then I've also run into not one but two cases where there wasn't a whiff of insanity. Both of them used to spend time with ascetics. One of them would go to Tarapith, that den of mystics, every Sunday. The other was embroiled deeply in office politics. Both hanged themselves. All these incidents are true. The age of making up stories has ended – why should people believe me, and why should I bother to make them up either? Some of the lunatics and suicides I've seen were tragedies of love. But this isn't the time for stories about women. Although the first person to whom I told the story that I have eventually decided to recount here was my wife. A woman, in other words.

And this was what led to all the quarrels and demands. For what? That I must see a psychiatrist. I was an able-bodied man – why should I abandon the business I ran and go see a doctor for the insane? She paid no attention. Her brothers came. Collectively they forced me to see a woman psychiatrist. What an enormous fuss they made! But it turned out to be a good idea. Very pretty. Western looks. And matching conversation. Very cordial. I liked her so much that I told her the story too. For years now I've been taking the tiny white pills she gave me, three times a day. Sometimes I take a blue one too. It gets wearisome, vexatious. But I like the woman so much that I can't help but trust her. I try to tell myself that I've recovered from an illness. Not that I'm ill.

The story that this preamble leads up to is not about lunatics or suicides, however. In fact, it's been three whole years. I was returning home by train from Madras. I have to travel indiscriminately on business. To save money I travel second-class on the way out, but on the way back I give in to my longing for luxury and inevitably buy a first-class ticket. There was no one else in the four-berth compartment. I was comfortable. Somewhere near the Andhra-Orissa border I woke up and found everything dark. The train wasn't moving either. Pitch-dark. You couldn't see anything out of the window. Once my eyes had adjusted to the darkness I realized that the train was standing at a small station somewhere. A deep-indigo night sky. Hints of low, black hills. A few lonely stars. People moving about. The glow of torches. Getting out, I was told that a goods train had been in an accident. It would have to be moved and the line repaired. Only then would our train resume its journey.

Almost without warning, the lights came back on. I went back to my compartment. At once I discovered that someone else had entered in the darkness. The man was – not probably, but almost certainly – not a South Indian. His appearance and way of talking made that obvious. In his forties. Fair, well-dressed, handsome. Slightly greying hair. His fine shirt and trousers, gleaming shoes and the tie around his neck gave him the appearance of a successful salesman of a multinational company. I wasn't entirely wrong, but I still don't know the name of the company or how big it was. So big that it was almost mysterious and obscure.

After some small talk both of us lit our cigarettes. He was the one to offer his expensive cigarettes. When I asked him whether he wouldn't mind a little whisky, he said he didn't drink. So I drank by myself. There was no sign of the train leaving. Neither of us spoke for a while. Almost startling me, the man suddenly said: 'Keep this business card of ours. Might come in useful.' The card was black, made of some kind of paper with the feel of velvet. On it, an address in an unsettling shade of bright yellow. Nothing else. A Waltair address. Nothing else on either side of the card. Neither the name of a company nor a phone number.

'That's not our actual address, mind you. You have to take a roundabout route to reach us. But when you write to us, add your address with all details. Our people will certainly get in touch with you. It may take a little time. But they will definitely meet you.'

'What exactly is this business of yours? Seems to be some sort of secret, illegal affair . . . But then you've got business cards too – strange!'

'Look, our company doesn't have a name. No name. We help people die – you could say we gift them death. Of course it isn't legal, but . . .'

'You mean you murder them.'

'Absolutely not! Murder! How awful! We aren't killers. It will be done with your full consent. Different kinds of death, in different ways. You will choose your method and pay accordingly. You want to die like a king? We can do it for you. We will fulfil whatever death wish you might have, no matter how unusual. You'll get exactly what you want, just the way you want it. But yes, you have to pay.'

I had a long conversation with the man thereafter. I'm recounting as much of it as I can recollect. As much of the strangeness as actually penetrated my whisky-soaked brain in the anonymous darkness of the station. As much as I've been able to retain three years later.

His position was that, for a variety of reasons, each of us harbours a unique death wish within ourselves. That is to say, a pet notion – and desire – of how we'd like to die. Like a romantic, someone might want to leap from a mountain into a bottomless ravine on a cold, misty evening. Others want their bodies to be riddled by bullets. Yet others, to be charred to death in a fire. Someone else wants poison in their bloodstream, so that they begin with a slight warm daze and bow out as cold as ice. Some want to be conscious at the moment of death, while others prefer to be halfway to oblivion. One person wants to be strangled. Another is keen on being stabbed. Some people wish for death in a holy place, the sound of sacred chants ringing in their ears. But wishing doesn't guarantee fulfilment. No matter what, the majority of deaths are uninteresting, drab and dull. This company meets the demand for exciting deaths, fulfilling its clients' wishes. I remember some parts of the salesman's pitch verbatim.

'There's a theoretical side to this too. Our R&D is extremely strong. You'll find non-stop research under way, not only on the practical side of death but also on other aspects, covering data from *The Tibetan Book of the Dead*, *The Thanatos Syndrome*, Indian thoughts on death, Abhedananda and Jiddu Krishnamoorthy, to the latest forms of murder, suicide and clinical death. Forget about India, no one in the world is engaged in this sort of business. It wouldn't even occur to anyone. We've been told of a few small-scale attempts in Japan, but this isn't a matter of automobiles or electronics, after all. They may have their Toyota and Mitsubishi, but those poor fellows still can't think beyond hara-kiri. All those bamboo or steel knives – so primitive. Not at all enterprising. Incidentally, do you know which country has the most suicides in the world?'

'Must be us.'

'No, sir, it's Hungary. Magyars are incredibly suicide-prone.'

They offered access to all kinds of death. They would fulfil even the most intricate and virtually impossible proposals. A man from Delhi had always imagined dying when his jeep skidded on an icy mountain road. It was organized. If you wanted to die of a specific disease, their medical team would check on its feasibility. But they would not engineer someone else's death at your request. You could only arrange for your own death through their services.

I learnt a great deal from the conversation. Apparently, many people lived such bewildered lives that even though they had a vague idea of how they'd like to die, they could not express it clearly. The company had a choice of pre-set programmes for such clients. The grandest of these was the 'record player'.

A gigantic record player was placed in the ocean at a distance. A huge black disc was set in it, the disc of death, turning at thirty-three and one-third revolutions per minute. The record player was placed on a rig similar to an offshore oil-drilling platform. You had to get there on a speedboat.

The fortunate man desiring death was made to sit on a chair over the spoke, shaped like a bullet or a lipstick, reaching upwards through the hole at the centre of the record. The record player played an impossibly tragic melody – Western or Indian. Rachmaninoff's *Isle of the Dead*, or the wistful strains of a sarangi, as you wished. Several thousand watts of sound enveloped the client in a trance. Revolving on the surface of the ocean along with the record, he was also transported to a place beyond the real and the unreal. When the music ended, the stylus entered the glittering space in the middle of the record with the sound of a storm, striking the man a mighty blow that ensured his death even before his body hit the water. His head was either torn off his body or pulverized. As soon as the corpse fell into the sea, hundreds of sharks swam up at the scent of blood. This was a very expensive affair. Very few people could afford it. To date, not more than two or three people had heard the symphony of death.

'Who are they?'

'Excuse me, but clients are more important to us than even god. We cannot possibly divulge their identities. Although we are practically friends now, you and I. Do you remember how Mr —— died? You should.'

'How could I not remember? Such a horrible plane crash!'

'It was a plane crash all right, but that was what he wanted.'

'But what about the other passengers? Surely they didn't want it.'

'Sorry. It's prohibitively expensive. Because there are other victims.'

'But they were innocent.'

'Innocent! My foot! In any case, there's nothing we can do about it. None of them told us to kill them. But if they insist on taking the same flight, what are we supposed to do? Moreover, this was his choice. Yes, choice. We made all the arrangements to fulfil his request, using the money he paid us.'

'But. Why did he do this?'

'He had got rid of Mr —— the same way. Not through us, of course. Lots of innocent people had died on that occasion too. So he wanted a similar death.'

'How many more such cases have you handled?'

'Numerous. But why should we tell you about all of them? Do you think all such cases can be discussed? Should they even be discussed? We offer many services. We sell suicide projects, for instance. Not as expensive. Lots of other things too. Let me just tell you this, all the famous people who have died recently – from the Bombay mafia leader being gunned down to the Calcutta film star who committed suicide with the phone in his hand and forty sleeping pills in his stomach – it was all our doing. And then there are always the political leaders. It's very easy to help them – all of them prefer a heart attack.'

'So you people help only the famous? Give them the gift of death, that is.'

'We're still trying to consolidate our business, you see. The company's a long way from breaking even. But yes, pride in our performance is our major capital at present. Later, of course, we'll have to think of the economically weaker classes too. To tell you the truth, poor people are much more trouble. The bastards aren't even sure whether they're alive in the first place, how can they be expected to think of death? And besides, they're unbelievably crude.'

'What about those even lower down – miles below the poverty line – beggars?'

'Impossible! Last year our R&D people studied the death wishes of beggars in three metropolitan cities – Calcutta, Bombay and Madras. Their findings were – how shall I put it – silly and delightful. Childish demands.'

'Such as?'

'In most cases the image involves eating. For instance, some of them want their limbs, heads and bodies to be stuffed with meat, fish, butter and alcohol till they explode. They desperately want liquor. Then again, some of them want god to take them in his arms in the middle of Flora Fountain in Bombay. Infantile, and so naive.'

'But you have to say they're imaginative.'

'That's true. They're bound to be, since they're human beings. But yes, we get a lot of valuable ideas from children. Just the other day our R&D unearthed a fascinating story from an American newspaper.'

'Tell me, please.'

'A boy, you know. About twelve. Somewhere near Chicago. The little fellow had dressed up as Batman. He was Batman constantly, jumping from roof to roof with a pair of wings clipped on. No one took him seriously. Even the girls used to laugh at him. Child psychology, you see. So none of you can recognize Batman, he said. One day he was found in a deep freezer, frozen after several days in there. You'd be astounded at the kinds of cases there are. Batman! Actually it's not like I don't drink. Pour me a strong whisky, will you? What's this whisky called? Glender! Oh, it's Scotch. I've never heard of this brand.'

I poured a few whiskies. For the salesman. And for myself too. After I poured several, he left like Batman, swinging and weaving. I wove my way to bed too. The train had started moving. I could still hear his voice ringing in my ears ...

'But yes, there's a grand surprise in death, especially in accidental death – a thrill that we never deprive our clients of. Say someone has booked a death to be run over by a car. But not all his efforts will allow him to guess when, where, or on which road he will die. The virgin charm of sudden death will always remain.'

Who was this man? What company did he represent, for that matter? The gift of death – the idea couldn't exactly be dismissed out of hand. Despite my best efforts, I hadn't been able to do it for three years. Secondly, don't we have our own visions of death, after all? Would it be fulfilled in this one life, in this life? For instance, I have a specific sort of death wish of my own too. But then the death by record player is very expensive. Naturally. I live with doubts and misgivings like these. These things lie low when I take my pills regularly. When they raise their heads I visit the psychiatrist. She changes the medicine. Blue pills instead of white. In the darkness of power cuts I pull out that man's black business card for a look. The disturbing yellow letters are probably printed in fluorescent ink. They glow in the darkness. I don't mind showing the card to anyone who gets in touch with me. You can check for yourself by writing to them. It might take a little time, but their people will certainly get in touch. You can be sure about this. They will definitely meet you.

MANORANJAN BYAPARI

Hangman

The man was of middling height, dark-skinned and strongly built. His was clearly not a body nurtured by the generous affection of milk and butter. It had survived the ravages of many a winter and summer.

His torso was covered with a dirty T-shirt, and his legs with a wraparound cotton lungi, the bottom of which he had hitched up above his knees in a unique style. This reduced the chances of tripping when running.

Picking up the newspaper at the tea shop, he turned over the pages idly till his eyes stopped at a report on page five. 'Nata Mullick severely ill.'

Nata Mullick was not a celebrity or politician or film star or athlete. Why had the newspaper published a report about his illness? The man began to read with care.

By our Special Representative

Nata Mullick, the only hangman in Calcutta and the entire state of West Bengal, has been admitted to hospital after being diagnosed with heart disease. Doctors have recommended complete rest for him.

This has led to some trouble for the authorities at Alipore Jail in Calcutta. A state of uncertainty prevails over whether the two convicts sentenced to death will now be hanged on the date finalized for the execution.

The man read the report several times, trying to make sense of the news behind the news. Abruptly, he pounded the table with his fist, sending his now-empty tumbler of tea to the ground.

An open drain ran past the tea shop filled with dirty, contaminated water. Monta, the shopkeeper, was washing cups and saucers with the help of a dented bucket. Turning to the man on hearing the sound, he said, 'What's the matter?'

'News of those two.'

'Who?'

'The ones sentenced to death.'

'Can you read out what they're saying?'

Monta had expected to be pleased by the news, but he was disappointed on hearing the details. 'So they haven't been hanged.'

'Nor *will* they be hanged.'

'They'll be spared?'

'Looks like it.'

'Really?'

The man gestured in a way that could mean either yes or no. Various possibilities began to swirl in his head, all of them suggesting that the wealthy convicts – a father and a son found guilty of murdering the son's wife – were using all the resources at their disposal to avoid being hanged.

'The bastards will live,' the man said. Jumping to his feet, he vented his anger by tightening the knot of his lungi and prepared to leave. Monta looked at him questioningly. 'I'll pay later.'

'Do you remember how many you owe me for?'

'It was seventeen yesterday, add one more.'

'And where are you off to?'

The man pointed with the index finger of his right hand in a direction that suggested anywhere between where he was and the western horizon.

'When will you be back?'

'Can't say.'

'What if someone asks?'

'Tell them I'm at the crematorium.'

The man was looking for Shonkor Mullick. He was perpetually to be found at the crematorium, for he disposed of dead bodies. Nata Mullick was a distant cousin of his.

No hangman could hang anyone alone and unaided. The fear of

imminent death made the convict so desperate that they sometimes attacked the hangman violently. So the hangman needed assistants to restrain the convict. The guards at the jail helped too. But all of this went only as far as leading the convict to the gallows. After that the hangman had to take over.

Shonkor Mullick had assisted his cousin at a hanging once. It was him the man was looking for. He made an appearance about an hour later. Spotting the man from a distance, Shonkor went up to him with a smile and greeted him, not obsequiously, but with something like a military salute.

'Where have you been all this while? You disappeared completely. Long spell in prison or something?'

The man said, 'You've been gone too. Been waiting a long time.'

'Went to Chetla. What you get here these days is junk, can't get high on it. Want some?'

A dead body had arrived. An elderly man, so there were no heart-rending cries. The quiet conversation of a dozen people with saddened faces did not disturb the peace of the crematorium. The man said, 'You helped your cousin hang someone once, Shonkor. You told me about it, unless it was someone else who did.'

'That was a long time ago. Why are you asking me about it now?'

'No particular reason. Just wanted to hear the story.'

'No, I'm sure there's a reason.'

'No reason at all. An experience like this is . . . a big thing isn't it.'

Shonkor burst into laughter. There was an innocence in the flash of his yellowed teeth. 'I'm not an idiot. Are you telling me you walked ten miles in the middle of the day to hear a story about a hanging. Tell me the truth. Are you going to hang someone?'

'Will you help me if I do?'

'I have burnt at least three or four thousand corpses with these hands. I have no problem burning the dead. But turning a living man into a dead one is something else. I did it once with my cousin. What can I say, I didn't sleep for three months. All I did was drink.'

'All the evidence proved he was guilty of a horrible crime. Keeping him alive would have harmed society. That's the kind of person he was. And besides, someone sentenced to death by the courts is already dead in a sense. What's wrong with killing a dead man?'

'But in front of your own eyes?'

'There's a body in front of your eyes. The doctor has certified him dead. You're going to burn the body. Are you sure he's dead?'

Shonkor began his story. 'I was twenty-two or twenty-three at the time. In the morning Nata-bhaiya told me, "We have a case after many years. I'm all by myself here, it won't be easy. Give me a hand. Nothing to be afraid of. You'll have to have several stiff drinks first." I don't know what I was thinking, but I said all right. In the evening we went to the jail. That was the rule. You had to spend the night in the jail.

'So Nata-bhaiya brought a rope from the storeroom. He checked it properly. Thick rope, polished with wax. Wouldn't tear even if a truck pulled at it. Still he tested its strength with a sack of sand.'

'What did you have to do?'

'I poured five or six buckets around the pit and cleaned it thoroughly. Then I went to the jail gate. They gave us a room to relax in. Dinner was mutton, along with liquor. Imported . . .'

'Did you sleep after that?' The man interrupted Shonkor.

'Sleep!' Shonkor sighed deeply. 'You think sleep was possible? Drank all night. Got fully drunk.'

'And then?'

'I don't remember what time it was. A priest came. He was going to read some holy book or the other to the convict. The convict had already been bathed and dressed in new clothes.'

'Did the convict bathe himself?'

'Impossible! How can anyone cooperate when he's about to die?'

'What happened?'

'The convict knew he had been sentenced to death. The president hadn't pardoned him. So he could be strung up any day. So he knew. As soon as the sentence came he had been put in a separate cell.'

'The condemned cell.'

'So as soon as the guard went to unlock the door he knew. He attacked like a tiger. Convicts don't have too many things in their cells. A plate, a blanket, a bucket to piss and shit in. So he used the bucket like a club to hit the guard . . .'

'And then?'

'So the other guards used their heads. One of them covered himself with two or three blankets. Then three or four guards held the door open while the one wrapped in blankets entered and overpowered the convict. Then his hands and legs were tied up and he was brought to the bathroom. Someone poured a few mugs of water on him.'

The wood on the pyre was crackling. Blue smoke coiled upwards. The red flames danced. The smell of roasted flesh spread everywhere.

Shonkor continued after a pause. 'He was powerfully built, but I don't know how it happened, after the water was poured on him he went limp. He knew there was no escape. His legs were untied. He put on the new clothes himself. Listened to the holy book being read to him.'

'People say a convict's last wishes are fulfilled before they're hanged. Is this true?'

'All that had been done much earlier. At least a year and a half had passed after the sentence. By then he had eaten everything he wanted, met everyone he had asked to meet. There was nothing left to be done. Except the hanging.'

'What did you do after that?'

'He was taken to the hanging pit.'

'Did he walk on his own or did he have to be dragged there?'

'Don't ask me more about that. He was taken there. His hands had been tied in front of him, now they were tied at the back. Then he was hoisted on to the wooden platform and his feet were tied. His face was covered with a black cloth. That was it. The superintendent waved a handkerchief, and Nata-bhaiya turned the handle. The platform he was standing on parted in the middle. The convict dropped into the pit.'

'Who else was present?'

'The superintendent, the jailer, an officer, nine or ten guards and the doctor.'

'There was a doctor too?'

'Who would write the death certificate otherwise? The doctor would check the body half an hour later, only after that . . .'

'One more thing. At the very last minute, before the handle was turned, what did the man do? Didn't he say anything?'

'Nothing much, only said god's name. But Nata-bhaiya followed the rules and told him, look, I'm not doing anything wrong. The judge has given you this sentence according to the law. I am only following orders. Then the convict told him, god knows I'm innocent.'

'Was he very poor?'

'Extremely poor. We found out later.'

'What was he hanged for?'

'No one is hanged unless they've murdered someone.'

'Do you know whom he killed?'

'I cannot say.'

The man had found out all he had to. It was time to go now. His heart bled for the unknown convict who had been hanged. No one lied when they were about to die, it was a time for remorse and regret. Why had the convict claimed innocence then?

The calculation was clear, he was poor. Or else eminent lawyers would have pleaded his case, used technicalities and saved his life. Someone without money could not give eyesight to blindfolded justice. The wretched man had died. But those two would use their wealth to cripple justice.

With these thoughts running through his head, the man walked across Kalighat Bridge and went up to the main gate of the Central Jail. It was two in the afternoon, and there was a crowd outside. The guards were moving about cautiously. The crowd was expectant, waiting to meet their relatives and friends among the inmates.

The sky was overcast, with the sun peeping through with some effort now and then. There was a mild chill in the air. Was it raining somewhere?

The man stopped and pondered over something before walking up to a tree to which a letter box was attached. Those who had come to visit the convicts had to write down all the details on a piece of paper and put them in the box. An old man sat beneath the tree, ready to write the application for a price of two rupees.

He said as soon as the man stopped in front of him: 'Convict's name? Father's name? Address?'

'Give me paper and a pen, I'll write it out myself,' said the man.

'Two rupees.'

'I'll pay.'

Walking a short distance away, the man wrote a letter slowly, put it in the letter box, returned the pen to the old man, gave him two rupees and lit a cigarette.

A guard emptied the letter box half an hour later and took the contents for sorting to the deputy jailer's desk. Going through the applications, the deputy jailer stopped at one of them. If it had been posted by an enemy, it was meant to insult the jailer. And if by a friend, it was a joke. Why had the convicts' letter box been used to seek an audience with the jailer?

The jailer and deputy jailer were almost of equal rank. Therefore their relationship had room for a sense of humour. Glancing at the jailer over the rim of his reading glasses, the bald deputy jailer said, 'Here you are.'

'What's that?'

'An interview with you.'

The letter was addressed in wavering script to 'The Jailer, Alipur Jail, Kolkata.' The jailer began to read it out of curiosity, having trouble deciphering the words, which were arranged haphazardly. The meandering lines chased one another around the sheet of paper. With great difficulty, he read:

Respected Jailer,

I have learnt from the newspaper that no executioner is available to conduct the hanging of two murderers sentenced to death and imprisoned in your jail. I believe such murderers do not have the right to live even one more day anywhere in the world. I am willing to perform the above-mentioned task with pleasure and without remuneration. I will be obliged if you grant me the opportunity.

Sincerely
Jibon

Impressive! The writer had tried to compose his letter with some care. He had referred to a social perspective, and then 'with pleasure' and 'without remuneration'. What was going on? He wasn't mentally ill was he?

Still, it looked like an opportunity to have some fun. Laughter was a valuable commodity, it was essential to laugh for some time every day to maintain one's mental health. Here the entire time was devoted to criminals. There was neither leisure nor reason to laugh. Now here was an idiot giving them a chance for some humour. Why not make use of it?

'Send him in.'

The deputy jailer told the guard whose job it was to usher visitors in, 'Ramdhin, go fetch this man named Jibon.'

Jibon came in. The jailer surveyed him from head to toe, and then glanced with amusement at the deputy jailer.

The enormous desk was not maintained very neatly. A hundred years of dust seemed to have gathered on it. The surface was filled with thick registers, pens, paperweights, a glass of water, an ashtray, an image of a goddess and many other useless objects. Jibon went up to the desk.

'What is your name?' said the jailer gravely, without offering a smile.

'I wrote it in the application. That's the name the guard used to call me here. Jibon.'

'What do you do?'

'Nothing worth mentioning.'

'How do you manage then?'

'I do this and that. Only one stomach to fill after all. I manage.'

'And what is this and that? You have to tell us.'

Jibon wondered whether to tell the truth. He didn't seem to have a choice. What should he do? Might as well come out with it.

Taking a little time to make up his mind, he said, 'There was a raid on a drinking dive the other day near where I live, sir. The new officer in charge at the police station is a tough nut. Said what we used to pay the officer before him wouldn't do. Prices were rising. Asked for three hundred a month. That wasn't a problem, sir, but then he had one more instruction. There had to be one arrest from every drinking dive every month. He couldn't meet his quota unless twenty cases were filed a month. So sir, Bonomali . . . he has a dive too. Used to drive a rickshaw before, but had to stop after getting tuberculosis. He can't do anything else, he sells country liquor beside the railway line.

'So Bonomali came up to me and said, I'm too sickly to survive police custody and jail, Jibon. Why don't you get arrested instead of me? I'll pay you fifteen rupees for every day you have to spend there.

'So, sir, I pretended to be Bonomali and went into custody. I was inside for five days, I earned seventy-five rupees. Everyone benefited, Bonomali as well as me. The judge had slapped a fine of a hundred and fifty rupees, Bonomali would have had to pay it unnecessarily. To tell the truth, sir, I'll have to go to jail quite often on Bonomali's behalf.'

'Which jail were you in, Jibon?' the deputy jailer asked through narrowed eyes.

'Didn't you notice, sir?' Jibon answered quickly. 'I was right here, file number seven. Next to the flower garden, sir – that garden was my handiwork.'

'A garden in five days!'

'Not this time! The last time I was here. I was inside for nearly two years.'

The jailer had not seen him, or if he had did not remember him. It wasn't possible to keep an eye on which of the thousands of prisoners were gardening. There was no need to, either. Besides, all convicts looked the same.

But the deputy jailer felt Jibon looked familiar. 'I know you will come here again, Jibon,' he said, 'but do you remember how many times you've been inside already?'

'No, sir,' Jibon answered honestly. 'Who remembers when you're in for a day or two or a week or two. I served a full sentence only once, that was for nineteen months.'

'Where do you live, what's your address?' asked the jailer.

'I don't have an address, sir. But sir there's this space in Jadavpur Rail Station, opposite the ticket counter, between the tea stall and the bookshop, that's where I sleep at night. I can be found there after ten o'clock. And during the day I'm usually in Monta's tea shop near the bus stop.'

'That's all very well, but what about other kinds of work, like killing people . . . I'm asking if you have any experience of hanging anyone.' The jailer proceeded to elaborate. 'Whatever the work might be, whether it's digging holes or hanging murderers, those with experience get first preference. Do you have any such experience?'

'No, sir,' Jibon said candidly, 'I have no experience of hanging anyone. But . . .'

'But?'

'But I've killed with a knife.'

'How many?'

'One. Only one of them died. I've used knives a lot.' Jibon continued with a mixture of shame and pride, 'Knives and guns are the weapons of cowards. A brave man will fight with his hands. But, sir, those days are gone … Everyone is armed nowadays. So I had no choice but to …'

Jibon felt his excuse hadn't gone down well, for neither the jailer nor the deputy jailer was responding. He continued, 'There was a goon in our neighbourhood named Baadol, he was nearly six feet tall, well built. He had a fight with me, and then one day he fired at me. Now I had no fire-arms, sir, so I had to use my knife on him from the back. Otherwise, sir …'

After a long pause the jailer said, 'Yes, but how can we rely on you, you're completely inexperienced. Since you read the newspapers you must know that any job of importance needs people with at least five or six years of experience. Which you don't have when it comes to the noose.'

'I do, sir, I had garrotted a fellow once, he would have died, his tongue was hanging out. He would definitely have died if everyone hadn't forced me to let go.'

'That won't do,' the jailer said, shaking his head.

'I can do it, sir,' Jibon pleaded. 'Have faith in me, you won't regret it.'

Both the jailer and the deputy jailer were silent. An idea began to take shape in Jibon's head. The convicts have purchased the authorities, so they're making excuses to refuse my offer. But I'll see this through till the end. I'll appeal to the minister of jails if need be. I won't let those two murderers go free.

The jailer said in the same grave voice as earlier, 'There are rules, Jibon. Nothing can be done on a whim.' Pausing, he continued after a few moments, 'I understand what you're thinking. You want to perform a noble task. Very well, we still have a year to go. Why don't you gather some experience in the meantime. We will consider your application after that. Can't you go out there and become a pro at it meanwhile?'

'You won't change your mind later?'

'We need people who can get things done.'

'All right, sir, I'll be back.'

'Yes.'

It was getting on for evening. The sky was quite dark. It looked like rain. Out on the street, Jibon began to wonder whom to kill to acquire the necessary experience to become a hangman. Whom could he pick?

A parade of faces moved past Jibon's eyes, some of them unknown, some familiar. Any of these could help him fulfil his objective. Couldn't he lay hands on even one of them under cover of darkness?

SYED MANZOORUL ISLAM

The Weapon

I

Ponir had always been troubled by his name. He had no idea why his father had named him after cottage cheese. He hadn't had the chance to ask him, either. His father, who used to work in a shop in Islampur selling cut-price fabric, had died suddenly after a three-day fever. Ponir was ten or eleven at the time, a student in Class Five at the Suritola Primary School. What had Ponir's father been ill with? A malignant form of pneumonia, apparently, but neither Ponir nor his mother, nor even the local doctor, had had any inkling. The doctor had treated him for flu. But then, why blame the neighbourhood doctor when the diagnoses of even well-known physicians are wide off the mark? They've managed to send gastric patients to their graves by giving them bypass surgeries, confusing gas-induced chest pains with heart attacks. Haven't you heard of such cases?

How did we find out the truth about Ponir's father, then? Why, that's just what we do. As storytellers it's one of our responsibilities to know these things. How else are we supposed to tell our stories?

Ponir Ali didn't know whether his father was fond of cheese. The fact was that he had never seen a slice of cheese in his life, for they couldn't afford any. Perhaps his father had in fact loved cheese – who could tell? But Ponir had a grievance against the dead man – why did he of all people have to be named after cheese? Why not his younger brother, the one who had died at the age of three months? He too had remained as elusive as cheese, beyond their reach.

Asking his mother hadn't helped. She never answered such questions.

When Ponir's mother told him, 'You have to leave school and get a job,' he knew it was fated to happen – it was the unchangeable truth he had to live with. The great Cicero had said, 'Whatever is unchangeable is the truth.' Even the venerable Confucius had said, 'The unchangeable truth is the ultimate truth.' He had learnt these from the aforementioned book. He had also learnt: 'Never disobey your mother.' According to Principal Azadur Rahman, it was Haji Mohammed Mohsin who had said this. This was possible. Ponir not only understood the unchangeable truth his mother had conveyed, but also learnt that there were other truths behind it. He realized the predicament that the family was in. Phuli and Duli were growing up. He had observed their torn clothes. The constant shrinking of the portions of food at home and his mother's deteriorating health had not escaped his notice either.

Still, he asked for more time – until the end of his Class Eight exams. He took the scholarship test without success, but passed the end-of-year exam and was accepted into Class Nine, even scoring quite well in maths. One winter morning, though, instead of swishing his way to school in his uniform and trainers, bathed and with his hair slicked and combed with oil, Ponir set out more or less in silence – as though he were a midnight suitor out to prowl the neighbourhood like a wary cat – for Nantu Mian's Car King garage in Dholaikhal. Nantu Mian ate his lunch at Bogdadia Restaurant after three in the afternoon. That was where Ponir's mother had requested him to give her son a job. Nantu Mian was a taciturn man. He told her, 'Send him to me, I'll hire him only if I like him.'

He liked Ponir at first sight. The boy appeared alert and educated and in control. Nantu Mian hired him but issued two operating instructions at the outset. No weeping. (Ponir had tears in his eyes after his separation from school.) Nantu Mian believed that only women wept. Tears did not melt human existence. Life was hard – like the motor parts and nuts and bolts in his garage. His second instruction to Ponir was not to wear trainers. 'You see, Ponir-mian,' Nantu told him, 'personally I have no objection to your wearing shoes. They're yours; you're free to wear them. But the other boys won't take it well. They don't have shoes. This might get you into trouble.' Ponir understood. He accepted both instructions. A few days later Nantu Mian issued a third operating instruction. He had observed Ponir bringing a book to work in a polythene bag. He glanced at the book occasionally as he worked. He never had time to read it, but now and then he turned it over a couple of times before putting it back in the bag. The other boys stared and laughed. But Nantu Mian's problem was not with the book – he didn't approve of anyone bringing a bag to work. Last year one of the boys had spirited away a carburettor inside a bag. He did not suspect Ponir – there was no reason to – but the sight of a bag made him uncomfortable. He told Ponir, 'You see, Ponir-mian, books are wonderful things, but this garage isn't a place for reading. The boys will just laugh at you.'

Ponir understood. He wouldn't bring the book any more. Nantu Mian felt guilty. After all, it was a book they were talking about – and now he had banned books! Smiling, he told Ponir a rhyme, hoping to entertain him:

> Go to Banglabazar if you need books
> And to Dholaikhal for iron scraps and hooks.

If any of you read copiously and have books at home, and happen to live in Dholaikhal, please don't be offended. I am not the one who composed the rhyme, it was Nantu Mian, and he composed it to provide a moment's distraction to a sorrowful young man buffeted by the blows of life.

It wasn't as though Ponir-mian was not remotely entertained. But he was hurt. He was aware that working at a garage meant saying goodbye to his studies. But did that also have to mean banning *Memorable Sayings of Venerable People*? Did his daytime relationship with his favourite object have to be severed? Nantu Mian's instruction made him feel he would have preferred to have been asked to leave a foot or his ears or even his brain behind at home. Ponir took two decisions (the second an alternative to the first) on his way back home that evening. First, that he would drop *Memorable Sayings of Venerable People* into the open manhole on Bongshal Road; or, second, that he would himself jump in. When he considered the second possibility, he also thought about jumping in front of a truck, or, as a last resort, in the path of a train at Gandaria. However, he rejected the second possibility even before he thought it through. For some time now, his mother had been bleeding from chapped lips. Every time he had tried to examine them she had pushed his hand away, which meant, leave me alone; or, my dear Ponir, what difference does it make whether a poor person is bleeding from her lips or not? How many things can you fix?

Thankfully the skin had not peeled off entirely. Ponir had decided to buy a balm for his mother's chapped lips as soon as he got his first pay. He was close to the manhole at the time he had considered leaping into it; peering in, he had seen human excrement floating beneath the edges. He wanted to throw up. He couldn't bring himself to cast *Memorable Sayings of Venerable People* into this hole.

Ponir decided it would be better to hide the book and not read it any more. There, on the half-deserted road, he wept in silence. Then, returning home, he displayed flashes of temper with his sisters, and didn't eat dinner.

But no one seemed particularly bothered.

Ponir put *Memorable Sayings of Venerable People* in a polythene bag and dropped it in an empty kerosene tin hanging from the roof beam. The tin wasn't entirely empty, though, for it contained small mementos from his school life – pencils, erasers, marbles. He had already sold his textbooks and notebooks after the exams, as he did every year.

This tin was his own property. His mother never touched it. Nor did Phuli and Duli.

He couldn't help telling his mother the saddest story of his life. She listened in silence, saying nothing and showing no sympathy. If Ponir happened to be our son, we would have drawn him into our arms, wept with him, taken him to the ice cream parlour and bought him a cricket bat. Ponir's mother did none of these things. She only tried to straighten his unkempt hair with her fingers.

Ponir's mother's detached action burst the dam that had been holding off his tears.

5

If you heard Ponir's heart-rending sobs you would think he was a shy, soft-hearted boy. But that was not the case. He was not soft at heart at all. In fact, you could call him quite hard-headed. How else could he have carved out a place for himself in the adult world in less than a year? No one ever had the opportunity to show the slightest pity for Ponir, not even Nantu Mian. Ever since Nantu Mian had told him, 'No crying, tears don't melt the heart of this thing called life,' he hadn't wept even once. Instead, he had made others weep. There was something about the way he looked at people or talked to them that made everyone uncomfortable. He said little, and never shirked his work. But Nantu Mian noticed that everyone except two or three friends maintained a distance from him. Why? Nantu Mian didn't know; he concluded that it was a matter of Ponir's personality.

We believe that Ponir's appearance was made more formidable by the soot and grime he was constantly covered in. He was a grease monkey, after all.

It wasn't that Ponir never cried. He did, but never when people were around, and then only once in a while. The first time was when Nantu Mian had had a few words with him. Very gently. Not operating instructions, only advice. A couple of questions. Some things the garage owner wanted to know. And the second time, when Nantu Mian had given him a raise after a year, pressing 400 taka into his hand. 'Buy your mother something, Ponir-mian,' he had said.

Holding back his tears, Ponir had bought lip balm for his mother from the pharmacy. Vaseline. Her lips were like the earth in summer, permanently cracked. She had all but returned the jar when she found out the price. But she did put the balm on her lips before going to bed.

Not that Ponir had felt any emotion on seeing this. He was his mother's son, after all.

6

My story has been progressing in a straight line so far – from Gulistan along Bongshal Road, for instance. But it will become more complicated now, turning towards Nawabpur, and then negotiating the congested roads of Adalat Para leading to Patuatuli. It might even get lost up a blind alley. Or down a manhole.

What can one do anyway if that happens?

One morning Phuli told Ponir that Dish Baidya was stalking her, and she wouldn't go back to the garment factory any more. Oh, I forgot to tell you. Phuli had been working at a garment factory for a year and a half. We – meaning Ponir, Ponir's mother and us, all of us – had been having trouble with Phuli. She could not be married off. Neither Ponir nor his mother could afford it (not that Phuli was ugly, she just wasn't particularly pretty either). Nor could we have her get married at short notice, even if we tried. Who would come forward to take her hand? What about the handsome, rich, young garment-factory owner, you might ask, the heart-throb of neighbourhood girls, who drove a maroon Nissan Patrol wearing sunglasses, a Havana cigar dangling from his lips? Didn't he look approv-ingly at her once, and even smile? Well, if he did marry her, our story would no longer remain a story but would turn into a fairy tale or film. Could he really be that mad? So to protect everyone's interests we made Phuli take a job at this young man's company, Pari Garments & Apparel. This will make things very easy for us. Need we add that the young man, whose name was Naushad, never had set eyes on Phuli after that one encounter, for his office was elsewhere? An assistant manager had given Phuli her job. The company needed someone. Since Phuli was someone, she got the job. Simple.

If you'd like to know more about Naushad: he was already taken. The girl he was going to marry was named Shakila. She was the retired income tax commissioner Badrul Haider's second daughter. Haider owned a five-storey mansion and an enormous shopping mall named Afsana Plaza. Shakila studied English literature at Eden College; she was also famous for her modelling and T V work.

We must be crazy to compare Phuli to Shakila. Life wouldn't forgive us if we did. Still, all of us were pleased when Phuli settled down. But Dish Baidya put a spanner in the works. He worked for a cable T V – what we call 'dish T V' – firm in Bongshal, going door to door to collect monthly subscriptions. He was known as Dish Baidya because there was another Baidya in the neighbourhood.

By our reckoning, Ponir was now seventeen. Dish Baidya was twenty-five. So what? One evening he confronted Dish Baidya in the alley leading to Bogdadia, planning to teach him a lesson for stalking Phuli. Ponir was accompanied by Delwar and Motaleb, his friends from the garage. Dish Baidya was with Leftie Bikash. Both of them bad characters. But so what? Ponir hammered Dish Baidya with a wrench from the workshop, emitting war cries all the while. We had no idea he had such a powerful voice.

The attack was so sudden that Bikash fled at the first blow. Eventually, Dish Baidya did too. By then he had discovered why he was being beaten up. But despite being a bad character he was neither a hooligan, nor particularly brave. So he fled not just to save his own life but also to depart from Phuli's forever. Ponir's friends were astonished at his boldness. They had remained spectators. And yet they worked at the garage – grease monkeys through and through. And once they were out of the garage, they looked fearsome. As they did now, in the darkness of evening in the alley leading to Bogdadia.

There were two outcomes to this incident. First, a new player named Ponir had arrived in the first division of hooligans in Bongshal. Everyone now realized that he wasn't to be rubbed up the wrong way. His rite of passage was complete. Ponir was an adult now. This was how he was accepted in Bongshal and in the world. Second, he lost his head.

He had discovered an intense and thrilling source of joy. Dish Baidya hadn't even resisted. It was possible that, even at seventeen, Ponir's arm was as strong as a monkey wrench, that his fist was as powerful as a small gorilla's. But Dish Baidya was no pushover, he was actually taller than Ponir. So?

Ponir's victory had less to do with strength than with courage. You will see that a diminutive but brave man can overcome even an extra-large-bodied wrestler who has zero reserves of courage. We used to have a dog named Bundle, who had once chased a bull of regular proportions out of our alley. The bull was foaming at the mouth, as though it would have a heart attack. And Ponir's war cries had their own impact too. Working at the garage had turned Ponir Ali into a dictionary of foul language. By contrast, Dish Baidya belonged to a decent family. You could say he was half vanquished by Ponir's expletives.

7

Two years passed. Ponir was now an important figure in Bongshal. An influential member of the Bongshal branch of the youth organization of the ruling party. Ponir had a godfather, though. Hasan Bhai from the neighbourhood. He was better known as Phuchka Hasan. For some reason, the people of Bongshal were never content with the names given by parents – they inevitably added a nickname or a surname, especially to those who were well known. Why Phuchka Hasan was named Phuchka Hasan – the first name coming from the popular roadside snack – was a mystery to Ponir, possibly to Hasan as well, and even to us. But people said he used to sell phuchka at one time in the alley leading to Bogdadia. Hasan denied this. But his first wife didn't. Hasan had divorced her. She told us that it was the truth. She had given half her life to Hasan, the poorer half, when Hasan had to sell phuchka for a living, phuchka that she used to make. Hasan was a millionaire now. His first wife was one too, having secured a flat, a shop and a car as part of her divorce settlement. Moreover, she had married Sunny, the younger brother of Amir Khosru, the owner of Bogdadia.

Never mind all that. But we acknowledge that Phuchka Hasan's first wife may be bitter. She could even have made the whole thing up out of a need for revenge. Who knows? Phuchka Hasan was the ward commissioner. And a close friend of Nantu Mian's. He often turned up at the garage for a chat. One could say Ponir had caught his attention soon after Dish Baidya was thrashed.

Dish Baidya had complained to Phuchka Hasan, who promised him that he would take it up with Nantu Mian. Had Ponir not been an employee of Car King, he would have sent someone to pick him up for some quick justice. But Car King belonged to his friend Nantu. He decided to investigate personally. After meeting, and talking to, Ponir, however, he had a change of heart. He sent for Baidya. As soon as Baidya appeared with an ingratiating smile on his face, Hasan took off his slipper and hurled it at him, saying, 'How dare you fuck around with someone without knowing who they are, shitface? Don't go anywhere near Ponir ever again.'

Dish Baidya vanished into thin air. I was told he had taken a job with a satellite dish supplier in Mirpur 10. He had just one dream now: 'Mohammedan Sporting Club will play at Mirpur Stadium sooner or later. Ponir will come to watch. I won't let the bastard get out of Mirpur; I'll bury him here.'

Mohammedan Sporting Club was Ponir's favourite football team, but it never played at Mirpur, which was reserved for cricket.

It was an unreal dream. Only Dish Baidya could have such a dream. But let him, if that was what made him happy.

Phuchka Hasan's entry has benefited us in two ways. First, the story of

Ponir's conversion to a goon is now sufficiently credible, for it is Ponir's life as a goon that is the main subject of this story (why would it be titled 'The Weapon' if that were not the case?). Phuchka Hasan was a dangerous man – he had no match when it came to delivering silent but brutal terror. We've been told that the mothers in Bongshal made up fearsome rhymes about him when putting their children to bed . . . 'Now my child sleeps they keep the nasty Phuchka away', etc. Do any of you remember the incident of the slum near Dholaikhal being razed? A criminal group had taken control of the slum after night-long mayhem, killing and maiming people, setting homes on fire, humiliating the women, tossing old people into the pond; and the next day, the Home Office minister had suspended the officer in charge at the police station, patted the head of a girl from the slum in sympathy and left. And what happened after that, sir? How could anything happen when Phuchka Hasan was there? Ponir was the bodyguard for the very same Hasan, flexing his monkey-wrench-like arm and his infinite courage. Tell me, was he meant to be a boy scout or a goon?

The second favour that Phuchka Hasan has done us (Ponir, Ponir's mother, Phuli, Duli and your worthless storyteller) is this: he made arrangements for Phuli's marriage, and gave Duli a job in his garment factory. Had the story not ended abruptly, he might have arranged for Duli's marriage too, relieving us of our burden. But that has not been possible. Which is a cause for some regret for us. Still, a story is not life, for whose natural end you have to wait sixty-seven or so years. Don't you agree?

Phuli got married to Lattu the contractor. He had washed up on Bong-shal's shores while his family was still marooned in a remote village, deep in the interiors of Damudya. The period before Lattu's emergence here was shrouded in darkness – he became visible only after he had surfaced. Until very recently he had travelled on buses, but now he rode a motorbike. He could have bought a car, but the street he lived on was too narrow to accommodate one. Most of his work was at the city council, though he got a lot of projects from the districts too. He was a favourite of Phuchka Hasan's, though not a terrorist.

Surprising all of us, Lattu and Phuli turned out to be a happy, love-struck couple. On some evenings Lattu took Phuli to Crescent Lake on his Honda. Despite being a contractor, he was a romantic at heart. With some education he could have worked in the field of arts and culture – or joined a poetry recitation group, at the very least. If you saw him sitting at the edge of the lake by the red light of the setting sun, draping one arm around Phuli's shoulder and shelling peanuts with the other hand to feed her, you would find it difficult to think of him as anything but a dashing hero in a film.

8

Two aspects of Ponir's life could not be reconciled with the simple equation of being a gangster. One was Nantu Mian, Phuchka Hasan's friend, although they had nothing in common, the way friends do. Ponir had lost his father when young. His mother had not played the traditional role of a mother – he had received none of the love and indulgence that normal parents give their children. Whatever he had got was from Nantu Mian, whom he considered a father figure. Nantu Mian knew this too. You could say he thought of Ponir as his son.

Sometimes Nantu Mian would say to Ponir, quite despondently, 'You're not the person I thought you were, Ponir-mian.'

A conundrum. What had he imagined? How had Ponir turned out? 'What did you think, chacha?' asked Ponir. 'What sort of person was I supposed to be?'

Nantu Mian looked at the floor and sighed. 'Don't get into so much trouble. Why must you get involved? Do you really need to be part of what Hasan Mian is doing?'

Nantu Mian was a reticent man. So he was unable to speak his mind clearly – to say that Ponir should distance himself from Hasan, stop terrorizing people and be a good man. Not that everyone in the world can speak their mind. And this leads to so much trouble.

But Nantu Mian couldn't possibly tell Ponir in as many words to abandon Hasan, who was his friend. Still, he had dropped all kinds of hints. He usually made his case through a question. For instance: 'Why do you create trouble in the neighbourhood?', 'Why did you beat up that young man?', 'Why did you have to ransack Aftab Mian's shop?' But Ponir had not realized from this interrogative conversation how disappointed and pained Nantu Mian was, deep down. Never mind Ponir, Nantu Mian couldn't even talk to his own children clearly, although he had never thought of Ponir as anything but his own son.

Ponir was wracked by doubt. He felt miserable too. But what was he to do? And besides, there was the thrill of it all. He couldn't give it up. There was money, his mother was recovering; she ate well and dressed well now, every evening she watched TV on the set that Ponir had bought her (black and white, yes, but so what?) – even if none of this mattered, how could he ignore the excitement? Aftab Mian's screams while Ponir ransacked his shop had brought that delight back.

After all, hadn't Aftab Mian given an inhuman thrashing to Ponir's friend Delwar's younger brother that very morning? Revenge was sweet. And electrifying.

Still, what Nantu Mian said shook Ponir. He suddenly began to think of Nantu as a venerable person – like Cicero, A. Monty, or Lutfar Rahman or Ramendu Sundar Tribedi. Ponir didn't really know who they, these famous people, were. He had come to know them in the form and the spelling with which Principal Azadur Rahman (Ponir had no idea who he was, or what institution he was principal of) had presented them. And he had been captivated by them. What could Nantu Mian's memorable saying be? Ponir pondered. He couldn't come up with anything instantly, but was convinced that Nantu Mian had been born to become venerable. After much thought he recollected two of his sayings. Not that they were of inferior quality. But the language was colloquial. This didn't matter to Ponir, even if Principal Azadur Rahman might have a problem. The quotes were:

1. Unclean people cannot appear before god. (This was what he told the grease monkeys covered in soot and grime as they left at the end of the day.)

2. The dog has no work but it always runs. (He said this often, for he did not approve of anyone rushing about without reason.)

Later, Ponir discovered a third saying of Nantu Mian's, the reference to guns and bullets in it deflating him to some extent – and deflating us too at the thought of the intrinsic irony of the statement:

3. Guns don't kill people, people do. If not with a gun, with a stick. If not with a stick, with a brick. If not with a brick, with bare hands, blows and punches. (And yet our Hasan walks in the air because he owns a gun, his feet never touching the ground.)

As a matter of fact, there was a silent war between Hasan and Nantu. Nantu wanted to bring Hasan back to an honest life, telling him, 'You're my friend, Hasan. Change yourself.'

Hasan would laugh at first. Then he would be annoyed. And, even later, enraged. Ultimately he would become furious whenever Nantu said anything. He had even vented his anger in public. Smashing Nantu Mian's glass-topped table, he had said, 'Save your grease for your own machines, Nantu Mian. Don't try to reform me. I advise MP-sir. Even Minister-sir heeds my suggestions. And you dare tell me all this nonsense?'

Hasan's public display of wrath has helped us greatly, for the story can now advance quickly towards its (targeted) culmination.

No matter how many names of MPs and ministers Hasan might drop, he was still nothing but a ward commissioner, on good terms with the officers at the local police station. Why would senior police officers even give him the time of day?

Hasan brought his Toyota Sprinter to Nantu Mian's garage. He was having problems with the ignition. He had driven it to the workshop himself. 'Have it repaired,' he told Nantu Mian. 'The driver will pick it up in the evening.'

He took a rickshaw home for lunch. Just as he sat down to his meal after a bath, the police arrived and arrested him. Phuchka Hasan couldn't believe his eyes. 'You dare arrest me? Me?' There was an uproar. 'Are you out of your mind, man? You've come here to arrest me?' he challenged the inspector. The inspector said, 'Not mad, my brother, but wise. You're under arrest now. I have orders.'

'Whose orders? What the fuck!' Hasan roared. The people upstairs, the inspector indicated, pointing to the sky. Then he added, 'There were arms in your car. Weapons.'

Hasan realized there was a problem, a conspiracy of some kind. An enemy manoeuvre. It was all so complicated. He also knew that possession of arms was a harsh charge – he could be jailed for up to fourteen years. In other words, someone was playing a game with him.

Hasan calmed down. Quietly, he asked, 'There were arms in my car?'

'You're behaving as though the sky has fallen on your head,' said the inspector. 'Come now, it's time to go to the police station.'

Phuchka Hasan returned home the next day after getting bail.

Exhausted, a wreck. About 100,000 taka had been spent. He felt tense and angry. Hasan fell back on the sofa and shut his eyes.

He opened them after a while. They were red. Blazing like flames. The inspector had told Hasan that Nantu Mian had opened the car door and shown them the weapon. A Pakistan-made pistol had been found under the seat. And fresh bullets in the air-conditioning pipe.

Hasan knew that as far as he was concerned there shouldn't have been a pistol and bullets in his car. He was never so careless. He wasn't naive. Fresh bullets in the air-conditioning pipe? Hasan chuckled. But who had framed him? Several names occurred to him. MP Sahib had told him, 'Find out who did this, Hasan. I don't like the way things are going.' The MP was worried too. Losing Hasan meant one of his pillars was crumbling. The elections were coming. Hasan visited Nantu. Nantu said, 'Yes, I showed the police where the arms were. But don't you see the positive side, Hasan? This is a lesson for you. It's time you gave up using weapons. Reform yourself.'

Hasan uttered a loud expletive. Then he asked with a wink, as though he were posing an amusing question, 'Did you plant the weapons in the car, Nantu Mian?'

Nantu was astounded. He thought Hasan was being terrifyingly funny. So terrifying that his hair stood on end. Winking back – as though he had got the frightening joke – he said, 'Who else could it have been? The car keys were not with you.'

Nantu Mian chuckled. Still chuckling, he said, 'Stop using arms, Hasan. Give up your ward commissioner's job. Come, you and I will open a phuchka shop again.'

Nantu laughed at the top of his voice. The garage boys had never seen him laugh this way. They looked at him in amazement. One of them was Ponir Ali. He noticed that Hasan's winking eyes were bloodshot. There was no laughter in them, only rage.

9

Anyway, Hasan finished Nantu off one day. His suspicions had deepened. The officer in charge at the police station had told him plainly, 'Nantu

Mian has framed you, Commissioner Sahib. And he's supposed to be your friend. Some friend!'

The inspector had sworn with all seriousness that this was true. He didn't want Hasan to suspect that it was he who had framed him. He knew that Hasan had powerful patrons; senior political leaders had visited the police station to plead for him. He did not want to be transferred out of here just yet. He would have to keep Hasan happy.

Ponir soon found out that it was his mentor who had eliminated his father figure. He could not fathom what Nantu Mian's crime was. Nantu had sought nothing but Hasan's well-being. Then why did such things have to happen? He simply couldn't reconcile them.

10

For three nights Ponir couldn't sleep. He dreamt of Nantu Mian's bloodied face. The bullet had passed through his forehead. Phuchka Hasan had fired at close range. Ponir could tell. Although he had said he knew nothing when the police questioned him. He wasn't anywhere near the garage at the time. He was at Phuli's home till eleven; the murder had taken place around eight-thirty or nine. Lattu the contractor had backed Ponir's statement. Lattu would bribe the officers at the police station all the time. What choice did the inspector have but to believe him?

On all three nights Ponir had dreamt that Nantu was passing on some memorable sayings. Was it Cicero, or was it Churchill? Startled into wakefulness, he had discovered that his arm had turned stiff. As though it were a monkey wrench, which would leave nothing undamaged once Hasan's neck came within its reach.

Eventually, he did receive a message, at an hour between sleep and wakefulness. We did not hear it, only Ponir did. Or he thought he did. As a result he wandered around in a frenzy all day. All the way to Sawarighat, where he took a boat out into the river in the hope of some peace. He didn't find any.

II

Evening fell. Another day done with, Ponir told himself. But he was wrong. On his way home in the darkness he kept seeing Nantu Mian's terrified face with the bullet wound. It was smeared on the wall of every building. He could again hear Nantu Mian's memorable saying. He entered his home as though he had seen a ghost. Duli and his mother were watching television. A TV series. Their concentration was sky-high.

Ponir went into his own room. He had one of his own now. His mother and Duli lived in another one. The room in which they were watching TV was actually Phuli's. Lattu stayed there too from time to time.

Ponir quietly pulled out the kerosene tin. It was kept beneath the bed these days. He had put a five-star pistol wrapped in polythene into the tin a few days back. He needed the pistol tonight. He had taken a decision.

He was a man possessed. He wouldn't be swayed. He inserted his possessed hand into the tin. For the pistol.

A polythene bag emerged. Very well, it was tonight, then. Feeling heady, he held the bag open beneath the light. Only to be startled. What five-star pistol? This was his book, *Memorable Sayings of Venerable People*. Why was it here? He tried to fling it away but couldn't, just as he hadn't been able to last time. Principal Azadur Rahman had to be considered a lucky man. Twice Ponir had tried to throw the book away without success. We have never heard of this happening to any other book.

Ponir removed the polythene cover carefully. The ageing volume, received as a prize at school in another lifetime, emerged in the dim light of the bulb. He had forgotten those old days when he had put the book in the tin. The pages looked torn and crumpled by the heat.

But the silky feel had not disappeared. Nor had the smell. And there it was, the first page. With the handwritten inscription, 'For Md Ponir Ali, a reward for punctuality.' His eyes stopped at this page, which was like magical moonlight, like Halima's eyes. (Oh, we forgot to tell you. A girl named Halima had stolen Ponir's heart. She worked with Duli at the garment factory and lived at Juginagar. Ponir would visit her every night on his way back from the garage, but would leave her after a brief conversation. He was supposed to have visited her tonight as well.) The page was as beautiful as the white lilies that grew next to the fence around the house where Halima lived.

Ponir turned the book over in his hands, gazing at the inscription twice, thrice, countless times. Then he leafed through the pages, feeling the nearly stilled heart of the book with his fingertips.

Muttering some of the quotes from *Memorable Sayings of Venerable People* to himself, Ponir felt as though his senses were being assaulted by a sudden shower of rain from the other side of the darkness on this Srabon night. How tragic that these sayings had remained unuttered all this while! He hadn't read out even one of his favourite quotes to Halima.

Duli was calling him to dinner. The door was locked. Bangladesh Television was playing its news theme, 'We Shall Not Forget You'. It was 10 p.m. 'Coming,' said Ponir, and picked up the book. He was supposed to have been somewhere at nine! An hour had passed in an instant. *Memorable Sayings of Venerable People* had claimed him completely; he was overcome by the moments when he used to set off to conquer the world in his school uniform, oil-slicked hair and squeaking trainers. He realized that he had tears in his eyes.

Ponir went out of the room with the rustling packet holding *Memorable Sayings of Venerable People* in one hand and the pistol wrapped in polythene in the other. Stopping briefly at the kitchen door to tell his mother, 'I'll be back soon, ma,' he left without giving her the time to respond. Then he strode out to the main road.

On Bongshal Main Road, Ponir found the open manhole gaping at the moon. And the poor moon was trying its best to cover the sludge and shit overflowing from it with a tender glow.

Ponir paused for a moment at the manhole. Then he flung one of the polythene packets into the thick mass of waste. It sank at once.

He would now head towards his destination with the other packet.

AMAR MITRA

The Old Man of Kusumpur

Fakirchand of Kusumpur set out on his way to meet the Big Man. A bundle of meagre belongings hung on his back from one end of a cane stick that rested on his shoulder. Old Fakirchand walked with a slight stoop.

It was moments before sunrise, and the March morning was soft and cool with a genial air and the earth still pleasant to walk on. The cocks were still crowing. Swarms of little children were already out in the open. Old Fakirchand walked slowly, as though measuring each step, and raised both hands to his forehead in obeisance to the rising sun. Yes, his eyes felt better and so did his body. He touched his rheumy eyes with his cold hands in the brisk morning air.

Fakirchand was about three-times-twenty, but already the world appeared hazy to him, his limbs trembled, his skin hung loose and innumerable wrinkles criss-crossed his face. At this age, the ripe old man felt the desire to meet the Big Man of Khanyadihi, situated on the bank of the River Subarnarekha, some twenty miles away, beyond the forest of Durgadih.

He had been passing through a state of mental turmoil of late. He decided to go and see the Big Man, whom he had never met before, because his sorrows were not one but many. His eyes, for instance. Fakirchand knew the Big Man would refer him to a village doctor, a wizard, the very sight of whom would heal his eyes. What good was it to remove a cataract, he reflected – clear it once and it comes back again. But the Big Man had many medicines, he knew of many wild herbs. Oh, it was ages since he had last seen the good earth with clear, transparent vision.

His son, too, caused him much pain. The fellow had eloped with a village girl to distant Chakulia, where he had managed to get himself a job of sorts. But life at this age, without a son, was not worth living. What point was there in having given the boy life if, at this fragile age, he was to be left to fend for himself? old Fakirchand brooded as he walked along. He knew the Big Man would have an answer. He expected him to find a way to bring his son hurrying back, abandoning the woman he loved.

And about his plot of land, the Big Man's advice, he knew, would be vital. Fakirchand was a loner. His wife was long dead. The task of keeping possession of his land was driving him to his wits' end. His opponents did as they pleased; they carried away every sheaf of unhusked rice that stood on his field. Just one word from the Big Man and Fakirchand would know how to treat the rascals.

And even though his wife was dead and gone, Fakirchand's sixty-year-old blood still ran warm in his veins. If only the Big Man named a suitable girl! Even now the old man's eyes lit up, his mouth watered, and passion swelled within him at the sight of an attractive woman.

And so Fakirchand had prepared himself for a meeting with the Big Man of Khanyadihi. He had dreamt of his own death the night before. The villagers, a bumptious lot, were hovering like a bunch of vultures, waiting for him to die. They would swoop on him the moment he drew his last breath, tearing at his possessions. But Fakirchand would not let that happen. He would meet the Big Man and tell him all.

Fakirchand had been hearing of the Big Man ever since he had moved to Kusumpur fifteen years ago from beyond Parihati. It was only after he came here that he found himself a home and a patch of land. The village was rife with tales of the Big Man's great deeds. All things moved, it was said, according to his wishes, everything changed according to his dictates. Fakirchand had never cared for the Big Man before, but now he did. He felt restless.

One could never tell how the mind would behave when the body grew old and infirm.

Fakirchand's wife had gone to heaven, and his son had run away with a girl, leaving him alone to guard his own little kingdom – a thatched hut and a piece of land – like the Yaksha of the legends. Many in the village wished him dead, but he was not a person to give in easily. If only his eyes were healed, he would once more live it up with the warmth of his blood, he mused as he walked.

Leaving the dusty bushes and the dry ponds of Kusumpur behind, Fakirchand found himself in a gently undulating, open, barren field of saffron gravel. The sky soared infinitely above, the moor stretched unhindered to the horizon, and the light poured down from the heavens in a warm, incessant stream. The old man made his way in this thick light, charting his course to a distant destination that lay beyond the moor, beyond the villages and beyond the forests.

Fakirchand's mind grew dim. He remembered with difficulty the days when he had first come to this region. It seemed a long, long time ago. It was when an awe-inspiring flying machine of war had broken apart in the sky and come crashing down on the plains of Nishchinta. Fakirchand now heard a drone, like from one of those machines of yore, approaching from afar. He turned his head and looked heavenwards into a brilliant and dazzling sky. A helicopter, hanging from its revolving blades, flew by towards the air base of Kalaikunda.

The sun changed colour, the light thinned into a brassy glare.

Fakirchand crossed the field. The day was still cool, but the sky seemed to have receded, as he approached a narrow dirt track winding through a wilderness of tall grass and thorny shrubs.

He crossed this too, and stood before a canal in which waist-deep water still flowed. With summer advancing, it would be reduced to a mere trickle, but after the rains it would again swell to a height more than that of a man and a half.

There used to be a bridge across the canal. But it had disappeared. Fakirchand looked left and right, but found no trace of it. Had he come the wrong way? No, not quite, he thought. The old banyan tree stood as before next to the Baburbani canal. The tree was there, but the bridge was gone, without a trace.

Fakirchand studied the water with his foggy eyes and sensed a sharp current underneath. He stood helpless on the banks of the canal, which was the only source of water in a sprawling, drought-prone place. He knew there were layers of silt beneath the water and a treacherous current. He remembered old Nakphuri, who died of drowning while fishing in the canal one monsoon month and was washed five miles away to Kadamdihi.

It was a hopeless case, thought Fakirchand, surveying the surroundings. His body was too infirm, his eyes too weak to brave a crossing. Memories of Nakphuri came back repeatedly like horrifying and cautioning visions, making him sink into a stupor. And as he stood transfixed, not knowing what to do next, the day grew brighter as the sun rose higher in the sky. It was just then that the notes of a flute wafted into his ears, bringing him back to his senses. He scanned the surroundings for the musician who was playing so sweetly, and, before much time had passed, a dark-skinned man with a flute appeared like an apparition from the void. Fakirchand had found another human being at long last.

'Where are you going, old man?' the dark-skinned man asked, lowering the flute from his lips.

'To meet the Big Man,' Fakirchand said, taking a step forward.

'The Big Man? Who on earth is he?'

It was Fakirchand's turn to be surprised, and he let out a taunting laugh at the young man's ignorance. How was he to describe the Big Man – it was as impossible as divulging the secrets of the bird and the bee. So he broke into a song, hoping that the dark-skinned man would understand the allegory:

> Who spreads the smell when the flowers bloom?
> Who brings rain borne by the clouds?
> The flowers blossom and he makes the scent flow.
> The clouds gather and he makes the rain fall.

The dark-skinned man listened in wonder while Fakirchand told him many, many things about the Big Man.

'Are you telling the truth?'

'Yes, I have no reason to lie. You don't know of my sorrows. My son has deserted me; my wife is dead. I have no one at home. My eyes don't see well. But I know the Big Man will set everything right.'

'Oh! Then he must be as powerful as god!' exclaimed the dark-skinned man, whose skin was as lustrous as the first clouds of the monsoon.

'Yes, very much,' Fakirchand agreed.

'Then proceed,' said the dark-skinned man, and turned to take his leave. But Fakirchand held him by the arm.

'How will I cross the canal?' Fakirchand asked.

'How do I know?' The dark-skinned man tried to free himself.

'Carry me across,' Fakirchand pleaded in a tremulous voice.

'What will you give me in return?'

Fakirchand promised everything. He would tell the Big Man about him so that the dark-skinned man was left without sorrows. 'I'll ask the Big Man to make you happy.'

'Really?'

'Yes, of course, I am not mentioning the Big Man for nothing.'

With a quick, effortless jerk, the dark-skinned man lifted Fakirchand on to his shoulder and went down into the canal. As he waded through the waist-deep water, the dark-skinned man told Fakirchand, in fragments, the tales of his woe.

His name was Chhotosona Mandi, and his life seemed as barren as the fields of March. He was deeply in love, with the daughter of one Bankim Hansda, and the girl loved him too. But it meant nothing. Hansda would never give him his daughter's hand.

Fakirchand's body quivered with pleasure at the thought of marriage. 'But why wouldn't he let his daughter marry you?'

'Because I have no house, no land.'

'Ah, the greedy swine,' thought Fakirchand with laughter building up inside him as Chhotosona Mandi stepped out of the water on to the canal's other bank.

'I've helped you cross, so be sure to tell the Big Man about me,' said Chhotosona Mandi. 'Tell him that a youth as fresh as the clouds loves a woman of Asanbani whose name is Bishnupriya.'

If only the Big Man brought them together, his sorrows would be over. He wished he could go along with Fakirchand, but his hands were tied, for he had to go and work as a labourer. But he would be at the same spot the next day, waiting for Fakirchand's return. He would help him across the canal again and would expect to hear the good news.

With these words Chhotosona Mandi let himself go into the bright sunlight and blew into the flute again, the strains of which were carried far by the wind as he disappeared out of sight on the other side of the canal.

Chhotosona Mandi's affair was indeed a sad one, thought Fakirchand as he resumed his journey, and resolved to tell the Big Man everything.

The old man made slow headway along the dry, saffron dirt track, on one side of which was a low-lying field, with a small thickly wooded hillock on the other. The day was warm. It was the last day of March. The wind was laden with the smell of sal, mahua and myriad flowers.

Twenty years ago, he was strong as a buffalo. Some of that strength must have still lingered; how could he have travelled so far on such a hot day otherwise? With a limp body and clouded eyes he trudged doggedly on.

Gradually, the day grew white with heat. Unfiltered sunlight struck his dark, glistening body and broke up into flares as though from sparklers. He felt his throat drying up, his face felt hard and baked, his mouth tasted bitter and his body burnt like desert sand.

The old man's eyes became dimmer still, and flights of hallucination crossed his fading vision. He was in the midst of a wood and ravines. His progress slowed down. He gasped for breath. With his tongue he sought more air and wetted his dry, parched lips. He knew it was still a long way to the Big Man's house and felt intimidated.

Then a strange thing happened. Old Fakirchand heard people singing. He wondered, who were this joyous lot who sang when the sky rained fire? He followed the sound and the forest soon thinned, revealing a clearing. Men and women, tribal Santhals all of them, were gathered there, singing without a care in the world despite the oppressive heat. Silently, Fakirchand drew closer, his head dizzy and darkness enveloping his eyes.

'What's happening here?' he asked, running out of breath.

The Santhals looked at him curiously.

'Where does it come from?' asked one man.

'Would you like some rice cake?' asked another.

Fakirchand felt as though his skull would crack because of the heat. He sat down in the shade of a young neem tree.

'We are doing our religious rituals,' he heard someone say.

'Give me some water to drink before I die,' mumbled Fakirchand, loud enough to be heard.

Some of those who were standing around him called for water, and others brought it in a shining pail.

Fakirchand first applied some to his scalp before drinking to his heart's satisfaction. His sight came back to him and he took a long, deep breath.

'Why are your rituals being conducted here?' Fakirchand asked.

Someone said something but he was too sated to be coherent. The women started singing again.

Fakirchand screwed up his eyes to have a look. Someone ordered the singing to stop.

'An outsider is here among us,' the voice said. 'We must speak to him. No singing now, please.'

'Where are you going?' asked a veteran Santhal, too drunk to stop swaying.

'Khanyadihi.'

'Where do you come from?'

'Kusumpur.'

'Kusumpur to Khanyadihi – that's a long way to go! But why are you going there anyway?' the Santhals seemed eager to know.

Fakirchand felt more at ease now. He ran his eyes over the faces that crowded around. All the eyes that stared at him were bloodshot.

'I am going to meet the Big Man.'

'Who is he, is he the forester or a forest ranger?'

'Rubbish,' retorted Fakirchand, surprised at their ignorance. So he told them all that he knew about the Big Man and his greatness.

'We don't need any Big Man here, we are happy without him,' said one.

'Shut up!' another one cut him short.

'We have our sorrows,' he continued, 'our sorrows pile up to the skies.'

Old Fakirchand batted his eyelids and cast sly glances at the shapely young women. 'Tell me of your sorrows and they will end,' he said absent-mindedly.

'Yes, we'll speak. Would you care for a drink?' asked one of the Santhals, nudging him.

'How can I? I am going to see the Big Man.'

'Then listen. Bad times have overtaken us. This festival can no longer be observed lavishly. We don't get good sal trees any more. The forester sends them all to Kharagpur. We can no longer sacrifice boars at our ceremonies and my daughter will, in all likelihood, run away with an outsider. We don't get timber, we don't get game to hunt. The Marang Buru is not happy with us. If we drink, the police go after us and pack us off to Jhargram.'

The man hid his face between his knees and cried. Those who stood around him cried too.

'Look, old man, you are like a god to us. Don't go away without accepting our offerings. If you don't like our liquor, have our rice; if you don't like our rice, drink our water,' they pleaded.

They forced Fakirchand to have the rice. But he had no taste for it. He felt like throwing up, but it was good that his belly was full. He stood up, ready to depart. The Santhals followed him. 'Tell the Big Man about us; tell him to give us back our good days,' they said as they saw him off.

'Be here tomorrow. I will have news for you on my way back,' Fakirchand assured them.

The old man set out again. He had not gone much further when he squeaked with suppressed laughter, but fell pensive again. He was moved by the sadness all around. 'I must carry these words of sadness to the Big Man,' he said to himself. The sun had dipped already. A deep booming sound reverberated through the somnolent wilderness. Were the clouds bursting? No, bombs were going off in Kalaikunda. A mock battle was on, ripping apart the silence.

The sun was going down rapidly when Fakirchand neared the forest of Durgadih. He still had this forest to cross, and two villages and a field beyond, before he could reach the banks of the Subarnarekha on which Khanyadihi was situated. The Big Man lived there – tall, fair and in the pink of health. He must have greyed by now; Fakirchand tried to form an image in his head. He had not seen the Big Man ever; whatever he knew was all based on hearsay.

He recounted the things he must say to the Big Man – about Chhotosona Mandi, about the Santhals and about himself. There was no point in surviving like the Yaksha – either he must have a wife or his son must come back, Fakirchand mused as he walked, without realizing that the sky had disappeared behind the thick foliage overhead.

He was deep inside a forest. Beams of sunlight pierced through the cover of leaves here and there amid vast pools of darkness. These forests had contained so much to fear in the days gone by; now they were different. Yet there were mysteries galore. The god Baram still made his rounds of the forests silently, invisibly, riding on his favourite animals. Beneath the towering sal trees lay heaps of horses and elephants made of burnt clay; somewhere in the forest's elusive depths one could still run into the seat of the demon goddess Rankini.

The old man walked along the eerie path and found himself in trouble again. Three distinct tracks branched off in different directions and Fakirchand did not know which one to take. He was faced with yet another confounding predicament. Again, he stopped and looked left and right as he often did when helpless, not knowing what to do next. And then he noticed something move at the foot of a sal tree. A man, was it? he wondered.

'Who is it that comes this way?' Fakirchand called out, feeling nervous.

The figure waved back at him, beckoning him near; he distinctly saw it with his hazy eyes. His heart began to pound in fear. 'A ghost, a genie, moving like a man?' Fakirchand asked himself. But there was nothing he could do. He was lost in the forest and had to seek help.

He moved closer and what he saw made his hair stand on end. Yes, it was a man indeed, who spoke in whispers. He looked hideous, his body decomposing in places from leprosy. His face appeared moist and bulbous and he lay limp on the forest floor.

'Which village do you belong to?' Fakirchand asked as he threw a coin towards the ill-fated man.

The man did not care to touch it. Other coins lay where they had fallen. Forsaken by society, of what use was money to him? Fakirchand stood transfixed and quiet.

'Death has had me,' moaned the man. 'Where are you going, to which village?'

'Khanyadihi, to meet the Big Man.'

The man sat up, but said nothing.

'How long has it been?' asked Fakirchand.

'It will be five years this May.'

Fakirchand felt uneasy standing near him. He could not bear the sight of that horrid, disintegrating face.

'Which way is Khanyadihi?' he asked the leper.

The man did not answer. 'If you saw the Big Man he would surely prescribe good medicines,' Fakirchand said again.

'Who is he?' asked the leper, this time his voice echoing in the forest.

A chill ran down Fakirchand's spine. He told him slowly, haltingly, all that he knew about the people of Khanyadihi. The leper listened with distended eyes and stretched forward to feel the old man, but Fakirchand stepped back, avoiding his touch.

'I'll tell you the road to Khanyadihi, but promise me you will tell the Big Man about my misfortune. If I am cured, I would like to roam the village streets again,' the leper said, his voice becoming increasingly hoarse.

He showed Fakirchand the way and the old man promised the leper to return with the medicine the very next day.

'If only the Big Man touched you once, your body would be healed,' he repeated.

Fakirchand resumed his march with haste. His heart was heavy. A fine youth wrecked by a terrible disease; the thought kept turning in his mind. He will tell the Big Man about him too. Had they not helped him, Fakirchand would never have found the way to Khanyadihi, where the Big Man lived. He was sure that the Big Man would provide succour to them all.

The sun slanted towards the river in the west. The old man walked listlessly on, and then suddenly, not far away, he saw the sandbanks of the Subarnarekha spreading like an endless white band across the earth. Khanyadihi must be there, the Big Man's house must be there! The exclamations exploded involuntarily in his head.

He walked even faster now. Oh, what immense suffering people endure, he thought as he walked. But without suffering who would know what happiness is? It was only in search of happiness that he had travelled this distance.

The evening grew sullen. Fakirchand ran out of breath with excitement. With his lean body, sagging skin and weak eyesight he had endured much strain. He felt awfully tired. His body seemed to bend and break. If only he could rest awhile. And if only his wife were with him and his son by his side, his pain would have half disappeared. He would once more sit back and stare at the world with ethereal pleasure. He would have his cataract removed, and if it reappeared he would go to Khanyadihi with his son. His son would carry him on his shoulder, or would arrange a litter for him if possible. The Big Man of Khanyadihi would then heal his eyes and make the world appear sharp and clear. But that was not to be. So, in the twilight of his life, he had gone to meet the Big Man all by himself, risking body and soul in an arduous trek on a terrible day in March.

He walked with a tremulous heart. Shadows stretched far and long. The sun went down in a pool of blackish red. Old Fakirchand felt melancholy, remembering his ruined family as the day neared its end.

At last he reached the banks of the Subarnarekha. But was this Khanya-dihi? Was this the place where the Big Man lived? The sullen wind had no answer; it only blew past him, hissing.

The river had swallowed up much of the village. A few structures stood scattered, reminiscent of a hearth. Babla trees crowded the place and wild bushes grew in abundance – not a soul was in sight. The old man strained his eyes with the hope of spotting a human figure, for this must be the Big Man's village. No village could exist beyond this; the river had taken a fearsome bend.

Fatigue and hopelessness began to overcome him. His body felt limp and bloodless. Perhaps this was not Khanyadihi at all, he thought; maybe he had taken the wrong road. Maybe it was somewhere else, somewhere nearby.

The dark spread itself gradually. The wind from across the river blew hard into the old man's face as he felt the darkness thicken around him. Still he looked for people, and finally he did chance to spot someone coming towards him with a lantern. Fakirchand pumped all his strength into his lungs and called out at the passing man, asking him to stop.

'In which village does the Big Man live?' Fakirchand asked.

'The Big Man?' The stranger stood askance in the dark.

With a quivering voice, Fakirchand told the man about the munificence of the Big Man, one who gave shelter to the tired, spoke unceasingly of life, solved insurmountable problems with inconceivable ease, the one to whom people went to seek succour for all suffering.

The stranger broke into harsh, metallic laughter.

'You dream of such a man on earth, old fellow? Such men don't live any more.' He shook his head and went his way, leaving Fakirchand standing alone.

A pale moon rose like an ochre egg. There was nobody in the vast expanse that lay between the moon and Fakirchand, not even the Big Man; only the sand dunes and the river seemed familiar. All else seemed shrouded in mystery. The old man's mind began to fail, everything seemed to go wrong. 'You didn't wait for me, Big Man. They say people like you don't exist any more. How will my suffering or Chhotosona's or the leper's or the Santhals' ever end if you are not there?' Fakirchand muttered to himself.

He walked down to the dunes where the grains of sand glittered in the faint moonlight. Standing on a sea of sand beneath a benevolent sky, Fakirchand cried out in frustration and anguish, 'How can I stand on guard eternally like the old Yaksha, how will I live with my clouded eyes, Big Man?'

The river was there, but the man was gone. He had departed silently, leaving behind all sorrows and sufferings; and yet faith persisted in the old man's mind.

'If you had to go away, why didn't you carry all human miseries with you?' The old man spoke to the river in whispers. He perked up his ears and listened to something – the sound of feet wading through water. 'Who goes there, is that Big Man?'

Fakirchand tried to dash towards the sound, but fell spreadeagled on the sand. He lay on the dunes like the sky lies on the earth, and all stirrings sank into a cosmic silence, broken much later by a flying machine, flashing its red and green light in the elemental darkness.

The following day the others kept vigil where Fakirchand had asked them to await him, in the forest and by the canal. But the old man did not return that day as he had promised. He did not come the next day either, or on the day that followed.

But one day he would, they mused.

(Translated by Anish Gupta)

SHAHIDUL ZAHIR

Why there Are No Noyontara Flowers in Agargaon Colony

Abdus Sattar was returning home; some people observed him after he got off the bus at Taltala and made his way towards his residence in the colony in the soft glow of evening, although this daily event, a thin, dark-skinned, middle-aged clerk returning home from the office, was nothing worth looking at. When he reached the road inside the colony – perhaps because it was the rainy season, or because of some unseasonal rain – the countless potholes in the run-down, brick-lined road were full of water, and where there wasn't any water the road was slippery and the treacherous mud made him hold his back high and crooked. Abdus Sattar hopped like an egret and traversed the road with the bottoms of his trousers rolled up to just under his knees, and when he reached the front of his building he stumbled on one such slippery patch and fell down; he then spread his hands behind him and sat down in the wet mud. Those who witnessed this scene burst out laughing, and then hurried towards him and lifted him up from the mud; contemplating the incident as he sat there, Abdus Sattar's own lips too quivered a bit and he said, 'I fell down,' and thus, after a long time, solely on account of having slipped and fallen down, he got the opportunity to exchange words with his neighbours. When he returned home he could only say the same thing to his wife, Shireen Banu, 'I fell down in the muddy slime,' and then, like he did every day, he went and sat on the balcony in the grey light of dusk. Sinking into the cane chair, he used to sit until night while his wife helped his two sons and daughter with their studies, after which they made a ruckus and then went to the flat next door and watched television; and all the while Abdus Sattar blended into the darkness on the balcony. He observed how dense and almost tactile the darkness became after the light of day was effaced; he just kept gazing, but that didn't make him happy or tired, just as he never experienced any feeling of tiredness in his clerical government job.

Sometimes as he sat like this, when the southerly breeze wafted in and the green potted plants arrayed by his wife on the narrow balcony of their flat swayed and their leaves made a fluttering sound, the air was suffused with the faint, petrichor-like fragrance of the noyontara flower that had been born from the soil in a pot fastened with a string to the railing. Abdus Sattar used to sit on the cane chair amid that flutter and fragrance, as if from time immemorial, and his wife Shireen Banu filled their flat with a variety of potted plants; besides the noyontara and patabahars, she had also planted rajnigandha seedlings on the balcony. Abdus Sattar may or may not have observed all this, he didn't say anything about it; whether or not he was mindful of the green world of foliage that had grown inside his residence remained unexpressed until the day he died.

Under Shireen Banu's indulgent tending, the trailing patabahar plants spread to every doorway of their flat; green, snake-like vines of money plants hung down from the cupboard, bookshelf and mosquito-net posts. When Abdus Sattar went to sleep after dinner, a long, clustering plant placed beside the dressing table by the head of his cot swayed as it respired; Abdus Sattar didn't notice that, he remained asleep; but his neighbours did notice, they praised Shireen Banu endlessly, and the womenfolk of the colony were beside themselves with excitement on seeing the sylvan assemblage inside the flat.

Following the arrival of Abdus Sattar and his family in this colony four years ago, his wife had brought about the consummation of the artistic practice of growing plants in pots, and these plants spread from their flat to those of their neighbours. All the residents of this building in the colony – i.e. the wives of the clerks, inspectors and junior officers in various government offices – began competing with each other to fill up the space inside their flats with plants. And thus, the balance in the relationship between nature and man that had, according to knowledgeable people, apparently been ruptured in the modern age, seemed to have been restored in this building. For that matter, the estrangement that occurred every day in the relationship between the residents of this building in the colony and people at large also seemed to have been repaired somehow by the green foliage of various shrub-like plants. All these young ladies and their menfolk in the colony finally learnt to discover the beauty of life; they found arboreal significance in their meaningless and isolated lifestyles, and all of them were grateful to Abdus Sattar's wife, Shireen Banu, for this. Only Abdus Sattar remained outside this circle; nothing struck him when he gazed at the lovely cactus inside the flat, and when something did suddenly come to mind, he then felt that this plant was graceful, incomparable and entirely thorny. Green creepers descended from every balcony of the building in which Abdus Sattar lived, and a reddish-purple-coloured pattern was formed on the front side of the yellow-coloured building by the noyontaras planted along the balcony railings.

When sunlight turned pale in the late afternoon, butterflies abandoned the shrubs at the aerodrome near Agargaon and began fluttering in front of the building, and the arrival of the butterflies and their hovering and fluttering continued for many days. The first day the butterflies arrived, the people in the colony were afraid that perhaps they would remain in their flats and lay eggs and build a kingdom of golden caterpillars among their verdant dreams. But their fear was at once eliminated; the butterflies didn't stay on in people's homes, for as the evening light waned they melted into the surroundings. This process continued in front of the building in the colony for a year, and through all of it Abdus Sattar remained alert, a motionless presence like some ageless and immovable piece of stone; when the butterflies ascended to the balcony and fluttered around there, yellow pollen from their flapping wings accumulated on Abdus Sattar's face, chin and earlobes. He gazed at them, and wiped the pollen off his ear with his fingers, and if a butterfly entered his shirt he freed it; it seemed he had got used to living in the domain of all these insects, it seemed he wasn't inconvenienced now – although a year ago, when the butterflies were first overwhelmed by the beauty of the noyontaras and began arriving there, the excitement it created in this city had interrupted the tranquillity of Abdus Sattar's life.

When news of the capriciousness of the butterflies spread by word of mouth, the city's tired, sad and drowsy folk became excited, and when one day a report accompanied by a picture appeared on the last page of a newspaper, the situation took a decisive turn. Every evening, even before the arrival of the butterflies, the road in front of this six-storey building in the colony was crowded with all the entertainment-starved city folk leading dreary lives; and when swarms of yellow butterflies arrived and danced around the noyontaras and created the appearance of a moving garden of marigolds floating in the air, the people gazed in speechless wonder; and they kept thinking that it wasn't humans but beautiful butterflies which led fulfilling lives.

The middle-aged man whom these people spotted through the gaps in the railing of one balcony, sitting amid the crowd of butterflies from beginning to end, was Abdus Sattar. Although he initially tried to remain indifferent to the comings and goings of all these people, he gradually became conscious of his surroundings; as the astonishment of those who came to see the butterflies was dispelled and they forsook their earlier conclusion about the fulfilment in a butterfly's life, they were once again afflicted by the fatigue of monotony. In order to drive away this annoyance, some of them began to throw clods of earth at the butterflies, all of which missed their target and fell on to the balconies of the building; and one day a clod like this hit Abdus Sattar while he was sitting on the balcony. Also, given the situation, peanut and ice cream vendors suddenly arrived for the delectation of the vexed folk, and the whole place resounded with their cries and the sound of bells. The guardians of the city too were prompt in this instance, and so that peace and order were not disrupted, a temporary police outpost was erected in a corner of the field in front of the building; and then people from the Forest Department turned up one day and put up a hoarding on bamboo poles on the side of the road in front of the colony, on which it was written that the butterflies were only for observation and they could not be caught or harmed in any way; if anyone did that, they would be punished under the Wildlife Protection Act.

When the colony took on the scruffy look of a dusty, noisy fair, and it occurred to Abdus Sattar for the first time that perhaps it would no longer be possible for him to sit in this spot, which provided him with the greatest shelter in life, the people in the colony woke up one morning and heard on the radio that the government of the nation had changed the previous night; and, as a result, a situation was created whereby Abdus Sattar found deliverance and did not have to forsake his balcony. This new government of generals took many quick and significant steps in the interests of the nation and the people, among which was a project to modernize Mirpur

Zoo. A dozen chimpanzees were imported from Kenya on an emergency basis and were exhibited in a new cage beside the old monkey enclosure. When pictures and reports of these chimpanzees appeared in the newspapers, the vexed folk who were tired of monotony were roused; they ran towards Mirpur Zoo to see the chimpanzees, and the field in Agargaon Colony returned to silence; Abdus Sattar could again submerge himself, with shallow breaths, in this silence.

But most people in the world are always capricious; people are not mindful of the fact that their capriciousness is infectious, just as ripples are created when a stone is thrown into a pond; and one day some caprice like this, arising somewhere, was transported and flew through the darkness, landing on Abdus Sattar when he was sitting on the balcony. He picked up the object that had accidentally landed there, and even before he sniffed it he realized that it was a flower; and when he brought it close to his nose, he was certain that it was a rose; he kept the rose. The next day's rose fell about a foot away from his chair, but for the next five days no flowers landed there, and then on the sixth day two flowers arrived in quick succession; and in this way, roses kept piercing the darkness and flying on to Abdus Sattar's balcony. Abdus Sattar accepted the flowers, he took in their fragrance; but he didn't think too much about it. Then one day, when Abdus Sattar went indoors to eat dinner earlier than his usual time, his wife came and stood on the balcony to enjoy the cool breeze, and that day's rose then flew in. When Shireen Banu realized that a flower had flown in from the darkness outside she became unsettled, but she couldn't figure out this mystery; she remained seated with the rose in her hand. When Abdus Sattar came to the balcony after dinner, Shireen Banu extended her hand towards him in the darkness and said, 'Take it.'

'What is it?'

Shireen Banu didn't speak, but Abdus Sattar realized it was a rose when he took it.

'Who throws you roses?'

'I don't know.'

It then occurred to Abdus Sattar for the first time that this was definitely a mystery, but his mental investigation into it did not proceed very far.

'Is this why you sit on the balcony?'

Neither of them could see the other's face. Abdus Sattar said, 'No.'

'Do you feel ashamed to admit that?'

'Ashamed of what?'

'Then?'

'Then what?'

'For the last one month, I've been clearing torn, dry flowers from the balcony.'

'What of it?'

Shireen Banu then mumbled something softly. Abdus Sattar couldn't hear it properly, but he suddenly remembered that long ago a bluebottle had flown in from the darkness outside, and he asked, 'Do you remember the day of eighteenth March 1970?'

Waves of meaningless time had steadily dissipated in Shireen Banu's memory and she couldn't remember anything; she asked, 'What happened that day?'

'That was three months after our marriage,' Abdus Sattar replied. 'It was before your second visit to Dhaka after our wedding. I had gone to Sirajganj to bring you back, we were going to take the evening train on the eighteenth of March; you had got ready, your luggage was packed, there was a two-horse carriage waiting in front of the gate of your house on Kalibari Road. Everything was ready, everyone was on the balcony or in the compound, and you were inside, just about to come out. I was lurking in the darkness under the sweet-and-sour mango tree behind your house and pissing with the zip of my trousers undone; one of the shutters of the window at the rear of the house was open and I spotted you. There were biscuits smeared with honey on a saucer, you picked one up and ate it; some honey stuck to your lip and a big bluebottle came flying in from the darkness and sat on your lip. You flicked it away, wiped your lip and went out, and I was pissing under the mango tree then; can you remember that?'

They had nothing left but darkness and silence. Then after a long time, Abdus Sattar once again asked, 'Can't you remember? I know that the bluebottle had come from the dirty latrine in the clump of palm trees behind your house; can't you remember that?'

'No, I can't remember,' Shireen Banu said. 'I'm living with a madman.'

After that, Abdus Sattar kept receiving roses in the evening's darkness, and in the mornings Shireen Banu removed the dried-up blooms from the balcony; they were unable to solve the mystery of the roses that flew in. But a very simple answer to the puzzle was soon discovered. One day, when Fazlul Karim, who lived downstairs on the first floor with his wife, two daughters and a young son, moved out of their flat in the colony, the sound of Rahimuddin Bhuiyan's young daughter's suppressed weeping could be heard from the fourth-floor flat directly above Abdus Sattar's. No flower landed that night, and after that, just as rain ceases, the hitherto inevitable process of roses flying into Abdus Sattar's balcony too ceased. Perhaps there was a direct link between Fazlul Karim's young son departing the colony and the cessation of flowers flying on to Abdus Sattar's balcony; or maybe there was no connection between these two events, which happened at the same time merely by coincidence. Whatever the truth might be, Abdus Sattar remained indifferent to and removed from the mysteries that are at play in nature or within people, and these changes did not cause any change in his own life. He sat at dusk among the silent swarms of butterflies, he watched the darkness spreading, although the dance of the butterflies didn't continue for very many days after that either.

Just a few days after this, late in the evening one day, the city was rocked by severe tremors; cooking utensils came crashing down from all the kitchens in the colony, people screamed, they rushed down from their flats and ran towards the field. Abdus Sattar was sitting on the balcony that day as well; a few moments after the first tremor, startled, he realized it was an earthquake and he thought of going down. The building was then severely rocked a second time, and he could see that the pots of noyontaras placed on the railing and fastened with string had come loose and were about to fall down; he moved forward hastily, leant over the railing and put his arms firmly round two displaced pots. But as he leant over and then firmly grasped the two heavy flowerpots, the upper half of his body grew heavier and he lost his balance; instead of retrieving the flowerpots, his body went over the railing and descended with the pots. Abdus Sattar's trajectory was exactly like that of a bomber plane on a kamikaze mission.

Twenty-seven buildings in the city developed cracks as a result of that earthquake, a building beside the lake in Rampura tilted, and in Agargaon Colony all the noyontara plants, and Abdus Sattar, fell to the earth. Abdus Sattar's skull was smashed and spread like a bloody mushroom on the upper part of his neck, his brains spilt out and became one with the earth. After Abdus Sattar was buried, the grieving folk of the colony put their fallen noyontara plants back on the railings; only the widow Shireen Banu's plants lay on the ground below. After a few days, everyone's plants came back to life again and the butterflies returned, and Shireen Banu, who was feeling a bit better now, brought back her noyontara plants and planted them in new pots; but instead of springing back to life on the railing, they very soon died. After that, everyone in the building observed with astonishment and alarm that the leaves of their thriving noyontara plants were gradually wilting; and within a week, all the plants had withered and died. The people in the colony then obtained new noyontara seedlings and planted them, but all the seedlings once again withered and died in the same way. The people in the colony then invited a professor from the Agricultural College to look into the matter and advise them. The professor tested the soil and found nothing harmful, so he planted new seeds, but they kept dying as well. He undertook this process thrice, and all three times the noyontaras died for no apparent reason. The venerable professor arrived at the truth of the matter after a month of hard work, but he was unable to explain it to everyone; he merely advised the people of Agargaon Colony not to plant periwinkles for the time being. However, he wrote a long note on the subject in his personal notebook:

I still don't know whether or not such a thing is possible. The noyontara (*Vinca rosea*) plants were thriving; but as a result of the earthquake, there was a change. The plants in two pots came into close contact with the brains of a dead man. After the earthquake, when the other plants were taken back, they were doing well; but the two clumps that the dead man had tried to save began to die, and after that the other plants became afflicted too. On examination, no infectious fungus or disease was found, there was nothing harmful in the soil; rather, it was observed that all the necessary ingredients for the plants' nourishment and growth were present. The roots of the plants were examined and they were found to be adequately healthy and strong. All the seedlings that were planted on the railing, thrice in succession, are dead; but the four that were planted in the earth at the spot where the dead man's head was smashed have survived and are becoming robust. Does that mean that the plants have got into the habit of consuming some material from the brain? I am not yet certain about this, but my preliminary thinking is that perhaps this is not correct. One of these four plants was removed from there and planted elsewhere, and the elements that make up the brain, like sodium, magnesium, chloride, phosphorus and so on, were added to the soil, but there was no positive result. I've tried using the fresh brain of a cow, and for that matter (something very secret), a few days ago I brought a human brain in a polythene bag from the morgue at the Medical College and tried mixing that in the soil too; it didn't work. The seedling was dying, and finally, after replanting it with the other three seedlings, it sprang back to life. It's difficult to figure out why the plants thrive in this particular spot (the soil there was tested and no other special characteristics were found); there's only one special feature of the spot, which is that a person's head got smashed there, a person who, I've heard, was a bit crazy, and at the time of the earthquake he fell while trying to save two pots of noyontara plants; in that case, is it something that's personal for these plants? It could be. But my thinking on this subject of the noyontara plants in the colony dying when they are removed from a particular spot is that the plants are simply committing suicide. That's because I have not found any real reason for their death. I cannot say anything more about why these noyontara plants die. I do know what sentient beings plants are. And in this regard, the desire for suicide first spread from one plant to another because of the close proximity of the plants, and the butterflies performed the role of messengers in this process; I suspect that subsequently the soil too might have played a role. If contact with the butterflies can be avoided, and if they are planted on soil brought from elsewhere, noyontara plants may perhaps grow again in Agargaon Colony. I was able to save one seedling by this method, inside a polythene bag. But one can only conduct an experiment in this way, not raise a garden. This note of mine is perhaps not as accomplished as a scientist's paper; but I see nothing wrong in writing down whatever I have observed and thought.

The four noyontara plants planted by the professor from the Agricultural College were in the earth in front of the building in Agargaon Colony; he had thrown away the seedling that grew inside a polythene bag. But subsequently, at some point in time, people from the Public Works Department arrived and laid a metalled road in front of the building, and they paved the grassy patch between the road and the building so that no trash would be dumped there. They thus removed the final four noyontara plants and cleared that space, and ever since then there have been no noyontara plants in this colony. However, as advised by the professor from the Agricultural College, if one were careful in taking note of the butterflies and the soil, and tried hard, perhaps noyontara flowers would once again bloom here in the future.

(Translated by V. Ramaswamy)

ANITA AGNIHOTRI

Crater Lake

. . . I didn't quite know how to get here. The crater lake is somewhere in this district, but no one knows exactly where. In rural areas people keep track of neighbouring localities or at best nearby villages, not much more. There's a train from Mumbai to Jalna, a passenger train. If I'd got off at Jalna Station I could have got there in three hours. But I had wandered off aimlessly to an area well north of Aurangabad. Then, as I stood drinking water at a roadside tap in the middle of the afternoon, in a place called Malikapur in Buldhana district, I asked for directions. An old bus conductor said, uh-huh, you've come the wrong way, girl, you have to go another 150 miles east. I was in a wretched state by then. My hair was caked with dust, my clothes were stiff with dirt; the bus wouldn't go all the way — so a lumbering jeep again! I was also worried about not being able to see anything once the sun had set. The sun sets before six here at the onset of winter.

I hadn't had anything by way of food all day. This area abounds in custard apples. Wild custard apples. They don't need watering or anything, nor any formal cultivation. Shivaji's mother Jeejabai is supposed to have spent her childhood at a village named Sindhakher. The farmers' wives were sitting at the bus stop there with mounds of custard apples. I wrapped a few in paper and tied them up in my sari. I've been eating them in the jeep. My hands are smeared with their juice.

. . . No one from our family has ever been to Buldhana district. It's on the northern border of Maharashtra, adjacent to Madhya Pradesh. But not as saline as Vidharbha or Marathwada. Maybe the hills would have appeared brown if I'd come here in summer. Now, after the monsoon and autumn, at the beginning of winter, there's an exquisite expanse of

mountain ranges spanning the horizon – the hills cascade like waves on either side of the road, as though the earth has taken my hands to draw us into its playing fields. I can see a profusion of natural lakes in this region – pools of water lie everywhere, the sky reflected in them. Cultivation is limited to acacia and cottonseed . . . cottonseed and pigeon pea. They plant different crops in alternate rows. In places there are sugarcane crops – the cane trees stand like confused, prematurely aged householders. The corn farms are being prepared for ploughing after the harvest. The soil is black. Here the soil is black everywhere. I've heard as much ever since I was born. I've been told the soil in Bengal is pale. And red too in some places . . .

Shakya was stretched out on the grass. Not the manicured grass of a lawn. The rough but loving lap of wild grass, shrubs and weeds all growing together on uneven land. This was the western bank of the lake, sloping downwards to the edge of the water. The incline on the northern bank was far less steep in comparison. Other than this one bank, the lake was like a deep bowl, with the water gathered at its bottom. It was afternoon now. Sparrows and jackdaws were twittering; crows spoke up harshly now and then. The irregular shadow of a stunted plum tree was waving in the wind. The letter from his mother lay on Shakya's chest. It was thirty years old. She would never post her letters.

There was an old government bungalow on the edge of the lake. It may have been young once, but now it lay in a stupor of disuse and neglect. Shakya's sparkling-white Innova was parked in front of the bungalow. Balaram the driver was painstakingly cleaning the traces of mud and grime that had appeared on the car from the journey. He had collected a bucket, water and duster from the bungalow on his own initiative. Shakya's elder sister Urvashi had just disappeared inside to find out whether there were arrangements to freshen up. There was a well-maintained guest house run by the Tourism Department close by. Shakya and Urvashi had booked rooms there. But still this bungalow was important to them. Their mother's letter had referred to it.

Urvashi emerged from the bungalow, the end of her yellow sari flying. Her gorgeous hairdo had not been altered in the least by four hours of air-conditioned travel, she had no straggling locks on her forehead. Her nail polish and lip gloss were both in place. The caretaker at the bungalow had cleaned the bathroom to the best of his abilities, and laid out brown but freshly washed bedclothes. But he had not been able to get rid of the grime, cobwebs and similar memories amassed over the years at one stroke. The barbed-wire fence that ran along the edge of the lake was sagging and invisible in places. Slipping in through one such gap, Urvashi was descending the slope gingerly. The letters folded on his chest, Shakya was watching her. Thirty years ago, his mother was exactly the same age that his sister was now. But his sister was much prettier and more glamorous than his mother. His mother couldn't have imagined travelling in a milk-white car, dressed in a silk sari like this. She had arrived at the crater lake with dirt caking her clothes, dust in her hair, custard apples tied in her sari. But she had arrived as evening was about to fall, a terrible anxiety in her heart – she wouldn't be able to see anything once the sun had set. Shakya and Urvashi had travelled at leisure to avoid this rush. First by plane to Aurangabad. Then in the car to Buldhana, passing Sillod on the way. Any unfamiliar place appears quite bearable if you arrive in the after-noon. Besides, reclining in silence here at the edge of the desolate deciduous forest, they would be able to hear the cries of different birds, even the sound of shedding leaves. They could wait for the sun to set.

As he gazed at his sister, Shakya bled invisibly from a piercing regret. If his mother had been alive today, he could have brought her here by plane and a white car. She would have walked down that slope, one hand on his sister's shoulder and one hand on his, smiling in shy embarrassment. She had died ten years ago, leaving her children not riches and money but innumerable letters. Unposted but stamped and sealed letters. Just like she wrote letters when she was home, she also wrote them from different sta-tions, roadsides, bus depots, post offices; every now and then she would set off from home. Within her limited means, she would travel by bus, by train, sometimes on foot, and then come back home and write about her travels to her two children.

Shakya felt that travel had been like a drug for his mother. In his grandfather's home her day was devoted to her chores, her cooking, the daily routine. Her father was not well off. He had to suffer both the eco-nomic and psychological pain of having his married daughter live with him all his life. But still he had tried to take care of Shakya's grandmother and mother as much as he could. His mother must have felt desperate at times. Out of boredom, out of loneliness. Knowing that she had no way to be with the people whom her heart longed for constantly, she used to go off travelling every now and then. The letters were her travelogues – of her sojourn at home, of her wandering ways.

Even when the severity of summer turned the hills and the soil in this region an arid brown, when the heat scorched the rainless earth, a green, fresh, mixed jungle remained alive on the sloping banks of the lake. Its deep, bowl-like structure restricted the swirling of the wind, there was the effect of the water vapour, and besides, the surface of the lake was high – for all these reasons, the woods near the lake remained full of shrubs, vines and trees. Naseem, a young local, was pointing out various trees. Besides rain trees, myrobalans, flames of the forest, Indian beeches, banyans, marmalos and baby margosas, there were apparently a lot of sandalwood trees. Apart from these there were shrubs with local names like dhamal, chlat, karati, jhimula and paleri; there were a dozen varieties of vines too with local names – basan, papal, murad kong, sanjeevani, sagardutt . . . nature had planted a superb range of them around this lake. Scientists from all over the country and the world visited this place, examining the vines and shrubs, the soil, the saline level of the water; the research on the soil and rocks here was part of experiments involving the planet Mars. Numerous species of snakes, iguanas, deer, peacocks and monkeys roamed the jungle bordering the lake; birds of many forms and colours inhabited the place. Naseem said he had seen different kinds of parrots, weaver birds, owls, ducks, tailor birds . . . he had seen swans play in the water, flamingos fly through the air . . . were his enthusiasm and intensity making the picture a little extra-colourful? This unemployed young man named Naseem was landless, he lived in a shanty in the village adjoining the lake. Tourists brought a breath of fresh air to the anaemic life he spent with his younger siblings and parents. Fine cigarettes, fat tips, variety in conversation.

By the way, is there someone named Kalidas here . . . a book . . . my mother had written about him, she had met this writer . . . could he be asked to join us?

You mean Kalidas-chacha? asked Naseem. You might find a copy of his book if you searched in the shop at the bus stand – but he has lost his eyesight. He cannot see any more, he cannot even step out of his home.

I was worried the sun might set before I reached ... I had made no arrangements to stay the night, it wasn't possible either. I wasn't worried about that. I would certainly find a place to hole up for the night. But if there were no daylight ... to stand in darkness before what I had travelled so far to see ... that would be very hard. The sun rises late here in early winter, around quarter to seven, but it sets before six.

The jeep kept stopping everywhere, picking people up, piling large loads on the roof. I had found myself a seat at the side, the custard apple seeds tied up at the end of my sari, the wind in my face, harvested land on both sides of the road, waves of an unfamiliar smell rising from the hills with outstretched wings, spreading over the land.

The small village is named after the lake. Lonar. Sounds salty, desolate. It was small but famous. That's why milestones by the road carried its name ... I was counting thirty, twenty-five, fifteen, twelve ... and wondering what the first sight would be like. Would the water and the reflection of the sky in it shimmer up before my eyes as soon as I reached Lonar ... would I be able to see it from the jeep, did the road go past the lake ... or was it further away ... stray thoughts.

Five-thirty ... five-thirty-five, forty on my watch ... it seemed to be running a little too quickly. As soon as we entered the narrow road beyond the shops clustered around the crossing at the village, there was a huge herd of cows and bullocks, the dust raised by their feet and the ringing of the bells at their neck, seemed to be ushering in the evening early – I was begging and pleading with the driver to avoid them and move on ... we had left the village behind, still no sign of the crater lake, had I lost my way again? The other passengers couldn't care less, nor the driver, all of them were on their way home after their day's work at the market, the accounts done; the driver, of course, travelled on this road every single day. Eventually the jeep screeched to a halt by a pile of pots and pans and pitchers and a potter's shed on the side of the road, get off here, he said – we're going in a different direction ... The sun had dipped into the horizon. The sky was filled with a sad orange and purple light. Who knew how much further it still was. Adjusting the bag on my shoulder, I ran in the direction they had pointed. The back of an old government bungalow was visible. The wooden gate was open ... as soon as I raced in through it ... how do I tell you this ... a day from 50,000 years ago returned to me ...

...The bottom of the lake held the condensed, flaming reflection of the sun. The sun wouldn't sink directly in the water, however – because the crater lake was like a deep bowl, soil and rocks had been ejected from the earth to line the lake with hills, like the raised rim of a bowl – the sun would go down behind those hills ... it did too ... it seemed to have been waiting only for me to arrive. Then, very slowly, with reluctant footsteps, it hid its plumage of light at the corner of the lake. Still a purple darkness tinged with blue remained in the sky, the soul of an indescribable, fading light mixed in it.... In that faint light I saw a lake, its perimeter covering three, maybe four miles, its egg-shaped expanse of water lying like still, white, transparent fabric, surrounded by a dense, green, silent, dusk-wrapped forest, the calling of homebound birds floating out of it, the chirp of crickets, the sharp buzz of insects brushing their wings against one another rising into the sky and mingling with it ...

A strange overflowing joy was entangled with tears in my heart, as soon as my eyes adjusted to the darkness I saw someone else sitting close to the barbed-wire fence – so I wasn't alone. It was Kalidas Purandare ...

Picking her way to where Shakya was stretched out on the grass, Urvashi sat down carefully beside him. Avoiding the thorns, insects, water and everything else. This was the wrong sari to wear, you know, she said, unfolding the letter lying on Shakya's chest to read it.

How strange, isn't it, bhai, how ma came rushing with so much effort to have only about a minute of daylight – today we'll watch the sunset properly, peacefully, savour the whole thing, Urvashi said.

Shakya shook his head without getting up. No, even with all our planning and organizing and waiting I don't think we'll get what ma had got from the setting sun in those couple of minutes. Ma was full of anticipation and excitement, joy and sorrow, all at once. We're far more wary and dispassionate now, we're successful. Ma wouldn't have recognized us if she saw us now.

She had used the words 'salty' and 'desolate' about this place. Naseem had said the salt trade here was quite old. When the water from the lake evaporated from the rocks the salt would remain. These mounds of salt used to be extracted from the water of the lake in the monsoon. Was it because of the meteorite that they wouldn't dissolve in the water – or did they retain rock dust?

According to the *Rig Veda*, King Dandaka had his capital at Madhumati Nagar – the town was buried in an explosion. Then the story was resumed in the era of Kashyap's wife Diti. Her sons Gayasur and Kolhasur had been killed by Vishnu. Lavanasur ran away in fear with his sisters to Lonar. The lake was supposed to have had a stone roof then. The fleeing Lavanasur had not managed to escape. The roof flew off at a kick from Vishnu, landing forty miles away at Thakkal. Vishnu was given the title of Daityasudan, demon-slayer, and the dead demon's blood was converted into saltwater with medicinal properties. It was necessary for a tribal leader to die in order for the tale of the Aryan gods' conquests to have been written, the leader's death sentence had been pronounced after dubbing him a demon – all this was concealed in the folds of time. Lonar was converted into Vishnugaya. People seeking redemption had been bathing here through three eras, Tretayug, Dwaparyug and Kalyug, to salve their sins . . .

Kalidas Purandare, of course, had major objections to all this bathing business. An inhabitant of Lonar village, he had read widely around his college education – mathematics, history, astronomy. Scientists from Harvard and the Smithsonian Institution of the US would also talk to him. He used to spend all his time near the lake – observing the flora and fauna and the rocks was his fixation. Another obsession of his was writing letters – he was perpetually writing voluminous letters to the president, the prime minister, the environment minister – this ancient cosmic wonder could not be saved unless cultivation, washing of clothes and dumping of temple waste in the water of the lake was stopped. The rich biodiversity and forest resources around the lake would be destroyed. The local people knew all this, but they used to consider Kalidas an eccentric, they would laugh about him with affection; they didn't even consider the possibility of their daily activities being disrupted because of Kalidas's letters. They had been disrupted, however. Naseem had told him all this. Shakya had tried to imagine how many sunrises, afternoons, dusks, sunsets and nightfalls Kalidas Purandare must have witnessed as he wandered around the lake and roamed the passages in the dense forests around it. He had published slim volumes with his own money, and had his letters typed out and sent in the mail. Now his eyes were sightless.

At the end of the letter their mother had written, 'When you grow up, both of you must come here. You will, won't you? My joy won't be complete till I have shown all of this to both of you. Kalidas has said he'll give me a photograph. Taken by a studio photographer here. But will it really reveal anything?'

Was there a photo with the letter, Shakya?

No, didi. It didn't come to me, at any rate.

It had been ten years since their mother had died. Shakya realized now that she had been afflicted with a terminal disease – but they had not recognized the symptoms at the time. Shakya's wedding was just a few months away. She had agreed to live with him and his wife immediately after the wedding – that was enough to make Shakya happy. His elder sister had been married five years earlier. His father and grandparents had virtually kept her hidden at the time. Apparently her appearance could wreck the wedding. Fearing scenes and confrontations, his sister had agreed, shedding tears in private. Their father's temper, cruelty and blind malevolence were not unfamiliar to them. Shakya had left home in a rage. He had gone to his mother. It was she who had pacified him and sent him back. His sister would be even more miserable without Shakya. When you get married, I'll come and stay with you, his mother had said then too. Let your sister's wedding take place peacefully.

What had his mother been like? Orthodox or modern? Clever or plain silly? Stubborn or reckless? Her life had simply slipped through her fingers – she had not been able to do anything about it, she could only sit by and watch. She hadn't exactly sat by, actually, she had kept herself busy. She had travelled, and tried to discover herself in different settings, incidents, mysteries.

His father had had a social standing, education, degrees, networking, fame – enormous popularity as a teacher. That was why students, their parents and other teachers alike had overlooked his licentiousness. But his mother had not been able to overlook it, and she had not been able to accept it. She had wanted an honourable coexistence as his wife, but had realized soon after the wedding that love and affection could not be expected of her husband. It had become impossible for her to live with his regular deception, treachery, unending affairs and, alongside, the minutiae of conjugal life. There was no use complaining to her husband's parents. They were unwilling to acknowledge any flaw in their son's character. Especially when the son was as bright, sharp and successful as he was. If you can't get along, divorce him and leave. She had hoped that having children would strengthen the bonds of love and caring, that her husband would stop looking around and return to his family. That did not happen. Urvashi was born. Shakya too. Their father was not the least unwilling to have children. A tiger never changes once it has tasted blood. It scours different regions, human habitations. Shakya's father had not changed either. When Shakya was about three, his mother had wanted to leave home. Go ahead, who's stopping you, his grandparents had told her. But don't you dare take the children with you. An immoral wanton mother cannot take care of her children, that too by herself. If she had opted for a divorce she could at least have fought for custody of her children. After taking into account her own father's economic condition, she could not take the decision. She had also considered the fact that her son and daughter would always carry the label of being the children of a divorcee. Shakya's grandparents knew his mother, her capacity for battle, well enough. So they had pushed her towards a divorce. She did not want to take that option, stopping out of doubt and fear. But her patience had run out after bearing the torture and torment every single day. So she had returned to her parents' home. Shakya was very young, his sister was in Class Two. So what if she was gone, his grandparents couldn't care less. They proceeded to bring their grandchildren up with great enthusiasm, ensuring they went to good schools and learnt good manners. Their father continued to fly freely, like a kite in the sky; between them they ensured that their mother's name was wiped out of Shakya and Urvashi's lives, their hearts. What a strange life it had been! Shakya used to dote on his grandparents when he was a child, even afterwards in fact, till the other day, when he got his first job. The day he learnt of his mother's terminal illness, a fire began to burn within him with the realization that his favourite people, the old man and woman, were actually cruel, so cruel. They had never asked his mother to come back, not even once. They had never loved her. They had deprived Shakya and Urvashi of their mother's touch. There was no forgiveness for such cruelty. Urvashi had not managed to be so harsh. She had maintained a working relationship with her father and grandparents. But not Shakya. Breaking all shackles, he now belonged to his mother alone, the mother who wasn't there, who would never come – to that mother. His mother would often develop a low fever at night – Shakya had not known. He had not come to know where the pain was, where it hurt. His grandparents had destroyed his instincts as a son – how else could he not have realized what was going on? If her illness had been diagnosed early enough Shakya could have ensured she was cured. The thought agonized him, it had the impact, the pain, of a scorpion sting.

The day declined. The colour of the land around the rim of the lake, where there was a dense mixed forest on three sides, with several ancient temples concealed in its folds, was changing in tandem with the changing colour of the light. No matter how much Kalidas Purandare disapproved, people were bound to use the tracks deep within the forest to visit the place on full moon nights, on new moon nights, on days earmarked for rituals, to deliver the things they had pledged: clay lamps, wicks soaked in clarified butter, dried flowers and leaves, and paper packets which had held sweets would be scattered everywhere. Priests would chant a variety of incantations melodiously on the stone steps of demon-slayer Vishnu's temple. The sound of bells being rung and metal dishes being beaten would waft out of the temple of the goddess Kamalaja. The afternoon rolled towards dusk. The trilling of birds ascended into the forest and the adjoining sky. It rose into the branches of different, unknown trees. The sun dipped. Many years ago at this time of the day, their mother had been rushing helplessly and desperately towards the crater lake, changing buses and jeeps, hoping to beat the sunset and the darkness.

Look there, Shakya, it's not as dense, there are fewer trees, something like a stream seems to be running through it. His sister pointed to the north-west. The slope was the most pronounced in that direction – Purandare had written that this was the direction from which the meteorite had hurtled towards the ground, at a very acute angle with the earth, the massive friction on impact had raised a storm not just of dust and wind but also of pain – shooting up from the bowels of the earth like crushed lava, it had spread across distances and leapt up into the sky, and then, when everything had settled down, the split-open earth had turned into stone, forming the edge of the gigantic opening in the ground . . . years of rain had filled this void, forming the crater lake. The meteorite had been alkaline at its core, which was why the saline taste of the water had not dissipated even after thousands of years.

Meteorites, small and large, hurtle towards the earth this way on innumerable occasions, in every year and every season they drop into the earth's atmosphere. Asteroids are circling the sun, covering an enormous distance, halfway between the orbits of Mars and Jupiter. Meteorites are the pulverized skin or particles of their bodies. Some of them are burnt into oblivion in the atmosphere, some meteors avoid the gravitational pull of the earth to drift further into infinite emptiness. And some embed themselves in the green, many-hued earth of this planet, ripe with shades and emotions.

Plunging swiftly through the atmosphere 50,000 years ago, did the meteorite get caught in a trance of enchantment? Was it attracted by the Buldhana mountain range with its spread-out wings? Did the contrast between the green vegetation and the black soil raise in its heart the hope of a shelter? Then before its surprised eyes rose this alluring village of Lonar, swollen like a sail billowing in the wind. Of course it was not called Lonar then, for Lavanasur had not yet been born, the demon's blood had not yet gushed out because of Vishnu's kick; cultivators and shepherds were engaged in earning their quiet livelihoods in homes woven with leaves and shrubs. How hopefully the meteorite had kissed the doorstep of its new home while breathing in the scent of the vegetation and soil of the earth!

And the very next moment a tumultuous uproar rose in the forest, heat, lava and agony spurted up into the sky ... and the meteorite was interred in the depths – as though it would not be released from its pain unless it escaped to the centre of the earth. But the centre – that was so far away, the path to release was blocked by layers of earth, rock and molten metal ...

The meteorite realized its way was blocked both in the sky and in the depths of the earth; turning its back to the world, it buried its face in the ground, the rainwater filled the emptiness of its barren shelter ... its back turned ... yes, Shakya was reminded of his mother turning her back – for in the last few months of her illness she used to lie facing the wall, the old wall of her father's home, in her narrow bed. Shakya had arranged for a home of his own, taken a loan from the bank, a block of flats was being constructed bit by bit ... I'm going to take you to live with me, ma, just try to be well in the meantime ... perhaps she had tried, but his mother had not managed to get well. Deprived of love, tenderness and caresses for many years, every bone in her body, her marrow, her blood was converted into cinders ... his mother was burning, the froth and the blood poured out thickly, her face, hands and legs swelled ...

The meteorite is there, didi, somewhere beneath the lake, for it had nowhere to go, instead of wandering around the rim if only I had tried swimming in the water this afternoon ...

Going up to her brother, Urvashi put an arm around his shoulder. The image of Shakya swimming in the saline water looking for remnants of the ancient meteorite brought a smile to her lips, tears to her eyes. She knew Shakya would never be able to salve this wound ... the one within him. Loving his mother, not being able to be with her, not being able to get her to live with him and give her a little happiness ... now all he had was a lament in his heart, the emptiness of the storm in the forest, the failed effort at forgiving – forgiving himself, forgiving his heartlessness as a child ...

The sun had descended to the edge of the lake. Its perfect, vibrant image was visible in the transparent water, as was the crooked reflection of the range of hills. Before it rose in another direction, over another hemisphere, it had deliberately paused for a moment, in search of someone ... had anyone come today to take a look at their home and habitation by the last light of the sun?

Brother and sister were returning in the orange-purple light. Picking their way carefully through the gap in the barbed-wire fence around the lake. The lights were switched on in the old government bungalow. Like a lit-up platform where no more trains would arrive.

A thick layer of dust covered the leaves of the custard apple tree. It had not rained in a long time. The tree was bent. Some wild custard apples were concealed under the leaves. Hard, unripened. The ripened fruits fell to the ground, the village boys took them away, cows ate them if they were within reach. It was not supposed to bear fruits any more after all these years – but kept doing it out of habit. The weight of ages had coiled around its trunk, vines wound around its body, its branches and twigs. The tree was waiting. In one sense it was not supposed to have been born here, there had been no certainty that the custard apple seeds which had fallen out of the end of the sari would have taken root here. But one of the seeds had sent down a root. The custard apple tree had come to life at the edge of the land formed by the earth that had erupted from the lake.

Were those Shakya's fingers brushing the dusty leaves of the tree? The end of Urvashi's yellow sari flew up to touch it. The custard apple tree felt a thrill in its body. A frisson of joy ran through it.

They were leaving. The white car had its ignition switched on. The ground shook. Who knew when they would return? People didn't keep coming back, after all. Exhaling softly, peacefully, the tree looked as far as it could into the darkness.

SHAHEEN AKHTAR

Home

I

The mobile chirped like a bird.

'I just fell asleep! How can it be morning already?'

Bindubala sat up in bed, buzzing like a mosquito. Was it day or night? Rubbing her eyes with the back of her hand, she looked around blankly. Until she remembered the borrowed mobile she had been using for the past three months to make endless 'missed calls', the bird continued to tweet from under her pillow.

'Haaalloo, who's this?'

'It's Rima.' The actress. 'My body's aching all over, I need a rub-down. Make sure you come at eight. My shoot starts at ten . . . Don't forget.'

There was a bitter taste in her mouth. Occasional sour belches. Bindubala turned on the light to look for her watch. It should have been on top of the trunk by the bed, where she stored her blankets. Had a thief come in the night? Shukhlal's eyes were as wide open as his mouth. He stared even in his sleep. The bravest of burglars would have a heart attack at the sight. How did a son inherit the traits of a father he had never seen or known? That man was worse than a thief! When Bindubala tried to close the boy's eyes, he groaned and turned on his side. Just like his father. The watch slipped off his wrist on the bed. 'How dare he!' About to slap him, Bindubala restrained herself. They said a child smacked while sleeping could die of it. So instead she just gnashed her teeth in anger.

'How many times have I told you not to touch my things?' she asked the sleeping boy. 'If you were awake, I'd give it to you so hard you'd forget your father's name!'

Was the rage directed towards her son or towards the actress Rima? It was a quarter past one in the morning. Bindubala gulped down some water – was this any time to call!

As soon as she turned off the light, a vision of Dhaka came to her, as familiar as the back of her hand . . .

Rima's house. New Eskaton. Eight in the morning. But Bindubala was supposed to be at Paltan at eight. At Roksana madam's house. It would pay 250 taka – she couldn't afford to miss it. An elderly woman, all she wanted were oil massages. It took barely thirty or forty minutes. From Paltan she'd go straight to Mohakhali. It was all right to get there by ten. Shathi madam went to bed late after her Thursday night parties. She got up late too. Bindubala would need at least two hours in Mohakhali. She had to make a mixture of honey, herbal cream, lotions, banana, lemon juice, carrots, cucumbers, oranges – all kinds of things – and rub it all over Shathi madam's body. Then she'd have to dry her client for twenty or twenty minutes with the help of a table fan, until she looked like a dehydrated fish, before rubbing the grime off of her body with cream or olive oil.

An ample woman. It was hard work and the pay was meagre, considering. Just 200 taka. From Mohakhali she'd take a three-wheeled van, followed by a rickshaw, to Banani.

But now Paltan and New Eskaton were clashing. The actress Rima's call had messed things up. Both appointments at eight, both worth 250 taka, both old customers. She could get away with skipping the Paltan madam this once. The actress had a problem. Watching her on screen, you'd never know that shooting endlessly in the sun had turned her skin as black as a crow's egg.

'The shoot's been cancelled. She's sleeping,' declared the shrewish woman at the door. She was picking dead grains from the rice. 'Can't disturb her now.' Normally this woman tailed her daughter on set like a bodyguard, constantly stuffing paan into her mouth from her handbag. Two of Rima's sisters were slicing fish and vegetables with a kitchen knife nearby. They didn't have a maid.

'So what if the shoot's cancelled! My time is valuable. Wake her up.' Bindubala was irritated. What a way to start the day! Paltan was gone. Now she'd lose Mohakhali too. If Shathi madam woke up at ten and went to bathe, no amount of begging would make her agree to a massage.

She was very moody. Drinking at parties made her short-tempered the next day.

One of Rima's sisters got to her feet, went up to the door and came back. She was dependent on her actress sister and didn't dare disturb her sleep. The other sister did the same. The mother concentrated on chewing her paan and picking out grains. The jar of herbal cream was empty – what was she going to use for the massage? In the next room, a young assistant was taking the cheap satin outfits for the movie *Queen Salma* out of a bag and folding them. Rima's mother sent him out to buy some herbal cream. After all this, the massage finally began at nine.

Bindubala's anger melted as she rubbed herbal cream mixed with cucumber and carrot juice all over the actress's body. This was the rule. You could not take care of someone with anger in your heart. The rage would be transferred to the hands. How could the client feel comfortable if the fingers rebelled and turned into pincers? Why have you been summoned over the phone, Bindubala? It's for this little additional care that they do all this in secret. Your fingers will sink into their skin, but they mustn't leave a scratch. The skin will become soft and smooth. This was a bonus for them. That's why you're valued more by the unmarried, the divorced, or those with unfaithful husbands. Just as they want some comfort for their bodies, they also want to use skin care to stop ageing. If they got physical pleasure elsewhere, they wouldn't spare even loose change on you – just remember that. Think of Tonika madam in Paribagh. When she got married in her old age, she dumped you at once. But you were called again before three months had gone by. Bindubala was no pushover. Let three more months pass, she wouldn't go before that. For now she should focus on massaging the actress's flour sack of a body.

'Why are you getting so fat? You're an actress – try to stay slim.'

Rima only smiled. Once the herbal cream started drying on her face, the cinematic smile would vanish quickly enough. She had folds of skin around her throat like a blanket. Bindubala sweated as she massaged the skin upwards towards the chin with her palms. Considering the rate at which Rima was getting fatter, 250 taka would not be enough. As soon as the actress turned over on her stomach, Bindubala began to massage her back and came to the point.

'What are all these new rules they're making in the city? They're taking rickshaws off the road. Are they trying to turn this into a foreign country – like America?'

The actress had no patience for such nonsense. She had a thousand other worries – between the theatre, movies and promotional work, she had schedules for at least ten different performances. And, amid all this, newspaper interviews. Such a busy artist! So little time! She pointed to the prominent protrusion between her shoulders – meaning, stop talking and massage it hard.

The layer of herbal cream had been removed. But Bindubala kept massaging the protrusion with all her strength. And though her fingers and arms ached, the mountain remained as it was, refusing to be flattened. It seemed the woman would get her money's worth this time. But what about her own travel expenses?

'I had to walk to your house after getting off the bus at Bangla Motor. Such a long way! I walked a while, then took a rickshaw. Still had to pay the rickshaw-driver the full ten taka. It's all very well for actresses – they have cars.'

'You want to buy a car? Oh my goodness!' The actress giggled, resting her chin on the pillow. 'Join the movies – you'll soon have a house and a car.'

Just see how vain she is because she's in films. I spit on such acting. I'm not allowed to think of buying a car, but hasn't she herself risen from the gutters? She won't even hire a maid. She'd rather make her mother and sisters slaves. Allah will judge them all. Her only brother is a gangster – the police are searching for him with a fine-tooth comb.

When the actress went into the bathroom in her panties, Bindubala sat thinking to herself. It was no use asking such people for more money indirectly. Like their bodies, their skins were also thick.

It was now a quarter past ten. After leaving the actress's house, Bindubala gave Shathi madam a 'missed call'. It would be eleven by the time she got there, first by rickshaw, then on foot to the bus stop to get a bus. Madam was not calling back. Perhaps she had already gone in to bathe. There was no use rushing all that way now, it would only be a waste of money. Bindubala waved her hand to stop a bus to Gulistan and got on. Where would she go now – should she go to Paltan? But could she expect to do an eight o'clock assignment at eleven? Still, she clutched her ticket to Paltan tightly and settled regally into a double seat. But the pleasure did not last. Was her body a honeytrap? With so many empty seats, why did the thug have to sidle up to her? What could she say, he had paid for his own ticket, after all. Bindubala moved away till she almost melded into the metal frame of the bus. But the man was adamant. 'Do you want a job? Good salary. Ten thousand cash per month. Other perks too . . .' He whispered at first, but gradually his voice rose. *Why don't you do it yourself? You wouldn't have to ride this ramshackle bus if you earned ten thousand a month.* Bindubala's thoughts remained in her head. She didn't say a word. Instead she got off the bus before reaching her destination for fear of creating a scene.

She needed to cross the road in front of PG Hospital at Shahbagh, but a formidable police sergeant in dark glasses was blowing his whistle loudly. There was a five-taka fine for not using the overbridge. Sometimes they punished you by making you hold your ears and do squats in the middle of the street. Pay for everything, and humiliation on top of that. These people didn't consider others human. How much longer would Bindubala have to live in the slums with her son? She had her eye on a piece of land in Joydebpur – a barren field on the edge of the wilderness. The plot of land did not change position but the price kept rising in leaps and bounds. One month, she had found that if she scraped together all her savings, she would need to add just 10,000. The next month, the price increased by another 10,000, and now she was 20,000 short. This game had been going on for the past two years.

A dream mansion loomed in front of Bindubala. Paribagh Eastern Tower. Tonika madam lived on the fifth floor. She got married just three months ago. Now she kept sending messages. She had probably lost Bindu-bala's phone number during the wedding chaos. So what? Someone who used to offer a glass of iced lemonade as soon as Bindubala entered couldn't possibly become a stranger only because she was married. Besides, just before her wedding she had passed on her own mobile phone to Bindubala to make it easier to stay in touch. Bindubala only had to pay for her calls. A penniless Bindubala had no right to be sniffy with someone who had done so much for her.

Bindubala did not have to sign herself in at the entrance to the Paribagh Eastern Tower. The uniformed guard took the opportunity to chat. 'Where were you hiding all these days? Madam asked even yesterday on the intercom – Tara Munshi, did you see Bindubala passing by?'

Bindubala did not look back. She ran to the lift, tucking her bag under her arm. The tinkling of a spoon in a cup rang in her ears. Beads of sweat gathered on her forehead, like on a glass of cold lemonade. Before she could press the button the lift doors opened and first a man and then Tonika madam tumbled out. Bindubala stepped back quickly. Madam looked like she had seen a ghost. By the time she drew Bindubala aside and asked her to come on Thursday at exactly three o'clock, when her husband wouldn't be home, the man had already started his car. Madam was running, Bindubala right behind her. The car door opened slightly. 'Who's this?'

'An old housemaid.' The door slammed in Bindubala's face.

2

'Don't get married, all right? Marriage makes the female race dependent.'

'Hmm. But *you* did.'

'Not by choice. My sisters forced me. I was young. Didn't understand a thing.'

As she massaged her client's fingers to soften them, Bindubala recounted the story of her wedding. The family elders had become drunk from the local liquor even before the groom's party had arrived. Their bodies limp and their bones rattling, they had danced wildly. Bindubala's only uncle – her mother's brother – who was supposed to give the bride away danced so violently in his drunken state that he fell into the yard along with the door when he heard the groom's party had arrived and broke his hip. He died a disabled man, who never stood upright after the incident. That day, her uncle's brother-in-law had given her away instead. Bindubala said, 'I've had bad luck ever since then.'

Both the masseuse and the client realized that something had snapped. Bindubala kept dipping her fingers into the bowl of oil. For eight years she had wondered whether her husband's untimely death had been a blessing or a curse – without arriving at a conclusion. But what was the use of pondering over this any more?

The wood was gone, the wooden flute would play no more. 'My ears are ringing. I can't hear a thing sometimes.'

'Do you want to see a doctor? I know an ENT specialist. He'll treat you free of cost.'

They say strangers are better than friends, and wild beasts are best of all. Look who was advising her to see a doctor now, and who had led her by the hand to destruction one day . . .

Bindubala was a new bride at the time. There was a lockout at the jute mill. The workers had not been paid for two months. Ramlal left in the morning and returned home empty-handed at night. Every morning he threatened his wife, 'Don't you dare take a step outside.' Her mother-in-law had always worked as a midwife and had a good reputation. It was she who came up to Bindubala with an oil lamp one day, saying, 'Bou, how long will you go hungry? Come. No one will know.'

Bindubala had enjoyed the whole thing. A complicated case. It was quite late when she returned after observing her mother-in-law at work. As she pushed open the door and tiptoed into the room, a massive slap landed on the left side of her face. She had been hard of hearing in one ear since then.

'My life has passed in sorrow. Not a day of happiness.'

'Who's happy, tell me. Look at me – am I happy?' Bindubala felt today's massage was not going well. They were wasting time on idle talk. It was not easy to control which way the mind ran – it outpaced the wind and needed to be stopped in its tracks. Although her husband beat her, he would also pull her close and kiss her, comfort her where it hurt. Wasn't physical pleasure also pleasure, just as physical pain was also pain?

'You're too shy. The madam in Baridhara never has a stitch on.'

'Let her. I'll never be able to do that in my life.'

'Yes, it disgusts me too. I'm a widow, a vegetarian, but my business is with bodies. Allah will forgive me – this hard-earned money is helping bring up a fatherless child.'

Of course, there were advantages as well as problems with having no clothes on. The madam in Kochukhet had breast cancer. And it was Bindubala, not a doctor, who detected it. Her hands had run into something hard on their way from the underarm to the breast. Not once but three or four times. She pinched the area on the side of the breast with all five

441

fingers. Madam said, 'You're tickling me. Stop, darling!' By that time the lump had slipped from her grasp like a smooth, shelled nut. Neither madam nor Bindubala knew that it was a life-threatening disease. Then the best doctors were consulted, and she was rushed to Bangkok and Singapore. If she did better one day, things took a turn for the worse the next. It was the last stage. Bindubala got a call from the airport. She dropped everything and rushed. All the bags and suitcases lay scattered around the living room. She hadn't even changed her sari. 'Come with me,' she said. Her husband sat on the sofa, cupping his face in his palm. There was no more hide-and-seek. 'My husband is home. Sleeping. Not now. Come when I send for you.' Bindubala had been turned away from the door many times with these words. Today, she entered the bedroom in full sight of the husband. In the middle of the room lay not a human being but a skeleton. Madam lay down on the bed with the sheet drawn over her. 'It's been so long since I've had a massage from you. Just oil will do. And be gentle.' A little later, suddenly roused from her reverie, madam sat up. Her eyes were bloodshot. 'I took so much care of this body, and now it will mingle with the earth in the grave!' Bindubala put her Seiko watch on her wrist. It was ten minutes and five or six seconds past two in the afternoon. Madam was hurrying her from the back. 'Bindubala, tell me quickly – do you want to see the doctor or not? I'll call him before I go in to bathe.'

'My ear isn't ringing any more.' Bindubala's ear ached every time she remembered her husband. She felt feverish. How could she tell the doctor any of this? It would have been another matter if the man were alive. Bindubala said, 'Madam from Dhanmondi gave me a missed call. She'll be furious if I don't see her on time.'

Perhaps the current madam didn't like this. Instead of going for her bath, she was still standing in the veranda, clutching the grille, when Bindubala went out through the gate and turned into the street. Her eyes were blazing – either with anger or with jealousy. Why so angry? Whom are you jealous of? Bindubala pondered, turning her eyes away from the veranda as she walked. Fate has forced you to be lonely. Can Bindubala afford to stay for a meal with you and chat the day away? Besides, Bindubala doesn't belong exclusively to anyone. Everyone is equal to her, everyone has the same identity – of a client. Give me money and I'll give you comfort. That's all. Not that Bindubala could keep her head if anyone was in trouble. She plunged in like a moth drawn to a flame. By the time she tried to fly off, her wings had been singed. Why did she have to be swayed by what the jewellery-store owner's wife told her and start doing the rounds of holy men? Husbands got up to all kinds of mischief when they had cash at their disposal. The jewellery-store owner's wife had clutched her hands and begun to weep during a massage. 'Save me, Bindubala didi! He has fallen for a whore, and now one jewellery set after another is being smuggled out of the store.'

Bindubala was not moved. What did it matter if things she had never seen in her life were being smuggled out? But when the jewellery-store owner's wife said, 'My parents are very poor, they can barely manage two meals a day, if he divorces me I'll be on the streets,' Bindubala took notice. Forgetting her work, she rushed about in search of amulets to tame one's husband. And when all was well once again, the jewellery store-owner's wife pretended she had never known Bindubala.

Bindubala spat through the bus window. Now the penniless woman goes to a penniless beauty parlour for a massage. Six hundred a pop. Never mind the amulets – I used to take such good care of her. Would giving me 200 taka make her poor? All they do at the parlour is give you a short massage with some cream, then wipe you down with hot towels. Forget about removing the grime. The penniless woman pays 7,000 to get her hair done each time, that's how rich she is.

3

The rich, the poor, the beggars – everyone wants to be well off these days. They want to throw their money up in the air like confetti. But Bindubala was stuck at 10,000. The price of the land had been increasing by 10,000 every month for the past two years. The cantonment madam said, 'I'll get you work – lots of work. Even if you work night and day, you won't be done. Want to do it?'

But there was just the one Bindubala, with only two hands. The girl who lived in the room opposite hers, old enough to be married, sat all day with her arms folded across her chest. Without a touch of oil or soap, her hair flew stiffly in the wind. Every now and then she'd say, 'Aunty, teach me how to give massages.' Today it was Bindubala who called the girl. 'You keep saying you want to learn. Suppose I teach you and you start work. You get customers. And then you get married. What will you do?' Instead of replying, the girl ran indoors. Perhaps she had been embarrassed by the talk of marriage.

Bindubala was worried. Would it be right to turn down a golden opportunity? Every assignment at the cantonment was worth a lot. Not only because they paid 250, but also because it was a safe place. There was no fear of thieves or gangsters. It was also a strike-free zone. She wouldn't miss work because of a strike. Everyone angled for such opportunities. Bindubala only wasted the time it took to stand up from a sitting position. Leaving enough food for the day beneath the bed, she locked her son in the room. When Shukhlal got hungry, he would climb down from the bed to eat, spending the rest of his time listening to Hindi film songs on the cassette player and peeing through the crack in the door. He was a good child. He was overjoyed at the thought that his mother would return a day later with chips and Coke.

It was dark when Bindubala got off the bus. A long dirt road lay ahead of her. Those who had been to the market were returning home to the village with their purchases. Everyone here was from her father's part of the country. But no one guessed that she was a member of the local Robidas community. Bindubala's manner of dressing had changed so much that they assumed she was a woman from the city.

When she was in Dhaka, Bindubala had heard that her sister now worked as a day labourer, digging the earth in a gang of five. After her husband died, she had lived for a year off the money she had made from selling their pet pig. Since then her job as a day labourer had paid for running the two-member household of her daughter and herself. Poor thing. This sister used to be her father's favourite daughter. Bindubala felt as though she was walking not on a dirt road, but over her sister's heart . . .

'A long, long time ago, when the British still ruled, some men were forcefully brought from Gorakhpur, Ballia, Munger and Bhojpur to build roads hereabouts. For one thing, water was scarce at home, and then there were no jobs – how would people survive? My grandfather and my great-grandfather took the opportunity and came here. By the time the work was done, they had forgotten the way home. Such fools!'

'I won't go to Dhaka, Bindubala. I'll lose my way.'

'What rubbish, didi. I know Dhaka like the back of my hand. I know every road, every backstreet. I'll show you everything.'

Her sister did not prolong the conversation. Who could appreciate the untimely arrival of a younger sister from the city, full of unwanted advice? Having spent all her time with the rich madams, her sister also wanted to be rich. All she ever talked of was money.

'Listen, didi. Don't stay quiet like a fool. You're my sister. I will teach you the work personally. You will take two assignments a day. Two-fifty plus two-fifty – that's five hundred. Fifty for meals and bus fares. You can save the remaining four-fifty. We will pool our savings and buy a piece of land in Joydebpur by the woods.'

Her sister had no interest in buying land on the edge of the wilderness. But although she occupied government property, the public could burn down her home and evict her at any time. She'd be forced to flee. Even now she had a shifty look. Although she was meeting her sister after such a long time, she just couldn't sit still. She would run into the empty threshing room at frequent intervals. On the other side of the room, her daughter Dukhuni sat cooking rice on a fire made with dry leaves. Bindubala glanced frequently at Dukhuni from the yard. 'The girl is maturing. Such a beautiful child. Her dark skin looks so lovely in the red light of the flames. Raw turmeric would suit her better than herbal cream.'

Dukhuni's and Bindubala's eyes met through the smoke. Embarrassed, the adolescent hid her face between her knees. Bindubala laughed. The next time their eyes met, there was no trace of shyness. Dukhuni ran to her aunt and whispered that her mother was drinking cheap liquor behind the thresher before going back to feed the fire with dry leaves. Four of the five people in the group appeared from the threshing room, staggering. Each of them was covered in mud. They couldn't wait – they had hit the bottle as soon as their work was done, without even stopping to wash. One of them was didi's elder brother-in-law's daughter-in-law – her mother and mother-in-law themselves brewed the liquor. The other was didi's own sister-in-law. The third was her husband's cousin's wife. All four were widows. Independent women. They had to hide behind the thresher to drink because Muslim traders passed by on the road.

They gathered openly in the yard later at night – a congregation of five widows drinking on a moonlit night around a plate of snacks to chase their liquor. In the beginning, Bindubala drank a lot. As soon as the guest from the city emptied her cup, didi's brother-in-law's daughter-in-law refilled it, merrily shouting, 'Cheers!' Bindubala got drunk beneath the open sky. She seemed to dance from star to star. And amid all this, the lucrative assignments at the cantonment kept pecking at her head like a vulture. 'Don't be obstinate, didi. Listen to me carefully . . .' Never mind the other three women, even Bindubala's own sister paid no attention to what she had to say. She herself forgot. Now and then a flock of fair-skinned, naked, plump bodies floated like swans across her mind's eye. Spreading their wings, they flew above her head. Bindubala slurred, 'Skin, didi, skin as soft as butter.' Her sister was drunk too. She said, 'You were as dark as fried meat when you were young, Bindubala. Baba used to say, this girl can never be married. I will make a pillar for my house with her.' She could never stop once she had started talking about their father. She used to be his favourite. 'Every time I walk past the cremation ground I hear baba say, I couldn't get Bindubala married. Is she well?'

When her intoxication deepened even more, the image of a young stork struggling to fly appeared in front of Bindubala's eyes. Who was this? Looked like Lipi madam – she'd been murdered by her lover in broad daylight. Her husband was at work and her child at school. Of course, Bindubala had to have chosen that very day to show up at her house to give her a massage. She had just covered Lipi madam's face and neck with a paste of mashed lentils and was about to layer it on her arms when there was the sound of an ear-splitting motorbike horn. Madam was naked. She bid farewell to Bindubala in that state and leapt to part the window curtains. Lipi madam had been very fair and petite; her body used to be extremely soft – like a baby stork's. Bindubala couldn't recognize her from the photograph in the newspaper the next day, although the paste had dried and stuck to her. For a long time afterwards Bindubala was afraid to take the lift alone – what if Lipi madam pounced on her saying, Bindubala, please clean the paste from my face and neck, I'm very uncomfortable.

Bindubala tried to push herself into the gang of four and hide, but they shoved her backwards, giggling. Everyone was drunk. No one was bothered about anyone else. They fell over one another laughing, their white teeth glistening in the moonlight. Lipi madam's teeth had been pretty too. Her laugh could shatter glass. Bindubala had often waited with a bowl filled with a paste of mashed lentils, while Lipi madam shattered glass with her lover in the next room. How could the man have killed such a woman just out of greed for money?

Bindubala's vomit flooded the yard.

At dawn, Bindubala bathed, ate some leftover rice, and was ready to leave. Her conscience kept pricking her. What was the point of having abandoned her work to travel so far? Didi had refused to go to Dhaka for fear of losing her way. 'Your daughter and you live in such filth, didi.' Bindubala brought her purse out of her synthetic-leather bag. 'Here, keep this money. Buy some soap and soda.' Didi blew her nose with her finger-tips and wiped her eyes with the end of her sari. 'I have nothing but bad luck. I work on the streets. I couldn't look after you, Bindubala! What will I say if baba asks?'

The other three women from last night rushed to Didi as soon as Bindubala left the yard. The difference between them and the city guest was stark in the daylight. They followed Bindubala, kicking up dust on the road they had themselves built. The gap between them was the distance between the poor and the rich. As Bindubala walked on ahead, they stood with their arms round each other at the end of the road.

The four friends were still standing in the same position when Bindubala got on the bus. The morning sun had cast their long, tender shadows over the tyres. She wondered how a woman who exploited all of Dhaka, competing with the daughters and wives of the rich, could have a sister, born of the same mother, among these four figures. Her sister had not agreed, so if she did want to buy the piece of land in Joydebpur she would have to work twice as hard when she returned to Dhaka, enough for herself and her sister. At times the thought of didi filled her heart with anguish – perhaps one day her life would end on the very road where she laboured. Bindubala's father had also died on the streets, his head propped up against the box in which he stored his cobbler's kit.

'Robidas, you have come a long way. What do you want from me?'

'Lord, I want to earn enough every day.'

This was the blessing of a livelihood that Robidas had asked of his maker.

When Bindubala's husband Ramlal died, his only possession was a Seiko watch – a wedding gift from didi's husband. Ramlal too had died on the streets, though his had been not a natural death but a bus crash. Five days after her husband disappeared, a pregnant Bindubala went out herself to search for him. Ramlal had gone to visit his younger sister's in-laws in Sripur. He was supposed to have returned the same day. He was not the kind of man to get drunk and collapse in a ditch somewhere for five or six days. What could have happened?

The skeleton of a crushed bus had been left in front of the Sripur police station. When the sergeant opened his drawer and brought out a Seiko watch, Bindubala crumpled to the floor. After she regained consciousness, she was taken to the government graveyard and shown Ramlal's torn shirt strung up on a bamboo pole. It was covered in dried blood. The barren area had about a dozen new graves for the unclaimed bodies from the bus crash, with no separate arrangements for Hindus and Muslims. There were still four or five graves with bamboo poles displaying bits of the clothes worn by the victims. Relatives could use them to identify the dead. If they could, they would carry the decaying bodies in gunny sacks back to their own homes and perform the last rites. Where was Bindubala's husband Ramlal's home? During the wedding vows, she had only heard him say '*Baliya astaan*'. My home is in Baliya. Where was Baliya? How far was it? Her husband hadn't known either. Bindubala simply returned home with the Seiko watch.

The watch was strapped round her wrist now. When he was alive her husband had not wanted her to work outside the house, and now she was using the same man's watch to make appointments with her clients – or cancel them if necessary. The watch now showed that it was eight in the morning. Even though it was a weekend and traffic was thin, it would still take her at least three hours to reach Dhaka. Bindubala extracted her mobile phone from her bag. The actress Rima had gone to Malaysia for filming. She wouldn't make it to Roksana madam's house on time. Eight in the morning meant eight in the morning, after all. She was an elderly lady who didn't like punctuality being taken lightly. That left Mohakhali,

Banani and Baridhara. If Shathi madam in Mohakhali did not get Bindubala's call she would go in to bathe at exactly ten. It was the same with Banani and Baridhara. She needed to call them all immediately and ask them to delay their baths by an hour.

Bindubala travelled towards Dhaka, making one 'missed call' after another.

(Translated by Arifa Ghani Rahman)

KABERI ROY CHOUDHURY

Getting Physical

'Our village had a lovely name, you know. Dharabaari. The district of twenty-four parganas had not yet been split into two. It was a large area, all told. Trees, a river, ponds – what you'd call the countryside. You people were nowhere around then. You cannot even imagine the life we led back then. Have you ever been to a village?' Ramanimohan arched his eyebrows.

Joba said, grinning, 'Gouripur and Birati in the early seventies is as far as my village tourism goes.'

'Nonsense! As if you can call them villages! Haven't you read Sarat Chatterjee? That's the kind of village we had. It wasn't just the other day, you know. Nineteen thirty-eight.'

'What was it like?'

'Beautiful. Pollution? We hadn't even heard of it. A glorious existence. Swimming in the ponds, stealing fruit, romping in the fields. What more could we ask for?'

Joba had been listening to Ramanimohan open-mouthed. She tried to conjure up a picture of what it must have been like.

'Penny for your thoughts.'

'Me? Nothing.' Joba was embarrassed. She didn't like putting her emotions on display.

'Something, surely?' Taking off his glasses, Ramanimohan revealed the astonishment in his wide eyes and looked into Joba's.

Joba felt uncomfortable. But she was back to her animated self the next moment. 'I was trying to picture the village from your description,' she said. 'I love imagining things I've never seen. All I do quite often is imagine things by myself. Let's say I'm at a party or gathering that I'm not enjoying very much – you know what I do? I start thinking about a hundred different things. Or let's say I'm on a long-distance journey. My mind starts wandering, and before I know it I've reached my destination. But then the word destination has a different meaning for me.'

'How do you mean? I don't understand.'

'You'll laugh. Do you know what I do? In my head I go to places that may not even exist on this planet. Or, if they do, I'm not aware of it. Now let's say I'm on my way to Delhi while such thoughts are playing around in my head. Consider. Have I really reached my destination?'

'Excellent! You're a very interesting person!'

'I haven't actually travelled a great deal. That may be why I love imagining. You don't need tickets to board an imaginary train, after all. By the way, the name Dharabaari is very sweet.'

'The name has a history. Although it's hearsay. Apparently it used to rain a lot there at one time. No one knows why. So Dharabaari – pouring rain.'

'Don't you go back now?'

'Of course I do. Whenever I'm back in the country. Roots. No matter how large the tree, the roots will always pull it back towards the soil. What days those were! I used to go to the local school at the time. Torrential rain, water and mud everywhere, lake and river and land were indistinguishable. Splashing through the water to study. Trapping fish in mosquito nets. I had a girlfriend, do you know? She used to thread a garland of flowers for me every day, just like Saratchandra's Parvati. Delicious. Just like a sweet-and-sour mango.'

'What was her name?'

'Manjuri.'

'Do you run into her now?'

'How would I? She got married when she was still a child. Back then village girls were made to get married by eleven or twelve. I met her two or three times after her wedding. I went away from the village too, to Calcutta. I entered college. All the relationships built on the village roads began to slacken.'

'Don't you miss her?'

'Why should I? I'm not particularly emotional. Women are like a trance to me. They come, and then they leave. Like dreams, you might say. We can do as we please in our dreams, we can shake the foundations of any relationship in our dreams. Don't you agree? And women keep me alive, Joba. You could say they're resources for my survival. When I look at women I think of food, somehow. They appear to me as tender mangoes, or ripe berries, or juicy coconuts, or slices of orange or grapefruit . . . You get the picture.'

Ramanimohan was chuckling. He ran his fingers through his salt-and-pepper hair. His eyes dancing behind his glasses, he said, 'Do you think I haven't looked at you too? I have already.'

Joba wasn't put out in the slightest. She had been introduced to Ramanimohan at a friend's house. He was a friend of her friend's father-in-law. So although she addressed him as 'dada', as one would an elder brother, he belonged to her father's generation. Nothing to be afraid of. And besides, she was attracted by people's personalities. So she took a quick decision. Why not study him a bit? Human nature, after all.

'What are you thinking? That I'm a strange man, right?'

Why is he saying this? Joba didn't respond. I'm telling my eyes to observe, ears to listen and mouth to shut up, she told herself. So Joba changed the subject. 'Aren't you going to introduce me to your wife?' she asked. It didn't escape Joba's notice that Ramanimohan's face acquired colour at once.

The very next moment he said with a smile, 'Basanti is obsessed with gods and goddesses. Whenever we're in the country she rushes around from one temple to another. This morning too she's off to some shrine or other. You'll meet her one of these days.'

'Don't you go with her? You don't believe in god?'

'Frankly, no.' Surprising Joba, he asked, 'How old are you?'

'Thirty-four. Why?'

'My god! You don't look thirty-four at all. I would have said twenty-five or so. But I appreciate your boldness. Otherwise no woman who's as tender as a soft fruit would tell the truth about her age. You could easily have said you're twenty-two – no one would doubt it.'

'What's the point of hiding one's age?'

Laughter seemed to be at the core of Ramanimohan's nature. He laughed again. Full-throatedly. 'Your lips flutter so beautifully when you speak,' he said. 'Have you ever noticed? The way a glass of clear, sweet orange juice trembles. Sweet and delicious.' Not everything needed a response, Joba knew this. Some things just had to be ignored. Without being either agitated or astonished she said, 'Where were you during the attacks on the World Trade Center?'

Leaping to his feet, Ramanimohan said, 'What a horrifying experience that was. We had gone from our house in New Jersey to our daughter and son-in-law's home in New York just the day before. Terrible, terrible!' He closed his eyes as he spoke. For just a moment. The very next moment he said, 'You're a poet and writer, aren't you? Got anything you've written?'

'I do. Some poetry.'

'Read it. I want to hear it.'

Ramanimohan stretched out his tall, erect frame in his chair, extending his legs. Taking out her notebook, Joba began to read the poem she had written the night before. When she got to the tenth line, Ramanimohan sat up, saying, 'Read that line again, please.'

Astonished, Joba read out . . .

> The sex smell blood spit of others, their ejaculation, hit or miss –
> Rummaging through these, suddenly one day the girl
> Looked up at the sky . . .

Ramanimohan stopped Joba before she could finish. 'Enough!' he said. 'I don't need to hear any more.'

Joba was surprised. 'Don't you want to hear the rest?' she asked. 'The sense of the poem won't be obvious unless you hear the whole thing . . .'

'Please!' Ramanimohan cut her short. 'Am I supposed to learn from you what poetry is?'

'No, I'm not saying that.' Joba restrained herself. 'That's not what I wanted to say . . .'

'I know. I've got the essence of your poem. You have a way with words. And these lines of yours have elevated your poetry to a new dimension. No vulgarity whatsoever, and yet you've succeeded in bringing the real truth out beautifully. You're a smart girl, I don't mind telling you that I'm a slightly physical type. You wouldn't believe me, there used to be a pond just for women in our village. All the women and girls used to throng the place for a bath every afternoon. And I'd climb a tree and hide among the leaves to watch them bathing.' Ramanimohan paused for breath. 'Do you hate me now?' he asked.

Joba shook her head. 'No, not in the least. Go on.'

Ramanimohan picked up the thread. 'As I was saying, a woman's body is so exciting, you know, such a thrilling affair. I've seen not a few of them in my life. From foreign women to village girls, from green cucumbers to over-ripe coconuts, I've seen them all, but their appeal hasn't diminished even a bit. Thank goodness you're a liberal thinker. Not stupid and naive.'

Joba was astonished. She had never met anyone like him. How could a man her father's age talk this way to a woman he had known for only two days? Do I dislike him? Joba asked herself. If so, why? Is it because of his candid conversation? Is this broad-mindedness or perversion? If it's broad-mindedness, how should the word be defined? Does it refer to the uninhibited discussion of any subject, no matter how private?

Ramanimohan continued, 'As a matter of fact, there are many people like me. They are in love with women's bodies, but they pretend to be avuncular. Nonsense! Nothing but hypocrisy. I'm a plain speaker, you know. By the way, stand up for a minute, will you?'

'Why?'

'I'm asking you to stand up for a bit.'

'But you must tell me why.' Joba was surprised.

'I want to check the size of your waist.'

'And then?'

'This is it. This is where you Bengali girls lose out.'

Joba was astounded. What she said was, 'My waist size is not very attractive. Not worth checking.'

'How can you say that?' Ramanimohan was even more astounded.

'Why shouldn't I? Truth is truth.'

Now Ramanimohan took off his glasses. His eyes brimmed with curiosity. 'Smart comeback,' he said. 'I knew the first day I met you that you weren't like run-of-the-mill girls.'

Joba chuckled. He really was turning out to be an unusual man. She quite liked such people. It took all sorts to make the world.

'Really,' was what she said.

'Who named you Joba?'

She was startled once more. 'What do you mean?' she asked.

'Why do you keep asking what I mean? Who gave you the name?' Despite the smile on his face, Ramanimohan scolded Joba mildly.

'I don't know. But I like your name. Ra-ma-ni-mo-han! Charmer of women.'

Ramanimohan was laughing loudly. Wild laughter. 'Well said!' he remarked, still laughing. 'But your name has a scent of sex in it, did you know that?'

'Oh my god!' Joba was turned to stone.

Ramanimohan continued, the gentle smile still on his face: 'Bangla was the language we were taught in, so when they taught us about reproduction . . . the first forbidden whiff came from the union of the stamen with the pistil of the hibiscus, the joba flower. That was our first sexual text. And so much excitement over such a small thing. Ever since I met you I've been thinking of those flowers. They call it association in psychology.'

'Aren't you thinking of fertilization?'

Ramanimohan seemed to pull up short. He took a sip of water and lit a cigar. Pursing his lips, he looked at Joba for some time with a peculiar expression. Then he said, 'Very bold.'

Joba laughed. 'I don't think I said anything particularly bold.'

'Good. It's a joy talking with you. Don't people fall in love with you?'

'Maybe they do.'

'But they don't tell you?'

'Maybe they lack the courage. Maybe I don't give them the chance.'

'You're quite pretty. Warm. Don't you enjoy male company? What I mean is . . .'

'I know what you mean. You're talking of physical relations, aren't you?'

'Right.'

'I'm just a normal girl with normal requirements, Ramani-da. That's all.'

Ramanimohan nodded to himself absently. 'The more I see of you, the more you surprise me,' he said. 'Any other woman would have been embarrassed. And my experience says that they would have grown voluble. This is the mystery of womankind. Touch me, but don't watch me. Something like that.' Ramanimohan was pleased by his own sense of humour. An expression suggesting that he knew everything there was to know about women appeared on his face, not escaping Joba's notice. She tried to behave as normally as possible, saying, 'But you didn't say anything about the talent or intelligence or faculties of women, or even of their minds.'

Ramanimohan appeared to ponder this for a while, biting his lower lip as he gazed at Joba. Various feelings played over his face. Then he said, 'Good question. Then let me confess frankly that intelligent women seem mannish to me. Women should be soft and beautiful.'

'But didn't you say I'm quite intelligent? What about that?'

'No, my dear. It's your body that does the talking.' Ramanimohan chuckled. His eyes were enraptured. 'Which is why your intelligence hasn't hardened you. You're a very sweet girl. A juicy fruit.'

He was quite a character. Joba armed herself mentally. Let's see how far he goes. 'You're very lively even at this age. Your wife must be very proud of you.'

'Are you crazy? Do you think wives like all this?'

'Why not?'

'Basanti's an excellent wife, ideal for the family. I'm a different type. But women like Basanti are perfect for the home. I see the world differently, though. For instance, I can tell you candidly that I like you. Is that bad?'

'Not at all. It's not abnormal to like someone.'

'I'm getting a whiff of my village from your body after all these years. Do you know what the tender black fuzz peeping out of your armpit through your shirt sleeve reminds me of? Of the hair rising out of a java apple. And your breasts? You may have restrained them, but they look like a pair of restless pigeons, trying to break free and fly away.'

The blood was pounding in Joba's head. But, maintaining her smile, she said, 'What else?'

'Your waist's like a stick of cane. Because you're in jeans it's obvious that your thighs are like tender butternut squash. Your bottom is admittedly a bit on the heavy side, but it's nice nevertheless.'

'No simile?' Joba asked with a questioning look.

Ramanimohan couldn't stop smiling. 'What a fine girl you are,' he said. 'Your bottom's like an upturned mandolin ... Am I not right?' His eyebrows danced. 'See what a good eye I have?'

'Definitely worthy of admiration.'

'You can't have anything without the body, see? Haven't you read how Radha is described? All this platonic love is just a sham. Those who wrinkle their noses when you talk about physical love are hypocrites. Those who believe in the primacy of the body never resort to shame or hatred or fear. Even death can be prevented by lovemaking, they say. They can even drink substances ejaculated by the body without hesitation. It's called Charichandra Sadhan.'

Joba smiled mentally. She was familiar with this. But still she gazed at Ramanimohan, feigning great interest.

'Do you know about the moon when it comes to physical love? Those who believe in physicality think of the human body as possessing twenty-four and a half moons. Thus . . .

> The body with its twenty-four and a half moons
> Ten on the arms, ten on the legs, two on the cheeks
> One each on the lips and brow, and half a moon above . . .

When a man and a woman make love with their moon-studded bodies, they say there's a moon on the moon. Do you get it? Life is arid without the body.'

Joba drank a glass of water and prepared to leave. 'It was fun chatting with you,' she said. 'I didn't even realize when morning turned into afternoon.'

Ramanimohan was out of his chair too, saying, 'No one's ever bored chatting with me. So when are we meeting again?'

'We will. You're in India for some time, aren't you? When do you go back to New Jersey?'

'Next month.' Ramanimohan seemed lost in thought. 'Are you free tomorrow?' he asked.

'Yes. Why?'

'Want to take a trip somewhere close by?'

Joba prepared herself in an instant. 'Why not,' she said, 'but where?'

'Impossible. Planning is for clerks. I don't plan my travel. Come over tomorrow. We'll see.'

Joba looked at him with soft eyes. Ramanimohan melted. Even the chaste can be seduced, he told himself. He was thrilled. When Joba had left he went into the kitchen and told his wife, 'The girl who was here is very lively.'

Basanti was silent. She was cooking. Nuzzling his wife's neck, Ramanimohan inhaled her scent. 'It's good for women to be progressive, you know,' he said. 'So many women have never . . .'

Basanti interrupted him. 'You're getting old. Adventures won't suit you at this age. It's time for your bath.'

Ramanimohan had made up his mind to take Joba to the river. Go on a boat ride. He had woken up early. After a bath with fragrant soap, he put on a pair of blue jeans and a long shirt the colour of warm blood. His heartbeat quickened. He kept glancing at this watch. Joba would be here at nine. The minutes seemed to stretch into hours.

Eventually the clock struck nine and the doorbell chirped. Ramanimohan ran to the door, only to be astonished when he opened it. A boy of about fifteen stood outside. He seemed to be holding a bowl covered with strips of paper in various colours. Ramanimohan was irritated beyond measure. 'Whom do you want?' he asked.

'Didi sent me.'

He was furious with Basanti. Whenever she came to Calcutta she got into an orgy of buying vegetables and flowers. Most annoying. 'So which variety of grass have you brought today?' he asked. 'Go right in and hand it over to my wife.'

The boy looked at him in surprise. 'Didi sent these for you,' he said. 'Here you are.'

This time Ramanimohan was more surprised than irked. Tearing open the wrapper, he discovered to his utter consternation a brass tray, on which were tastefully arranged a stick of sugarcane, two tender pieces of butternut squash, a pair of Java apples, two ripe quinces, two orange slices and a single cowrie. Baffled, he could make nothing of this at first. 'What's all this?' he asked. 'Who's sent this?'

'Didi. There's a letter too. She's asked for a reply. You can give it to me.'

Picking up the letter on the tray, Ramanimohan read it swiftly.

Respected Ramani-da

You know the doctrine of the body. You are extremely erudite. But your application is far too unidirectional. Your behaviour is nothing but a display of masculine power – like an elephant drunk on arrogance. This is probably why you can declare with aplomb that an intelligent woman appears mannish to you. Alas!

I have also studied certain aspects of the doctrine of the body. I am aware of how and when this 'ism' came into being. The proponents of physicality had placed human beings on a higher pedestal than religion. This philosophy was formulated to break people's faith in temples and mosques and in the theocracy of both religions. And yet you yourself flaunt your high-born Brahmin origins with that supposedly sacred thread you wrap around your torso.

Women's bodies are like food for you. I apologize. I was unable to lay my hands on pigeons. I have sent you some quince as a substitute. The equivalent of breasts. I am sending you a cowrie too, symbolizing the vagina. Sending a mandolin would have been far too expensive. The rest are all in accordance with your demands.

Yours truly,
Joba

Entering the drawing room, Basanti was delighted at the sight of all the fruits on the tray. 'Did you go to the temple?' she asked. 'I had never expected you to change so much. Give them to me. Oh my god!'

SANGEETA BANDYOPADHYAY

Sahana or Shamim

Even after 9/11 Sahana had bought fish regularly. Also when the Godhra incident had taken place in her own country. Taking advantage of Paramesh's absence, she had bought fish every single time, overcoming her hesitation. So many people were dying every day in Kashmir, America was tearing Iraq to pieces. Militants nurtured by Pakistan's Inter-Service Intelligence were taking shelter in Bangladesh, even Kolkata wasn't safe any more. The air was thick with rumours, you felt afraid to step out of your home, being in a crowd was uncomfortable, the cinema hall made you claustrophobic – but still, skirting all these truths, Sahana had continued buying fish. When she entered the market she looked around, then casually approached the area where the fish was sold. She bought the fish, put it in her shopping bag and went home. She did all of this with her mouth clamped shut. Cautiously. Even rinsing the fish slices made her hands shake.

It happened every time – from the moment of buying the fish, through bringing it home in her oversized shopping bag, rinsing the slices gingerly, gathering the scales and the other parts to be discarded with an unerring hand, till she had thrown them away from the high-rise she lived in into the thicket of fig trees on the grounds of the British bungalow next door. Her hands shook, she found it difficult to breathe, her head reeled.

And how self-flagellating the act of frying the fish was. Constantly she felt as though Paramesh were standing next to her, crying, 'Flesh, flesh!' She started in alarm every now and then, certain that her fear would lead her to cause an accident. Her own carelessness would make her burn to death. The stench of her roasting flesh would mingle with the smell of fried fish.

But death would not bring deliverance. The forensic report would definitely indicate that she was burnt while frying fish. Paramesh's heart would no longer harbour the detached respect and love that people customarily felt for the dead. If there were any photographs of her in the flat, he would throw them away, damning her as a traitor. And then he would hate her as long as he lived.

Sahana mused about all of this as she cooked the fish. She usually felt overwhelmed when she was done with the cooking. Unable to control herself, she ate the fish with some rice, experiencing an acute sense of satisfaction. But as soon as she had eaten, she began to gasp for breath. Fear seized her, weighing her down like a huge slab of stone. She didn't even blink till she had washed and scoured the utensils, the ladles, the table, the oven – the entire kitchen, in fact – until they gleamed. She sprayed freshener in every room, poured phenyl into the sink. Picking every single bone with her nails, she put them in a polythene packet and threw them out into the thicket next door. She poured soap on her hands, rinsed her mouth out with mouth freshener, shampooed her hair – she showered! She showered!

Not a trace of the smell remained. Still she sprayed the freshener once more in every room and sniffed both sides of her palm. Sometimes, unable to handle such anxiety, Sahana pounded garlic into a paste and fried it in oil. All smells were certain to be buried then.

But the situation had not been remotely like this when they had met and exchanged hearts. Fish had not appeared a significant issue during those early days of their romance. In fact, she had never felt as though she were treading a path of sacrifice in the process of linking her life to Paramesh's. She had accepted the whole thing without protesting. Although she realized now that she had indeed wanted to protest – but hadn't been able to.

'I'm vegetarian,' Paramesh had told her. 'You mustn't eat anything non-vegetarian at home.'

'What about elsewhere?' she had asked.

Silent for a couple of seconds, Paramesh had shrugged.

'I don't mind chicken. But as for fish, you'll have to give it up completely, at home or elsewhere. I simply cannot tolerate the smell of fish, Sahana. I throw up on the spot. It makes me so sick that I've had to be hospitalized in the past. I hate fish. Moreover, Sahana, I cannot dream of kissing or making love to someone who eats fish. I can't enter someone who, in one way or another, is fishy.'

Holding up the middle finger of his left hand and shaking it, Paramesh had conveyed both meanings of the word fishy to her, 'So you have to give it up.'

By then Sahana had fallen in love with Paramesh. If it had been only love, it might have been different, but she had also become psychologically dependent on him. She had realized that she would have to give up fish if she wanted Paramesh. She had inexorably and almost effortlessly uprooted the very desire for fish from her heart. She had trained her sights instead on all the other kinds of food in the world. For two years she had not eaten any fish. Then she was possessed again by its taste.

And she began to eat fish in secret, and started to fear Paramesh. For she was only too aware that if Paramesh came to know, their relationship would end. Alternatively, a conflict would erupt, the kind of conflict that we are familiar with. The more Sahana began to fear Paramesh, the more she began to loathe him too. Hatred. Or, one could say that the more she became aware of Paramesh's abhorrence for fish and those who eat fish, the more determined she became to retaliate with a proportionate degree of revulsion for those who did not eat fish. She seemed to feel a certain responsibility to do this. She found her self-awareness offering ammunition for her opposition to, and disillusionment with, Paramesh.

'Those who eat fish and those who don't are poles apart, separated by a deep gulf of mutual contempt.' When she grew deeply emotional about fish, she argued with trepidation, 'Why should I be deprived of fish, Paramesh, just because you don't enjoy it, just because you cannot stand the smell of fish? Why should you impose your behaviour on mine? I'm not you, I'm a person of my own, I shall remain a distinct person. Isn't this a mistake on your part, Param?'

Paramesh became furious, telling her about total surrender. 'Even if I'm wrong,' he replied, 'I expect unquestioning submission from you in this regard. Remember that there is no alternative if this relationship is to be maintained in the most peaceful form it is capable of being in. Or else, as you know, terrible things may happen, you'd better not blame me then.'

Sahana's former lover Manish returned to her life at this precise juncture. Because hate spirals upwards and the reasons for the hatred fade while the object of the hatred becomes the most important thing, Sahana entered into an illicit relationship with Manish more or less needlessly, simply out of loathing for Paramesh.

Paramesh came out sharply against eating meat and fish one evening at a small party at a friend's house. 'The most extreme form of enjoying meat is cannibalism,' he declared. 'Human flesh is the most delicious of all!'

Sahana wept buckets that evening, sitting on the toilet in the friend's house. Finally, she ground her teeth. 'So it's hatred? So much hatred?' On the way back Paramesh's face appeared to be composed of nothing but a glutinous green substance. The next day she not only cooked some fish, she ate it too in Manish's arms. Then, drawing strength from ultimate hatred for the first time in her life, she let Manish have sex with her. But she could see that this hatred was working in its entirety on her and her alone. Since Paramesh could perceive nothing of it, since he had no inkling of this nightmarish loathing, the only person who had to bear it was Sahana herself. Poor Sahana! Not only was she the one who hated, she was also the one to suffer from its impact. Just like cheating – as long as the person being cheated on is not aware of it, they don't have to bear the burden of being deceived, it is reserved entirely for the deceiver. And again, the moment the person being cheated on gets to know everything, they're no longer being cheated. And yet the person who had done the cheating continues to bear the entire burden, as before! In other words, people can cheat, but people can never be cheated on – it really was entirely one-sided.

In the same way, Sahana cheated on Paramesh, but Paramesh wasn't cheated. Sahana hated Paramesh, but Paramesh did not feel hated. Sahana remained perpetually saturated in her own loathing. Yet whenever during the day or the night Paramesh wanted to be intimate with her, he smelt strawberry, gulabjamun or mint on her breath. He was able to relax his body completely and kiss her fervently. He could say, 'Don't you love me any more, Sana? Why is your mouth so cold?'

On the other hand, Sahana frequently discovered when trying to cook the fish she had bought that it had rotted. Rotted completely. When having sex with Manish she discovered she did not want him, during intercourse with Paramesh she suffered from guilt, disquiet and fear – and

463

she filled the rest of her hours with aversion. It was an unarticulated, unstated detestation which progressively crossed the limits of forbidden pleasure to rot just like stale fish. Yet Sahana could not simply separate the scales and bones and throw them away. She could not forget that Paramesh and she were repulsively unlike each other.

Paramesh had been in London on 7/7. Sahana didn't know anything about the explosions till Pubali called her in the afternoon with great anxiety, for she hadn't switched on her TV.

In a frenzy she tried to call Paramesh on his mobile. But a pre-recorded voice kept informing her that 'the subscriber is out of reach at this moment . . .'

Their friends gathered one by one. Manish, Pubali, Tushar, Vasundhara. Each of them tried in their own way to get some information about Paramesh. But evening stretched into night, there was neither any news of Paramesh nor any communication from him.

Despite their collective efforts her friends could not calm Sahana down. Her behaviour was out of control. Although they could make out her words, none of them could understand what Sahana meant.

'My hatred has killed Paramesh,' Sahana was shrieking, 'my continuous hatred.' In tears, she continued, 'Was it necessary to hate him so much?'

The day passed in a whirl. Paramesh did not return. A week later Sahana took a flight to London, along with her sister and brother-in-law. And returned without Paramesh.

There was no trace of Paramesh anywhere. No sign. It wasn't even obvious whether he was dead.

A couple of months later Manish visited Sahana. She seized his arm. 'I'm converting, Manish,' she told him. 'I'm going to become a Muslim.'

Manish was so astonished he was unable to speak. He could not grasp how this was related to the grief resulting from Paramesh's disappearance, or whether it was at all related.

'Paramesh used to talk of complete submission, Manish,' Sahana continued.

'We cannot live together until you become me, he would say. I could say that to you too, Param, I used to reply angrily.

'He would shake his head. Ultimate submission means unquestioning surrender, he would say. Where there is no scope for asking questions. Where questions don't even exist.

'Now that I don't know whether Paramesh will be back, Manish, I have found only one way to offer the ultimate submission he wanted. Only one. In a couple of days a senior Muslim priest will convert me. My name will be Shamim.'

Possibly understanding some of what Sahana was getting at, Manish reached out to move a few strands of hair away from her face. 'Is there no other way, Sahana?' he asked.

'No, there isn't, Manish. There's no shortcut. No room for bargaining. I cannot become him with anything less than this. All effort will go to waste. This is what complete submission means, Manish. When Paramesh comes back he will realize that, even if it took time, I have been able to accept him with my heart.'

Don't raise any questions about this story, reader. Before you can, I would like to remind you that this is a story of unquestioning surrender.

Biographies

Anita Agnihotri (b. 1956)

Anita Agnihotri is a writer of short stories and novels, a poet and a former civil servant. Much of her fiction, which is often intensely political, is derived from her experiences working in the Indian Administrative Service in some of the poorest regions of India.

Humayun Ahmed (1948–2012)

Humayun Ahmed was a novelist, short-story writer, scriptwriter, filmmaker, songwriter and professor. He wrote over two hundred books of fiction and non-fiction and was the most popular writer in Bangladesh in his lifetime.

Shaheen Akhtar (b. 1962)

Shaheen Akhtar is a novelist and short-story writer whose works have been translated into several languages. Her fiction is often set in historical periods and is frequently concerned with the position of women in the world.

Banaphool (1899–1979)

Balai Chand Mukhopadhyay, whose pen name was Banaphool, was a doctor by profession. His literary career spanned sixty-five years and included over five hundred short stories, many of them no more than half a page long. He also wrote sixty novels, numerous essays, five plays and an autobiography.

Bibhutibhushan Bandyopadhyay (1894–1950)

Bibhutibhushan Bandyopadhyay's first novel *Pather Panchali* was published in 1928, followed by *Aparajito*, its sequel. Both novels were made into films by Satyajit Ray, and together with *Apur Sansar* formed the critically acclaimed *Apu Trilogy*. He wrote a number of novels, short stories and essays exploring the relationship between humans and nature, and was considered one of the foremost exponents of short fiction alongside his novels.

Manik Bandyopadhyay (1908–56)

A committed Leftist, Manik Bandyopadhyay used his novels and short stories to chronicle the lives of the deprived and the forces working on them, against the backdrop of colonial rule in Bengal. More than thirty of his novels and three hundred of his short stories were published, and readers continue to discover new gateways through his fiction to the world and the people he wrote about.

Sangeeta Bandyopadhyay (b. 1974)

Sangeeta Bandyopadhyay's works of fiction, with women at their centre, have often evoked shock and consternation in many of her readers. She has written eighteen novels and over a hundred short stories.

Saradindu Bandyopadhyay (1899–1970)

A lawyer by profession, Saradindu Bandyopadhyay gave up his practice to become a writer. He wrote novels, short stories – including crime and detective fiction – plays and screenplays, and was actively involved with the Bengali as well as Hindi film industries. Bandyopadhyay's most memorable character was the fictional Bengali detective Byomkesh Bakshi.

Samaresh Basu (1924–88)

Samaresh Basu worked in a factory and was involved with the trade union movement and the Communist Party, which led to his imprisonment. He wrote his first novel in prison and devoted himself to writing on his release, often working on themes of political activism, middle-class life and sexuality. Two of his novels were briefly banned due to charges of obscenity. He also wrote under two pen names, Kalkut and Bhromor.

Lokenath Bhattacharya (1927–2001)

Lokenath Bhattacharya wrote novels, short stories, poetry and essays, many of whose themes and narrative styles place him among global writers. Despite his significant literary output, Bhattacharya was not well known to Bengali-language readers. He spent most of his adult life outside Bengal – much of it in France – and was something of a recluse, two reasons why he was partly overlooked by literary circles in the state. Fifteen of his books have been translated into French.

Nabarun Bhattacharya (1948–2014)

Nabarun Bhattacharya was best known for his magical realist fiction, in which he created radical, anarchic creatures and told avowedly anti-establishment stories. He was also a poet whose poems were deeply political.

Buddhadeva Bose (1908–74)

Buddhadeva Bose was a poet, novelist, critic, editor and translator who was one of the writers instrumental in ushering in a post-Tagore age for Bengali literature. He was an active member of the Left-leaning Progressive Writers' Association in the late 1930s and joined the Anti-Fascist Writers' and Artists' Association in the early 1940s. His distinctive prose marks him as a unique writer even fifty years after his death.

Manoranjan Byapari (b. 1950)

Manoranjan Byapari is a subaltern writer, socio-political activist and politician. He taught himself to read and write in jail, after being arrested for his involvement in ultra-Left politics. Born into a family of refugees who crossed the border from East Pakistan (now Bangladesh) into India after the Partition of the subcontinent, he writes directly from his personal experiences.

Sarat Chandra Chattopadhyay (1876–1938)

Sarat Chandra Chattopadhyay wrote a number of short stories, novels, essays and plays. Many of his works have been, and continue to be, adapted to films, most notably *Devdas*, which has had sixteen cinematic versions. He wrote sensitively and accurately about the plight of the downtrodden in both rural and urban Bengal, focusing especially on social ills and prejudices.

Kaberi Roychoudhury (b. 1972)

A writer with modern sensibilities, Kaberi Roychoudhury has written thirty-one novels, four collections of short stories and two volumes of poems. Her fiction spans both contemporary and historical settings.

Jibanananda Das (1899–1954)

Jibanananda Das was primarily known for his poetry, and acquired a post-humous reputation for being arguably the finest poet in Bengali after Rabindranath Tagore. A recluse and an introvert, he wrote prolifically, but did not publish most of his writings during his lifetime. Only seven volumes of his poems were published while he was alive. After his death, twenty-one novels, over a hundred short stories and many essays were discovered.

Ashapurna Devi (1909–95)

Ashapurna Devi, like many of the Bengali women of her time, had no formal education and was self-educated. But even without stepping out of the confines of her home, she wrote a series of short stories and novels consistently focusing on the socially, economically and psychologically restricted lives of women.

Mahasweta Devi (1926–2016)

Mahasweta Devi was a writer and an activist, a Leftist who worked for the rights and empowerment of the tribal people of eastern India. Over one hundred novels and twenty collections of her short stories have been published. In her fiction, she often depicted the brutal oppression of the tribal people and untouchables by powerful authoritarian upper-caste landlords, moneylenders and government officials.

Akhtaruzzaman Elias (1943–97)

Akhtaruzzaman Elias wrote only two novels, besides short stories and essays, and was an academic. His relatively smaller output was sufficient to mark him as a strikingly original writer. His literary works explore themes of Bangladesh's history, politics, economics and the poverty and exploitation of its people.

Sunil Gangopadhyay (1934–2012)
A poet, novelist and editor, Sunil Gangopadhyay broke away from traditional forms to create a literary idiom almost indistinguishable from the spoken word, while writing of things well removed from the ordinary. He wrote numerous novels, short stories, poems and essays and was a crusader for increased use of the Bengali language.

Gourkishore Ghosh (1923–2000)
A writer, journalist and the founder of a newspaper, Gourkishore Ghosh often drew from his reportage and editorial work to write his fiction. He wrote both short stories and novels, as well as a renowned column for newspapers under the pen name of Rupadarshi. He was jailed for protesting against the Emergency imposed on India in 1975.

Subodh Ghosh (1909–80)
Subodh Ghosh was a journalist by profession whose best-known work is a fictional retelling of romances of characters from Indian epics. His fiction, often set in the small towns of eastern India, was widely read, making him a perennial favourite. Many of his works were adapted into films in the Bengali and Hindi languages by notable directors, including Ritwik Ghatak.

Selina Hossain (b. 1947)
A writer and a diplomat, Selina Hossain has written twenty-one novels, seven collections of short stories, four collections of essays and four collections of children's stories. Many of her works focus on the emergence of Bangladesh as an independent country and the liberation war that led to it.

Syed Manzoorul Islam (b. 1951)
Syed Manzoorul Islam is a writer, critic and academic. He has written several novels and a large number of short stories, and is known for his absurdist, magical realist and surreal fiction.

Amar Mitra (b. 1951)

A novelist and short-story writer, Amar Mitra often blends history and magical realism in his novels and short stories, many of which are set in the small towns and villages of Bengal.

Narendranath Mitra (1916–75)

A journalist who wrote fiction alongside his work for newspapers, Narendranath Mitra captured life in Kolkata memorably through collisions between human nature and social reality. His stories were often adapted into films in Bengali and Hindi.

Premendra Mitra (1904–88)

Premendra Mitra was one of the most versatile Bengali writers, whose works spanned literary novels and short stories, science-fiction, fantasy, horror, poetry and screenplays. He was the creator of the memorable character of Ghana-da, a teller of tall tales inspired by Baron Munchausen.

Moti Nandy (1931–2010)

A sports journalist most of his life, much of Moti Nandy's fiction – novels as well as short stories – was centred on the lives and on-field action of sportspersons, engaged in sports ranging from football to cricket, tennis to boxing, athletics to swimming. Several of his novels have been adapted for films.

Parashuram (1880–1960)

Parashuram was the pen name of Rajshekhar Basu, who used it at first to write humorous sketches for a monthly magazine. He continued to use the same nom de plume for his satirical short stories, which have remained unparalleled in Bengali literature. A chemist by profession, he also compiled *Chalantika*, a monolingual Bengali dictionary, and translated parts of the Indian epics the *Mahabharata* and the *Ramayana* into Bengali.

Purnendu Pattrea (1931–97)

Purnendu Pattrea was a writer, editor, artist, illustrator and film-maker. His five-volume novella in verse, which is also a compendium of poems, tracing the lives of a young woman and an older man through early romance, her marriage and a renewal of the relationship, was a long-lasting publishing success in Bengali. He was one of the many multifaceted writer-artists who flourished in the world of Bengali culture in the twentieth century.

Ramanath Ray (1940–2021)
In his short stories and novels, Ramanath Ray developed a signature style of writing that discarded realism in favour of stark prose loaded with surrealism, irony and dark humour to comment on contemporary Bengali society.

Satyajit Ray (1921–92)
Satyajit Ray is known to most of the world as, arguably, India's finest film-maker. He was also as a writer of fiction, a translator, an illustrator, a music composer, an editor and a calligrapher. Ray created two of the most popular fictional characters in Bengali children's literature, the detective Felu-da and the scientist Professor Shonku. He wrote over a hundred short stories, many of which were for an adult readership.

Sankar (b. 1933)
Sankar is the pen name of Mani Sankar Mukherjee, who, in his teenage years, worked as a clerk for Noel Barwell, the last British barrister at the Calcutta High Court. His experiences during this time, and his subsequent work in the corporate sector, provided the material for most of the numerous novels and short stories he wrote before turning to non-fiction writing later in life.

Nabaneeta Dev Sen (1938–2019)
Nabaneeta Dev Sen was a writer and an academic. She wrote more than eighty books, including poetry, novels, short stories, plays, literary criticism, personal essays, columns, travelogues, translations and children's literature, and conveyed the idea of equality for women through all her writings.

Syed Mustafa Siraj (1930–2012)
Syed Mustafa Siraj was involved with Leftist politics and theatre in his youth. He wrote one hundred and fifty novels and three hundred short stories. Much of his fiction is located within the Muslim community in

Bengal. His most popular work is a series of thrillers with a central character called The Colonel.

Rabindranath Tagore (1861–1941)

Rabindranath Tagore was a poet, writer, playwright, composer, social reformer, educator and painter. He wrote more than eighty short stories, eight novels, four novellas and numerous songs, poems and essays, besides composing the music for over 2,000 songs. He won the Nobel Prize in Literature in 1913, and established a university, Visva-Bharati. Tagore's literary and artistic works reflect his modernist and liberal sensibilities.

Shahidul Zahir (1953–2008)

A writer and bureaucrat in his lifetime, Shahidul Zahir was known for his use of magical realism. He published four novels and three story collections, and several of his stories have been adapted into films, television series and plays.

TRANSLATORS

Pushpita Alam is a writer, translator and former editor.

Anish Gupta is a journalist and a prize-winning documentary maker who is associated as a translator with a fact-checking website.

Arifa Ghani Rahman is a professor of literature and writing and an experienced editor and translator.

V. Ramaswamy is a non-fiction writer and translator, and an activist working for the rights of the labouring poor.

Arunava Sinha is a literary translator and a professor of creative writing.

Gayatri Chakravorty Spivak is a scholar, literary theorist, feminist critic, writer and translator.

Notes

Abhedananda: Monk who propagated the teachings of the Vedanta, one of the schools of orthodox Hindu philosophy.

Dr Afaz Ahmed: Bangladeshi politician who became a member of the Awami League and a Member of Parliament.

Anna: A measure of Indian currency before the metric system was introduced. One rupee equalled sixteen annas, with each anna amounting to four paise.

Baram: A localized pronunciation of the name of Balaram, a character from Hindu mythology, where he is Krishna's brother. Baram is worshipped as a god by some tribes in eastern India.

Bishwanath: Bengali pronunciation of the name of the Hindu god Vishwanath, which is another name for the Hindu god Shiva.

Brahma, Vishnu, Maheshwar: The three Hindu deities representing the creator, the preserver and the destroyer respectively.

Brajabuli: Language coined for his poetry by the poet Vidyapati (1352–1448), on a base of the Maithili language with a smattering of Bengali added.

Dadubhai: A term of endearment used by a grandfather to address his grandson.

Draupadi: A character from the Hindu epic *Mahabharata*, who was married to the five Pandava brothers.

Durga Puja: A festive occasion spanning four days, when community celebrations are held in most neighbourhoods in Kolkata and across Bengal in accompaniment to formal religious rituals conducted to worship the Hindu goddess Durga. The celebrations usually take place in October.

Gita: The *Bhagavad Gita*, part of the ancient Indian epic *Mahabharata*, which outlines key Hindu ideas about duty, choice, redemption and the illusory nature of reality.

Godhra incident: On 27 February 2002, fifty-nine Hindu pilgrims were burnt to death in a fire on the *Sabarmati Express* at Godhra Station in the Indian state of Gujarat. The incident, whose cause is disputed, led to widespread violence in Gujarat between groups of Hindus and Muslims.

Haji Mohammed Mohsin: A prominent Bengali philanthropist who lived in the eighteenth and early nineteenth centuries.

Hari: Popularly used name for the Hindu god Vishnu and for several of Vishnu's reincarnations.

Janmashtami: The day observed as the birthday of the Hindu god Krishna.

Jiddu Krishnamoorthy: Philosopher who advocated freedom from religious conditioning and developed a theory of education.

Kali Puja: Annual celebration and rituals conducted in honour of the Hindu goddess Kali.

Kamalaja: An androgynous combination of the Hindu god Vishnu and the Hindu goddess Lakshmi, who are each other's consorts.

Khan Sena: The term used by the people of Bangladesh, before and after its independence from Pakistan in 1971, to describe the Pakistan army against which the country fought and won, with the help of India, the Liberation War.

Lakshmi Puja: A formal religious ritual conducted to worship Lakshmi, the Hindu goddess of wealth, in Bengal. The rituals are performed on a full-moon night, usually in October.

Ma Kali: The Hindu goddess Kali. Hindu goddesses are considered mother figures, hence the prefix Ma for mother.

Mahamaya: Hindu goddess who is a form of the Hindu goddess Shakti, referring to the fact that she wields the power of illusion or maya.

Mahashakti: A name used to refer to the Hindu goddess Durga, who wields great power.

Maiji: A respectful form, in Hindi, of addressing a woman, including spiritual leaders, with reverence.

Marang Buru: God worshipped by the Santhal tribes of eastern India as the supreme source of power.

Narasimha: One of the avatars of the Hindu god Vishnu, he is depicted as part-man, part-lion.

Panini: Grammarian and logician who lived in an unknown period between the seventh and fourth centuries BCE. His work *Ashtadhyayi* was a treatise on Sanskrit grammar that is considered the foundational text on the subject.

Patitpaban: The purifier of fallen souls, often thought to be the Hindu god Jagannath.

Radha: The human lover of the Hindu deity Krishna. Their romance is celebrated in many myths and legends.

Ramakrishna: The Bengali spiritual leader Ramakrishna Paramahansa (1836–86), who continues to have a mass following.

Rankini: A fiery Hindu goddess worshipped in many parts of Bengal, especially by people of tribal origin, often considered a form of the Hindu goddess Durga.

Robidas: The Bengali pronunciation of Ravidas, who founded a sect that was part of Sikhism until 2009 before branching out on its own.

Sacred thread: A length of thread worn around the body by some men who identify as Brahmin to signify their caste.

Saratchandra's Parvati: One of the characters involved in the iconic triangular love story *Devdas*, written by Sarat Chandra Chattopadhyay, the other two being Chandramukhi and Devdas.

Scottish: Scottish Church College in Kolkata.

Shakti: Hindu goddess representing power, energy or force.

Shakuntala: The heroine of the Sanskrit play *Abhigyana Shakuntalam*, written by Kalidasa (fourth–fifth century CE), most likely in the fifth century CE.

Shudra: One of the four traditionally recognized castes in Hindu society, the lowest in the hierarchy, associated with the regressive practice of untouchability.

Srabon: One of the twelve months in the Bengali calendar, lasting roughly from mid-July to mid-August, corresponding to the rainy season.

Tretayug, Dwaparyug and Kalyug: The last three of the cycle of four yugs or periods in Hindu cosmology, the first one being the Satyayug. By these calculations, the world is currently passing through the Kalyug, a 432,000-year-long period of progressively degenerating morals. Each epoch of four periods is supposed to last 4.32 million years, after which it starts afresh.

Vidyasagar: Ishwarchandra Vidyasagar (1820–91), Bengali educator, writer and social reformer. He spearheaded the movement for allowing widows to be remarried, and for the minimum age of consummation of marriage to be raised for women. He also set out a primer of the Bengali alphabet that continues to be used.

Vishnugaya: A holy place for Hindus named for the Hindu god Vishnu and the demon Gayasur, for whom Vishnu promised to name a holy place after slaying him.

Yaksha: A nature spirit, often appearing in Hindu, Buddhist and Jain legends.

Acknowledgements

I would like to thank everyone who has contributed to the making of this book.

Philip Hensher, for his conviction that such an anthology needs to exist, and for his suggestion that I put it together.

Simon Winder, for commissioning the book, patiently answering all my questions and asking me important questions back.

Eva Hodgkin, for her wonderful editorial work on the book.

Linden Lawson, for her meticulous copy-editing.

Rachel Thorne, for securing all the necessary permissions from writers, their estates and their publishers.

Sayari Debnath, for reading through and commenting on the manuscript.

And all the writers and translators whose work is on these pages.

Once again, thank you so much, one and all.

Credits

We are grateful to the following for permission to reproduce copyright material:

ANITA AGNIHOTRI: 'Crater Lake', translated by Arunava Sinha in *Anita Agnihotri: Seventeen*, Zubaan Publishers, 2011. Reproduced by kind permission of the author.

HUMAYUN AHMED: 'The Game', translated by Arunava Sinha. Reproduced by kind permission of his family.

SHAHEEN AKHTAR: 'Home'. First published as 'Astan', in Shaheen Akhtar's short stories collection, February 2008. Translated by Arifa Ghani Rahman in *The Book of Dhaka*, edited by Pushpita Alam and Arunava Sinha, Comma Press, 2016. Reproduced by kind permission of the author and Comma Press.

BANAPHOOL: 'What Could Happen?', translated by Arunava Sinha in *What Really Happened, Stories by Banaphool*, Penguin India, 2010. Reproduced by permission of the publisher.

SANGEETA BANDYOPADHYAY: 'Sahana or Shamim', translated by Arunava Sinha in *Panty*, Tilted Axis, 2016. Reproduced by permission of the publisher.

SARADINDU BANDYOPADHYAY: 'The Rhythm of Riddles', translated by Arunava Sinha in *The Rhythm of Riddles*, Puffin Books India. Reproduced with permission of the publisher.

SAMARESH BASU: 'Aadaab', translated by Arunava Sinha. Reproduced with kind permission of the Estate.

LOKENATH BHATTACHARYA: 'The Illness', translated by Arunava Sinha. Reproduced by kind permission of France Bhattacharya.

NABARUN BHATTACHARYA: 'The Gift of Death', translated by Arunava Sinha, copyright © Seagull Books. Reproduced with permission of Seagull Books. All rights reserved.

BUDDHADEVA BOSE: 'A Life', translated by Arunava Sinha in *A Clutch of Indian Masterpieces*, Aleph Book Company, copyright © Arunava Sinha. Reproduced by permission of Aleph Book Company.

MANORANJAN BYAPARI: 'Hangman', translated by Arunava Sinha. Reproduced by kind permission of the author.

KABERI ROY CHOUDHURY: 'Getting Physical', translated by Arunava Sinha. Reproduced with kind permission of the author.

ASHAPURNA DEVI: 'Deceiver and Deception', translated by Arunava Sinha in *Shake The Bottle and Other Stories*, Om Books. Reproduced with permission of the publisher.

MAHASWETA DEVI: 'Draupadi', translated by Gayatri Chakravorty Spivak in *Breast Stories*, Seagull Books, copyright © Seagull Books. Reproduced with permission of Seagull Books. All rights reserved.

AKHTARUZZAMAN ELIAS: 'The Raincoat', translated by Pushpita Alam. First published in *The Book of Dhaka*, edited by Pushpita Alam and Arunava Sinha, Comma Press, 2016. Reproduced by kind permission of Mrs. Suraiya Elias and Comma Press.

SUNIL GANGOPADHYAY: 'A Cup of Tea at the Taj Mahal', translated by Arunava Sinha in *Wonderworld and Other Stories*, Supernova Publishers, 2012. Reproduced with permission of Supernova Publishers.

GOUR KISHORE GHOSH: 'Sagina Mahato', translated by Arunava Sinha in *Galpa Samagra*, Ananda Publishers Pvt. Ltd, 2003, copyright © Gour Kishore Ghosh, 2003. Published by arrangement with Ananda Publishers Pvt. Ltd. All rights reserved.

SUBODH GHOSH: 'Unmechanical', translated by Arunava Sinha, Originally published as 'Ajantrik' in *Galpa Samagra*, Ananda Publishers Pvt. Ltd, 1994, copyright © Subodh Ghosh, 1994. Published by arrangement with Ananda Publishers Pvt. Ltd. All rights reserved.

SELINA HOSSAIN: 'The Blue Lotus of Death', translated by Arunava Sinha in *Gantha Miscellany*, Writers Ink. Reproduced by kind permission of the author.

SYED MANZOORUL ISLAM: 'The Weapon', translated by Arunava Sinha. First published in *The Book of Dhaka*, edited by Pushpita Alam and Arunava Sinha, Comma Press, 2016. Reproduced by permission.

AMAR MITRA: 'The Old Man of Kusumpur', translated by Anish Gupta in *The Old Man of Kusumpur*, Hornbill Press, 2021. Reproduced with kind permission of the author and Hornbill Press.

NARENDRANATH MITRA: 'Organic', translated by Arunava Sinha. Reproduced with kind permission of the family of the author.

PREMENDRA MITRA: 'A Coward's Tale', translated by Arunava Sinha. Reproduced with kind permission of the Estate of the author.

MANI SHANKAR MUKERJEE: 'The Priest's Manual', translated by Arunava Sinha. Reproduced by kind permission of the author.

MOTI NANDI: 'The Pearl', translated by Arunava Sinha in *Kick-Off: Stories from the Field*, Hachette India, 2017, copyright © The Estate of Moti Nandi and Arunava Sinha. Reproduced by permission of the publisher.

PURNENDU PATTREA: The poetries 'Kathopokathan', translated by

Arunava Sinha. Reproduced with kind permission of the family of the author.

RAMANATH RAY: 'A Letter to a Millionaire', translated by Arunava Sinha. Reproduced by kind permission of his family.

SATYAJIT RAY: 'Pikoo's Diary', translated by Arunava Sinha. Reproduced with kind permission of the Estate.

NABANEETA DEV SEN: 'The Miracle', translated by Arunava Sinha. Reproduced with kind permission of the family of the author.

SYED MUSTAFA SIRAJ: 'India', translated by Arunava Sinha. Reproduced by kind permission of the Estate for the author.

RABINDRANATH TAGORE: 'Dead or Alive', translated by Arunava Sinha in *Tagore for the 21st Century*, Aleph Book Company, copyright © Arunava Sinha. Reproduced by permission of Aleph Book Company.

SHAHIDUL ZAHIR: 'Why There Are No Noyontara Flowers in Agargaon Colony', from *Selected stories from the volumes Dumurkheko Manush O Onanyo Golpo*. Originally written by Shahidul Zahir and translated by V. Ramaswamy, HarperCollins Publishers India. Reproduced with kind permission of the author's Estate; the translator and the publisher.